Small Medium: At Large

By Andrew Seiple

Edited by Beth Lyons

Cover by Amelia Parris

D1606630

DEDICATION

To my Wednesday gaming group. Excelsior!

CONTENTS

Acknowledgments	i
PROLOGUE	1
CHAPTER 1: Chase Pursued	4
CHAPTER 2: Wolves? Where?	16
CHAPTER 3: A Hive of Scum and Villainy	25
CHAPTER 4: A Man of Wealth and Taste	35
CHAPTER 5: A Parting of the Ways	46
CHAPTER 6: Old Faces and New Places	56
CHAPTER 7: A Pound of Flesh	67
CHAPTER 8: Magic by Any Other Name	75
CHAPTER 9: Legacy of the Wizaard	86
CHAPTER 10: Awkwardness, Armor and Ambling	97
CHAPTER 11: House Odds and Ends	107
CHAPTER 12: High Stakes Gambler	115
CHAPTER 13: When Your Luck Runs Out	124
CHAPTER 14: Scrying Time	134
CHAPTER 15: Blood and Cannolis	145
CHAPTER 16: A Duel of Words	154
CHAPTER 17: The Tower	164
CHAPTER 18: CSI Arretzi	177
CHAPTER 19: Party Planner	186

CHAPTER 20: A Study in Verde 195

CHAPTER 21: Bad Lady, Good Doge 209

CHAPTER 22: Green and White and Red All Over 219

CHAPTER 23: No Plan Survives Fur's Contact 227

CHAPTER 24: Confessions of a Ringmaster 244

CHAPTER 25: My Name is Error 254

CHAPTER 26: Pwned 268

EPILOGUE 273

APPENDIX I: CHASE'S JOBS AND SKILLS 276

ACKNOWLEDGMENTS

To Amelia and Beth with gratitude.

PROLOGUE

Once upon a time there was a halven.

Against the customs of her kind and the pull of her own genetics, she desired adventure. And she got her wish.

She also broke the law repeatedly, lied to some very powerful people, and fled town to escape the consequences.

But the thing about adventure, as she would learn, is that you don't get to have the fun parts without a few bad parts, too…

Name: Chase Berrymore
Age: 15 Years
Jobs:
Halven level 9, Cook level 4, Archer level 5, Grifter level 6, Oracle level 8, Teacher Level 1

Attributes		Pools	Defenses
Strength: 55	Constitution: 32	Hit Points: 87	Armor: 0
Intelligence: 53	Wisdom: 87	Sanity: 140	Mental Fortitude:30
Dexterity: 94	Agility: 57	Stamina: 151	Endurance: 0
Charisma: 117	Willpower: 43	Moxie: 160	Cool: 36
Perception: 62	Luck: 116	Fortune: 178	Fate: 32

Generic Skills
Archery – Level 1
Brawling – Level 7
Climb – Level 15
Dagger – Level 2
Dodge – Level 12

Fishing – Level 14
Ride – Level 10
Stealth – Level 14
Swim – Level 7
Throwing – Level 24

Halven Skills
Fate's Friend – Level N/A
Small in a Good Way – Level N/A

Cook Skills
Cooking - Level 14
Freshen - Level 10

Archer Skills
Aim – Level 2
Demoralizing Shot – Level 1
Far Shot – Level 1
Missile Mastery – Level N/A
Quickdraw – Level N/A
Rapid Fire – Level N/A
Razor Arrow – Level 1
Ricochet Shot – Level 2

Grifter Skills
Fool's Gold – Level 1
Forgery – Level 1
Master of Disguise – Level 3
Pickpocket – Level 1
Silent Activation – Level 6
Silver Tongue – Level 3
Size Up – Level 1
Unflappable – Level N/A

Oracle Skills
Absorb Condition – Level N/A
Afflict Self – Level 1
Diagnose – Level N/A
Divine Pawn – Level N/A
Foresight – Level 21
Lesser Healing – Level 29
Omens and Portents – Level N/A

Transfer Condition – Level 3

Teacher Skills
Lecture – Level 2
Smarty Pants – Level N/A

Unlocked Jobs
Farmer, Herbalist

CHAPTER 1: CHASE PURSUED

Chase was running for all she was worth, when she heard the sound of her doom approaching.

Branches cracked and crackled behind her, and she didn't look back. She knew what she would see, and any seconds a backward glance would cost would be seconds she couldn't replace. Instead, Chase kept her precious burden close to her chest and forced her legs to go faster, eyes straining to pick out obstacles in the path ahead.

Though 'path' was beyond generous, here. She was fleeing through the deep woods now, places that had long been without people to keep the trees restrained. The game trails that wound between them were barely wide enough for her.

Her pursuers didn't have that problem. They didn't use the trails, and the wide branches overhead were strong enough to support their swarming forms.

They were small, smaller even than Chase, but they were legion. And they were *hungry*.

Furthermore they had very, very sharp teeth, so Chase *ran*. Which wasn't at all what she was made to do because Chase was a halven.

Halvens are small, pudgy, and have a disposition that rewards sedentary pursuits. They usually dwell in farming communities, eat prodigiously, and avoid things like adventure and life-and-death struggles at all costs.

Which made Chase all the more freakish, because she had too many dreams, and not enough chances of fulfilling them in her home. She'd left her home a shambles, skipped town with a known liar and rascal, and broken the law four times over in order to accomplish all of this. She hadn't even told her mother goodbye!

Mind you, there *had* been extenuating circumstances…

A flash of red, a ribbon tied to a tree, and Chase swerved toward it, taking the left-hand fork in the path.

She almost missed seeing the cord stretched between the trees but caught it in time to execute a quick hop.

PER+1

She was mildly surprised that she had gained perception, instead of agility. But as her eyes and hearing sharpened, just a bit, she wasn't too upset at the help. More perception meant less chance of falling to the traps.

And she HAD gained a point of agility just yesterday. The rules which governed reality in general seemed to dictate that it took more work to increase your attributes, the further up you got.

But now was not the time for that. Chase hugged her burden tighter, feeling the comforting warmth, as she charged through fallen leaves, sending them upward in a spray.

They were gaining on her, now. The rustling was coming from either side, not just behind her. Right on her heels, pushing themselves to leap down upon the tasty meal that awaited, ready to swarm down in a fury of teeth and claws…

Then another tripwire loomed out between a pair of bushes, and she was moving too quickly to dodge it—

But her feet went right through it and she stumbled in surprise, but recovered. *Illusion,* Chase knew. *I won't get that lucky twice.*

Some of the traps were illusions. Some weren't.

Not that it mattered, since she jumped the rest of the triplines she saw. And as her legs ached and her breath burned in her chest from the last leap, she got a consolation prize for all her hard work.

CON+1

Some of her exhaustion eased and she pushed herself harder… but it wasn't working. Above her, her foes chattered, sharp and shrill. They smelled victory. They would not relent.

And then, as Chase burst into a clearing, the way ahead split down two paths, both flagged with ribbons… and both blocked off by tarps strung between the trees. They looked identical. They moved identically in the cold breeze.

One is an illusion, Chase knew, and hesitated, slowed for a second.

Then a branch creaked right behind her, and she had no more time to hesitate. *That one?* She guessed and darted forward, put on a last burst of speed—

—and ran headlong into the tightly-stretched tarp.

Chase had a fleeting second to regret her choice as the tarp stretched out, then rebounded, hurtling her back…

…and sending the pie in her arms straight to the ground, splattering fruit and crust in a wide arc.

The exhausted halven closed her eyes as smushed strawberries rained down on her face. Her pointed ears furled in shame, as the horde behind her descended, and started to gorge their faces, arguing over the sweet treat.

Then came wet raspy heat on her face, and a strong odor of unwashed fur, and Chase opened her eyes to glare at the monkeys who had gone for the lower-hanging fruit, so to speak, and were licking her face clean. "Shoo!" she said, waving a hand.

They scattered, scolding her in incoherent babble, then surged in again to get the last few licks of strawberry from her hair. She sighed and let them, staring up at the sky.

A sky that was soon obscured by a shadow, a silhouette of a man as he peered down at her, face friendly but unsympathetic. It was a sharp face, with angular cheekbones and a pointy goatee, but it was softened a bit by his handlebar mustaches. And his snazzy red and black top hat clung jauntily to his head, defying gravity as he bent over and offered her a hand up.

"You were doing pretty well this time," Thomasi Jacobi Venturi said, hauling Chase to her feet. "You made it to the finish line, at least."

Behind him the other tarp disappeared, and a plush fox toy walked out from behind the illusion. "No, she made it to the fake finish line," he said. His name was Renny, and he was the second co-conspirator in the most black-hearted of operations; operation toughen up the halven.

It was the third co-conspirator that Chase loathed the most, though. And that Co-conspirator was Chase Berrymore herself. She'd been mad, absolutely mad, to ask Thomasi for help, to make her more like the traditional heroes she'd read about in the adventure books of her youth. *Those* heroes weren't pudgy, or weak, or fearful, or any of a number of things that Chase still *was*.

To be fair, she hadn't known the depths of torture they had planned for her, after she made her request.

"Did you get any gains from this time around, at least?" Thomasi asked, before he began taking down the tarp, gloved fingers flying with easy dexterity as he undid the knots.

Chase nodded, still trying to get her breath. "Perception. And… constitution," she wheezed.

"It must be nice to be able to get constitution from exercise," Renny said, glass eyes glittering as he considered her.

Chase glared back at him, brown eyes doing their best to commit ocular murder. But after a second, she relented. It wasn't really his fault. Renny was a toy golem, a sentient being animated by pure magic, and toughened in ways toys were not meant to be toughened. Renny could walk for days on end if he had to, carry large burdens without trouble, and endure damage that would reduce Chase to chunky pesto sauce. He didn't GET the idea of exercising hard, not really.

Besides, Renny was too adorable. Chase just couldn't stay angry at him for long. And he'd proven a hell of a friend, too. Thrown together by fate and caught up in an epic-but-scary adventure, they'd had to work together to survive. And at the end of it all, he had given up a chance to return home to keep her company and venture out into lands unknown.

Well, unknown to him, anyway. "We'll do a geography lesson tonight, I think," Chase said as she gathered the remnants of her stamina. "After dinner."

"Works for me!" Thomasi said. "I've been wondering how the borders shifted during my prison time."

Renny didn't say anything, but Chase noticed that his ears had perked up, and his tail was wagging slightly.

"Right. After dinner," Chase said, as her belly grumbled. Thomasi had insisted that she do this run on a mostly-empty stomach, and like a fool, she'd agreed. She cast one last look at the precious, shattered pie and the thoroughly out-of-season strawberries. They didn't have many of those left. Certainly not enough for a new pie.

"Come on, then. I've about got the fire going." Thomasi said and tucked the rolled up tarp under one arm, leading the way back to camp. Chase fell in behind him, brushing dirt off her dress.

"Clean and Press," Renny intoned behind her, and the dirt shuddered away to nothing, as did the sweat she'd recently coated it with. Which would have been a lot better but for the fact that Chase was still sweating. *Doesn't matter,* she thought to herself. *In a bit under an hour he'll have enough sanity back to do that again. I'll just ask then.*

The campfire was indeed crackling merrily, once they emerged into the cleared spot in the trees. Thomasi's wagon sat off to one side, tailgate open and displaying a loose array of junk. Its brightly colored sides billowed in the late fall wind, red and blue and gold, dancing in the breeze. Not far away, Dobbin the horse foraged in the grass for tasty morsels. He'd hauled the wagon and the trio of friends placidly and without complaint these long miles.

"You didn't get the pots and pans out?" Chase asked, surprised. "What were you *doing*?"

"I didn't know what was on the menu tonight," Thomasi shrugged. "Cooking isn't my thing."

Chase snorted. "Flour. Beans. Salt. Rice. Olive oil. The bottom of a jar of strawberries. A pinch of sugar. And some rabbit— thank you for that by the way, Renny. That list of ingredients should tell you we don't have many options left. It's not hard to figure out I'd only need a few tools, here."

"And like I've said many times before, I'm no cook. And you're leaving out all the herbs I've been scrounging up, for my share of the work," Thomasi looked sorrowful.

Despite her hangry-ness, Chase felt herself nodding. "You have helped. Never said you didn't." So she resisted the urge to bang the pots and pans around when she was hauling the various implements out of the back of the wagon.

"I hope you like arancini," she said, arraying the ingredients carefully around the campfire, making sure the herbs were in neat little piles. Thomasi helped with that, at least.

Then, once it was done, Chase started cooking.

An outline appeared in her vision and started filling up with a golden bar. Ingredients flew and whirled, as she grabbed the various tools called for with each component.

First came the flatbread. She had no yeast or anything else to make it rise, so it had to be flatbread. Which was fine, because she just needed it to be breadcrumbs. That was two cooking operations in of itself, and she lost a flatbread piece midway through, as the recipe failed. Gritting her teeth, the hungry halven tried again, and got it... along with a consolation prize.

Your Cooking skill is now level 15!

The rest of it was easier. The rice boiled with herbs, until it turned into herbal rice. Then the rabbit meat got separated out into tiny chunks and mixed with mushed beans. They were taking the place of eggs, but it seemed to work. Then all of it went together.

The end result, by the sixth or seventh step, was a set of fist-sized fried rice balls garnished with pine nuts, fontina, and parsley and stuffed with rabbit meat and black bean paste. They smelled delicious, and Chase risked burning her mouth as she plucked one from the pan and started to bite into it—

"Pickpocket," Thomasi said, and it vanished from her fingers.

Her teeth clacked together. She glared up at Thomasi, and considered taking a bite out of *him*, instead.

"You wanted to be competent," he said. "If I'd failed, you would have gained some perception." He took a big bite out of the arancini, and rolled his eyes heavenward. "Mfff! Gloriouf."

"Right. Sure," Chase sneered. "And the fact that you get to eat first is no factor at all in your decision, here."

"Mum whatfoevah," Thomasi said, through a mouth full of fried rice.

Chase ate, eyes watchful for more shenanigans, but Thomasi was content to share the rest of the repast with her. And it *was* a pretty decent meal, for all she was lacking a few key ingredients. That said... "We need more supplies. We'll have to hit a town tomorrow. Fortunately, we're not far from a good one." She pointed through the trees, at the multiple plumes of smoke highlighted against the setting sun. "That's Arretzi, up ahead."

"Mm. How big?" Thomasi asked, licking loose breadcrumbs from his gloves.

"According to my mother, it's huge."

"That's what she said," Thomasi grinned.

"Yes, that *is* what she said. Why else would I say that?" Chase explained slowly. Was he dense?

"Private joke."

"Ah. One of *those* things."

"Yes. Definitely."

Thomasi did this sometimes, he found random things and turns of phrases hilarious. Chase marked it down to his nature. Thomasi, among other things, was a player. What exactly that meant, she didn't know. But it did mean that he was weird.

So instead of trying to unravel the details of the joke, she focused on explaining what lay ahead. "Here. Actually, this is a good time for that geography lesson. **Lecture.**"

Your Lecture skill is now level 4!

Thomasi and Renny scooted in closer, watching Chase across the crackling fire.

"We're in the Barony of Lafiore. It's a small place, as it goes. A couple of dozen villages, and two small cities. The biggest one is the baronial seat... which we aren't going to, for obvious reasons."

"Quite," Thomasi said, mustaches twitching. "Baroness Floria's chief servant wanting us captured or dead, for example. Well, if she's still alive."

Renny spoke up. "Even if she's not, I can't imagine the Baroness wanting you running around free. Or any other player."

"Given how she treated us, I'm inclined to agree. Though her reasons are still a mystery. For now." Thomasi tossed a stick into the fire.

"You're burning lecture time," Chase scolded him. "My buff only lasts so long!" In actuality it had about twenty-eight minutes to go and she doubted that she'd need that much, but Chase knew that once Thomasi got going he had a habit of being a chatterbox. She didn't want to waste too much moxie on this task.

"Apologies, oh erudite educator," Thomasi stood and bowed, sweeping his hat off. "I'll owe you a proper gift once we're finished, as an apology."

"Uh, okay," Chase eyed him. "Anyway, about Lafiore. We're a small land, amidst giants. Our two biggest neighbors are Salami and Ferrari. They hate each other, which my Father says has kept us safe. They won't trade with each other and are constantly squabbling up north of here, but they keep it out of Lafiore. There are all sorts of agreements that make sure we can't go to war with either of them."

"I'm wondering if that's why you have the Law of Decades?" Renny asked.

"Ah," Chase said, cautiously. The law in question mandated that each person could legally only have one job per ten years of their life or fraction thereof and carried steep fines if broken. She had broken that law four times over, which would usually be enough to land her family into some serious debt and penalties under normal circumstances. But they had been far from normal circumstances.

As to why the law existed, Renny had raised an interesting point. Was it due to treaties with their more warlike neighbors? "That's... possible. I know that most travelers from other lands look at us weirdly when the subject of the Law comes up." She blinked. "I never thought of it that way."

"It makes sense," Thomasi said, shrugging. "Combining multiple jobs is a way to fast power. If your neighbors know that you're gimping your people, they won't see you as a threat. Although..." he frowned, pulling a stick from the fire, and doodling in the dirt. "Although, if that were true, I'm uncertain why it would apply to crafting jobs as well. There are probably some economic reasons. Somebody doesn't want too much competition, I'm betting." He cocked an eye at her. "Do you have trade guilds?"

"Yes, actually. All through the big towns," Chase shivered. Guilds made her nervous. Like most of her village she'd been taught that guilds were evil. Even if they weren't the old horrors from the guild wars decades ago the modern ones had issues. "When you get to level twenty-five in a profession, you can go and try to petition a guild to join. But it takes a lot of money, usually. Or politics. That's what the adults said, anyway."

"There it is," Thomasi said. "Trade guilds have been historically used to hold down the competition and ensure a hierarchy that benefits those above them. I'll bet someone burned a lot of influence and money lobbying to make sure it wasn't just adventuring jobs that got suppressed."

"I don't know about that," Chase said, feeling absurdly defensive about her home barony. "The Baroness is by all accounts a fair and kind woman. Surely she wouldn't let someone get an advantage like that just because of, well, money. Or whatever."

"Why is she a Baroness?" Renny asked.

"What? Well, she was the last Baron's heir. You know how that works, right?" Gods, she hoped so. She didn't want to try explaining the birds and bees to a magically animated plush toy. Even with Chase's considerable charisma, she expected it would be awkward.

"No," Renny said, tugging on his tail with one paw. "I mean back where I come from baronesses and barons don't rule over multiple settlements. Or if they do it's a couple of small villages, and stuff like that. But your baroness has two cities."

"I don't know exactly why that is," Chase confessed. "Most of the lands around here have a baron or baroness, and some lords and ladies. Some of the lands are very small and some are pretty large... Salami's huge, for instance... but the highest noble I've ever heard of is a Count. He's down in Pansyli."

"I expect it's to do with the Wholly Gnoman Empire's dissolution," Thomasi said. "Nobody wants to go too high in noble ranks, because then they'll be seen as having ambitions to try and unify or resurrect the old empire. And that brings far more trouble than it's worth... unless you can back up your words, of course."

"Okay!" Chase said, trying to reign in her frustration. "My lecture buff's timer is still going, so if I might continue, please?"

Thomasi lifted his hands in apology, pausing to chuck the stick back in the fire.

Renny nodded and waved a paw.

"So the city we're going to is the second-biggest one in Lafiore. It's on the border of Salami, right on the Aryes river. It's the great city of Arettzi, famous for its craftsmen."

"Well of course there are bunches of handmade things in our etsy," Thomasi said, mustaches quivering with contained mirth.

"No, Aretsy. AH-retsy," Chase said, making sure he heard her right. But Thomasi still looked like he was trying not to laugh. Well, whatever. He was weird. "ANYWAY. The city has a lot of guilds, like you mentioned. And it's got plenty of supplies, so we can stock up. Then you can do your thing and get us papers to cross the border into Salami."

"My thing?" Thomasi looked at her, puzzled. "I'm not sure what you mean."

"Your thing! Lying! You know what I'm talking about, you're a bigger Grifter than I am!" How could he not get what she'd been driving at?

"I do." He sighed. "But you believed me when I said I didn't. And that's the problem. Your willpower is mush."

"I... oh." His look of confusion had been flawless. "Maybe... you're too good?"

"I am good. I've had lots of practice. And don't get me wrong, from what Renny told me about that part inside the prison, you're pretty good too. You just haven't had the practice."

"I managed to do fine in Bothernot, for like, years," Chase said, sulkily.

"Yes, but in both cases you were up against amateurs. Willpower is what aids you in noticing lies, strange as it sounds." He sighed again. "You're good with falsehoods. You're bad at defending against them. That is a problem. Normally I'd prescribe taking a willpower-boosting job, but I don't have any I could montage to you."

"I do," said Renny. "Elementalists get good willpower."

"Mm. Could go that route," Thomasi said. "But... what's your willpower right now, anyway?"

"**Status,**" Chase said, and eyed the numbers that defined most of her existence. "Forty-four. **Close Status.**"

"Too low." Thomasi shook his head. "Taking on a new job to shore up a weakness just means it'll retard your growth with that attribute. No, painful as it is, you're better off training it up."

"I do have Teacher," Chase protested. "That job boosts willpower."

"Oh, right. Sorry, are you done with your lecture? I quite forgot."

"I am. I was hoping for a level, but I need to do more lecturing. But you got the gist of it, where we're going, I mean. And, uh, that's most of what I know about Arettzi."

"Mm. See, it's not good to depend on crafting jobs for attribute growth. They're nice when they happen, but there's no need to rush them. Although... I was going to offer you one more tonight."

"Oh?" Chase squinted at him. "You think we have time for a montage? We'll be exhausted come the morning!"

A montage was an ancient ritual that locked master and student into a flurry of activity, training exercises sped up to an absurd point. If done successfully, it ended up with the student learning one of the master's jobs. It also took about half a day, with no breaks allowed. Most halvens avoided this method, since it left them exhausted.

"Pfft, no," Thomasi waved a gloved hand. "I don't know the job."

Chase frowned. "Then why would I want it? I only have a single crafting job slot left. And how am I supposed to unlock it, if you can't montage it?"

"Because it's a simple one to unlock, if you have the right tools," Thomasi said, and moved to the back of the wagon. "Remember how I said I had a gift for you?" He rummaged around and came out with a small metal case.

"A gift?" Chase crept clearer, not knowing what to expect. Thomasi once had six full wagons full of junk. After a building fell on them, he'd been reduced to one full wagon and whatever junk he could salvage. Also a pack of monkeys and Dobbin, but that was beside the point. The point was that he could have anything stuck back in the wagon. And apparently he'd found something just for her.

"Yes," Thomasi said, flipping the metal case open. Then he rummaged back in the cart again.

"Paints?" Chase said, confused, as she looked at tiny colored glass jars, brushes, and mixing wells. "Why on Generica would I want to be a painter— oh..." She said, as Thomasi pulled out a small bundle, and realization clicked into place.

They were cards. Small cards, each one with a drawing of Thomasi's top hat on the back, and a red, blue, and gold background. But the other side was blank, just simple white pasteboard.

"I had them printed up long ago. The paint set I got somewhere along the way... I think it was a prize from one of Chilli's games. But combined, I think you can put them to better use than I, yes?"

"Yes," Chase breathed. "My fortuna deck... this is what I need. Thank you."

"I told him that you'd been missing your cards," Renny tugged on her skirt, and she glanced down to him with gratitude. "We can't fix them, because they're messed up and missing some, but you can paint new ones, right?"

"I think so," Chase said, marching over to the fire and pulling up a stone. "I'll have to go from memory... but I've got a skill for that, thanks to Teacher. And I can check them with my book." She patted the pack on her back. It had an explanation of each card, and some rough art that she could use as a guide.

Although, come to think of it, she didn't have to. She could change the art a bit, couldn't she? Personalize it, make it *her* deck. Yes! Yes, that made sense. "Thank you," she said again.

Thomasi beamed. "Don't mention it. Besides, it'll benefit me in the long run. Fortune tellers and circuses go together like pasta and tomato sauce, you know," he took a seat next to her, and placed a set of old posters nearby. "Here. For practice. I don't know how many you'll have to go through to unlock Painter."

The answer, arrived at two hours later, was about five paintings worth.

Congratulations! By painting a basic painting, you have unlocked the Painter job!

Would you like to become a Painter at this time? Y/N?

For a second, she hesitated. It was her last crafting job slot. She'd have to mess with *guilds* if she wanted to change it around, once set.

But…

It DID feel right. "Yes," Chase breathed.

You are now a level 1 Painter!

DEX+1

PER+1

You have learned the Fast Dry skill!

You have learned the Painting skill!

Your Painting skill is now level 1!

Sighing, and blinking the bleariness from her eyes, Chase leaned back and considered her "masterpiece." It looked a little like Greta, her sister, smiling and waving goodbye. Or maybe hello? It was hard to say. "Thank you again, Thomasi," she said… and found nobody by the fire, when she turned. "Uh," she said, looking around… and saw a snoring bedroll not far away.

"It's very late," Renny told her from across the fire. "I've been feeding the fire for a few hours now so you had light to work by."

"Oh," Chase said, glancing up at the sky. The waxing moon *was* farther along on its track, near the top of the trees, by now. Chase blinked, then frowned in irritation. "Agh! And now I'm weirdly refreshed, thanks to the new job. It'll be harder to get to sleep."

"Will it? Is that how it works for flesh people?" Renny asked.

"Flesh people sounds creepy, and yes. Kind of. I mean, I COULD go to sleep if I tried. But…" she cast a glance down at her new paint set, and then over to the cards. The blank cards, just waiting to be turned into a proper deck. "I could fast dry them as I went," she muttered. "Then it's just half a minute a card. Thirty seconds a card is nothing, really. And I can knock them out fast, so I can practice with them tomorrow…"

"Are you sure that's a good idea? You'll be grumpy if you don't sleep. Most fl— most living folks are."

"Ah, it'll be fine," Chase said, opening her pack and cracking open her fortuna book. "It'll only be an hour, at most. Then I'll get a proper night's rest. Besides, we'll be coming to the city tomorrow. I won't have time for painting then."

"If you're sure," Renny said, backing off and letting her do her thing.

Washing her brush of paint and drying it on a rag, Chase bent to the task.

The halven girl got no sleep, but she *was* right about one thing.

She didn't have time for painting cards, in the days to come.

CHAPTER 2: WOLVES? WHERE?

"I told you so," Renny scolded Chase as she stumbled down the hillside.

"Grnfrfl," she muttered back.

"What was that? That didn't sound like you saying thank you." Renny smiled as he strolled by her side, bushy tail wagging.

"Be nice," Thomasi scolded. "You're going to be in her pack for most of today once we get nearer to the city. She's going to have plenty of opportunities to smack it into things 'accidentally.' You might want to keep that in mind."

Chase tried a sinister grin. It probably came out more like a hungover grimace. She was running on pretty much no sleep.

Oh, the first attempts at painting eighty cards had taken about half a minute per card. Forty minutes, all told, and a considerable number of skill ups.

But then she realized that about half of her attempts had failed, once she reviewed the finished work. So she'd had to paint over previous attempts, and that was more painting skill gained, and then she'd had to go and touch up the *good* ones of the lot she'd completed before, and then the *second* good batch didn't quite match again…

By the time she was finally satisfied and the sun was sneaking up behind the trees, she'd learned two things.

Firstly, that when it came to her own artwork she had an annoying streak of perfectionism.

Secondly, was that despite her best efforts, fifteen years of growing up in Bothernot had instilled her with a halven work ethic that wouldn't let her leave a job half-finished.

Who knew? Chase asked herself in the privacy of her head. Mainly because talking out loud hurt too much, and she didn't want to mutter to herself any more than necessary.

Renny, normally the silent one, seemed to be relishing the chance to turn the tables. "What a beautiful day it is!" he announced, practically skipping along. "The falling leaves are pretty, the birds are singing, and the air is crisp, fresh, and..." he stopped. "The air smells bloody. Why does the air smell bloody?"

Thomasi stopped. "We're close to the road. Bandits, perhaps?" His eyes flicked back and forth beneath his cowl, and he lifted his walking stick warily. In preparation for moving through the farming villages around Arretzi he'd shrunk the wagon down and they'd both donned disguises. But disguises wouldn't matter against sufficiently bloodthirsty bandits.

"I'm not sure," Renny said, breaking off from the path and moving through the woods.

"Hey—" Chase bit back a shout and followed him. Not only would shouting have made her head hurt, but if there *were* bandits around, it probably wasn't a good idea.

Her ears twitched under her headscarf as she heard Thomasi mutter "The whole point of these disguises was to present *less* of a target to bandits, why are we going *toward* bandits? Need to teach these kids about self-preservation..."

She tuned him out and focused on following Renny. He tended to forget that other people didn't have the perception scores that he did.

If it were summer she probably would've lost him, but fortunately for everyone fall was well into season and the foliage was a third of what it normally was in the warmer months.

And as they got closer, Chase could smell it too. She wouldn't have known it was blood if Renny hadn't told her, but it smelled foul. She was glad that the monkeys and Dobbin had been shrunk down and stored away with the wagon; she'd been around enough farm animals to know that they wouldn't have liked this sort of smell at all.

The last leg was down a hillside, and Chase half-slid, half-climbed down, emerging onto a large ledge that held stone fire rings, cut and carved logs, and a foreboding-looking hole into the side of the hill.

The ledge was strewn with bodies. Quite a few bodies, though it was hard to tell how many. They were small and black and in so very many pieces, and Chase fought to keep her dinner down. It wasn't the first time she had seen corpses, but these... these were gory. She turned away and breathed until she was in control of herself again.

WILL+1

She laughed then and felt horrible for laughing. But it did help.

And the pressure eased even more, as Renny said, "They're all goblins."

"Goblins. Not children," Chase told herself, and that made her feel good enough to risk another look around.

Behind her, she heard Thomasi step down the hillside. His footsteps paused, and he swore. "This wasn't bandits," he finished, after he was done cursing.

"No. It smells like wolves." Renny said, staring nervously at the cave. He hugged his tail to him, keeping it high and out of the bloody splotches.

Chase looked from the bodies over to the carved logs. They had the starts of some ugly looking faces on them, and pointy ends. "What are those?" she wondered aloud.

Thomasi's voice was a whisper. "What?"

"The logs. They have faces. Goblin faces, I guess."

"Totem poles. They put them around settlements to warn people away," Thomasi said, coming closer. He stayed well away from the gory mess, though. "These are new, which means this tribe was new."

"I wonder…" Renny mused and headed toward the cave.

"Hey!" Chase snapped, ignoring the pain from her throbbing skull. "Be careful."

"I know what I'm doing," Renny said. "Adventurer, remember?"

"That isn't necessarily reassuring," Thomasi said, following the little fox. "I've known too many adventurers."

"Just give me a second," Renny said.

And then he disappeared.

Chase wasn't too worried. Renny was a Sensate, someone who focused on illusions and manipulating the five senses. He could disappear. That was a thing he did, sometimes.

Except wait, he hadn't said the skill he was using. He had to speak in order to use his Sensate illusions! Chase started forward, worried, but just as she was about to take her first shuddering step into a big clotted puddle, Renny reappeared.

"Ah," Thomasi said. "It's a dungeon."

And it took every bit of self-control that Chase had not to bolt down the hillside. Her ears strained to stand upright in alarm under her headscarf, and she shook, realizing just how *close* danger was. "Let's go," she whispered. "Let's go!" she said again, risking the shout.

Thomasi considered her. "That's not a bad idea."

"We could explore it," Renny offered. "If this is a new settlement then it's not that big, probably."

"No, and I'll tell you why when we're out of here," Thomasi said.

"Come now and mind your feet."

"Paws," Renny corrected. "At least let me search the bodies. There may be something useful."

"Can you find us down the path?" Thomasi asked.

"Yes. Once I'm away from all this blood. It's kind of overpowering."

"We'll go slowly. Catch up fast."

Thomasi went slowly. Chase didn't. All her grogginess had just been replaced by fear.

A fear that seemed to puzzle her human companion. "Slow down," he commanded as she started to outpace him. "And tell me what's wrong. Please."

"It's a *dungeon*," Chase said. "Those things are full of wicked monsters that eat people!"

"Well you're not wrong," he said, tugging on his goatee. "As reasons go that's a pretty good one to be afraid. But still, it's only goblins."

"Goblins are bad enough. But it's a *dungeon*. They spit out monsters over and over, and they draw in horrible people who raid them! People who do stuff like break into your house, and rob your chests, and try to sell the stuff back to you as if they hadn't nicked it not five minutes ago —" she broke off. Thomasi was trying to restrain laughter. "What's so funny?"

"Ah, well. You're not wrong about the impact dungeons have on nearby towns. But you no longer have a house, or really much to steal at all. We don't have to live around here, either. So what's to be afraid of?"

"Well..." she paused. "Well." No, she didn't have a house anymore, did she? This was adventuring. Even if she wasn't an adventurer, not in the *bad* sense of the word, anyhow. "I'm certainly not going to raid the dungeon. Or break into anyone's house and take their things."

"You might change your mind, given the right house," Thomasi said. Then he half turned. Chase heard it a minute later and turned as well, as brush crackled behind them... but it was just Renny. She slowed her pace, as did Thomasi.

The pause gave her time to consider. Her perspective on dungeons, the almost primal fear they inspired, all that had come from Bothernot. It had been taught by halvens who were happy and comfy and didn't want their home to change or to have to deal with anything risky or exciting in the slightest.

But now Chase wasn't a part of that anymore. She had gotten her wish. She was adventuring, now. The old reactions might not be the best ones. Although, Thomasi *had* insisted that they leave. So maybe her instincts were good after all.

It was all very confusing, and another reminder that her hometown had left its mark on her. Though now that she saw this particular string, she knew she could fight it, perhaps eventually snap it, if she had to.

"Did you find anything useful?" Thomasi asked.

"No," Renny said, and he had a small frown on his face, wrinkling his muzzle up adorably. "Somebody else had already searched them."

"Oh, so adventurers killed them," Chase said, relaxing.

"Maybe. But I didn't smell humans or anything else except wolves."

"You're certain of that?" Thomasi asked.

"Very."

"Did you smell them inside the dungeon when you went in?"

"Um... let me think." Fortunately, Renny was very intelligent. His memory wasn't perfect, but it did the trick this time. "No. No I didn't."

Thomasi nodded. "Then we need to keep moving, on the off chance the killers are still in the dungeon. We don't want to be anywhere near here when they come out."

"Wait," Chase asked, confused. "Why should we worry? He just said he didn't smell any wolves in the dungeon."

"And if that were a normal cave you'd be right: we wouldn't have to worry. But it's a dungeon." Thomasi rapped his walking stick on the ground as he moved, glancing down at her now and again to make sure she paid attention. "It was possible that the goblins had wolves. Some goblins are wolfriders, after all. If that was the case, then there would be wolf smell in the dungeon... it would have been their lair. But if there was no wolf-smell in the dungeon, it means that the wolf-things likely killed the goblins outside, then went inside to run through the dungeon. Which means that they're in one instance of the dungeon."

"Instance?" Chase frowned.

"That's an odd word for it," Renny added. "But I know what you're talking about. When a group goes into a dungeon together, it creates a unique pocket dimension. If another group goes in more than a few minutes later, then the dungeon creates a new pocket dimension for them. The two groups can never actually meet or interact in the same dungeon."

"Pocket dimensions. Yes, it would seem like..." Thomasi cleared his throat. "That's a good explanation. It also makes dungeons a good way of ditching pursuit. Vaffanculo hid out in one for a long time once the purges started."

Chase winced. "*Please* just call him the Necromancer. His name is just rude."

"Hid out in one?" Renny looked up to Thomasi.

"Yes. He went into a dungeon and stayed in there, knowing that nobody could come in after him, not while he was in his own private, ah, pocket dimension. Would have worked if he hadn't run out of food. Undead-themed dungeons are bad for that sort of thing and unless you go through some seriously hard quests first, it's difficult to make cannibalism work."

He said that last horrific sentence so matter-so-factly, and it made Chase look at him from the side of her eye. He *probably* didn't mean anything by it. Still, he'd said it awfully cavalierly.

"Why didn't they just seal the dungeon? His enemies, I mean?" Renny asked.

"What do you mean?" Thomasi asked.

"Why didn't they run through it and take the core out?"

Thomasi stopped, so abruptly that the pair of smaller friends turned to stare at him. They watched him open and close his mouth. Then his eyes narrowed and he moved his hand up to his lips... then hesitated and lowered it again. "I've honestly never heard of a thing like that."

"I haven't either," Chase confessed, and that seemed to set him at ease. She shifted to catch Renny's eyes. "What's all this about seals and cores?"

"Maybe it's not common knowledge here. Come to think of it I learned it from my guild school. Basically, every dungeon has a place in it where you can get access to a special place called a core chamber. It's usually behind the boss. It's full of... energy pylons. One of them holds a crystal that's the core. If you take it out the dungeon closes shortly afterward, and everything left in the dungeon is either destroyed or ejected outside, all at once."

"Really?" Thomasi asked. "That sounds like poor design, to me."

"Well, it's the only way to shut down dungeons permanently," Renny said. "Although you can take the core and start up a dungeon somewhere else with it. Then you can sit in the pylons and copies of you go out into the dungeon and fight adventurers and stuff. If you want to, I guess. I'm not sure how exactly that part works, we weren't taught that."

"So there is a way to get rid of dungeons? That's good," Chase said. Her head hurt less now. Still, she knew she'd need plenty of rest tonight. All this excitement and fear was bad for her nerves.

"Yeah," Renny said. "It's dangerous to leave dungeons alone for too long. They just get more powerful. But the treasure's good, so usually adventurers come through and keep them from getting too tough too quickly. And our Council has specialized troops that can move in and seal dungeons if the need arises. How do people handle it here?"

"I'm not sure," Chase said. "We're taught to run if we find anything that even looks like a dungeon and report it to the capital. I guess they maybe have people that do the same thing. We've never had one, so it's never been an issue, really."

Renny nodded. "If there weren't wolf-things around, I could go back and show you how to seal one. I think so, anyway. If it's just goblins in there it probably wouldn't be too hard. But doing that would kick the killers out of the dungeon and us with them, so that's probably a bad idea."

"Wolf-things?" Chase blinked.

"That's what Thomasi called them."

She shot the human a quizzical look. "Not wolves?"

Thomasi hesitated, then his face smoothed, as he seemed to reach a decision. "No. Definitely not wolves. Do you know why I'm certain of that?"

"Not really."

"There's a few things. The first being that the bodies were searched. Wolves don't do that. Then there's the fact that this was within four hours of our campsite and the deaths were recent... I'm no Scout but that blood was relatively fresh, I think. But we didn't hear any howling last night. I don't know any wolves that wouldn't howl at a moon like that."

"Well, you're the Tamer, you'd know," Chase said.

"Just a little bit of a Tamer, but my zoology is pretty good."

"What?"

"Never mind. All those factors I mentioned, they tell a different story. One that tells me we want to be as far as possible from this place before the moon rises tonight."

"The moon?" Chase asked. There was something she wasn't getting, something at the tip of her mind.

"Yes. The moon's almost full, isn't it?"

And then it clicked. "Oh my gods!" she shrieked. "Why are we walking? We need to *run!*"

"What?" Renny asked, looking from her to Thomasi.

"Werewolves!" Chase said and picked up the pace... only to slow it again, when Thomasi refused to hurry. "Come on!"

"Ohh... werewolves," Renny said.

"Mmm-hm," Thomasi grunted. "But there's no point in running *now.*"

"There's every point in staying far, far away from werewolves!"

"True. But consider. Our campsite was within a few hours of the site of the massacre last night. The smoke would have been easily visible. So either they got wrapped up in the dungeon, or they're gone from this place. If they're in the dungeon, then while we *would* benefit from hurrying, we've still got a scent trail from the massacre site to us. We're better off hitting the road and blending in with the other travelers, in which case we don't want to show up exhausted and panicked. If instead they are gone from here, then they can't be far and we're better off making as little noise as possible and just strolling normally, to avoid drawing their attention to us."

It made a fair amount of sense, when Chase considered it. "What's your intelligence again? That's remarkably well thought out."

"I'm not telling. Not everything is about numbers," Thomasi said.

"That's the sort of answer you hear when somebody's actually pretty low," Chase said. "But you're right, it is your business. Sorry." Thomasi had a way about him, that made one feel like a friend, like she'd known him for years. She had to watch herself around him, avoid being *too* casual. And questions about attributes weren't something you normally tossed around lightly.

"No offense taken." Thomasi tugged at his cowl. "Figure we'll stop for an early lunch in a bit, then push on to the main road. And hope like hell no werewolves come barking up our back trail."

No werewolves did. Though they DID hear barking at one point, but it was from a farmer's dogs, while they were skirting his property. After a couple of more remote farms they found their way to the road, and gladly fell in, treading over the ancient stones, and passing mile markers that still held carvings in the ancient script. They passed travelers as they went, most in groups, wagons moving with farmers and tradesmen keeping hard eyes on them... eyes that invariably relaxed whenever Thomasi gave a hearty hello and fell in next to them to chat merrily about the weather and their journeys and life in general.

By this time Renny was firmly in Chase's pack, and Chase had her headscarf tightly wrapped around her ears. With those concealed she looked like a very young child, and she reinforced the image by keeping her mouth shut, clinging to Thomasi's legs whenever someone tried to talk to her, and generally acting shy.

Chase ended up with a double handful of treats and sweets for her troubles, and Thomasi's explanation of how he was taking his daughter to see the city was accepted without any visible disbelief.

Their plan, hatched days ago, seemed to be working.

Thomasi and Chase had expected trouble from the authorities, if said authorities had survived the little incident in Pandora Prison. So they'd left the roads days ago, traveled in the backwoods, even though it took more time. When the terrain got too rough Thomasi had shrunk the wagon and they'd walked. When it was nice and flat, the wagon came out and they rolled.

But the fact of the matter was that the authorities would probably be looking for the Ringmaster of a circus, a toy fox golem, and a halven

girl. Some traveling storyteller and his daughter, on the other hand...
well, that was nothing to fuss about.

And for the first few hours, the plan seemed to be working...

...up until the point they hit the line. The city's walls lay in the
distance ahead and houses and shops rose to either side along the
outskirts, but a solid mile of stopped carts, grumbling pedestrians, and
people on shuffling horses sat between Chase and the gates. Her stomach
sank. There was no way this wasn't trouble.

"What's all this then?" Thomasi asked the teamster in front of him.

The stout man turned, and eyed Thomasi over a cartful of turnips.
"There's Scouts and Wizards with the guards at the gate. They're
checking people."

"For what?" Thomasi's face radiated innocent concern.

"No idea. But it was like this yesterday, too, from what Jocomo says."
The Teamster jerked a thumb at an elderly man currently in the process
of moving up and down the line, selling some kind of fresh bread. The
smell made Chase's mouth water. Lunch *had* been hours ago, after all.
And she hadn't even had brunch, or mid-dinner, let alone dinner yet...

She tugged on Thomasi's cloak and muttered, "Hungry, poppa."

"Well," Thomasi said, and turned around to look behind him. There
were a few travelers, most of them a convoy from some brewery or the
other, with wagons full of casks and kegs. "If it's going to take this long
we might as well get something to eat. Firenzi, do you mind letting us cut
back in if we finish up in time?"

"Not at all!" said the thin man that Thomasi had spent a half-hour
chatting with for the last leg of the trip. "Go, make sure your daughter's
fed! Doesn't look like she's too used to missing meals, it'd be a shame to
start."

That made Chase's ears burn. *Why do some of them comment on my
weight? It's not my fault most humans are too thin.* But she restrained
herself, as Thomasi patted her shoulder and the two of them left the line
and headed out into the muddy paths of the outskirts.

Once they were in a relatively clear spot, Chase tugged on his cloak
again, and whispered "Now what?"

"Now?" Thomasi said, rubbing his goatee. "Now we improvise." He
pointed to the collection of buildings and streets off to the side. "Have
you ever been in the outskirts, the parts of a city that lie outside the
walls?"

"Er, no, I can't say I have."

"Come along then. And keep your mouth shut. This is probably going
to be a bit of a culture shock..."

CHAPTER 3: A HIVE OF SCUM AND VILLAINY

The wooden sign above the door showed many faded carvings of wheat, in various stages of growth. The name above those carvings read,

TAVERNA SEME

"Perfect!" Thomasi declared, as he took one last look around the street, that was made up mostly of dark alley entrances, mud, and a single patch of cobblestones stained brown about ten feet from the Taverna's door.

"Um," Chase said, drawing nearer to him so she could speak without being overheard. That seemed like a difficult task, given the number of eyes she could feel watching the pair from every alley. "I think your definition of perfect and mine are pretty different."

No sooner had she finished the statement, then the door of the tavern slammed open, and a man hurtled screaming through the air, landing with a thud on the cobblestones, cracking his nose so hard that blood spurted to join the stains already in evidence.

The door slammed shut again.

Chase realized her mouth was open. "That poor man!" she said, regaining her composure. **"Lesser—** ow!"

"None of that, now," Thomasi advised her, looking around.

The noise in the street had disappeared.

All of a sudden the tension felt a bit tighter. The air seemed heavy, harder to breathe.

Someone in one of the dark alleys coughed.

Thomasi slapped his forehead under the cowl. "Ah! Right! Sorry. Look, daughter, what glorious architecture!" He turned his back to the groaning man, and nudged Chase.

She glared at him, then back to the corpse, then back up to Thomasi again. "What?"

"Turn around," he said, barely moving his lips. "They don't want witnesses."

Her confusion no less for the explanation, Chase turned around, and stared back down the way they'd come.

It was a fairly odd sight when you got down to it, especially to someone who had spent all her life growing up in a tiny rural village. The outskirts of Arretzi sprawled beyond its walls, ramshackle buildings and streets that curved and dead-ended and got you lost with casual contempt. Lines of washing and mud and the smell of filth, and wild-looking dogs growling at passerby.

And what passers-by! She'd seen more people in the last few minutes than she had in her entire lifetime! Most of them human, but a few halven, and even one or two figures with what had to be elven features. Mostly women, those. Mostly not-very-well-dressed, those. They had skirts that showed their *ankles*, and Chase's upbringing warred against her admiration. Much easier to move around in, she reckoned.

But as they'd traveled, the people got meaner-looking, more poorly dressed, and dirtier. And the architecture changed to match. What got Chase was that it hadn't taken all that long, just perhaps five minutes, and the neighborhood had a completely different feel than the sturdy, functional shops and homes lining the way to the city's main gate.

"Thanks, squire," someone muttered from very, *very* close behind them, and Chase was grateful for her cool, as she refrained from jumping and screaming.

"It is nothing," Thomasi replied. Then after a few seconds more, he tapped Chase on the shoulder and turned back around.

The halven girl felt her ears twitch under the headscarf as she stared at the now-still man on the lone patch of cobblestones, wearing nothing but a pair of heart-spotted boxer shorts. "Is he, is he dead?" she whispered.

"Mm? No. They'll have left him alive. No point in bringing trouble." Thomasi ambled toward the door of the tavern.

"We were only looking away for seconds," Chase said, staring around at the alley mouths. "I didn't hear a thing!"

"Well they're good at their job. Always nice to see professionals at work, hm?"

"I didn't see a thing."

"Good, you're getting it!" Thomasi ruffled her head, and she glared at him. Then he stopped by one of the windows and looked over to the murky glass. "Hm."

"Can you see anything through that?"

"Of course not. But it's been what, about thirty seconds, all told, since that fellow hit the pavement? And it's roughly noon, give or take?"

"Um…" She looked up to the sky. It was a little hard to find the sun, the buildings around here were tall and crooked. *Much like this neighborhood's inhabitants, really.* "Yes. Near noon, or a little past."

Thomasi nodded and started counting out loud. "Thirty… twenty-nine… twenty-eight…"

At twenty-two the door thumped open again, and a dwarf came sailing out. Chase glanced back, winced as he bounced off the already prone human occupying the cobblestones, and thwacked against a nearby wall on the rebound.

Come to think of it, that wall had some brown stains on it, too…

Without missing a beat Thomasi marched in, and Chase scrambled to keep up with him. The very large and very surprised man who'd just ejected the dwarf stepped back, and everyone in the room stopped what they were doing to stare at the new arrivals.

None of them looked friendly. Most of them looked like they were missing parts. Even the women looked like they had their body weight in knives stashed away somewhere.

And about half of them were wearing cloaks and cowls… nastier than Thomasi's, but still in a similar style. After Thomasi spent a second looking around, the strange eyes shifted away from the unlikely pair, and the room of scum and villainy returned to their drinking, gambling, and muttering.

Chase tried to peer into every corner, and found that the room was oddly shaped, and pretty much mostly corners. Every table had been pushed into one, and everyone was seated facing the door, even though there was plenty of more space available.

Far out of her depth, Chase followed Thomasi like she was tied to him with a string, trying to avoid thinking about how her bare feet were sticking to the floor every now and then. *Shoes. I see now why humans wear shoes so often. Maybe I can get a pair. Maybe they won't be so bad?*

Thomasi stopped at the bar, and Chase pushed past a forest of legs from nearby standing patrons. Once she had a clear view, she peered up at the ugly man who wore an eyepatch with a copper coin set into it.

The man's eye was locked on Thomasi, who stared back and smiled. "Greetings, signore. My daughter and I require a private room to dine in. The finest you have!"

There was a pause.

The bartender roared laughter.

The men standing at the bar to either side roared laughter.

The rest of the room followed suit, until she and Thomasi were the only ones who weren't braying their amusement and spittle into their neighbors' faces. Chase felt sweat gather under her headscarf, and dearly wished she could take it off, just for a bit. But no, they were in a dangerous spot now, and she didn't want to make a mistake. Didn't want to jog Thomasi's elbow, when he was working. *Because that's what he's doing,* she knew. *He's playing a role, deliberately being out of place. Why? What's he trying to achieve, here? This is a deception of some sort. He knows what he's doing. I'm certain of it.*

"I think you should leave," the bartender said, and the laughter died away, all save for one guy still snorting in an otherwise quiet corner. The large man at the door sighed and started ambling over.

"Well, if you don't want my money, all right. I suppose I can wait for our master elsewhere. A pity, your food comes recommended."

The bartender held up a hand. "It is very fine cuisine. And I do have a room with a view upstairs. But they are, hm... not for everyone who comes in off the street, you understand." The ugly man he was eyeing Thomasi as he said this. The mention of a Master made him cautious, Chase realized. That brought an outside force into the situation. Casual ejection and robbery now risked consequences.

Thomasi reached under his cloak, and the bouncer hurried forward. To either side, Chase was suddenly aware of the standing patrons at the bar parting like waves, and so, so many hands gripping hilts of knives...

Metal flashed in Thomasi's hand, and those knives started to slide free of sheaths—

—only to relax as the disguised Ringmaster put a silver coin on the table. "For the food and drink."

Knives disappeared. But now Chase saw a brighter sharpness in the onlooking eyes. A calculating one that said that knives weren't entirely out of the equation.

Thomasi reached back into his cloak, and metal flashed again. "And this for the room's rental."

Yellow, this time.

Gold.

We're dead! Chase thought, sweat soaking into her headband, and fought to keep her face still. But an odd thing happened, as she started glancing around the room, trying to find a clear path to the door.

Most of the patrons had returned to their business.

In fact, scanning the room, she saw that most of them pointedly had their backs to the strange duo. A few were even sweating, and that made her feel better. *We're fear buddies!* She stifled a giggle at the incongruous thought. But she *did* feel better.

"I see," the bartender said, swiping a rag across the counter. The coins disappeared into the cloth. "Antonio, mind the bar. I will show our lunch guests to their dining room. This way, please." He shuffled out from behind the bar and motioned to what Chase had taken for another corner, but was upon closer inspection a cramped, narrow staircase. Well, narrow by human standards. Her small body navigated the turns with no trouble, and Thomasi was nimble enough to make his ascent look graceful. The bartender was the main one troubled, as his girth literally compressed at every turning.

The room he led them to was small and simple, and had a window looking out over the main street. It had a pretty good view of the bouncing spot, and the warped, bubbled glass showed two pinkish forms there, stripped to their underwear. "You say you are meeting your master here?" The bartender's coin-eyepatch gleamed in the weak sunlight as he turned his gaze back to Thomasi.

"In a manner of speaking. My master is meeting someone of great importance today, and I am here to smooth the way." Thomasi smiled. "You understand how it is."

"And you wish to have such a meeting here?" The bartender looked around.

Chase did, too. The wooden furniture was a bit battered and there were cracks in the walls, but the room was clean. A jar stood on a shelf across the way, with flowers in it, and a painting of a glowering bald man hung askew on a wall. By comparison to the common room downstairs, this was luxury.

"I do." Tom sat at the table. "With the gates being what they are, it seems the best option available to discuss business."

"Ah, business!" The bartender smiled. "Your master is a man of business."

"She knows her business, all right." Thomasi smiled.

"Mie scuse, I should not have assumed," the bartender said, a hint of oil seeping into his tone. One hand felt in his pocket, and coins clinked. He startled a bit, as if he wasn't aware of what he'd done. "Please wait here. I will have a suitable repast sent up shortly."

With a nod and a casual wave, Thomasi dismissed the man and turned to stare out the window.

Once the door shut, Chase went around the room, searching. Only one door in and out. No secret passages that she could see. Although... "Ha!" she exclaimed, as she pushed a chair over to the wall, and clambered up to the portrait.

"What are you doing?" Thomasi asked.

"I *thought* the eyes looked funny." She took the picture down, revealing two painted eyes on the wall behind it. "These are peepholes."

Thomasi laughed. "I'm not surprised. Go ahead and put that back, though."

"It's just like the Jinkies book I read. The murderer spies on people through... peepholes... like... these..." Chase paled, and her voice trailed off. "He's going to murder us, isn't he?"

"Nope," Thomasi said, turning back to the window. "And there goes the runner. Off down the street to the most important man in town. In the outskirts, anyway."

"Okay..." Chase replaced the portrait.

Then she nearly fell off the chair, as a voice behind her asked, "Can I please come out now?"

It was Renny, Chase realized. "Can he come out?"

Thomasi nodded. "I think we're safe. For at least ten minutes, maybe an hour if people are busy. Maybe more if they're being real idiots about it. Although you should probably be ready to hide, in case the bartender actually brings us food."

Renny squirmed free of the pack, and Chase hopped down off the chair, and swung him easily down to the floor. He looked around with interest, then moved over to sit under the painting.

"So what is this all about?" Chase asked, keeping her voice low. "Why are we here? Why did you flash gold in front of that many miscreants? Why aren't we dead in a ditch somewhere, murdered and robbed because of that gold? And what's this about a master? Who's she supposed to be?"

Thomasi smiled, though his eyes didn't stray from the window. "Chase. Do you remember what you asked me to do for you, almost a week ago now?"

"I asked you to train me to be the best adventurer I could," Chase said, crossing her arms.

"And I am. But since you're not a Model, a Tamer, or a Ringmaster, most things I have to teach you fall into the social sphere. Fortunately we're in a place where I can set you up for massive Grifter experience. If this works out, you'll level. My god, you'll level."

Chase pulled off her headscarf, and felt her ears perk with interest. "I'm listening."

"I'm sure you are. But you should be thinking, instead." he said, glancing at her, and his eyes glittered as he looked from her to Renny. "Wouldn't you rather earn even more experience, and figure it out yourself?" Thomasi's smile showed perfect teeth. "You have anywhere from eight to fifty-eight minutes, if my estimates are right. Tell me your deductions. Tell me why I did what I did, and what I'm up to, here. What *we're* up to, at any rate."

Chase puffed her cheeks out in annoyance.

But annoying as he was, he was right. She could gain experience from trying to crack his plans. And as a fellow Grifter, he couldn't object too much if she cheated, right? Still…

"It's going to be hard to do this without context. Can you tell me if some particular assumptions are wrong or right?"

Thomasi considered. "Yes, that seems fair. But they have to be specific. Don't guess wildly or broadly and expect me to answer."

"Okay." She pushed the chair to the table, then clambered up and stood on it, studying the cowled man's face. "You chose this taverna. But you weren't familiar to the bartender or the crowd. That could either be because you're a stranger here, or because you've been in prison for twenty years."

"Give or take," Thomasi said. "It wasn't exactly twenty. And that's not a comment confirming or denying either of your statements."

"Give or take," Chase said, rubbing her sore ear. Being cramped under the headscarf had done the long, pointy extremity no good. "You didn't know about the peepholes. So I'm going to assume that you didn't come here because you are familiar with the Taverna Seme."

"You are correct." Thomasi said.

A knock on the door, and Chase scrambled for her headscarf again. Renny disappeared into her pack, so quickly that she almost fell off the chair.

"Come in," Thomasi called.

A whip-thin woman in a patched dress stood beyond, hands full of tankards and pitchers. Her sour face was stretched in what she probably thought was a friendly smile. "Some beer? Some water? Some milk?"

"Is the milk fresh?" Thomasi asked.

"The finest for your daughter, sir," the woman simpered. It didn't seem like it fit at all.

"Then leave all three pitchers." Thomasi tossed a few coppers on the table, and the woman's eyes widened as she sat down her drinks, and scooped the coins away, in a blur of motion.

She didn't spill a drop, despite the fast movement. *Got to a be a job skill there. Barmaid? Waitress?* Chase pondered but kept it to herself.

"The milk's mostly fresh," the woman muttered. "The cellar's cold. But I can run out and get better for you if you want."

"I'll keep that in mind. How shall we call you if we need you again?" Thomasi's smile was brilliant, and the woman swallowed, flushing slightly.

Oh, I know that look, Chase grinned to herself. She fancied Thomasi.

Or perhaps his coins. Probably his coins. The end result was the same, really.

"I'm down the sidestairs, in the kitchen," the woman said, fussing with her apron strings, smoothing out her skirt... and drawing attention to the shape of her hips under the dress. Not so thin as the rest of her, there. "Just send your girl if you need summat. Or come yourself, if milord can spare the time."

"We shall see how the afternoon goes," Thomasi promised, and spread his hands.

The woman giggled, sounding like a hawk trying to imitate a baby chicken, and left... after a slow, lingering look over one shoulder.

Once the door was shut, Thomasi held up a finger, then lowered it a few moments later. "Add this into your logic," he told her. "And I advise skipping the milk."

Chase nodded. "I planned to. It wouldn't taste right." She poured water instead and scowled at it. "Safe, do you think?"

"Probably. We're upriver from the city, yes?"

Chase reviewed her mental geography. "Yes."

"I'd say it'll be fine. And if not, you can always pass on whatever debuff you get hit with to someone more deserving, right?"

Chase blinked. Her half-secured headscarf rose with her ears. "You're right! I forgot I could do that! Hey, stop laughing!"

"To be fair, she's only had the job a few days." Renny said, taking one of the chairs and hopping up on it. "Can I play the figuring things out game, too?"

"Up to her," Thomasi said, pouring himself a tankard of beer. "I don't mind."

"You don't know this tavern."

"Taverna," Chase corrected.

"Right. He doesn't know this tavern, so that means he chose it. Why did he choose it? What does it have that other taverns— tavernas we passed didn't?"

"Glass windows," Chase said.

"Nicely done!" Thomasi said.

"Why does this place have glass windows, and no other buildings around have those?" Renny asked.

"Because they're the only place that can afford them?" Chase asked. "The rest of this place looks pretty poor. I mean, this place doesn't look rich, but..."

Thomasi's mustaches twitched. "I'll point out something for free. Some of the buildings around here had broken glass windows once upon a time."

"But these are intact." Chase said, turning it over in his head. "They're intact because... there would be trouble if someone broke them."

Thomasi took another pull of the beer. "Good..."

"Why would there be trouble? Well, a lot of locals drink here. Would it be trouble because then they'd get kicked out, or because the owner would raise prices if his windows got broken?"

"No," Thomasi said. "Getting colder."

"I'm fine, thanks. It's warm enough in here."

"Not what I meant. Neither of those are reasons why the windows are intact. Oh, they might be contributing factors in the abstract, but they're not *the* reason."

"So..." Chase climbed up on the table and poured herself some water. Then she took her seat and leaned back, sipping from the oversized tankard. "They're intact because there will be trouble. You confirmed that. Trouble from the city guards?"

"I don't think there are any of those that come around here," said Renny. "Those two guys outside wouldn't have been robbed if that was so."

"Four guys, actually," Thomasi said, glancing back out the window. "No, five."

"We would have been tossed outside like them if things downstairs had gone wrong," Chase said.

"They probably wouldn't have stripped you," Thomasi said. "Professionals have standards, and you're a young lady, after all. Generica's nicely un-pervy that way."

"Uh, okay." Chase felt her face redden a bit at the talk of being stripped, or not, as the case may be. "ANYWAY. You flashed gold in there... but you flashed gold after you mentioned you were working for someone. And after you flashed that gold, the crowd lost interest."

"They did. You're on the right track..." Thomasi made circular motions with one hand, eyes glued to the window. "Speed it up a bit. My estimates were off. Just our luck to be the excitement on a slow day."

"They saw the silver and they wanted it, and they wanted to get it from you," Chase said, remembering the scene vividly. "But then they saw the gold, and it was like... it was fear. They were afraid. Why?"

"It's the same reason that they're afraid to break the windows here, isn't it?" Renny asked.

"Very astute!" Thomasi nodded. "You are correct."

Chase stared into her water, letting her mind roam. She weighed possibilities, considered tangents.

Below her, she heard a sudden cessation. The low muttering and noise of the common room that she'd dimly been aware of through the floorboards had stopped, all at once. The door to the outside shut, but it was the only noise in the silence.

Finally, she spoke. "The windows are intact... and people won't rob someone who's too rich here... because there are consequences. And that means there's someone who enforces those consequences."

"Someone who isn't the guard," Renny pointed out.

"Someone who is below us at this very minute," Thomasi said, turning to face her, then looking towards the door. "And will be here very quickly."

"Who?" Chase whispered.

"The local crime boss, I expect," Thomasi said. "Someone who can get us in or through the city. Though we might not want to let him know that right away." He smiled. "I've done enough business in places like this to know that you want to go slowly, slowly. Take your time. Show respect. Read between the lines and listen to what isn't said."

"Why are you telling me all this?" Chase said, ears flicking. She reached for her headscarf... and blinked, to find it gone from her hands.

"No. The ruse would be seen as rude, here. Besides, it suits our purposes better this way." Thomasi twirled the scarf he'd pickpocketed from her and handed it to Renny. "She gets it back after this is done."

"Hey!" Then she blinked. "Wait. You told the bartender that you were here to facilitate a meeting between someone very important and your master." Her mind churned overtime, chewing on a terrible notion. "And then you corrected him, because your master wasn't a man..."

Thomasi smiled wider.

And then she knew. "Oh you son of a... the crime boss is the very important guy! And I'm your master! You're going to play it like I'm in charge of you and make me do the talking!"

INT+1

Thomasi's grin was all the answer she needed.

Feet creaked on the stairs outside, and she turned, composing herself. "That's why you gave me advice... argh! Renny, can you get back in the pack, please?"

He complied, and she set it beside her chair, smoothed herself down and prepared for what was to come. Shooting one last sour look at Thomasi, she asked "Any more advice?"

"Yes. Don't get us all killed."

And with that comforting thought in mind, Chase heard three heavy knocks at the door...

CHAPTER 4: A MAN OF WEALTH AND TASTE

Chase stared at the door. Three knocks came again, a little lighter this time.

"Shall I?" Thomasi asked, shooting her a glance.

Why was he being so deferential— oh, right. They're close enough to hear us. "Let our guests in, Tom."

And as he moved in front of her, she took the opportunity to buff. She didn't have many of those, but the one that came to mind might mean the difference between life and death. **"Silver Tongue,"** she whispered, barely on the edge of sound.

A slight creaking from the side, and she kept her face still. That creak had been inside the room, and from the side the portrait was on. There were living eyes watching through the holes now, she reckoned. No need to alert them to the fact that she knew. It took an effort to keep from looking, though.

WILL+1

Once the door was open Thomasi moved back to stand next to her chair, and Chase stared at the biggest, greenest woman she'd ever seen in her life. She had to stoop down to get through the door, and when she straightened up, Chase saw that she had two large, yellow tusks jutting out from her lower jaw. Flat black eyes stared at her, then roved around the room, taking in everyone and everything. Only after a solid twelve seconds of perusal did she grunt and move inside. Her clothes were fairly fine, Chase noticed; a loose tunic, sturdy trousers with embroidery, and a fur cloak. Finer garb than any she'd seen in this neighborhood so far. Or on the road, come to think of it...

The second person through the door was a woman with a dog's head, a sleek Doberman's muzzle and ears. She was dressed similar to her

35

partner, with the cut adjusted for her figure and visible, short fur in the few places that her skin was bare. More worryingly, she also had a sword hilt visible on her belt. The green lady was unarmed but seemed like she could probably bench press Thomasi if need be.

Dog-lady sniffed once or twice, then her eyes widened. "Wolf— wait. Wait, no. Fox," she announced, looking toward Chase. "Faint, though."

The statement made the big green woman frown and scratch her head. "Don't have instructions about that kind of—"

"Shush. You, why am I smelling fox?"

Chase reached behind her, and the atmosphere in the room grew hard, hard and brittle.

An atmosphere that eased when Chase pulled out Renny and put him on the table. "One has to keep up appearances," she said, demurely.

The green woman laughed, and her teeth were as yellow as her tusks. She leaned back through the door. "They're clean."

"Good, good," came a man's voice. Elderly, warm, jovial, it reminded Chase of her grandfather. "Cagna, Lachina, mind the door. We are expecting company, after all."

The man who entered took his time about it. A genial human, with a shock of white hair, thin on top. He was portly and walked with the help of a cane. His face seemed loose, even though he was fat. As if he'd been even bigger at one time and had shrunk down unevenly. Eyes glittered back in their hollows as he scrutinized them and smiled at Chase. "Well well." Then his glittering gaze roamed over to Thomasi, and his breath hitched in his throat.

"Tom, get the seat for our guest," Chase said, steepling her fingers together. "Show some respect, hm?"

"Of course," Thomasi helped the man to his seat, and poured him a tankard of beer.

The older man took it, eyes never leaving Thomasi's face.

Chase took the opportunity to glance away from the portrait and guards and mouth, **"Silent Activation, Size Up."**

Then she took a good, hard look at the stranger.

Old human?
Charisma – Moderately better
Perception – Mildly worse
Willpower – Greatly better
Wisdom – Moderately worse
Influencing conditions: Blessing – Willpower, Vow - Omerta
Your Size Up skill is now level 2!

More charismatic than Chase? That was a surprise. She licked her lips. That willpower, though… he'd doubled down on it, by the look of his condition.

This size up skill is insanely useful, Chase realized. *I should have been practicing it while we were on the road instead of playing keepaway with monkeys.*

After the old man was seated, Tom moved to stand by Chase's side, keeping his eyes downcast and his hands folded. The old man simply drank his beer a sip at a time, considering the two of them. He seemed in no hurry to speak. Chase, for her part, drank from her water and studied him right back. He had large hands, with several rings that ranged from plain to gaudy. Though his hands shook when he moved the tankard, she could see calluses along the fingers. If she cared about halven conventional wisdom that would have meant that he was trustworthy, since he'd obviously worked for a living.

But they were very far from Bothernot, and she was pretty certain that whatever crime he was bossing, this man wasn't trustworthy.

But then, neither am I.

He seemed patient to wait, and that was fine. She had formulated her first few moves in this game, and Thomasi had said that he'd back her.

So here goes... "Signore, I am thankful you came to dine with us," she said, putting on her best smile. "It is a fine day, and I am grateful that you accepted my invitation. May I ask your name, nonno?"

Nonno was the old word for Grandfather, and it was a gamble.

"Don't call me signore, I work for a living," the man said, but his eyes twinkled. "Nonno is fine. You remind me of my youngest, once upon a time. Mind you, she wasn't halven." He smiled. "Buzo downstairs told me that your man was setting up a meeting between his master and someone of importance."

"He did. And all are here, now, Nonno." Chase stood on the chair, leaning her elbows on the table, steepling her fingers below her chin. "Tom works for me, you see."

"Ah..." Nonno leaned back in his chair and chuckled. "There are less expensive ways to meet with me, you know."

"Your pardon, but I didn't know them. And I'm willing to believe that most of them would take more time. I felt it worth the expense."

"Ah, but some things are not to be rushed. We have a saying in Arretzi. Piano, piano. You know it?"

This one was a struggle. Chase ran back through her lessons in the old tongue... there were a few words that were all about the context, and this one hadn't come up often. Still, she could guess. "It means slowly, slowly," she decided.

Nonno's smile had missing teeth. One of the sockets was stained black, and Chase kept the disgust from her face. *How could anyone let their teeth get that bad? It would make it hard to eat, and that's terrible!*

"Slowly, slowly," Nonno said, tapping his fingers on the head of his cane. Just a simple bronze ball, that had nicks and tarnish on it. "Yes. That is the way I would prefer to do business, most days. For those I do not know so well, at any rate."

"I apologize, Nonno," Chase lowered her gaze to the table. That vow he'd taken nagged at her. The word 'omerta' meant something like humility, so perhaps he'd appreciate a display of the same? "Like me, time is short."

The self-deprecating humor got a chuckle. "But not too short to have dinner with your Nonno?" he asked.

She didn't look up. "For that honor, I make time."

"Then I think perhaps we can have dinner. Anything else... piano, piano. Yes?"

"Yes," she said, smiling.

So she chatted with Nonno, asking questions about the city, and listening attentively as he spoke of his family, the weather, his business down at the wharf, and the prices of olive oil these days.

Honestly, after weathering a decade and a half of having to listen to halven farmers talk about things that absolutely didn't change over and over again, it was refreshing. She found herself leaning in, and the old man grew more animated as the discussion went on, waving his hands and laughing, and telling stories that she was pretty sure had never happened... or had been so exaggerated that the truth they were built upon was a distant memory buried somewhere deep into the details.

But not once did he ever mention anything illegal. Not once did he talk about any sort of crime.

Chase was starting to wonder if they had the right fish on the hook, so to speak. But a quick glance back to the door, and the two inhuman and dangerous figures guarding it, allayed those doubts.

As the food finally started to arrive, Nonno leaned forward with a sharp look in his eyes. "And where were you from again, mia piccola nipotina?" Nonno asked.

His willpower is massively good. I can't lie to his face. But his perception is bad, so some deflection could work. After chatting with him for so long, she thought she had a feel for his ways. "I'm from the north, Nonno. Not far, as it goes."

"But you are south now, not north," he said, accepting the plate of prosciutto and olives that the dog lady handed him. "Thank you, Cagna."

"Ah. I'm attempting to start my own business. Following the family path didn't work so well, in my case. Thank you Tom," she said, accepting a plate full of hammy goodness from her own 'servant.' He also handed over a set of silverware, honest-to-gods fancy silverware that didn't match the rest of the taverna at all. *Probably stolen,* she realized.

"Your own business? Makes sense," The old man nodded. "Many young people chafe under the yoke of their elders. Sometimes a walk about is enough to cure that, or sometimes it does turn up new opportunities."

CHA+1

Chase turned her sigh of relief into a small moan of appreciation. The prosciutto *was* quite good. The thinly sliced uncooked ham made for a good contrast against the bitterness of the olives, and the vegetables and bread that Cagna laid out shortly thereafter made the meal a good elevenses. Not a solid halven lunch, but as short as food had been these last few days, it made Chase less worried about all the weight she had been losing.

A few muttered words from the doorway made her glance back in time to see the thin woman staring disconsolately into the room, holding up another tray and glancing back and forth from Cagna to Thomasi, her face forlorn.

"No," Lachina told her, and plucked the tray from her with ease. Without missing a beat Cagna moved over and deposited it on the table, scooting it a bit closer toward Chase. *Biscotti,* Chase recognized, and swallowed a sudden burst of saliva. She'd rarely had the thin cookies. And that bottle in the center meant *oooh, dessert wine, too!*

That was dangerous. And expensive too, wasn't it? Wine was supposed to cost more in the cities than back at home. "I have to admit, I'm impressed by the fare," Chase said, pushing aside the stack of emptied plates next to her.

"Ah, I told Buzo to give you your money's worth for the meal. As for the room, do not worry, it is my gift to you, for such pleasant company." Nonno smiled again.

Wait, we paid for that. We paid gold!

And against Chase's better judgment, her self-control slipped. She felt her face flicker in surprise, felt her mask slip—

—and the gleam in the old man's eyes showed that he'd caught that shock. She hastily reassembled her smile, but a trickle of fear oozed through her heart. Low perception or not, there was nothing wrong with his mind.

"Something wrong, signora?"

Signora, he calls me now. Not tiny granddaughter, like he did earlier. That's a bad sign. She took another pull of water. "Nothing, Nonno."

"It occurs to me, that I never did ask what business you wished to start. I am very interested in the answer you have to that, my dear. I am

39

in business myself, you see. And like any honest Merchant, I can tell the difference between true coin and false."

He reached into his pocket, and Thomasi tensed beside her. But all Nonno did was put a gold coin on the table.

A very familiar gold coin.

And Chase's heart sunk as she remembered one of the Grifter job's basic abilities.

Fool's Gold. Oh Tom, why? I know you have real gold! I saw some in the wagon!

The tray of cookies sat so close to her, and Tom was filling a small cup with sweet, sweet wine that she had only heard about before, never tasted, but her mouth felt like it was filled with ashes.

And the old man's eyes were boring into her.

Nonno was waiting for an answer.

And he would be very, very good at catching any direct lie.

"I apologize, Nonno. The business I am planning to start does not involve false currency. I thought this room rented with real gold. It was my mistake."

The old man was silent for a moment. He chewed a biscotti as he thought, slurped at his wine through broken teeth. "I do not think it was your mistake. I know well the Grifter's gold. And this coin is truly an amazing example of it. If the circumstances had been different... if things had been less strange... I think even I might have been fooled." And slowly, his eyes lifted from Chase to Thomasi. "She is not practiced enough to make such a thing, is she?"

Thomasi looked to *her*.

"Answer him," Chase said, and forced her trembling hand to take a biscotti. If this went bad, she'd at least have a cookie for the road. Or before she died.

"No, she is not," Thomasi said. "Not in my career, at the least."

"Ah... Much becomes clear," Nonno said, leaning back. "Your servant has done you a disservice. But he has done it in your name, Nipotina."

Chase weighed her options. Nipotina was back, and she hadn't missed that hint. The old man liked her, at least a little. *Audacity. Try audacity. But first...* She took a pull of water, and hiding her lips, mouthed, **"Silent Activation, Foresight."**

Time froze. Everything stopped, and noise faded. In that silent and still spot, inside the beats between the seconds, she saw a blurry outline in front of her. The outline leaned forward and said the words she'd decided to say.

And though she couldn't hear them, she saw a ghostly outline lean out from Nonno tilt its head, considering her. Then it laughed and slapped the table. Chase caught motion below and saw one of her ghostly outline's hands turn slightly, with its thumb up.

And then, in a rush of sound and sensation, time unfroze.

Your Foresight skill is now level 22!

This was the Oracle's greatest advantage. This was Foresight. And while it had its disadvantages, it had the very big benefit of letting her try a course of action without committing to it.

But commit she did, as she leaned forward slightly. "If Tom is at fault on my behalf, then I too am at fault. I take full responsibility for his mistakes, Nonno."

And with relief, she saw the old man tilt his head, consider, then laugh and slap the table. "Good, good! You are a good girl! You do your family proud."

Slowly, she turned one hand up on the table, giving as large a thumbs up as she dared before turning the motion into another grab for biscotti.

"Responsibility, Cagna, that's always good to see in the young. Would that my boy had such, hm?"

"He's young still sir, he will learn," the dog-woman said, breaking her silence for the first time since she'd entered the room.

"Bah! He's thirty, he's a man." Nonno smiled. "This girl is half his age and has twice the coglioni. Try the vin de santo, child, it's quite good."

The sweet, sweet wine was indeed everything she'd been told it was... but the slight tingle in the aftertaste told her she shouldn't drink too much. Not now.

"What to do..." Nonno mused, while she drank. "You must understand, I have to discourage people spreading the Grifter's gold among the good, honest businessmen I support. If I didn't, then everyone would go broke overnight. It would be chaos."

"I understand completely. What can we do to make it right?"

"I'm open to suggestions. And I do like gifts. Please, surprise me." His smile was bright, but his eyes were shining, again.

This is another test, Chase thought, irritated. It wasn't enough that Thomasi was testing her, now ancient, oddly-paternal gangsters were trying to put her through the wringer. *Damn it! I bargained with a god, why do I have to go through this?*

And with that memory, came inspiration.

"As a matter of fact, I think I *can* offer you a gift, Nonno." She reached into her pack and pulled out a well-worn wooden case.

"Oh?"

"I can tell you your future. It's all in the cards," she said, smiling widely… only to have the smile falter and die, as the old man's face turned to stone.

"This is what you offer me? Arretzi's got plenty of fortune tellers, with their crystal balls and cards and runes and crystals and cazza. They tell me they call up my grandfather's ghost and use ropes to levitate the table, and stuff like that. This is worthless."

"It's not!" Chase said, glaring at him. "Every time I've thrown the cards, every time they've come true!" Granted, she had only thrown them once, but still, it counted. "I bargained with a god to get this skill!"

Nonno laughed, harsh and barking, completely at odds with his previous manner. He leaned forward, sneering…

…and that sneer broke in the face of Chase's stubborn glare. "Child," he asked, his voice without emotion. "What is your business?"

"I am an Oracle of Hoon. All else is secondary."

That was a gamble.

But he'd called himself a Merchant, he was into shady business… from what she'd gleaned from her meeting with the god, it was worth the risk of mentioning it.

"All right," Nonno nodded, eyes fixed on hers. "Tell me my fortuna. And we'll see if it's a good enough gift."

Chase nodded. "Shuffle the cards and think of your question while you do so. Do not tell me the question."

The old man complied. Several times he dropped cards as his hands shook, their joints knobby in their cages of flesh. But eventually he handed them over once more.

Chase nodded, and took the top card, placing it into the center of the table between them. "This card represents you, as you are now."

It was a man in bloodstained leather armor sitting on a throne, while all around him disreputable sorts prostrated themselves. The King of Rogues, upside down, and Chase wasn't surprised to see it. But reversed… that wasn't good. As soon as he glanced down she mouthed **"Silent Activation, Foresight,"** and tested out the results of telling him honestly what the card signified. Her face paled as she saw the results. *No, no. That's bad.* Time returned, and she felt the pressure building in her chest, the pressure that signified the possibility of a backlash if she deviated too far from her predicted action.

But she'd used Foresight enough to know how far she could push it. So long as her action wasn't TOO off course from her original test, the paradox would fade. Well, either that or it would disable her Foresight for a day. Then she'd be stuck with an irate crime lord and her best weapon would be useless.

So instead of telling him how the reversed King of Rogues

represented a financially inept figure who was obsessed with material wealth, or a fantastically, stupidly, stubborn man, she took a pull of her wine and mouthed **"Silent Activation, Silver Tongue."** Instantly the pain in her chest peaked... and ebbed. She hadn't lost Foresight to paradox yet.

"The King of Rogues is a man of wealth and power, very respected."

"Nothing I don't know already," Nonno grunted.

Your Silver Tongue skill is now level 4!

Chase blinked away her relief and drew the next card with a shaking hand. "This card signifies the problem at hand." Then she deposited the card above the King of Rogues. It showed a blazing wall of fire with eyes, sweeping through a forest. "The Elemental," Chase whispered. She'd seen this one before. In exactly the same spot, come to think of it. Did that mean... no, what were the odds this was another problem with Vaffanculo, or undead, or something on his scale?

"What? What is this crap?" The old man asked.

She used another silent activation, and foresight combination, and found the old man's ghostly projection receptive to an honest answer. So she told the truth.

"This signifies a powerful and dangerous entity, but a neutral one. Something that's just acting according to its nature."

"And this is my problem right now?" The old man asked, exchanging a significant look with Cagna. "You're sure of this?"

"It's what the cards say so far."

"Continue," he grunted. But now the sneer was off his face.

"This card represents your ally in the face of this trouble..." she said, and laid down the third card, to the left of the King of Rogues. It was a wise-looking sage, lecturing a class of students. But it was upside-down. "The Trainer..." Another gulp of wine, another silent foresight, and another ten moxie and fortune goodbye. She was getting nervous and lightheaded, now. But the skill worked, and she confirmed it was safe to say the truth. "Normally the trainer is a good ally to have. But a reversed trainer means a person who has poor planning skills, or untried talents. Someone who can't teach you much about your primary skillset."

"Hmm... Go on." Now the old man was rubbing his face. Using Silent Activation? Maybe. He HAD to have some Grifter levels.

"The next card is the crux of the choice, the decision that you'll make that most affects the problem." It was the Trainer again! She blinked. How... no, wait. She'd used some of the better-preserved cards from the older deck as models for the new art. This was the older one. Somehow it must have gotten mixed in with the newer cards.

"That's the same card!" Nonno said, staring. "I shuffled the deck. I was watching your hands. No way you fixed that."

"I didn't," Chase said. "This... we can flip another card. This card shouldn't be in here—"

"No. Tell me what it means."

"Well... this is right side up. The Trainer right side up represents resourcefulness, power, and inspired action. Someone who knows what they're doing."

"And what does it mean when my ally is my choice?"

Chase gnawed her lip. "It means that choosing to work with a seemingly unreliable ally to resolve your problem will prove your ally's worth."

"Interesting. Very interesting."

"There's one more card," Chase said, quickly. "This represents your greatest enemy, the biggest obstacle to resolving the problem." And as she flipped it to the right of the King of Rogues, her breath caught in her throat. "Oh my gods..."

The thing on the card glared up from the table, green scales filled with innumerable broken arrow shafts, red eyes shining hatred. Fire gouted forth from jaws that could swallow a horse without opening fully, as the great dragon declared itself the King's enemy. And what's more, it was *reversed*.

The old man swore.

"Yeah," Chase whispered, and used another silently activated foresight. Skills climbed again, but she barely paid attention. "The dragon's bad enough. But reversed, it represents a powerful and smart monster. Something that's almost impossible to defeat, that wants you gone. In this spot... Oh my. Oh my."

Silence, for a long minute. When Chase dared to look up, the old crime boss was by the window, hands folded behind his back.

Chase noticed that he'd left the cane at the table. And his hands weren't shaking at all now.

"I was going to dispose of you, for causing a fuss in my domain. For trying to insult one of my friends by passing Grifter's coin. I still may." Nonno was gone, now. The man speaking was the wicked man she'd been expecting. That he was old made no difference. An old wolf still ate young deer.

She opened her mouth to respond... and Thomasi's hand fell on her shoulder. Chase swallowed her words instead.

It was the right choice, as the old man continued. "But I wonder, Oracle, can you tell me the sort of monster I face, here? Can you tell me what occupies my mind, these last few days? If you can do that, you might be someone I could use, here."

Chase licked her lips. She glanced up at Thomasi…

…and behind him she saw Cagna, looking worried. The dog-woman looked to her, then slowly, deliberately, tapped her nose. She turned it into a scratch, but she was definitely trying to get at something, here.

Her nose. Something smelled. She'd smelled something. When she came into the room she smelled fox, but she told the old man no wolves.

And then Chase's mind clicked over to the cave they'd found. The wolf scent all around, and Thomasi's conclusion.

"Nonno?" She said, and the word was alien in her throat now, but she said it anyway. "You have a werewolf problem."

LUCK+1

The old man's gasp turned into a cough, and she watched his back twist with tension. And after a tense second more, he turned, and Nonno's genial, blackened smile was gaping wide once more.

And then her vision was words… including a set that left her staring in surprise.

You are now a level 7 Grifter!
CHA+3
DEX+3
LUCK+3

You are now a level 9 Oracle!
CHA+3
LUCK+3
WIS+3

Congratulations, by combining skillful lies with actual oracular vision, you have unlocked the Medium job! You may not have told the actual fortune, but the customer got the one he needed to hear!

Would you like to become a Medium at this time? Y/N?

CHAPTER 5: A PARTING OF THE WAYS

"It's bad for business," the old man said, after they had all gone back to their lunch. Chase was feeling a bit tipsy from the wine, and Thomasi and the two bodyguards had pulled up chairs and joined the feast. A test had been passed, a barrier had been broken, and the crime boss had decided to work with them.

Even the eyes behind the portrait had withdrawn, replaced by their painted covers. The thin, rangy woman who had first served them water was now the primary server, and she seemed more comfortable now that her domain had been returned.

Cagna ate with surprising daintiness, taking small bites, and moving her muzzle as little as possible. Lachina, by contrast, gobbled her food with abandon. She was practically hunched over her plate, eyes moving like one of the others would take it if she was too unwary.

Thomasi ate sparingly, and only of the healthier food. He had removed his gloves for this repast, and now he held up the fork and studied the silver in the light of the window. "A simple werewolf test, yes?"

"Yes," The old man admitted. She would call him Nonno to his face, but he would never be Nonno in her mind again. Not after he'd shown his true face, back there. "The touch of silver burns them," he continued. "A good friend of mine is a Tamer. He confirmed this old legend is true."

"I'm a Tamer myself, but I'm not high up enough to know much about werewolves," Thomasi shrugged. "I know that some Tamer Tier Two jobs will turn you into one if you're not careful. Maybe some Berserker paths, too."

"Tier Two jobs?" Chase asked, putting her desert wine down, and reaching for another biscotti. "What are those?"

To her surprise, Cagna answered. "They're jobs that come about as a result of combinations. If someone mixes the right skills from two basic jobs together at the right time in the right way, then you can unlock a Tier Two job."

Thomasi nodded to the dog-woman. "They're powerful but focused. Usually a good idea to nab one if you find it, though. Unlocking one means you're doing the things that they're focused on doing anyway, so they're almost always guaranteed to give you an edge."

"Unless it makes you a werewolf," the old man said. Then he cursed a bit. "—wolfmen all up my rump. City's locked down because of those stugats."

Chase almost choked on her biscotti at the vulgarity.

"Ah, THAT'S why," Thomasi nodded. "We had wondered."

"It's bad for business," the old man said. "My friends on the river, they come to me and they say Massimo, we have such amazing things for you, and I must tell them no, I am sorry, I have no place to put them. With the gates being checked as they are, I cannot carry enough in to clear out my storage. I have piles of things I do not want scrutinized greatly building up in spaces that were never meant to hold so much for so long. And the money I must pay! It is too much, I tell you."

He waved his hands as he spoke, and they did tremble from time to time, but nowhere near how they had earlier in the meal. Chase was certain that had been a con, a ploy to throw her off her guard. And it had damn near worked. There was a lesson there, for the future.

Thomasi spoke again. "Surely there are other ways besides the gates, to get into the city. And out, of course."

"Of course," Massimo confirmed. "But surely you would not wish to depart so quickly. A business such as yours would do well in this city," he cast a genial smile over Chase, and she smiled back. "Too many frauds in the quartiere mistico. Not enough of the real deal. And I could be persuaded to talk with some of my friends inside the walls. Help set you up with a store, some starting capital, whatever you need to bring your wisdom from the gods to the ears of us poor sinners."

Chase was smart enough to know that saying no at this point would be a very bad idea. "Arretzi does seem like a beautiful city, from what I have heard by those who praise her. But I am worried about these werewolves. They are your enemy. They would then be my enemy, too."

"Dogs," Massimo snarled, his genial mood vanishing. "Not useful ones, either."

Cagna shifted and exchanged glances with Lachina but said nothing. Massimo didn't even notice as he continued. "They hunt in the outer ring here, where the guards don't come and they think nobody shall be missed. We find the bodies— what's left of them. And my people, they come to me, and say that I have promised to protect them. They are afraid. After all I have done for them, they forget who I am! Three stinking days of this, and they forget my name!" Massimo's loose-skinned face shook, jowls quivering.

"It's only been going on for three days?" Thomasi asked, his face the picture of shock. "How are people certain it is werewolves?"

Surprisingly, it was Lachina who rumbled a reply. "Werewolves terrorized this city decades ago. Everyone learned the signs. But the people weren't certain this time, not at first." Her voice was deep, so deep Chase almost spilled her wine in surprise and thought some unseen man had snuck into the room.

Lachina continued. "Don Coltello disposed of the remains. But then it happened *inside* the city, too, and the people who quiet such troubling things were not as... efficient..."

"And there were witnesses," the old man said, glumly. "One out here that I gave some money and advice to go take a vacation. But my money was wasted, there were more witnesses in the city. And then the damned Bianchi patriarch petitioned Doge Fedelta to do something about it. What's more, he petitioned in public! And so, our gates have the Doge's own household servants watching them. His huntsmen, his mages... it will not catch any sort of werewolf worth catching. It is... eh... it is... a thing to appease the masses, ah how to say it."

"Bread and circuses," Thomasi smiled.

The Don barked laughter, and Chase found herself giggling. Or maybe that was the wine. Was she tipsy? It would be stupid to say status and check. "Yes, bread and circuses," the old man said. Then his smile disappeared again. "I am the opposite of that. I take care of things without fuss. Without drama. These curs... it is not the first time werewolves have hunted in our city. I have killed them before, but I was too quiet about it, perhaps. Now I wonder if perhaps an example would be better."

"You've handled werewolves before?" Chase asked, blinking.

"Eh, me and the other dons, yes. Long ago. A mated pair decided to make this city their hunting ground. We tracked them down, chased them into the river, and filled it with her blood. I was the one to finish the chase and take the trophy. I still have the female's skin on my wall." The old man's grin had no mirth about it; it was a thing of wicked glee. Then it faded. "The male fled and got away. He was the runt, though, not a big threat on his own. Ironic, because he was the taller of the pair."

"Do you think he might have returned for revenge?" Thomasi asked, leaning forward and considering the old killer.

Don Coltello smiled, his eyes flat. "Cagna, show them your blade."

Chase stared, as the dog-woman pulled it free from the sheath, up to the first foot. It was oiled black metal, all save for the edge, which had the gleam of silver. After a few seconds, the bodyguard slid the sword back into place.

"It was the first thing I thought of," Don Coltello said, rising and looking out the window again. "But if he comes for me, he'll die. I'm not so worried about that. I am worried about my people. If these wolves came at me, they would die. It would be easy. But they're not coming at me, and tonight is the night of the full moon. They'll change. They'll feed. And my people's fear will grow. Or worse, Arretzi's fear will grow. And then the business of the city will come out here and get into my business. It will be bad all around."

"How can we help… Nonno?" Chase asked.

In the reflection of the warped glass of the window, she saw the old man's face smile in smug satisfaction. Then he turned around, spreading his flabby arms wide in benevolence. "I can kill wolves. That is no hardship. But first I must know where they are. You… you can find these wolves for me." He leaned on the table, both fists pressed against it, towering over her. "Do that, and I will be a very, very generous man."

Chase nodded. "We can try. Hoon has helped me so far, and I think werewolves are pretty bad for trade, so I don't imagine he wouldn't lend a hand here again. But... he helps those who best help themselves." Technically that saying was from the farming god, Old Koss, and she'd grown up hearing that over and over again, but she didn't think the Don knew the difference. "What can you tell us before we start looking?"

"Ah. That would take too long. But you are mistaken in one thing, mia piccola nipotina."

"I am?" Chase looked up at the old man.

He folded his hands over his gut. "You said when *we* start looking. You will look. Your man, Tom, will remain and help me look out here, and take care of a few small business matters."

A jolt of cold dread seeped down Chase's spine. Especially since quick, sidelong glances showed that Cagna and Lachina had tensed, ever so slightly.

PER+1

Refusal would have consequences. She was beginning to understand how things worked in the Don's circles. She still owed him for dragging him over here and passing that phony gold.

"Don, forgive me for speaking up," Thomasi said, settling a hand on Chase's shoulder. She jumped, but let it be. "The young lady, she is in my care. As a servant of her family, I would feel some concern about having her unchaperoned in an unfamiliar city. You understand my worries, of course."

"You think I don't?" The Don studied him for a moment, then smiled. "You are a good consigliere to your master, here. You do her credit with your concern. I would not be so rude as to let a young lady walk unescorted, especially with beasts about! She may choose one of my servants, here, to attend her in your place while she is in Arretzi."

Thomasi's hand patted her shoulder. "I see. That does allay my concerns. Thank you, Don Coltello."

"In that case..." Chase said, sitting back in her chair and making a show of studying the two women. Her choice was clear, thanks to the dog-woman's small show of help, earlier. "I choose Cagna, please, Nonno."

The Don's face was unreadable as he nodded. "Then Cagna you shall have. And now, my child, I must go. Tom, come with me. We have much to discuss."

"May I have a few minutes to consult with Thomasi before he goes with you, please?" Chase said, taking Renny off his little corner of the table, and putting him back into her pack.

The Don considered, then waved a hand in idle indulgence. "There is a room across the way. You may discuss matters there."

They had to pass the stairs to do so, and for a second Chase thought about grabbing Thomasi's hand and bolting. But only for a second. They were in one of the Don's strongholds, and he would certainly have stationed someone at the door. Besides, fleeing now would not help them get through Arretzi. It would probably make it more difficult, actually.

"This is a fine game you've gotten us into," Chase said, once they were in the sparse bedroom that the Don had pointed out, and the door was firmly shut.

"Technically it's called a con," Thomasi muttered, kneeling to whisper. "Right now, he thinks we might be from one of the northern crime families. From the Capital, probably. He'll check into that, but it will take time. Our job is to be out of here before he finishes."

"Is that why he's keeping ahold of you?"

"That and he'll get some use out of me. He was sizing us up, just as we did him. My attributes probably surprised him. I imagine I'll be making fool's gold and doing other services for him while you go on your werewolf hunt."

"We know at least one place they've been. That's something the Don doesn't."

Thomasi took her shoulders. "Do *not* go back there. Not without some heavy backup. It's the middle of the wilderness, and they might not be

Scouts, but that's still their playground. They'll literally eat you alive, if you do that."

"Then what am I supposed to do?" she spread her hands. "I don't know how to hunt werewolves!"

"Improvise. Stall. How many levels did you gain back there?"

"Two! And... a new job. Maybe." She bit her lip. "If I take it."

"Two levels, just from sitting and talking your way through this! What did I tell you?" Thomasi's grin showed pride. "You're a fast student. You can stall, have faith in yourself. And in me! At some point I'll give him the slip and come for you. After that we can get gone. Pretend to hunt the werewolves and keep your head down."

"How will you find me?"

Thomasi snorted. "By the time I'm done, the Don's people will be my people. I haven't spent years becoming a social juggernaut for nothing. Relax, I've got this."

She wondered about that. But time was short, and she didn't think the Don would grant them enough to argue about it. "Okay. Okay... Do you have any more advice or help you can give me?"

"Absolutely. Your friend should only talk to you when you're alone." He patted the pack... also clinking coins together as he dropped them in. "I'm giving you about half of my loose change. None of it is fool's gold. You can probably put it to good use... hm. You've never been in a city before, right?"

"No."

"Don't keep all your coins in the same place, stash them around your person. Don't pat the pockets or wherever, it shows thieves where to grab from. Don't make eye contact for long and mind your own business when possible. Follow Cagna's lead. Her perception is a bit better than mine."

Chase's mouth fell open at that. She didn't know exactly how many levels Thomasi had, but she was pretty sure he was up there.

"Okay," Chase said. "Okay," again, a little more firmly, as she shut her mouth and steeled herself.

He considered her for a moment longer, then sighed and reached into his pack. "Here. In case the worst happens."

And to her vast surprise, Thomasi handed Chase his Ringmaster's hat.

Her eyes grew wide, as he demonstrated how to collapse the hat into a cloth circle, then extend it to full length again. "Don't repeat this until you need it, but to use the hat say the following words; 'activate direct attention,' and then choose either away, or toward what you want people to focus on. Got it?"

"I do." Then, to Thomasi's surprise, she hugged him. "Thank you. Be safe."

His arms trembled, just for a second, before he hugged her back. "You too," he said, and cleared his throat. "Sorry. I haven't been hugged in... well. It's been a while."

She squeezed him harder for a bit, then let go. He followed her out of the room a few steps behind, as befitted his pretended position.

The Don smiled his gap-toothed smile at them as they returned. "Good, good. Are you ready to hunt my prey?"

"Yes. It will take time and hard work, but I am ready."

"It will take three days."

"Um... excuse me?" Chase blinked. "Did I hear that correctly?"

The old man's face was as still as a pond, as he explained. "Three days. Tonight is the first night of the full moon. The werewolves must kill every night of the full moon, and the full moon lasts four nights. If the werewolves kill all four nights, then stop, then even if they are hunted down afterward, the city will not know. The fear will grow until the next full moon. My business will continue to suffer, needlessly, for a month."

Thomasi tugged on his goatee. "But if, over the next four nights, a night comes without a werewolf murder, then it will prove that the werewolves are gone. Which isn't exactly certain proof, when you think about it, but it's probably going to be good enough for most people."

"You understand." The Don nodded, clearly happy. "It's the cowards I have to calm down. Smart people will believe me if I tell them the wolves are dead. Cowards trust only their fear. And there are far more cowards than smart people in this town."

While he lectured, Chase shot Thomasi a concerned glance and met his eyes. Three days didn't leave much room for Chase to stall. Would Thomasi really be able to escape Don Coltello's hospitality and rejoin Chase?

After a moment, Thomasi winked, and his grin showed utter confidence. "Well! Three days shouldn't change things much."

"Ah, okay," Chase nodded back. She would have had a lot more faith in his confidence if she didn't know he was very good at lying.

The Don thumped his cane on the floor. "Shall we depart, then?"

"We shall... Nonno." She didn't like saying the word now. But it was expected.

They left together, and Chase gasped as she turned the last corner of the twisty steps. The room below was completely empty of people. No one behind the bar, nobody at the wide open door. Not a soul visible.

It was a very real display of power, and Chase got its meaning at once. There would have been no one to stop them if they had fled. But they would not have gotten far.

The stripped bodies of the men had been removed from the street. The mouths of alleyways still gave the impression of surveillance. Chase's newly-sharpened perception detected shadowy forms in a couple of them. Pedestrians passed on the street and that, at least, was normal.

The Don's cane clacked on the stained set of cobblestones, as he smiled benevolently at her. She wasn't fooled but took his hand with her own smile. "Goodbye, Nonno. I hope to see you soon."

"I hope so too. You have three days, mi piccola nipotina."

And with that, he departed, shuffling away with Lachina holding one arm, working his cane with the other.

"No questions until we're inside the city," Cagna told her.

"You have a way in?"

"What did I just tell you?" Cagna sighed and strode off. Chase hurried to follow her.

It took a fair amount of work to keep up with Cagna. The lady had long legs and walked with absolute confidence and certainty. The thickening crowds of people gave way before her, and Chase followed close behind to benefit from her wake.

Due to the standard halven situation among taller folk, Chase spent a lot of time staring at Cagna's legs, catching a glimpse of her tail now and again as she turned and her cloak slipped aside. She had a hole cut into her trousers for the appendage, and it was curly and black.

For a few moments it bothered her, and she couldn't say why. A dog-woman was a strange thing, that was true, but Chase was way out of her comfort zone to begin with, and Cagna had at least been helpful...

Then she realized that it wasn't the tail; it was the trousers. No woman or girl in Bothernot wore trousers.

Chase looked down at her skirts, and how she'd gathered them in her hands to keep from dragging in the mud. Why *didn't* women wear trousers, back home? It was something she'd never questioned before.

Out on the main road, the line stretched on as long as before. Longer, even. But Cagna ignored it and walked toward a small door on one side. Chase followed, shooting awkward looks at the people she passed. They seemed to be universally unhappy, grumbling to themselves. The merchants and travelers near the front were staring at a small group of people, half of whom wore fancy pantaloons and carried pikes. They had breastplates and helmets over their shirts and seemed just as unhappy as the people in the line.

The other half of the group was dressed in fine leathers, but most of the men and women themselves were rough-shaven, with messy hair and muddy boots. In the middle, an old woman wearing starry robes and a conical hat stood glaring as the breast-plated group opened up a merchant's crates, going through each one and holding up items for perusal. The steaming-mad merchant next to the wagon berated them loudly and was ignored for his trouble.

But Cagna passed all this and went and rapped on the door.

A panel at the top of it slid open, and a red-nosed man stared out. "Your business?"

"Don Coltello's business."

The panel shut. The door opened. And Chase heard angry yells from the line behind them, as the two stepped in. The red-nosed man wore pantaloons and a shirt in similar green and yellow colors to the group outside, but no breastplate. He mopped sweat from his brow with one glove, and glanced up and down the arched stone hall, warily. "How is the Don?" he asked, voice uncertain.

"He is well, and he sends his regards." Cagna gave him a small pouch. "For your family, Bernardo. Your little one is what, almost eight now?"

"He is." The pouch disappeared, and Bernardo smiled. "Come, there is no need for friends of Don Coltello to wait in such a line."

Bernardo led them through the halls, past open doorways in the stone, that showed small offices and barracks. To Chase, who had just toured a prison a week ago, it all looked very familiar. Disturbingly so, and she shuddered as memories of blood and death ran through the back of her mind, screaming.

But no, this place had a different feel to it, she decided. It was by no means friendly, but it wasn't sinister. The few cells she passed had somber looking people in them, but they were well lit and fairly spacious. The offices were full of working people, chatting back and forth, and shuffling papers.

The crest of a shield with a hammer and sewing needle adorned every wall, just as it adorned every breastplate she'd seen up close, Chase realized. These were the guards of Arretzi, and they seemed to know their jobs pretty well.

Then just as Bernardo had his hand on a door handle a gong sounded, echoing through the halls.

"What was that?" Chase asked.

Cagna glanced at her but let the question slide. "They're moving someone important through. Who? I didn't see anyone like that on the walk up."

"I'm not sure," Bernardo said, taking his hand from the door. "But we can't go out there, not if a dignitary is passing."

"We can't wait here," Cagna pointed out. "You know of our

understanding. It would be... *unseemly* to linger."

Bernardo's nose flared, and more sweat gleamed on his brow. "I know, I know this thing... ah... let me think." He chewed his lip, then seemed to come to a decision. "Come! We can watch them from the murderholes. The guards there will be watching the dignitary, they won't care about you. Then once the gate is clear we can leave."

Cagna just nodded, and Chase followed as the two of them made their way up two flights of stairs.

It gave a sense as to the vast scale of the wall; the place was a fortress in of itself. If all of it had passages and rooms through it, then it gave Pandora Prison a run for its money, she thought.

Then it was through and into a large, open room with cauldrons sitting on pillars ever ten feet. An arrangement of chains filled the air, tracing from the cauldrons to gears up above them, worked into the support beams of the roof.

The floor next to every cauldron had grated metal set into it, and around the room men and women wearing guard uniforms stared down into the well-lit space below.

"This way," Bernardo said, and led them to a corner of the room, and an unused grate.

A black coach was below, with two very dusty horses receiving care and food from attendants. A crest adorned its side but the angle was bad, and Chase couldn't make it out.

As she watched, a ring of guards with halberds leveled surrounded it.

"What's this?" Cagna asked.

"Standard prisoner transfer procedure," Bernardo pointed off to the side. "See? Here come the Jailors."

"Six of them?" Cagna's ears twitched.

"That's odd," Berndardo's nose flared again. "Normally you get one, maybe two for the really dangerous ones. Six..."

And then the coach's door opened, and to Chase's horror and shock, she recognized the woman who stepped out.

"The Camerlengo!"

CHAPTER 6: OLD FACES AND NEW PLACES

Only when Cagna and Bernardo looked at her, did Chase realize she'd spoken out loud.

But how could she not?

Chase had last seen the Camerlengo in Pandora Prison, had left her there to the tender mercies of a psychotic wrecking ball of a prisoner that the official had tortured or tormented somehow. Chase had left the two of them to sort it out among themselves and fled for her life, knowing full well that the Camerlengo would hold a grudge if she survived.

Well she had, and now she was in the same city as Chase, and that was a problem.

But it is a problem for another day, Chase told herself as she grabbed control once more. She met the eyes of her curious comrades and shrugged. "What? It is the Camerlengo. I saw her once in Lafiore."

"What's a Camerlengo?" Bernardo asked.

"Someone who guards a noble's interests," Cagna explained. "Usually a cleric or someone with some pull in the church."

"Yeah, she does errands for the Baroness," Chase said, happy that the attention was off her. She leaned back over the grate again and studied her foe.

A tall, thin human woman, with her white-streaked brown hair done up in a bun, and a pair of spectacles perched on a hawkish nose. She was wearing traveling clothes, all black, and she had a silver pendant on. Chase squinted, and was thankful for her recently-boosted perception, as the shape of the pendant became clear to her improved eyes. *A ruler?* It looked like that, a flat, long rectangle with some sort of markings at regular intervals.

The Camerlengo spoke with the five hulking men and nearly-as-hulking woman surrounding the coach. They nodded their black-hooded heads, pulled out sets of manacles, and began chanting.

"Lockdown, No Escape!" they chorused in near unison, and then the closest one threw the door of the coach open.

It was almost the death of him.

A form exploded outward, swinging chain-wrapped fists, and bowling into the large Jailer. They both went down, and the remaining Jailers hurried forward, piling on, trying to subdue whoever was trying to escape.

Chase blinked, as a sudden suspicion filled her mind. *No. No, it's impossible. Why would she bring him here?*

The pile of fat Jailers gave a sudden heave, and a large form surged out of it, sending them flying in all directions. It straightened up and glared at the outer ring of guards surrounding the coach. Glowing, battered remnants of armor showed under links of chain, and a wild black mane of hair twitched as he stared around, looking for a way out.

Dijornos. She *had* brought Dijornos here! And Chase didn't know why. Why not take him to the baronial seat? Why bring him to Arretzi?

The guards pressed in closer, halberds leveled. Dijornos sneered and started toward them...

...only to trip and fall on his face.

There was a chain around his ankle. And as Chase watched, one of the fallen Jailers got back up and tugged on the other end, which was firmly wound around the fat man's wrist.

Dijornos struggled to his feet... but then the other Jailers moved, and swung heavy lengths of chain, battering him, locking manacles into place all around his body. It was like watching a pack of wolves take down a bear, and it ended the only way it could.

"Hogtie," they told him, as chains snapped and wrapped around the prisoner.

"Quiet you!" they snarled as he tried to shout in response, either activating his own skills or just roaring defiance. The end result didn't matter, as Chase watched his mouth snap shut so quickly and with such violence that a tooth went flying. Or maybe that was one of the Jailers putting a boot in, it was hard to tell given how close together they were.

Chase chose her next words very carefully. "Whoever he was, that guy never had a chance."

"Not really, no," Cagna said, keeping her voice low. "Jailers are a Knight and Animator Tier Two combination. That fat counts as armor, and once they land a chain on you, it's over."

The trio watched four of the Jailers haul Dijornos' trussed up form away out of view. The remaining two stepped up to the coach, and sent chains snaking upward, to grab a smaller bundle from above. This one sagged limply as it came down... a woman in a prisoner's hood, her clothes tattered. She seemed much less imposing than the last prisoner, but the Jailors treated her just as roughly.

And they were wise to do so. *This has to be Speranza,* Chase knew. She'd be gagged or unconscious or both, of course. Her powers were far too dangerous to risk around large groups of armed men.

"Well, that was weird," Bernardo summed up as the Camerlengo turned her back to the proceedings and waved at someone out of view. "But if she's transferring prisoners into the city, then they'll be at least an hour. We're safe to leave while this is going on, she's somebody else's problem."

It would be nice if that was true, but Chase didn't think she'd get so lucky twice. With her fate being what it was, and the Camerlengo showing up here and now, it seemed like Hoon was letting her know that their business wasn't done just yet.

"Let's go then," Cagna decided. "Nothing more to see here."

Bernardo snorted. "You missed your calling in life. Normally it's guards who say that."

Chase was at exactly the right angle to see how Cagna's tail twitched, then tensed. Just for a second.

But the dog-woman said nothing, and the three made their way down from the murder holes, down flights of stairs once more, and through mostly-empty halls.

Finally the last door opened into daylight, and Chase blinked, letting her eyes adjust...

...and she was glad she did.

For a second she just stared at the sight before her. She had thought the outskirts of Arretzi to be crowded beyond belief, full of more people than she'd ever imagined seeing in one place.

She had been woefully naive, she saw that now. She saw it in the throngs of people that walked the streets, in the wagons that rolled by, teamsters shouting for those walking to make way. She saw it in the high, sturdy buildings that lined the cobblestones, multiple stories worth of buildings, the least of them towering over anything back home in Bothernot.

And it wasn't just the sight of it, there was the noise, too. Countless conversations, shouts, doors opening and shutting, music somewhere in the distance, barking from distant dogs, and gods knew what else blended together to make a cacophony quite unlike anything she had ever encountered in her fifteen years of a quiet rural life.

"Are you coming?" Cagna's voice registered, as if from a distance.

Chase snapped out of it, and gave the woman a close-lipped smile, knowing somehow that she had to keep her lips shut otherwise it would be rude. "I thought you told me no questions until we're inside the city?" Chase said and patted the woman's arm with a friendly swipe.

Cagna stared for a second, then she literally barked laughter. "So I did." She took a big step and put her feet on the cobblestones just outside the door. "Well now I am. You coming?"

"I've got nothing better to do," Chase said, and followed her out.

Bernardo said nothing, but merely shut the door behind them. The pair ventured out into the city, and Chase focused on Thomasi's advice.

Don't stare.

But oh, that was much easier said than done.

Every street held a spectacle, every plaza had a performance. The throngs turned into crowds the further they got in, and every passerby had a story that she itched to know, but never would. There were humans and halvens and even a few dwarves throughout the crowd, and once a pair of stags loped by, carrying what might have been elves. Other, more exotic races abounded, from an owl-woman dumping washwater into the gutters from the side of an inn, to something nine feet tall and gray, with craggy skin and blue tattoos.

And the shops!

Every place that didn't hold a house or a big building of some sort was crammed with stalls and storefronts and merchants hawking their wares, from freshly-baked bread to metalware, from fine pottery to worked wooden toys.

Chase stopped at one point to watch what was obviously the work of a Tinke. A metal boat sailed and bumbled about on a blue tarp stretched out in the window of his shop, the tiny wheels below it just visible, and steam piping like mist out of a hole in the mast.

"Come on," Cagna's voice was harsh, but her hand was gentle as she sat it on Chase's shoulder. "I don't blame you for being a bit of a country mouse, but we have a job to do."

Country mouse. "Is it that obvious?" Chase looked up at her.

Cagna's muzzle wrinkled in what could have been a smile. "I was one myself. No shame in it. But if I'm noticing, others have too. The Don's grace won't protect you against the local pickpockets, other people run those groups."

"So where are we going, anyway?" Chase said, taking one last look through the Tinker's shop window, and stifling a wistful sigh at a set of toy gnome soldiers.

"The Don keeps a villa for his business in town. It's a good base of operations. Also got some baths so you can knock the travel dust off your boots... feet, I guess," Cagna said, glancing down at the halven's bare extremities. "After that, you tell me. I don't know how you do what you do. You know what you need to do, and I'll help you, but you have to tell me what you need. And not *here*," Cagna said, raising a hand as Chase started to speak. "We don't talk about this on the street. Capisce?"

"Capisca," Chase agreed.

A ten-minute walk later, and they reached the villa. A good thing too, since Chase's halven stamina was dangerously low. She was on her second emergency roll by the time Cagna slowed up and said, "This is it."

It, in this case, was a large walled compound, with two stories of a fancy, white-columned house visible over the wall. It was on a street of similar structures, sharing walls with its neighbors. Cagna fiddled with the gate, which opened with a creak.

Not knowing what to expect, Chase followed her in...

...and stared in amazement at the sights around her.

A paved courtyard sat between the wall and the villa house, the stones in the ground broken in patterns to let orange trees and decorative shrubs grow with carefully-cultivated profusion.

Across the way stood the manor house, two stories tall with a sloped roof, large enough that Chase's entire village could live within it and have room left over for their household pets, too.

Another building, more like a cottage, sat off to one side of the wall. An old man sat in a chair on the porch of the cottage, watching them with serenity, lifting a bottle of something quite-probably alcoholic to his lips as they entered. Across from the cottage, a small stables held a horse placidly chewing on a nearby overhanging branch, straining to get at the hard green balls of fruit just out of its reach on the already-stripped tree.

"You're the new one," the old man called. "Cagna, right?"

"One of the new ones," Cagna confirmed. "You're the gardener."

The old man nodded. "I am. The master, he's out right now. I don't know when he be back. He don't tell me that."

"We're not here to see him."

The gardener shrugged and turned back to his drink.

"Only a few servants here," Cagna said, as she led the way to the main door of the villa. "Four or five inside. Him outside. No guards unless there's trouble with the other families. Goes without saying, but you shouldn't talk business with the servants."

"I hadn't planned to."

"Good." Cagna held the door for her.

The inside was just as impressive as the outside, all white painted walls and fine furnishings. But something seemed off, and as Cagna led her upstairs and past large rooms, she put her finger on it.

There were square spots on the walls where paintings used to hang, but no longer did so. A few stands here and there held statues or sculptures, but even more stood empty. And a couple of the upstairs rooms were totally stripped of furniture, with marks in the rugs and on the tiles to show where furnishings had once been.

Times were perhaps a bit harder on the Don lately than they had been in the past. That was potentially useful information that she filed away for later.

Finally, Cagna dropped her off at a door. "This is a guest room. The key should be on the hook inside. It connects to a bathroom, so feel free to rest up and do whatever. I'll be downstairs if you need me. You're halven, so the cooks will need advance warning, I'll wager."

"Thank you," Chase said. "It would be nice to have a civilized meal schedule again. I've been traveling with a human so long that I've lost entirely too much weight."

Cagna's tongue lolled out of her mouth, and her eyes twinkled. *Is that amusement? Yes, yes it is,* Chase realized. *How do I know that?*

"I usually don't hear THAT complaint too often," Cagna said. "Sure, we can fatten you up. See you around, country mouse."

Once Cagna was gone, Chase surveyed the room, and found it to her liking. Sized for humans, yes, but there was a stepstool next to the oversized bed, and the door handles were low enough to reach if she stood on her toes. Glass windows, much nicer than those in the taverna, let in light and dust particles danced in the midday sunbeams.

Shutting the door, Chase pulled over a chair, clambered up it, and retrieved the key from its hook. A little fiddling got the door locked. And then, before anything else, she put her pack on the ground and opened the straps. "It's safe."

Renny crawled out, and stood, looking around. "That was frustrating."

"I'm sorry. It can't have been comfy, cramped up in that little pack for so long."

"No, I didn't mind that. Golems don't get as uncomfy as living people seem to. We can be still for days or weeks if we need to. What I mean is I could only hear what was going on, I couldn't see anything except when the pack was at just the right angle. And even then it was mostly just a lot of legs."

"Welcome to my life." Chase sat on the floor and put her back to the wall. "We're probably safe to talk here, so long as we don't shout."

"Okay... so what was that about the Camerlengo? And Jailers?"

Chase told him what she'd seen. At the end of it, she found she was hugging her knees to her chest.

Renny picked up on it, too. He patted her knee. "Don't worry. From what I saw it's a pretty big city. So long as we stay out of her way, we'll be done and gone in a few days."

"Maybe. Thomasi wants us to stall until he gets to us. But I don't know if we can do that. Moreover, I don't know if we should." Chase wrinkled her nose, as she stood. "I'm going to take a bath," she said, heading toward the other room.

"Okay," Renny said, padding along after her.

He stopped when Chase did. "What?"

"Where are you going?"

"I figured I can talk to you while you're in the tub."

"Um, no. I'm going to be *naked*."

Renny shrugged. "So?"

"This never came up? Didn't you have two women in your adventuring party before?"

"Yes. And?" He stopped. "Oh, are you talking about how Gadram used to bathe separately from them? And find excuses to be somewhere else when they were changing clothes?"

"Yes, exactly."

"Well that's fine, I'm not a dwarf," he started toward the bathroom again.

"Nope. Look..." Chase said and felt her face flush as she started explaining.

Finally they compromised, and dragged over a big screen so he could sit behind it and talk while she was in the tub.

Oh, did it feel good to slip into warm water again! Chase sighed and settled into it, feeling her aches leave with the dirt. Renny's Clean and Press skill was great for cleaning clothes, but skin was another matter.

"So Thomasi wants us to stall?" Renny asked.

"Oh, right. You weren't in the room for that conversation. Yes, he's confident he can give Don Coltello the slip, or find a way to turn this situation to our advantage. But he decided that before the Don surprised us with a time limit. Thomasi's good, but I don't know if he's *that* good. So I'm going to fall back on my dad's advice, here." She felt a pang of loss, saying that. Only a week she'd been away from her family, and it felt like a lifetime, now. When she thought about it, this was the longest she'd *ever* been away from them.

Her eyes stung a bit, and she closed them. *You wanted adventure,* Chase told herself. *Hard to adventure with your parents along.*

Then she remembered Greta and was almost undone entirely. She felt her ears droop and fought to keep composure.

"What did your dad say?" Renny asked from behind the screen.

That let her push the sadness aside and focus on business. "He said one should always hope for the best, and plan for the worst. So, let's try to hunt some werewolves. It's a good idea, anyway. They're killing people and if it's the same guy as before, then he'll have a grudge against the Don and the other crime lords. Which means they might attack us, since we're on sort-of-friendly terms with the Don now."

"Do you think they're the werewolves I smelled at the dungeon?"

"Almost certainly. That was really near to the city, and wolves are territorial, I think."

"Then that's an advantage. If I smell them again, then I'll know. Except... except it's going to be hard to smell anything while I'm in the pack."

"Yeah. We need a way around that. Can't your illusions make you look like someone else?"

"They can, but... well, there's two flaws. The first is that the spell fades after time, and I have to speak to renew them. Anyone who knows the skill is going to get suspicious if they hear me casting Phantasm all the time. The second is that if I want it to move, I have to account for every little detail of the movement. It's tricky, and I'm good, but it still ends up being a little noticeable. Especially when I try talking."

Another thought occurred to Chase. "It would be noticeable to werewolves, too. They're supposed to have great senses of smell... no. No, bad idea. Which is a pity, because that first part would be easy to fix."

"It would?"

"Yes. I could montage you the Grifter job, and you'd be able to silently use all your skills. It would also get you that Master of Disguise skill, too. That would probably help with all of that. Except, no, wait." Chase slathered her arms with soap, scrubbing as she thought. "A montage would take most of a day. We don't have that kind of time."

"I could get it instantly, I already unlocked that job months ago. But I don't know if I want it."

"What? Why wouldn't you? It would work beautifully with your illusions! Maybe not so much the air thing, but you chose your Elementalist job for combat anyway, right?"

"No, actually. I thought it would help with the illusions as well. I wanted to put solid air behind them, so that they were kind of real. For example, you could touch one, without me having to add in a fake sense of touch. Or worrying about the illusion failing entirely against someone who disbelieves it."

"Oh..." Chase thought, as she scrubbed. "You could put up a fake wall, then put a wall of solid air behind it. Stuff like that, right?"

"Right. But the problem is that it takes a lot of skill. Air doesn't want to be still or solid. Air wants to move. I'm a level ten elementalist, my skill is up in the forties, and I still have trouble getting it to stay inside the lines of the illusion, more or less. Throw in a moving illusion and it's really, really tricky. It's like trying to sew up a pair of socks while you're reading a book at the same time. It takes a lot of focus."

"Well, what attributes do you use for your illusion spells?"

"Charisma."

"Then you should definitely go Grifter! Charisma, dexterity, and luck; those are the attributes it boosts. And more luck is always good."

"Dexterity *would* help with my knifework," Renny mused. "And it would be nice not to have to say spells to activate them. But…"

"But?"

"I don't like lying to people."

"Well, here's the thing," Chase said, putting the soap aside, and rinsing herself. "How many jobs can you have, total? Adventuring jobs, I mean?"

"Six. I've got two so far."

"If you take it and never lie to anyone, then you'll still get Silent Activation and Master of Disguise. You can stay at level one in it forever, if you really want to avoid lying to people. Though I wonder why you went into illusions if you're so against deception."

"It's because I like dreams. And I wanted to help people see the ones that I used to have."

"What?" Chase sat up in the bath, propping her arms over the edge, staring at the screen. "I thought you didn't sleep?"

"We don't. Not normally. But there's a Shaman spell that lets them put people to sleep and gives visions. I think it's like what happens when you dream. I really liked the dreams I had, and I could never get anyone to tell me what they meant. So when I went to the teacher she pointed me toward this job. I liked it, and it helped me get a lot more sociable. I was pretty gruff and shy before. But it worked out, and here I am."

"Here you are," Chase agreed, climbing back out of the tub, and swathing herself in a human sized towel. Then another one, just for her hair. "Where are my clothes?"

"I cleaned them." Renny paused, then tossed them over the screen. With an audible splat, her blouse ended up in the water. "Oops."

Chase sighed and chucked it back over. "Once more, with feeling, if you please."

"Clean and Press. You really think I can be a Grifter and not lie?"

"I think that's up to you. It's better to have a weapon and not have to use it than it is to not have one and need it. When I swore to myself that I'd take every adventuring job that I could, life got... immeasurably... better." Chase froze. "I'm an idiot."

"What? Why?" The blouse came sailing over again, and Chase snagged it before it could go into the tub.

"I completely forgot! Today's been such a bustle... during all the excitement with the Don, I unlocked a new job. It's called Medium."

"Medium? Spirit Medium?" Renny sounded eager. "That's a great one! You can talk to ghosts, and manipulate soulstones, and... wait. I thought you needed Necromancer to get that one."

"Not Spirit Medium. Just Medium. **Status. Help Medium.**"

It displayed what she'd seen before. And no matter how she tried, the same information came up regardless.

Congratulations, by combining skillful lies with actual oracular vision, you have unlocked the Medium job! You may not have told the actual fortune, but the customer got the one he needed to hear!

Would you like to become a Medium at this time? Y/N?

"I don't know about this," Chase said, biting her lip. She read it aloud to Renny. "It looks like it's to do with fake fortune telling."

"Wouldn't it be called Fortune Teller if it was? The fact that Oracle is in there means that there's something beyond that. And besides, wasn't a fake fortune what placated the Don, and got you out of trouble with him?"

"Out of trouble's a subjective term, this is a different sort of trouble," Chase muttered. "And the fortune wasn't fake, I just had some help, and maybe left out a few things about how horrible a leader he was." She shrugged into her clothes as she spoke, leaving the towel in place around her hair.

"And hey, what was that you were just telling me?" Renny asked, staring up at her as she came out from behind the screen. "Better to have a weapon, isn't that right? And this is a Tier Two job you've unlocked! If it works out that's probably going to be a pretty big weapon."

Chase had a number of arguments she could bring to bear, but the more she thought about it, the more her curiosity grew. And what had Cagna said, earlier? That if you unlocked a Tier Two job, it was usually a good idea because it meant you were doing something it could help with anyway?

Still, the little fox did look a bit smug to turn her words back on her. "I'll make you a deal," she decided. "You take Grifter, and I'll take Medium. Does that sound fair?"

"It does," Renny put up his paw, and they shook on it.

Chase ignored how cutesy he was when he did that sort of thing and said **"Status. Help Medium."** And then, with only the barest hesitation, she said **"Yes."**

You are now a level 1 Medium!
CHA+5
LUCK+5
You have learned the Bad Fortune skill!
Your Bad Fortune skill is now level 1!
You have learned the Crystal Ball skill!
Your Crystal Ball skill is now level 1!
You have learned the Good Fortune skill!
Your Good Fortune skill is now level 1!
You have learned the Séance skill!
You have learned the Stack Deck skill!

Chase felt her toes curl as she felt pleasure, her pools of energy filling completely up, all the aches and pains that had been soothed from the bath now gone entirely. The fact that she was a better person now was just icing on top of it, and as the glow of leveling faded the halven felt sorrow as she was left herself once more.

It really feels like I'm tapping into something bigger, she mused. *Like that time Hoon showed me the world. Like the only thing holding me back is the notion that I should be held back. That if I tried just a bit more, I could...*

She could what?

But the thoughts faded like the dreams she'd discussed with Renny, so she busied herself by checking in on her new skills, one help command at a time.

And at the fourth skill, she paused. "Renny?" She whispered.

"Yes?"

"I think I know how we're going to find those werewolves..."

CHAPTER 7: A POUND OF FLESH

"That's a great idea, except for the part where it'll get you killed for necromancy," Cagna told Chase.

Chase frowned, took another sip of tea, and reached for a fifth cookie. The cook of this estate had risen to the challenge of a halven appetite and prepared a nice after-lunch service for the family's guest.

"Séance isn't necromancy," Chase said, waving the thin wafer around to punctuate her argument. "It just calls up the memory of the departed to answer a few questions. It can't be used to bind ghosts or anything like that, the skill description is very clear."

The Doberman-headed woman scratched between her own ears. "See, that distinction won't matter to the people whose departed you're going to be calling up. And the law is pretty clear that any unauthorized messing about with the dead in any way is necromancy. We had quite enough of that sort of thing back during the guild wars. The Doge is a fair man, but even he's got his limits, and breaking the law like that would get his attention in a very bad way."

"You work for a criminal, and you're worried about such distinctions?"

Cagna's mouth snapped shut. She glanced around, and leaned in. "Be careful what you say. You can do that inside these walls, while nobody's around. Outside is another matter."

Chase kept her gaze steady on Cagna's almond-colored eyes. "I'm no fool. I wouldn't have said that if anyone was around. But my point stands. Why can't we break the law? What's the point of being a criminal if you have to worry about such things? Bad laws aren't worth keeping."

Cagna sighed. "Look. I'm pretty sure Don Coltello called in a Necromancer for the deaths that happened in the outskirts. I'm also pretty sure nothing came of it. Na na na, hold on." She held up a hand to forestall Chase as the halven girl started to protest. "He did that because that happened in his territory, and the guards that watch there are paid well to look away. He did that because he could get away with it and there would be no proof. Here? In the city? There are guards we can't buy. What's worse, two of the deaths involved noble houses, and one of them was a guild official. You do something they see as necromancy to one of their own, they won't call in the guard. It'll be an Assassin with a strangling cord and a midnight burial out in the lime pits."

Chase closed her eyes. It didn't seem fair... but then the world wasn't fair. Still, it was a very good investigative skill, and this was just the sort of situation for it. There were victims, they might have seen something, and only some hurt feelings and bad laws were in the way of her using it.

She munched on the cookie she'd taken, finishing it off. With her energy full from her recent level choice, she couldn't even get satisfaction from the food. But she ate anyway, because she was used to it. And while she ate, she thought.

"How many murders inside the city, total?" Chase finally asked.

"Four."

"Two in noble houses. One from a guild. Who was the last?"

"The last one was the first killed, actually. A leatherworker's daughter, in the quartiere carne."

Chase ran the phrase through her knowledge of the old tongue. "The meat district?"

"I guess so." Cagna shrugged. "More like the flesh district."

"That's kind of gruesome."

"Not really. It's... ah, why should I try and explain it? Better to show you. You'll see."

"I will?"

"Judging by your line of questioning, you'll obviously want to talk to the victim's father. He is in the quartiere carne. So your fuzzy little feet are going to end up walking those cobblestones, and mine will be right alongside yours." She shrugged. "Honestly I wouldn't mind. They have some good eats out that way, and the smells are divine. The place is fun, too. Got all sorts of shows and spectacles."

"Shows and spectacles? In a meat market? What, do the butchers juggle knives or something?"

Cagna laughed, and leaned back in her chair, scratching under one arm without a care for the vulgarity of it. "Something like that. You'll see, you'll see."

"We'll see," Chase nodded in agreement, then scooped up her pack. Renny's head peeked out of the top of it, and he was completely still.

This arrangement let him keep an eye on things, and if need be, he could now silently activate his illusions and slip out to do whatever golemy stuff he needed to accomplish.

The trek across the city seemed easier now. With everyone at home or off to a taverna or ristorante for lunch, the streets were a little less crowded.

Less crowded by city standards was still an absurd amount of people by rural halven village standards though, and Chase found herself studying people as they passed. She was careful to keep from staring, and her much-enhanced charisma seemed helpful there. Her height was a bonus as well, and for the most part nobody seemed to take offense.

And what she noticed, after studying so many people, was a common thread.

They looked agitated.

They traveled in groups, their eyes picked out the dark places between buildings and they walked quickly, speaking little. There were few smiles, and the even rarer laughter that she heard now and again had a bit of an edge to it.

But it was the way they looked at Cagna, keeping eyes on her like she'd go mad and start cutting throats at any moment, was the final hint that Chase needed. "They've got this whole town on edge, don't they? The wer—" she cut off her words as a group passed near. "The, uh, killers, I mean."

"Oh yeah," Cagna said, locking her face straight ahead, keeping her hands in sight at all times. "Normally we don't get hostility here. Dog beastkin, I mean. But this is... bad for business. Scared people start suspecting anything that looks canine. It doesn't help that I've only been in town a few months. I'm a stranger, and that's dangerous now."

"You're not local?"

"No. I get around. Me and Lachina, we both came here looking for work and found it."

"Has it been good?"

"Mostly." Cagna tilted her head, thinking. She scratched behind one ear as she did so, and Chase stifled a chuckle. She was glad she'd done so, as the dog-woman looked back at her. "Just so you know, I've got a code I have to follow. There's things I can't do or it weakens me. So you don't command me to do something, and you don't ask it without running it by me first."

"Is your code the reason you helped me, back when I was telling the Don's fortune?"

Cagna considered that, then shook her head and looked away. "Yep. You guessed it."

But Chase looked at the way she set her shoulders and heard the faintness of her voice. Cagna was lying.

Then they reached the end of the last street, and her concern over that fell away.

The plaza before them was a riot of color and crowded with cheering onlookers. In the middle among some large statues, a group of barely-clad acrobats flipped and swung from ropes attached to the weathered stone structures. They perched on outstretched hands, dove between the legs of stone horses, and flipped over the empty space between standing stone warriors, making the crowd gasp as they dared a three or four-story drop.

"Oh!" Chase gasped, slowing to watch the show.

"Come on," Cagna said, after a minute. "I forgot we had a troupe through. This works in our favor, actually, the leatherworker's shop won't be as crowded."

"Do performances happen often, here?" Chase asked as she followed Cagna, trying not to shove her way through the forest of legs that made up the gawking onlookers.

"If they're naked enough."

"Wait, what?"

"This is the quartiere carne, the district of flesh. It's where meat, skin, and hides are displayed and traded, and the guild that runs this part of the city made some really loosely worded laws that people have been taking advantage of. So any business here pays lower taxes if they're putting flesh on display and able to make the case that it's involved with their business. Really it's meant for butchers and the like, but once the bordellos started getting in on the action, well..." Cagna gestured up, and the crowd parted just long enough for Chase to see a high-balconied villa, with some very pretty, very under-dressed women calling down to the passers-by below.

As Chase watched with shocked eyes someone called back up, and the woman put her hands to her bodice and started to tug it down.

But then the crowd closed back up again, and Chase, her face feeling like it was on fire, hurried to catch up with her guide. Cagna hadn't even broken her stride.

It took quite a long time to pass through the crowd, and the halven girl focused on navigation, sneaking glances at the performers as she went. To her surprise, once they were around some of the larger statues, she saw circus wagons at their base. Gaudy and golden and green, they seemed to match the city's colors. A sign on the side proclaimed them to be the 'FABULUS FLYING ACROCATS!'

Fascinated, Chase tried to drift over that way without losing sight of

Cagna. For her troubles she got a glimpse of a pair of performers walking into one of the wagons, and one of them did indeed have catlike ears and a tail... and six small breasts, hidden by a triple bikini. Her companion was human though, and he laughed as he gestured up at the rigging they'd just descended from.

"Hey!" Cagna literally barked.

The performers whipped around and the catgirl's hair literally puffed up like an angry cat's fur.

"Sorry, sorry," Chase apologized, knowing her words were lost in the noise of the crowd, and ran back to the irritated enforcer.

"You will be, if you don't stick close to me," Cagna growled. "These bordellos, and the other places? They don't always have willing people working in them. Plenty of sickos who'd pay good money to do horrible things to a little woman who looks like a kid if her ears get trimmed back."

Chase's ears flicked in shock, and she cupped them protectively.

Cagna's scowl turned into a chuckle. "Relax. You're with me, and all you'd have to do is mention the Don's name. That would probably make them hesitate until it got resolved."

"Oh. Does he, uh, does he run the... those houses, then?"

"No. That's another family. But they're on pretty good terms. Your 'Nonno' finds them stolen or desperate women in the outskirts when they need new stock. You remember that the next time you sit at his table."

The crowd thinned at that point. They'd come to the far edge of the plaza, where it broke off into twisty little streets and alleys. Cagna picked one of the dirtier-looking ways and strode downhill.

Chase followed but hesitated when the smell hit her. "Oh, oh that's foul."

"We're in the tanner's row now. The components they use aren't pleasant. Did you know that one of the lower level skills you get from that profession protects your nose against unpleasant smells?"

"No, no I didn't—"

"Kff!"

The noise came from behind her. Chase turned, staring. She saw no one. There were people back up the street at the main plaza, yes, but no one on this mostly-empty block.

"Kff, Kff!" It was behind her again and now her pack was shaking, straps pulling on her back, and Chase realized what it was.

Renny was *sneezing*.

"What the hell?" Cagna barked.

Chase cupped her face and went "Kff!" as best she could. "Kff kff!" she said louder, trying to mimic Renny's tones.

Cagna sounded confused. "Um."

Chase heard Cagna's feet on the cobblestones and whirled around to put herself between the curious enforcer and the fox. She found Cagna squatting down on her haunches, stretching out a hand. "Are... you okay?"

Chase sniffled, and rubbed her face, licking her hand across her palm so that her spit might be mistaken for snot. "Sorry. Give me a minute, please."

"I could loan you a scarf if you want. It smells like me, but it might cut the chemicals."

Chase felt her pack shake silently a few times. Renny had done something to kill the sound, but he was still sneezing. Cagna's eyes drifted over Chase's shoulder, and the halven girl hurriedly faked another sneezing fit. "Yes, please," she finally wheezed, once the pack stopped shaking.

Wordlessly, Cagna handed her a bright red scarf. It was more of a bandanna, really, square and with crease-marks where it had been repeatedly folded into a triangle. Thankfully, at some point while she was winding it around her face, Renny stopped sneezing.

The scarf *did* help cut the stink a little. Chase looked up at Cagna once her nose was covered, thinking to thank her, but found the dog-woman gazing past her, eyes narrowed.

"Do you see something?"

"Someone, maybe. Perhaps nothing. Come on, the sooner we get this done, the better."

A sudden worry crossed Chase's mind. "If there are werewolves here, could you smell them?"

"Not over the chemicals," Cagna said, standing and resuming her walk. "My nose isn't that good."

Nervous and feeling a target on her back, Chase took a filtered breath and followed.

Her unease waned a bit as they traveled. The twisty street opened up at various points, showing more of the district, and that helped as well. There were plenty of people in smaller plazas, enjoying different shows. None of them were as grand as the statue-traversing acrobats... acrocats? But they seemed entertaining in their own way.

One plaza had a makeshift stage, with a commedia in full swing. Another held firespinners, doing tricks with a bunch of fiery, ball-like things with eyes that Chase assumed were elementals. Circus wagons of all shapes, sizes, and colors were always nearby.

But as they went, the further they got from the main plaza, the more the odor grew, and the sketchier the performers looked. The quality of the act seemed to dictate one's proximity to the best stages.

The neighborhood got seedier and seedier as they went. It never quite matched up to the outskirts, but by the time Cagna finally held up a hand to stop Chase, they were at a nearly-deserted plaza, ringed by shops that had bars over their windows, instead of glass. Across the plaza a lone wagon stood, faded red and blue and gold next to a roped off area. The biggest and most well-muscled human Chase had ever seen lay in the middle of the ring, curled around a bottle and snoring. He was wearing a loincloth, and off to the side, a blue pointy hat sat emblazoned with gold stars. His wagon sign proclaimed him to be the MUSCLE WIZAARD. It also offered a purse of silver to anyone who could pin him in the ring. Chase wondered if that offer applied if he was drunk and unconscious at the time but decided probably not.

Something about the wagon drew her eye, but before she could say anything Cagna grabbed her shoulder. "Focus, please. We're here."

Chase let herself be led over to a well-worn door, under a pair of wooden gloves hanging from a sign. They creaked in the faint wind, and Chase coughed under her bandanna. Her throat was dry, and she was down quite a lot of stamina from the walk. She'd replaced her emergency rolls with tea cookies, but she didn't want to eat them here. The tannery stink would ruin the taste.

Regardless of her companion's exhaustion, Cagna pounded on the door until it opened.

A sallow, swarthy man about twice Cagna's weight stared back at her. His clothes were worn and dirty, and his face unshaven.

"We're closed," he said, blinking in the light... then freezing, as his eyes focused on Cagna's muzzle. "What! What is this?" he roared, and hauled out a long, thin knife.

Across the plaza, the drunken 'Wizaard's' snores paused.

"Stand Down," Cagna told him, and the large man froze. He returned the knife to its sheath, then looked down at it in shock, as if his hand had moved on its own.

Perhaps it had, Chase thought. That was a skill Cagna had used, there.

"Go away," the man said, and his voice wavered, hoarse and on the edge. "What do I have now? I have nothing. Go away. Leave me alone."

Cagna opened her mouth to say something, and Chase punched her leg. This would take a gentle touch. **"Silent Activation, Silver Tongue,"** Chase mouthed beneath her scarf.

Your Silent Activation skill is now level 8!

Then she pulled the garment down and spoke. "Signore? Signore, I am very sorry for your loss. I... I too have felt this loss. May we speak with you? I know it is painful, but I will lose more if we do not. I will lose someone very dear to me, and I do not want the monsters who did this to claim another because I failed."

Your Silver Tongue skill is now level 7!

The man blinked, and he looked down, noticing her for the first time. His face was almost comical in its amazement. "I... who are you?"

"My name is Chase. This is Cagna. May we come in? I promise we mean you no harm, and we will leave when you ask us to."

The man grunted and fished around in a pocket. Then he offered a single coin, that glinted silver in the midday sun. "Touch this first." His other hand hovered near where he'd stowed the knife.

Chase did so, and Cagna flicked it with one finger. When neither of them seemed hurt by that, the man nodded, returned the coin to its pouch, and pointed at Cagna. "She stays outside." His finger traced down to Chase. "You can come in."

Cagna's ears flattened. Chase punched her leg again. "It's fine. I've got this. Please?"

"It's your hide." Cagna shrugged, and walked toward an old stone bench, then sat on the least-stained part of it. "Scream if you need me."

But Chase wasn't watching her. She kept her gaze on the man, watched him ease as the beastkin retreated. Once she was sitting, he gave Chase an almost-apologetic nod, and stepped back from the doorway.

Steeling herself for the next part, Chase pushed down her unease and followed him back into the reeking darkness of his shop.

CHAPTER 8: MAGIC BY ANY OTHER NAME

Signore Castillo was a hard worker. It wasn't his fault that the guilds undercut his prices, and he was being slowly forced out of business.

Signore Castillo was a good husband It was definitely not his fault his wife couldn't see that and fled with some idiot minstrel, leaving him to raise a young daughter alone.

Signore Castillo was a good father. Why, he'd been in the middle of saving up to hire a matchmaker, to find her a good husband!

Signore Castillo was a good boss. That his daughter stayed up late at night working while he slept, that was just her devotion to keeping the shop going. Nothing more.

All this and more Chase heard from Signore Castillo as she sat in his shop, with the displays and racks pushed up against the wall.

All this she heard, while both of them did their best to pretend the coffin didn't exist.

It sat there on a low table, lid open, showing white cloth within. Plain cloth, but well made... probably the best a small tradesman could afford. Even then it had to have cost a fair amount of silver.

He loved his daughter, and that was enough now. And he seemed to take comfort into pouring his woes out on Chase, who had barely said more than "yes," or "go on," or "I agree," since she'd gotten through the door.

"I tried, you know? I tried. And this is what we get! What she... got..." Signore Castillo swallowed, hard. He moved to the clutter of junk surrounding the shop's counter, rummaged around in it, and pulled out a bottle. But it was empty, and he groaned in disappointment. Daunted but determined, he dug further into the mess.

Ah, this wouldn't do. The room already stank of alcohol and sweat.

Chase needed answers, and the more he drank the less useful those answers would be.

Still, he was wild with grief. She had to tread carefully. Fortunately, her skillset lent itself to that. **"Silent Activation, Foresight,"** Chase whispered. Time slowed, her ghostly self tested the words she wanted to say, and she nodded to see that the reaction was good.

Your Silent Activation skill is now level 9!

Time resumed and she said, "Signore, I wish to pay my respects. Have they taken your daughter to church already?"

That stopped him. He looked over to the casket, face crumpling. "No. No, they took her bod— they took her. They took my little Friatta."

"Who took her?"

"The guards. Useless! Two days ago I tell them werewolves killed my daughter." Signore Castillo threw his hands up and paced the room, letting his temper slip. But NOT at Chase, which was what she'd been worried about. He went on, moving into a full-blown rant. "They tell me there are no werewolves in Arretzi! They lie to my face! Then the very next day, Giuseppe Morrino calls upon the doge, and says werewolves slew his son!"

"And then what did the guards do?" Chase persisted.

"They took her, is what. They took my little girl." He leaned against a wall. Then he punched it twice, thrice, hard enough that a red '3' drifted up from his head as Chase winced. "They took her because they say her body might have clues. Bah! She is dead, it was werewolves, that is the end of it! She can't rest. She can't go to church until they're done. She can't..." The big man sagged. "I want my little girl back."

"What? Why? What could her body tell them?" Chase blinked. "Surely they wouldn't use necromancy..."

"What? No, no. No." That seemed to shock him out of his angry sorrow. "They told me the Doge is entertaining a scholar at court. That he can look at wounds and figure out what made them. I say cazzate! She was killed by a werewolf! A werewolf broke in here and killed her! What more do they need to know?"

"The how of it does seem pretty unimportant," Chase agreed. She gnawed her lip. "I'm more curious about why a werewolf would go after her."

"What are you saying?" The man squinted and brushed his hands down his apron. "She didn't do nothing wrong. It's a werewolf, they don't need a reason."

"I didn't say she did anything wrong." Chase held up her hands. "This happened at night, right? You said she worked late?"

"Yeah." The Signore sagged. "Lots of business. It's the end of the fur season, all the hunters and woodsmen are coming in with their pelts. Gods damned Clothiers guild undercutting my prices, we gotta work bulk and work cheap to make up the difference. That and we ain't far from the gate, so we get lots of work. The lights would be lit. Only lights lit around here at night, so it must have looked in the window, and..." he shuddered.

Chase looked over at the windows. The bars over them seemed intact. "Did it come through the window? Did you have it fixed?"

"No. The windows were shut. The door was shut. It must have used magic to get inside. That's the only thing I can think of." But his voice sounded uncertain.

"What did the guards do, exactly? Besides taking her?" Chase rubbed her chin. This didn't sound like a werewolf sort of killing.

"They poked around. They looked at the... the mess. They cleaned it. They looked for clues, didn't find anything. They took her and left. They said they'll bring her back. I asked when, they said 'when the scholar is done.'" Signore Castillo seemed to shrink into himself, voice going hoarse. He turned back to the pile of junk, searching through it again. With a grunt, he hauled out a bottle and this one was still corked. He opened it, sniffed, and took a pull.

Oh damn it, Chase winced. The next part would be tricky, but she had to move quickly. Another silently activated Foresight confirmed that it would be worth the risk. "Signore, what if I told you I had a way to get in touch with your daughter? Without necromancy."

He didn't sound offended, just sure of himself when he replied. "I'd say you were lying to me. Her body ain't here, she ain't haunting me, and there ain't no soulst—" he coughed, abruptly. "Mf. Nevermind."

"He knows about soulstones," Renny whispered in Chase's ear, and she jumped a bit. She'd forgotten he was here! "That's not usual in a place where necromancy's illegal, right?" The fox continued, barely audible to her.

"You know about soulstones?" Chase said, scrutinizing the leatherworker.

Signore Castillo stirred a bit, then looked up at the wall. Chase followed his gaze to where taxidermied birds sat on perches. "I got some clients. Hunters who work for certain patrons. They bring in animal remains and black gems, and I have to put the gems inside the remains." He took a slow pull of the bottle, scrutinizing her as he did so. "I don't ask questions, you understand. But I hear things. And I ain't stupid."

"You're a wise man," Chase agreed. "My magic is different. All it would take is help from a living relative."

"And then... what? What would it do?" The man seemed honestly curious, but she could tell by the way his face twitched, that he was trying to keep from being too optimistic.

"It would call up a memory of her. The skill says that the longer it's been, the weaker the memory will be. So..." Chase shrugged. "I don't know what will come of it. But if you're willing to try, I'll do it for free."

The last part seemed to break through the merchant's distracted, mildly-tipsy state of mind. He stared at her with new suspicion in his gaze. "Why? What do you get out of this?"

"I told you, that a friend of mine is in danger because of this beast. Or these beasts, however many there are." Technically true. Thomasi *was* in danger, but he had more to worry about from the Don than he did the werewolves. Still, the leatherworker didn't need to know this particular distinction. "If she can help us find them, then that's worth doing my work for free, here."

Signore Castillo searched her face, eyes narrow and suspicious. But after a minute they eased. He nodded and put the bottle down. "All right. What have I got to lose?"

That's some major charisma experience, there, Chase thought. If she hadn't leveled just this morning she was sure it would have been a boost.

"We'll need... We'll need this table, a few candles, and... do you have any of her hair? Or a portrait of her?"

He pushed the curtain in the back of the shop aside and went up, coming back down after a minute with a hairbrush.

They stood at opposite ends of the small table. Chase put the hairbrush in the center of it, arranging the candles in a loose circle and lighting them one by one. Then, after some prompting, the large man took her hands.

Chase took a breath, closed her status screen, and whispered, **"Seance. Friatta Castillo, we call to you. Friatta, your father calls to you from across the veil. Come to us, Friatta Castillo. Show us that you are here."**

Somewhere a horn sounded, low and deep. Metal rattled around the room as everything shook, just for a second.

Signore Castillo gasped, his eyes going wide. He tried to pull his hands away from Chase, but she held fast, held with all her might. Her recent adventures had granted her better strength, but it was probably the man's surprise more than anything else that let her keep hold. "No!" she commanded. "It's a fragile link! **Friatta, come to us!"**

And then she was there.

Her father choked a sob as a woman rose from the hairbrush, green and wavery and faint, caught in the act of combing her hair. She looked around, surprised... and then her face fell into sorrow, as she stared into her father's eyes.

"Are you Friatta Castillo?" Chase asked.

One of the candles flickered, guttering out, and Friatta seemed to go a bit mistier. Chase blinked. *So quickly?* There were five candles left burning, and she had the feeling that once the last was out, Friatta would be gone. Silently she thanked her massive wisdom for the insight and focused her mind on the matter at hand. "Friatta, we have questions. Can you answer them?"

Friatta turned and tried to speak.

But her lips moved silently, and Chase shook her head. "I'm sorry. We can't hear you."

"Friatta!" Her father could take no more and tried to embrace the spirit. To Chase's horror, his hands passed right through her, and tore out wispy strands of goop. Friatta jerked back in shock and stared down at the holes in her form.

Her father wept into his hands, as his daughter's substance dripped off them, oozing into nothing. "I'm sorry! I'm sorry Fritta! I was drunk! I could have saved you! I was drunk and didn't wake!"

Another candle went out, and Chase shook her head. She was close, so CLOSE... "Stop that, sir! Friatta, was it a werewolf that killed you?"

She had to repeat the question three times, but Friatta nodded her head vigorously when she finally looked up from her ectoplasmic wounds.

"Of course it was a werewolf!" Signore Castillo roared.

"Shush!" Chase commanded. "Friatta! Did you know the werewolf?"

More nodding, and a puff of smoke, as a third candle puffed out. Three more to go.

Chase made a grab for the leatherworker's hands, but he wasn't cooperating now. He was frozen in shock, and his hands were out of reach. Chase didn't know if it would help anyway. She was trying to figure out how to salvage this and coming up with a fair amount of nothing.

Fortunately, she wasn't alone.

"Ask her for clues!" Renny said. "See if she's got anything that can help!"

"Friatta! Can you give us any clues?" Chase asked. "Anything that would help us figure out who the werewolf is?"

Friatta nodded and headed over to the pile of junk. Once there she put her hands on her hips and shot her father a matronly glare.

"I'm sorry. I should have cleaned up," he said, in a small voice, still sobbing.

Chase pushed back a laugh at the absurdity of it. Another candle went out, and the halven dove into the stuff, throwing it around with abandon... almost hitting the spirit, before she caught herself.

And every time Chase held up something from the pile that might be of use, the spirit shook her head.

Seconds crawled by, precious and finite, but finally, finally Friatta nodded and pointed, lips moving frantically.

Chase blinked and stopped her arm in mid-throw.

It was a knife. A tiny knife.

"This? This is..." This was a familiar knife.

But how was it familiar?

The answer came to her, just as the last candle guttered out, and Friatta started to fade. "This is a knife made for a halven!"

INT+1

Friatta's smile illuminated the room with green glow... and then it was gone with the candlelight.

Her father's despairing wail filled the darkness, and Chase studied it. Well-worn, obviously used and sharpened many times over. It wasn't a fighting knife, of course. Halvens didn't do that sort of thing if they could help it. This one was thin-bladed, with a sharp edge.

"Hey. Did you..." she looked at the sobbing wreck that was Signore Castillo. "Nevermind. Sorry. I'll just..." Chase searched around in the pile where she'd found the knife, and after a minute, she came up with a sheath that fit the blade.

But as she was putting the dagger away, she realized that the sheath didn't *quite* match the blade. The blade was old. The sheath was new. So new it was still creaking and stiff. But it fit the knife snugly, and it was definitely made for the blade.

"Sir," she said, but Signore Castillo didn't stop sobbing. "Sir, I'm sorry, but—"

"Get the werewolf!" someone shouted, right outside the window.

There came the muffled sound of wood hitting flesh, and Cagna yelped.

"Sir! Please, this is..." Chase looked from him to the door.

"Kill her!" A woman howled.

"...this is not gonna work." He was too far gone to his grief. Chase ran for the door, shoving the sheathed knife into her pocket as she went. It took a few tries to get the human-height door handle opened, but she managed.

She opened the door onto chaos.

The quiet street was now a battlefield. Cagna was running for her life, heading for the central plaza, with her shortsword out. A man choked and bled onto the street not too far away, and six other humans were chasing the beastkin with clubs and daggers. More people filtered in from the surrounding streets, drawn by the carnage. But they were either drawing weapons and grinning, heading toward the fight, or they were standing there and gaping.

"I'm not a wolf, you idiots! I'm a dog!" Cagna said, whipping her cloak off and around to tangle someone who got in too close with a gaff hook. **"Pommel Strike!"** she shouted and laid him out with a sword hilt to the head while he struggled to escape the cloak.

But a thrown cobblestone clipped her leg while she was doing that, and she yelped.

"Hey! Stop!" Chase shouted, and the five people who were chasing Cagna slowed and spread out into a circle.

One of them, a woman, looked back and grinned maliciously. "She's with the werewolf! Get her!"

A few of the oncoming thugs switched targets, and Chase paled.

She was very, very good at talking things out, but she didn't think she'd have the time for that, here.

"Run for it, girl!" Cagna shouted, moving to put her back against the Muscle Wizaard's wagon.

"Dropping illusions!" Renny said in her ear. "I'll buy us time!"

The world rippled around Chase, and then there were twelve of her all running in different directions. The thugs paused, then split up and tried kicking at oddly-nimble halvens.

Chase paused...

Then Cagna yelped, and Chase saw a crossbow bolt through the woman's sword arm. Her blade clattered to the ground, and the thugs closed in for the kill.

"No! We're not leaving her!" Chase shouted. "Draw them off of her and to me," she hissed in a quieter tone, as she ran toward the ring. There was a trick she'd used before to great effect, if she could get one of them near enough...

"Phantasm," Renny commanded, and the air rippled again. Cagna vanished, and the group closing in on her slowed. The mass of fleeing halvens followed Chase as she leaped, grabbed the ropes of the ring, and swung herself in. The halven girl reached her destination... the slumbering wrestler.

"Guards!" Chase shouted, as the thugs looked around for their vanquished quarry, and glared at the shouting girl. Another crossbow bolt flew, striking one of the illusionary halvens. The halven gave a convincing shriek and toppled, lying dead on the ground.

Chase looked around, marked the crossbowman at the edge of an alley, and grabbed a hurler stone out of her skirt pocket. Her throw missed him but hit the onlooker next to him, who screamed and fell to her knees.

Okay, I feel a little bad about that, Chase thought. But the woman's scream was inadvertently helpful, as it broke the crowd's shock. People fled in all directions, trampling and hindering the thugs who now pushed through, trying to get to the ring, trying to get to Chase. They were down to eight or nine perhaps, it was hard to tell.

"Where's Cagna?" Chase hissed at Renny.

"Over there!" He shifted the illusion a bit, and Chase saw the dog-woman kneeling, pulling the bolt from her bloody arm.

"Lesser Healing, Lesser Healing," Chase commanded, unsure of the damage.

You have healed Cagna for 28 points!

Your Lesser Healing skill is now level 30!

You have healed Cagna for 29 points!

But then there was no time for that, as the leading thug grabbed the ropes and hopped them into the ring. Chase reached down...

...and put her hand on the bulging pectoral of the drunk wrestler.

"Absorb Condition!" she yelled, and then without waiting even a fraction of a second, she ran over and slapped the surprised thug. **"Transfer Condition!"**

You are now deathly drunk!

A wave of distortion, nausea, and pain crashed into her, as her vision instantly went dark...

You are no longer deathly drunk!

And then she could see again. And *ow*, did that hurt.

Your Transfer Condition skill is now level 4!

The thug stared at her, raised his truncheon, and then promptly collapsed in a heap.

But then five more were vaulting over the ropes, lashing out at halvens.

"Get the stunty!" A man with a lopsided jaw shouted. "The rest have to be illusions!" He clubbed at one, and it popped.

Behind the mob, Chase saw Cagna fade into existence, wrap her hand around one man's mouth, and slam her sword hilt into one man's temple. But then the line on her pressed forward, and Chase fell back, trying to figure out what to do next, hating the fact she had to fight her way out, knowing that a good slash or bash would pop her like a grape.

"No good," Renny said, as his illusions started to fray, too many people seeing through them. "Get clear, I'll switch to lightning and elementals!"

Chase backpedaled—

And stopped.

Her back hit something solid.

Very, very solid.

And amazingly, the half-dozen thugs in the ring slowed and stopped, staring over her head. Quite a bit over her head.

"Who dares enter the sanctum of the Muscle Wizaard?" A basso voice boomed above her.

LUCK+1

And despite herself, Chase looked up.

Up into a very large, very bushy gray beard, and a cleft-jawed chin, at a face that had a pair of tiny spectacles practically wedged into the eyesockets. At the conical purple hat studded with frayed golden stars, now on top of a wild-haired head.

It was a bit hard to make that out, because there were some truly impressive pectorals in the way. They grew even larger when he rumbled **"Flex** and **Strong Pose,"** and twisted in ways that made his body bulge, almost seeming to put on inches of height and girth.

The woman who had set the thugs on Chase spoke, the slim rapier in her hand angling to point at the giant human. "This isn't your affair. Step off."

"Step off? Step off? I think not! You've entered **The Squared Circle!** There is a price to pay, and that price is in blood, sweat, and jeers! OOOOOOoooohhhh yeah!"

Suddenly, the ropes snapped taut. With a whistling noise, the drunken man tangled in them was ejected, flying dozens of feet in the air to crash to the ground with an audible CRUNCH.

One of the thugs at the back tried to slink out under the ropes... but even though there was a clear gap, somehow he got tangled. He yelled and the Wizaard chortled. "Cowards and ruffians all! I have your measure." Then he whispered, and Chase and Renny were the only ones close enough to hear it. **"Theme Song."**

Grandiose music suddenly filled the air, and while the thugs looked around wildly, Chase felt a big hand pick her up and gently deposit her behind the big guy. She could see straight up his loincloth, and quickly looked away, eyes burning. "So I'm not sure what all this is about," the Muscle Wizaard said, as the brassy strings and horns of the song died down to a lull. "But I've cast my scrying spell, and it tells me that you're going down harder than an ice elemental eating one of my specialized fireball suplexes! You surrender and throw down your weapons now and I'll go easy on you. Otherwise..." He slammed a palm into his chest, and the sound echoed like thunder.

The woman was uncowed. "Get me a shot at his back, boys! I'll end this in one swing! **Fight the Battles, Take the Hits, Fast as Death, Backstab!"**

Several of the others muttered their own skills, and Chase shrunk back against the ropes of the ring. Beyond them, she could see Cagna trying to climb in and failing, hands slipping from ropes that should have been easy to go over. Whatever magic this wizard had, it cut both ways.

"Get behind me?" The pointy-hatted Wrestler laughed, honestly amused. "Get behind me? Do you know who I am?" He lifted a finger to the sky and shouted **"Signature Move! You Shall Not Pass!"**

Silence for a bit.

Nothing happened.

The thugs shrugged, and started to close in. The Muscle Wizaard shook his head. "Well, I warned you. Time to let **My Muscles Do the Talking!"**

And he did.

What followed was a symphony of brutal destruction, as one man stood against six foes...

...and won.

Chase stared as a screaming man got bounced off the ropes, so hard that he did three flips before ending with a sudden crunch. "Do you think he's got some kind of silent activation?" she asked Renny. "That talking muscles thing?"

"Seems likely," Renny said, poking his snout further out of the pack. "Ooooh... I didn't know bones could bend *that* way."

"They uh, can't," Chase said, averting her eyes. "Oh! Look out, she's nearly behind... you..." her voice trailed off.

The woman with the rapier had used her friends as a distraction and tried to dart around the Muscle Wizaard. But she couldn't. It was like she'd just hit a brick wall and bounced off.

In fact, none of them could get around him. Wherever he turned, they were pushed back, forced into facing him head on.

And, as she watched him pick up a screaming thug and use him to beat the other thugs, she knew that facing the Muscle Wizaard head on was a very, very bad idea.

It wasn't entirely one sided. He didn't bother to defend himself, and although his comically large muscles seemed to shrug off blows that would seriously injure Chase, they still had weapons and he didn't. The woman's rapier traced lines of blood and gouged into him, and Chase awoke from her awe long enough to throw healing his way.

"My thanks, fair maiden! Bide a bit longer, almost done taking out the trash. OOOOOOoooohhh yeah!"

The deadly woman screamed as he closed in, bounded to stand on the ropes with long-practiced balance, and shouted **"Off The Top Rope!"**

Then he leaped.

Chase looked away, covering her eyes.

There was a crunch.

"Oh wow," Renny said. "Yeah, she's dead. That's the biggest red number I've seen in a long time."

"Don't tell me," Chase said. "Just... let's look this way... um."

"Ha, relax! All part of the kayfabe," the Muscle Wizaard said, and Chase dared to look.

To her amazement, the people she thought she'd just watched be brutally murdered were still twitching. A few were groaning quietly.

"It makes the yellow stamina damage I inflict look red," the Muscle Wizaard said, then winced. "Ah, shoot. Wait, that's a trade secret. Sorry, I mean it's maaaaaaaagiiiic!" he flexed. "For I am a merciful mage!"

A slow clap echoed through the now-quiet plaza, and Chase, Renny, and the Wizaard turned...

...to see Cagna leaning against a wall, applauding. "If you're done, we need to go. The guards will be here soon. We do NOT want to be stuck in cells answering questions for *days*," she said, giving Chase a significant look.

"Go? Guards?" the Wizard blanched. "Uh-oh. Um...." he looked over at the wagon. "Oh no, I don't have time to buy my horse back. I'll have to pull it again..."

Renny spoke up, wriggling out of the pack. "I think I can help with that part."

CHAPTER 9: LEGACY OF THE WIZAARD

The horse clopped its way through the busy thoroughfare, straining to pull the gaily-colored wagon. It was obviously having a bit of trouble with its burden. Fortunately, the flow of traffic was slow. Besides, the number of pedestrians in the street negated the advantages of speed anyway.

A sharp-eyed person might have noticed that the horse's legs weren't quite in sync, and that a strange wind blew out from around the area of the horse, causing the cloth of the wagon to flutter and nearby passerby to look around for the odd drafts. They might also have noticed that the horse never blinked and breathed irregularly.

But this was Arretzi, the city of crafts and business, and people were far too busy to notice that. Besides, there was something going on in the slums, and people were watching groups of guards head down, truncheons out, looking for someone to beat until the problem was solved.

Thankfully, no one knew that the problem was in any way connected with the beastkin who was driving. Cagna had a ratty, too-big cloak bundled close around her, and a floppy, comical hat pulled low over her eyes. Though the disguise was somewhat spoiled as she cast a look back now and again, staring at the three people in the back of the wagon.

There wasn't much to the interior of the wagon, really. A large bed, a trunk full of costuming and props, a few cooking tools, and books.

And the Muscle Wizaard himself, sitting on the bed, staring at Renny. Renny, who was standing in the center of the wagon, eyes closed, concentrating on making the lesser air elemental he'd summoned look like a horse.

Chase gave one final look out of the back of the wagon, pulling the curtains closed and turning to the large man. "So! You probably have questions. So do I. Shall we trade?"

"Hahaha! Of course! Seeking out hidden knowledge is the goal of every true wizard!" The big man slathered ointment on his arms as he talked, flipping his beard adeptly out of the way every time it threatened to get smeared by the goop.

"Good. Ah..." Chase, still riding the adrenaline from the fight, threw her judgment to the wind and asked the first thing that came to mind.

"Why aren't you putting on a show in the central plaza? That was amazing!"

The Wizaard's smile was warm enough to melt ice in the dead of winter. "Ah! Young lady, you make an old mage very happy, when you say such a thing... and years back, I could work such a stage. Years ago, in my prime, I was a titan of the turnbuckle, a sorcerer of the sweet sciences... I was all the rage in Gall! But..." he sighed. "Time is the end of all things, even the sagest of wizards. Well, time and politics." He scowled, pouting lips mostly concealed by his bushy beard. "After hearing so many stories about Laraggiungere, I had to come and see the place for myself. That... was a bit hasty." The Wizard sighed, and took off his spectacles, polishing them with a spare sock. "You either need to be in a big show or know somebody powerful to work the center of quartiere carne. I, alas, had neither. As such, I was relegated to the first available plaza. And there, sadly, I languished." The man deflated, losing a few inches of girth to another deep sigh.

His lungs must be the size of me. Each. Chase thought, distractedly. "I'm sorry to hear it," she said. "Is there any way we can help?"

"Ah! Young lady, you transgress the rules of this arrangement." The Wizaard gave her a mock frown, and Chase giggled despite herself. "Now it is MY turn to ask a question. Are you ready? Are! You! Ready!" he said, in his stage voice.

"Hahaha, sure!"

"What... is your name?"

"Chase Berrymore," she said, offering a tiny hand that disappeared into his massive mitt.

"Well met, Chase Berrymore. I am the Muscle Wizaard... but offstage, my friends call me Bastien."

"Thank you, Bastien. Is that a Gallish name?"

"It certainly is! I was born in a small village not far from the border. My turn! What is HIS name?" Bastien hooked a thumb at Renny.

"I'm Renny," the little fox spoke.

"And I'm Cagna," said the dog-woman, glancing back into the wagon. "There, we're done with introductions. So let's move on to the important stuff. Why did you step in back there?"

"You have to ask?" Bastien frowned at her. "Six on one, and that one a tiny young girl?"

Chase frowned. *I'm on a first name basis with a god. I could've handled that. Maybe. Probably? I mean Renny and I could. Maybe...* she shoved it out of her mind as Cagna spoke up again.

"So you're an altruist, huh? Not looking for a payout?"

"You are asking far too many questions for the exchange and violating the terms of the mystical contract!" The Muscle Wizaard shook a finger at her. "You meddle in forces you do not understand!"

"Cagna, it's all right," Chase said, moving up and laying a hand on the beastkin's arm.

Cagna shook it off, and glowered, ignoring the "horse" she was "guiding" entirely. "No it is NOT all right. I just got jumped in the middle of Dona Tarantino's turf by a gang. A freaking gang! This is the sort of stuff she should have in hand."

Bastien rubbed his beard. "I'll ask a question then, while I can; why did they assault you? I've seen many victims in my time, and you, my lady Cagna, are not one. You are quite clearly dangerous."

"It's because I'm dressed nicely and have a blade they could resell." Cagna growled. "Nothing more."

"They called you a werewolf—" Chase began, only to be furiously interrupted.

"Nonsense!" Cagna barked, sharp teeth flashing. "That was just the excuse!"

"She's right," Bastien nodded. "With the werewolves driving fear up in the city, it would, at the very least, let them excuse away the killing later. They would say ah, we thought she was a werewolf, excuse us please. So sorry." He glowered. "A lie to cover the most evil of intentions."

"What I'm saying," Chase waved her hands frantically, "is that it doesn't matter why Bastien saved us. It's what he did that matters, and I..." *I need allies, and this man has already proven he can save my life,* she realized and said, "I want to reward him for his good works."

"No reward is necessary!" Bastien protested. "Any good man would have come to your rescue!"

"I could have handled them," Cagna growled again. "Just would have taken some time, is all."

"Yes, but if they'd caught me they would have killed me while you were busy handling them." Chase said, patting her arm again. This time Cagna didn't shake it off. "You're good at your job, but there were just too many. We need somebody who specializes in groups, battling gangs, that kind of thing. You, you're deadly one on one. But it wasn't one on one. And how often will it be, really, until this madness is gone from the city?"

Cagna turned her muzzle from Chase to the Muscle Wizaard, clearly struggling for words. Finally, she lowered her muzzle and rubbed the bridge of it, in a sort of face-palm. "So what are you suggesting?"

Chase took a breath, and turned to Bastien, who had been watching the conversation with a bemused, almost fatherly air. But in his eyes, Chase could see the glint of hope. "Bastien... Mister Wizaard... could you perhaps spare some time to work for me? I can offer good wages and room and board until our business is done."

"Of course!" The Wizaard beamed and shook Chase's hand.

Cagna stopped facepalming and whipped her muzzle up, ears flat and alarmed. "What? Hey! I can't... the Don doesn't... I can't pay—"

"I can," Chase said, as the Wizaard's eyes flickered with worry. She pulled out the pouch Thomasi had given her and checked inside.

After nearly dropping it, and clenching her jaw to keep her mouth shut, she pulled out two gold and handed it over to the Wrestler. *If this is just half of Thomasi's loose change, then he must be rich beyond all my wildest dreams.*

"Is the money all right? Or do you want more?" Chase asked Bastien.

"All right? All right?" he laughed. "I had no idea how I was going to make it through the winter, let alone maintain my strict dietary restrictions. And you say room and board is included as well?"

"It is. We've got a big villa with lots of rooms available."

The dog-woman winced. "Hey! That's not your villa!"

"Shush," Chase shot Cagna a look. "There's at least five or six empty rooms upstairs. He can have one."

"You realize that the Don's son is living there, right? He might have something to say about it."

"Really? From the way the Don talks about his son, and the way he let us use it without talking to his son beforehand, I don't think that what the son has to say is such a big deal."

It was a bit of a stab in the dark, but judging by Cagna's grimace, it was pretty on point. "All right. But you're paying for him. And any special stuff his diet requires."

"That's fine by me. Heck, I can cook his food myself if I have to," Chase said. "It's the least I owe him."

The Wizaard beamed. "You owe me nothing, Lady Chase! I shall be your servant for this task. Whatever this task is. Uh... bodyguarding, I'm assuming, yes?" Now Chase could catch a cautious tone in his voice.

"Bodyguarding, yes. And help with... well, I might as well tell you.

I'm working with Cagna and her friends to find the werewolves."

"I see..."

"Does that change matters? If you want to back out, that's okay," Chase realized, belatedly. "I won't think any less of you. Werewolves are dangerous."

"Change matters? No, not at all!" The Wizaard laughed. "Right now I'm a face! Doing something like this is definitely good, that's just the sort of cause that my buff can help with."

"You're not concerned at all about going up against whirlwinds of claws, fangs, and murder. Unarmored." Cagna scowled at the Wrestler.

"No more than you are, lady," the Wizaard smiled.

"I'm better protected than you think. And I'm no lady."

"Signora, then. Sorry, my grasp of your tongue is a bit limited. I've only been here a few years."

"A few years..." Cagna considered him. "I thought Wizards got massive intelligence boosts. Learning the local language tricks shouldn't be much of a fuss for someone with that job."

"Ah! Er. Well. As to that..." The Wizaard coughed. "I'm, er, I'm..." he muttered something so fast Chase had trouble hearing it.

Cagna's ears twitched. "You're not actually a vizier? What is that supposed to mean?"

"I'm not actually a Wizard," said Bastien, taking off his pointy hat and staring at it morosely. "Where I come from only nobles or the very rich get to go to Wizard school. Or orphaned children of prophecy, and I'm no more that than I am the first two things."

"It takes *that* much money?" Chase said, frowning.

"Well... I had enough saved to cover it, once. The first year's tuition, anyway. But... by that time I had been Wrestling as the Muscle Wizard for a few years. But it turns out that unlocking Wizard takes a lot of math, and I'm, er... well, I'm bad at that. And then the admissions board heard about my wrestling career, and well... they didn't have a sense of humor about it." The Wizaard's face sagged, and he kept staring at his hat. "They made me change my name. Now I have to spell it with two 'A's and people think I'm stupid. I'm... I'm not stupid," he burst out. The rawness in his voice made Chase's heart go out to him, and she patted his knee. "I'm just very very focused, that's all," he muttered.

"There are other ways to learn that job than just the wizard schools," Cagna pointed out. "Rogue mages could montage you, it'd take a day and they'd do it for way less than the schools charge."

"Yes, I suppose, but..." he sighed. "In my darkest hours I've considered that. But it wouldn't be *right*. I don't want to skulk and lie to get the job, I want to BE a Wizard! I want to stand among my peers and learn the secrets of *true* magic. I don't want to have to hide what I am. I'm all about showing my stuff, and..." he sighed again, harder. "Besides, now that I caught the attention of the schools in a bad way, they spread word around. If I start using wizardly magic without their approval, they'll know I'm a rogue. And here and in the nearby countries, at least, they'll put a bounty on me for that."

"Is it really that cutthroat?" Chase blanched.

"It is around here," Cagna nodded. "Even a Wizard who hasn't been promoted by a guild can do some really dangerous stuff with magical experimentation. Same thing with Necromancers and Enchanters, and to a lesser degree, Alchemists. That's why they have their own guilds in most places, and why they make sure there are big penalties for running without a guild."

"Cylvania isn't like that," Renny said, and Chase and the others jerked in surprise, and stared at him with varying degrees of wonder.

Mind you, Chase was wondering how he was talking and managing the illusion at the same time. "Didn't you need full concentration to conceal the air elemental?"

"We're at the gate to the villa. I let both the illusion and the elemental go."

"Oh! All right. Good work, thanks. Um... Cagna, should we borrow the horse to pull the wagon—"

"No need," the Muscle Wizaard said, stepping out of the wagon. "If it's only into a courtyard, that shouldn't hurt my back too badly."

Chase opened her mouth to protest, then shut it again. "Let's at least get out so he has a lighter load."

Cagna snorted. "Right, because you're at least a whopping twenty pounds, and that thing—"

"Hey! I have a name!"

"—that named thing over there is about two or three himself. Ah, come on. We need to talk anyway." Cagna hopped out of the wagon, and unlocked the gate, motioning the others to follow her in.

The gardener was out of sight at least, that was something. The sun was getting low in the sky, and Cagna led Chase and Renny inside to a sitting room. "So," she said, locking the doors. "What the hell are you, little guy?"

"I'm a toy golem."

"I've seen golems. They're big hulking stupid things that do what they're told."

"I'm a special kind. I've been given a gift of sapience."

Cagna shook her head, turning her gaze to Chase. "So your parents ARE that rich."

"What does that have to do with—" Renny stopped talking as Chase rested a hand on his head.

"A little bit," Chase lied. "He's my other bodyguard. You understand why I didn't mention him before?"

Cagna actually smiled a bit. "I do. You've got more brains than I give you credit for."

A gentle knock at the door, and Cagna checked it, snorted, and let the Muscle Wizaard in. He'd traded in his hat and loincloth for a set of loose, flowing robes that hid his muscles. He could be mistaken for an elderly monk this way, Chase thought.

"Done so soon?" Cagna asked.

"Please! I started my career as a strongman. My warmups are harder than that little chore. So, what did I miss?"

"Pretty much just me telling Cagna I was a golem," Renny offered, hopping up on a nearby footstool.

"A golem!" the Muscle Wizaard exclaimed. "The most magical of made creatures! Say..." he rubbed his beard. "My act would do much better if I had a er, trained familiar doing cutesy things. It would draw in the kids! Are you currently employed?"

"He is," Chase said, before Renny could speak.

"Ah, bother. Well no matter, if you ever want to get into show biz, there's always room in my wagon! Ha ha ha!"

"That sounds fun! Sure, after I'm done here, maybe we can work together."

The Muscle Wizaard stopped laughing. "You really mean it? You're serious? Wow. I... yes. That would be good! I think we'd make a great team."

"Anyway!" Chase said, trying to regain control of the situation. "We're going to be working together to find and stop werewolves. So I think it's cards on the table time—"

"Again?" Cagna said, with a bit of snark in her tone.

"Metaphorical cards," Chase said.

"Metaphyiscal? What?" The Muscle Wizaard asked, seemingly confused.

"Meta... look. I need to know what you can do so I know how best to work with you," Chase said. "I've got broad strokes. I know what Renny can do, and I know what I can do. You, Bastien? You're a powerhouse. Cagna is murder on two legs. But if you have other things you can do, I'd like to know them, please. Fighting the werewolves isn't our goal, finding them is. What can the two of you do? Maybe you've got strengths we can play to, there?"

"As far as finding werewolves goes... I don't have much there, I'm afraid." The Muscle Wizaard shrugged. "Think of me as a Wrestler. My other jobs built toward that role and are mainly about combat and self-improvement. I... also, I don't like killing, much, I'm sorry. If you ask me to do that, I'll consider our contract terminated. Not that we have a contract." He frowned. "Should we have a contract?"

"I uh, don't think so," Chase said. "I don't like killing much myself. I'm not good in fights and killing when you don't have to seems like a good way to get in a lot of trouble. In fact that's what I'm good at, talking people out of fights. Negotiating. Stuff like that."

"Good luck with that if we run into the werewolves," Cagna said. "Full moon tonight. Their blood will be up. And it'll be blood on the streets when they hunt."

"And what do *you* do, young lady?" The Muscle Wizaard adjusted his spectacles, as he studied the dog-woman.

"Like the short stuff said, I'm murder on two legs. Leave it at that."

"Nothing investigative?" *Thomasi said she had very good perception. She has to have some kind of job that contributes to that.*

"No," Cagna said, but her eyes shifted, just a bit. Had that denial been a little too abrupt?

Something in Chase's expression must have given her doubt away, because Cagna waved a hand in irritation. "Once upon a time I got some Knight training. Then my country stopped existing, and I took to the wilds. Became a bandit for a bit. Got good enough at it that I unlocked Highwayman. But that was a long time ago."

"Highwayman!" The Muscle Wizaard frowned at her. "I don't know if my image will survive working with a robber."

Cagna snorted. "Please! It's a Knight and Bandit combo. I've got a code about who and when I can steal. And I don't DO that anymore... for the most part." She shifted her muzzle back to Chase. "Remember that mask I loaned you? I can disguise myself with it, make people forget the exact details about me. And I can command people to do things. And ride like the wind, if I need to. Does any of that help your plans?"

"Don't Knights use shields?" the Muscle Wizaard persisted. "And isn't armor a key thing, there?"

"Armor just slows me down. And anything can be a shield in a pinch. Cities are full of stuff or people that I can improvise with if I have to." Cagna shrugged. "Be different if we were in the wild."

It might come to that, Chase said, remembering the dungeon. *But not yet.*

"Okay. So now we know what we can do," Renny said. "What about that clue that the ghost showed us?"

"Oh? Oh! Right!" Chase hauled out the knife and the sheath and explained how her séance had gone.

"...sadly I don't think we can go back there," Chase said, biting her lip as Cagna and The Muscle Wizaard passed around the blade and studied it. "The owner fell to pieces pretty hard during the séance. I don't fault him for that, but I've known a lot of people like him. If I go back he'll blame me for how he felt. At best he probably won't cooperate, at worst he might report me for necromancy. Falsely!" She added, as the Muscle Wizaard shot her a dubious look. "That's not necromancy! It just could be mistaken for it by the common layperson." *Or me yesterday, to be honest. I've had this job for a few hours, I'm by no means an expert.*

"It's sized for a gnome. Or a halven," Cagna said, studying the blade. "Seen a lot of use and a lot of sharpening. Good eye on the sheath though, it's definitely new. The dye is fresh." She considered. "I could maybe get some guys together and go have a talk with the shop owner. Some quiet intimidation and he might tell us something more."

"You'd threaten a bereaved man over information he might not even have?" The Muscle Wizaard folded his arms. It took some effort.

"Lives are on the line, here!" Cagna growled. "It'll be night soon, and once that moon goes up, someone's going down!"

"I think it's a bad idea," Chase shook her head. "From what he was saying, his daughter ran the shop at nights, and he handled the daylight hours. What I think happened..." she took the blade back and stared at it. "What I think happened is that the werewolf brought the blade in to get a new sheath. He did it during the night and picked it up during the night. Or he planned to anyway, but... something happened. Maybe he lost control? I don't know. But the point is, there's at least a fifty percent chance that the shop owner never had any interactions with the werewolf in the first place."

"Unless the shop owner was telling the truth. That the werewolf just burst in there because it was the only shop with a light still lit that night."

Chase looked up at Cagna and shook her head again. "No. No, the door was unmarred. She let him in. Besides, the séance confirmed that she knew the werewolf. He *had* to have been a customer. She wouldn't have let him in that night... assuming it was a him. Gods, I should have asked that. There just wasn't time." She rubbed her face.

"You did the best you could," Renny tried to soothe her.

"It's not enough. Night's going to come soon, and someone's going to die." Chase started pacing back and forth, drumming her frustration into the ground. "There are three more murders I could be looking into, and I haven't even started! I don't know *how* to start."

"About that," Cagna said, hesitating for a second. "I uh, might have a few ideas."

"What? You didn't before. What changed?"

"What changed was you proved to me that you're taking this seriously, and that you can take care of yourself. To a point, anyway. Or at least that you're smart enough to hire help so that you don't have to risk your own rump." Cagna swept a hand around to indicate the Muscle Wizaard and Renny.

"Ouch." But Chase didn't contest the point. It was true, for the most part.

"So... the guild is definitely out of reach. They're looking into it themselves and we want nothing to do with them."

"Which guild are they, anyway?" The Muscle Wizaard asked.

"Soluzioni Semplici."

The Muscle Wizaard inhaled a sharp breath. Cagna barked brief laughter. "Yeah."

"I'm missing something," Chase glanced between the two of them.

Cagna glanced curiously at her. "Soluzioni Semplici is the biggest mercenary's guild in Laraggiungere. They also employ a large number of... professionals. They overlap with the Don's business, but not in a good way. We had best steer clear."

"Always a bigger fish," Chase nodded.

"So the guild's off limits, but I might have a few contacts who might... emphasis *might* be able to get us something from one of the noble houses. Neither of them is really high up. Some quid pro quo might get stuff done." Cagna scratched the back of her head. "I'll be out late tonight."

"How can I help?" Chase asked.

"You can't. Your part comes after I set things up. Get a good sleep then be ready to go early in the morning."

Chase tried to think of a reason to protest but couldn't. And exhaustion was creeping in. Even if her pools were pretty full, it had still been a hectic day. Lots of drama, and people had been trying to kill or rob her not even an hour ago! She shook a bit at the memory. "It has been a long day," she admitted.

"There was also mention of dinner, I believe?" The Muscle Wizaard asked.

"Yeah." Cagna said. "I'll introduce you to the cook. Ah..." She looked over to Renny. "Maybe you don't mention the golem, huh?"

"I'm my own golem! I have a name, you know." Renny protested.

"Sure kid, sure." Cagna rose. "We'll talk in the morning."

The chef was quite amenable to having more company over, and happily whipped up something with a lot of green vegetables and meat for The Muscle Wizaard. For Chase's part, she found it tasty enough, but a little light. Some bread helped fill in the gaps, there.

The bed was as soft as it looked, and this was a case where too-big furniture proved to be more of a blessing than a curse. She curled up in it, leaving Renny to putter around the villa. He'd offered to stay and watch over her, but she figured there wasn't any need.

Which made it all the more shocking when she woke up in the middle of the night to find strange hands pulling at her clothes and a tongue in her ear.

CHAPTER 10: AWKWARDNESS, ARMOR, AND AMBLING

"I am, once again, very very sorry about... that misunderstanding," Giuseppe Coltello said again, waving one free hand in agitation.

The other hand wasn't free. It held a very expensive ice pack against a thoroughly swollen black eye.

Chase, for her part, folded her arms and glared at him over the most luxurious breakfast spread she'd ever seen. It was a long way down the table, but Giuseppe flinched back anyway, looking like he wanted to bolt out the door.

Giuseppe Coltello was a human just out of his twenties. He had a physique that was just starting to turn to flab. His jawline was the same, his hair was a neatly groomed mass of yellow braids that he had assured her were all the rage in Toothany, and his hands were soft and unmarked by any sort of honest work.

His free hand caught her attention as it wobbled uncertainly in the air. Chase was relieved to see that his fingers had healed up well, after she'd nearly bitten one off and broken a few more for good measure. But not *too* relieved.

She'd already decided to forgive him in exchange for significant favors and maybe a cart of gold at some point in the future, but it was best to let him squirm, first.

"So let me get this straight once more, now that you're not screaming and begging for mercy," she spoke, and Giuseppe jumped, then cleared his throat.

"Yes?" he squeaked.

"You thought I was your paramour, come to surprise you by staying over in the middle of the night."

"I er, well, yes. She always shuts the door you see, to let me know she's in. And your door was shut, the doors are always open otherwise, it was an honest mistake—"

"And the fact that I'm half her height didn't clue you in?" Chase kept her face stony.

"But you're not! Not exactly. I mean... well first of all I was very drunk. I had quite a bit at the Contessa Della Lumbyardi's place, and she's only a foot or so taller than you, my love I mean, not the Contessa. Not that the Contessa isn't a dear, but—"

"Wait. Your mistress is only a foot taller than me?" Chase let a darker tone leak into her voice. "Do you like them short? Like children?"

"No! No no no! Absolutely, I mean, absolutely not!" The ice pack slipped to the ground as Giuseppe waved both hands in frantic circles, like a man hysterical and beset by bees. "She's a dwarf! My Tabita is four feet two, just the right size, for, er, ah..."

Okay, *that* caught Chase's attention. "I thought dwarves didn't usually, er, get involved outside of their own kind, so to speak."

"They don't. What we have is *special*," Giuseppe said, stars in his eyes. Well, less of a star and more a red harvest moon for the black eye on his left-hand side.

"And how do you think she would feel, if she knew that you'd felt up another woman? A halven? Dwarves are supposed to be pretty sensitive about their height," Chase said, taking a sip of breakfast wine, and following it with a bite of gooey cinnamon roll. "Be a shame if she got the notion that you only loved her because she's short. That you have a thing for every short woman you come across."

Giuseppe went pale. "Tabita wouldn't... I mean... I don't think she..." he blustered, then stopped. "Did I mention that I'm very, very sorry about this whole thing?"

"Only about three times since I got here," The Muscle Wizaard boomed behind him, and Giuseppe fell out of his chair.

Chase bit her cheek to keep from laughing. It had TOTALLY been worth keeping a straight face as the big man snuck in from a silently opened door, and stood behind Giuseppe, waiting silently. The Wizaard knew how to make an entrance.

"I'll say it as many times as you like," Don Coltello's son squeaked from the floor. "Only oh god, no!" he screamed as the Muscle Wizaard reached down...

...and helped him to his feet.

Giuseppe quivered, and looked up at the bearded bodyguard. "Don't worry about me, friend," the Muscle Wizaard said, smiling through his beard. "I'm only here to handle the things that she cannot. And she handled you just fine. But you might want to worry about Cagna."

Chase watched, fascinated, as all color drained from Giuseppe. "Oh. She's here?"

"She's here. Should be back any time now," Chase said. "So let's talk about how you can make it up to me quickly, before she gets back..."

It didn't take long. Chase had sized him up after the chaos was done last night and found his willpower equivalent to soggy parchment. This morning proved no exception, and he meekly agreed to both foot their investigative expenses for the next couple of days and owe them a few favors in the future. "Specifically, I want you to see if you can get us into one of the noble houses that lost a member to the werewolves. Who were they again?" Chase asked. She'd never gotten a name, so she was fishing, here.

Fortunately, Giuseppe was eager to take the hook. "Bianchi and Rossi," he said. "Of course! I shall pay my respects through my friends in those houses, and endeavor to allow you to visit in some capacity."

"Good." Chase finished her cinnamon roll and put the wine down before it could muddle her. She knew her limits. And, as the door opened again to admit a familiar face, she knew she'd be pushing those limits today. "Ah, there you are Cagna! Perfect timing."

"Cagna! Ah, hellohelpyourselftobreakfasthaveapleasantstay!" Giuseppe squeaked and literally ran for the far door, slamming it behind him and heading deeper into the villa.

"I didn't even have to growl at him this time," Cagna said, from her spot at the door.

"You look dog tired," Chase said without thinking.

"Only heard that one about a thousand times," Cagna muttered.

But it was true. Her ears drooped, her fur was mussed, and she slumped as if she was barely holding herself upright.

"Would you like a Clean and Press?" Renny offered as he faded into existence next to Chase, dropping the illusion that had concealed him.

Cagna wasn't surprised. "You know I smelled you, right? I knew you were here. So you can cut the theatrics."

"They weren't for you," Renny said.

Cagna looked around, then blinked, bleary-eyed and unimpressed. "Whatever. Okay, so two bits of news. I've got you the password to the Rossi casino."

"Their what now?" Chase asked. "I don't know that word."

The dog-woman gave her a strange look. "You're in the business, how can you not know about... whatever. A casino is a gambling hall. The Rossis back an illegal gambling hall, down by the docks. A lot of the family's servants and allies spend time there, and you might even be able to find one of the family who isn't grieving over the loss of Enrico Rossi." Cagna extracted a crumpled bit of parchment from her cloak and set it on the table. "There's the address and password to get in. Take the walking muscle-mountain with you."

"Muscle Wizaard," the big man corrected.

"Yeah no. The constables are looking for the Muscle Wizaard. Best to play it low-key for a while."

"I'm not very good at that, I fear."

"I know. Which is why I told the gardener to throw a tarp over the wagon until we can get the sign changed. And the second piece of news..." Cagna sighed. "There were two werewolf killings last night. In different parts of the city."

"So we're dealing with two werewolves." Chase rubbed her chin.

"At least. Could be more. Might have been a murder we didn't hear about. But anyway, the problem is *who* they killed. One was a constable on patrol near the river gate. That's a problem because he was with a whole patrol. Idiot stepped away to take a piss and got disappeared. Now the guards are shamed, and the whole city is whispering that they're useless against the werewolves. The other killing though, that's the big problem..." Cagna exhaled, hard. "The other murder was Dona Tarantino."

Chase's memory filled in the name with a context. "You mentioned her last night? Something about how it was shameful that she let gangs run loose?"

"Yeah. She's the crime boss I mentioned who Don Coltello sold... I mean, had dealings with." Cagna shot the Muscle Wizaard a look.

Chase thought that wise. *It's probably best not to mention how the guy we're working for trafficks in stolen women. Not to the Muscle Wizaard.*

Cagna continued. "Which means that it's probably vendetta. It's probably either someone related to that runt werewolf that got away all those years ago, or the runt himself, all grown up. The dons are having a meeting about this tonight. I'll need to be in attendance, which means that you should plan to be as well. Don Coltello wants to show that he's making progress and showing that knife you found in front of the Council will help him look good in front of the others."

Chase nodded. "I can do that. Anything else I should know?" She hopped down from her seat, and took the parchment off the table, glancing at it before tucking it away.

"No." Cagna said. "Some stuff for the meeting tonight maybe, but that can wait. Just be smart, don't make waves, and keep your ears high.

And..." she considered Chase. "You should probably go shopping. Get some armor, kid. You're going to be moving around rough areas and rough people, the less stabbable you look the better."

Chase tightened her lips.

"No, don't argue. This isn't your hometown, country mouse. People play for keeps, and arrows don't care who steps in their way. Get armor. Wizaard, make her do it."

"Yes ma'am."

Chase shot him a betrayed look, and he stared back, unconcerned. "I *am* your bodyguard. And I *do* happen to agree with her on this point."

"Right. I'm going to crash. Be back before dark." Cagna yawned, tongue stretching far out of her toothy muzzle, and headed to the back of the villa.

Half an hour later, Chase and her friends managed to locate a good-quality leatherworking shop near a large inn that catered to adventurers and other people with violent professions and lots of money. Some careful negotiation and a mention that she was a local and not an itinerant murder-hobo got her a sizeable discount... along with an unexpected charisma boost.

To her surprise, the Muscle Wizaard had proven very helpful at helping her pick out accouterments. "I've had long experience with a number of costumes," the Wrestler pointed out. "You're going to want light leather, something that you can move in without hindrance, but might slow down a stray arrow or turn aside an off-target thrust."

"What about on-target thrusts, and straight arrows?"

"Well, I'm sorry, but they'll probably kill or badly injure you regardless of what kind of armor you're wearing. So it's best to work with your mobility and not get hit by those in the first place." The Muscle Wizaard shrugged. "You're a halven, young lady. There's only so much we can do without magic... and I don't think you have the funds to access that sort of thing."

"Really?" Chase pushed her prospective purchases into the big man's arms. "Hold these while I go check." Thomasi had given her a LOT of coin. At least twenty gold worth, give or take!

Two minutes of conversation with the shopkeeper, and she came back, ears drooping, and with a new humility. "So. Uh. Magical armor costs... lots."

"Yes it does," The Muscle Wizaard nodded.

"Like more than my entire home village probably has, lots."

"Well, there's little need for them except among adventurous sorts, and they take components that are hard to find and expensive in most places," the Wizaard shrugged.

"It's a little different in Cylvania," Renny whispered from her pack. But he was loud enough for the Wizaard to hear.

"Ah yes! I've been curious about that place ever since you mentioned it. Can you tell me about it, my small friend?"

"Not here," Chase said, shooting the shopkeeper a look as he haggled with a red-haired woman wearing a chainmail bikini. "Too many ears."

While the store's owner was otherwise occupied, they escaped into the changing rooms in the back. The Wizaard and Renny took one, while Chase took an adjacent cubicle. The walls were thin enough they could discuss matters, and by turning the signs on the others to 'occupied,' she thought they wouldn't be interrupted.

Initially focusing on trying on the various pieces of armor and accessories, she found herself listening to Renny with interest, as he told the story of a land locked behind magic gone horribly wrong, wracked with civil war, and beset by demons.

It sounded like the sort of high adventure she'd craved as a child, and she stared at herself in the mirror as she realized that she was free to visit there someday, and have a look for herself.

She was finally free to do and go wherever she pleased.

After over a week it was starting to sink in.

The Muscle Wizaard was less interested in the adventure aspect of it, and somewhat more focused in his inquiries. "You say there's no Wizard guilds? Or schools?"

"No. The kingdom used to control the royal academy, but it got dissolved after the war. Now the official council arcanist is Mister Graves. He's not a Wizard, but he helps people get the arcane training they need. And there's plenty of Wizards around to take apprentices and teach whomever they want."

"But what about dangerous magical experimentation? Like Cagna said?" The Muscle Wizaard asked.

"She left out something pretty important. Experimentation like that takes a lot of money and resources. The council keeps an eye on where the money goes these days. And we're always short on reagents and crystals. You need those to make golems, and we're making a whole lot of golems these days."

"Why's that?" Chase asked, struggling into a corset.

"Because there's really not many people left," Renny said. "The wars went on too long and we weren't a big land to start with. So golems that don't have to sleep or eat or stop working are a really big help to the living folks."

"That's admirable!" The Muscle Wizaard decided. "To spend your life in service like that!"

"Oh, we get paid for our service. And we don't have to serve if we don't want to. Once we graduate from the Rumpus Room we can choose to go and do whatever we want. So long as it's legal anyway. But most of us want to help people. We're good at it! Teacher said it was because we're toy golems. We're made to be friends and help our people. We don't feel right unless we're doing that."

Is this why he stayed with me? Chase wondered.

She'd asked herself that many times over during their trip. When the chance had come to rejoin his group and return home, he'd decided to come travel with Chase instead. Ostensibly it was to explore more and learn more about this land. But it had always seemed like a thin explanation to the halven girl.

Was it because he considered her his people?

If so...

Chase was touched. And with that came the realization that she was fully responsible for his predicament. He'd bonded with her, it sounded like that anyway. She would have to take that into consideration, and make sure what he'd gained was worthwhile, more than what he'd given up.

"I want to go there," decided the Muscle Wizaard. "If there's no guild, and it's that easy to become a Wizard, then maybe... maybe my dream isn't quite dead after all."

"I know the way back now. It's a hard trip over a bunch of mountains."

"We can go together," Chase spoke. "After we're done here, we've got business in Gnome. But after that, I'm thinking it'll be best to get out of the country for a while. If you want to stick with us, that is, Bastien."

"I think I do," the Muscle Wizaard said. "So long as you're still paying. I'll probably need money to legally pay a Wizard to teach me."

"Money won't be a problem," Chase promised, adjusting the last few fittings, and slipping on the clothes she'd bought to go with them. "And now I'll need to borrow your eyes, please."

Chase stepped out of the booth, and the others gave her a good once-over.

"Um..." Renny said. "Did you put on any armor at all?"

"She's got shoes," the Muscle Wizaard said. "And bracers."

"I've also got a corset on under here. And I'm wearing PANTS!" Chase lifted her dress to reveal that her legs, in fact, were clad in leather trousers. Not the tightest she could have worn, but every halven knows to leave a bit of room for good meals and sedentary times.

"Are you sure that's enough?" The Muscle Wizaard said, running a hand through his beard. "I advised thin leather, but that's a bit too thin.

Maybe."

Chase grimaced. "It's costing me ten gold for all of this. And that's AFTER a lot of haggling. Anything heavier is probably going to be more than I want to pay."

"All right. It is literally your own hide if it doesn't work out," Renny said. "Oh! Hey, want me to stress test it for you?" Renny pulled a knife out of his bushy tail and waved it around.

"No! Er, ah no, that's fine. Let's just pay and go. We've got a camino to visit."

"Casino," the Muscle Wizaard corrected.

"Yes, that thing."

It took some navigation to figure out the location of the address that Cagna had given them. Her directions had been brief and of little use to the three people who were by no means permanent residents of Arretzi.

Several times Chase had to stop and ask directions. But after about half an hour of wandering, she saw the western wall narrow and slope down, and caught the gleam of water on the horizon.

It was also the point where the smell of fish started to pervade her nose. Behind her, in her pack, Renny sneezed once. "I'm turning my nose off," he whispered into her ear.

"Good," Chase advised, absent-mindedly. "We don't want a repeat of yesterday."

"Don't remind me. I can still taste those tannery scents in the back of my throat," Renny muttered.

Chase bit back a reply. Her feet were currently sweaty and hurting. Shoes took some getting used to. Granted, it was better than trusting her calluses to the bare cobblestones, and there were some truly dubious patches of dirt and substances starting to appear as they got closer to the waterfront, but still... still, it was an adjustment. It felt unnatural. Halvens were supposed to be barefoot, that's why they had good thick patches of fur there!

Still, the shoes were part of the armor, and the Muscle Wizaard assured her repeatedly that she'd get used to them. And a little bit of discomfort was nothing against the pain of losing toes, if random violence erupted again.

But eventually Chase's people-watching skills kicked in, distracting her from her footwear woes.

Yesterday she'd noticed a tension in the crowds she'd passed, an unease and wariness.

Today it was simmering. There was no laughter, not even nervous laughter. The streets had much less traffic... there were plenty of people out, but they were watching on corners, at stalls, or out of windows.

They were watching and whispering to each other, and scrutinizing everybody with cold, angry eyes.

This was what werewolves did to a city, she realized. *It isn't the deaths, though those are horrible. It's the fear that they bring, the paranoia that they inspire. That's the true horror of it; they could be anyone, and so everyone is suspect.*

She passed a small plaza where a group of children were playing a game that seemed to involve a lot of clapping and telling people to open and close their eyes. Not far, parents or other relatives watched, every one of them with a weapon of some sort near to reach.

"This crowd is ugly," The Muscle Wizaard rumbled. "If they don't get satisfaction or a distraction soon, they're going to riot."

"It's to that point already?" Chase asked.

"Beyond that point. If the Doge weren't so well-loved, there'd be mobs in the streets and fires everywhere," The Muscle Wizaard sighed.

"I trust your judgment. I'm more used to dealing with individuals and small groups. Still very much a country mouse, as Cagna would put it."

"About that one," The Muscle Wizaard asked. "How much do you know about her?"

"I've known her for a day. She's decent enough, although I don't think she was lying about spending time as a Bandit and Highwayman." Chase rubbed her chin. "But she doesn't sugarcoat what her employer does. It makes me wonder why she's working for him."

Now that Chase had the time to think about it, there were a few things about Cagna that didn't add up. Nothing she could put her finger on, but the dog-woman had secrets, she was sure of it. Whether or not they were secrets Chase could afford to let lie or something that she'd have to dig up for her own protection was yet to be determined.

But given the prospect, she knew which she preferred. Chase had spent most of her formative years finding out everything she could about the people who most had an impact on her life. She'd gotten to know them, dug out their secrets, knowing that it was the only way to protect herself and her loved ones.

How to go about it, though?

Now is the perfect time, actually, Chase realized. *This is likely the only time I've got where Cagna won't be with me. If I can get some clues from the Rossis or their employees quickly, then I can spend some time investigating her.*

"This is the address, I think," Renny whispered, and Chase and Bastien stopped, staring at a plain wooden door. It looked like its neighbors down the block, doors set into old brick buildings. The windows were black, though a few glimmers shone out of cracks in what had to be tar.

Chase knocked on the door, and it cracked open. "Yes?" Someone asked.

"Pesce spada," Chase said, stating the password that Cagna had given her.

"Ah, my friends! Come in."

The door opened wider, and Chase nodded to The Muscle Wizaard.

She had two goals for this trip now. And if there were answers to be had in this place, she'd find them...

CHAPTER 11: HOUSE ODDS AND EVENS

"There's only four rules," the doorman said, leading the way down a flight of stairs. Chase stared at the tails of his ill-fitting suit and did her best to navigate steps never meant for halvens.

"The first rule is to keep your mouth visible at all times, unless you're in the special line. That is because of the second rule, which is don't use any skills. Not even if it's one that has nothing to do with the games. We got people watching for that, you see. The third rule is simple; no fighting. This is a classy place, be respectful. The fourth rule..."

He stopped before a door at the bottom of the stairwell, and looked them up and down.

He timed his speech so that he'd hit this point at the same time as the door. Nice!

Behind her, she heard the Muscle Wizaard grunt in appreciation. Of course another showman would recognize such a subtle touch.

"The fourth rule is that who you are outside doesn't matter. In fact, most people don't want to know. If you are allowed to be in here, you are a noble to us. Doesn't matter what you are outside. Treat every other patron accordingly, capisce?"

"Of course!" Chase said, smiling brightly.

The doorman scrutinized her for a long moment, and Chase was certain he was using a skill. But at last he grunted, and opened the door.

Instantly a wall of sound rolled over her, and her ears flicked back. Laughter, cheers, groans, the ratcheting of metal and the clattering of wood.

Taking a few steps forward, Chase left a bare and unassuming warehouse behind, and stepped into a wonderland of the sort that she had never imagined.

Brightly colored cloth lined the walls, tapestries in red and gold and silver, depicting scenes of joy, merriment, and celebration. Everything from feasts to weddings to... oh my.

Chase looked away, blushing. *Humans. Humans are incorrigible.*

Putting her back to a fifty-foot-long tapestry that depicted an epic orgy, Chase surveyed the rest of the room.

Chandeliers of spun crystal and glittering wire dangled above, hundreds of candles illuminating the crowd below. A velvet carpet wound and zig-zagged a path through the room, which upon further observation seemed to be divided between distinct areas.

It was a very, very big room. She thought that several cellars had been joined together to make it, and instantly that brought to mind the shared basement between the Church and the Inn back in Bothernot. Chase went from amazed to on-guard and started searching for the exits.

"What's wrong?" Renny whispered in her ear.

"I can't find the exits," she realized. Even the door behind her had vanished, the doorman closing it silently while she was indulging her eyes. A tapestry hung there now, and logically Chase knew there was a door there, but for the life of her she couldn't see it.

"We just arrived and you already want to leave? Come, let's see what this place has to offer!" The Muscle Wizaard leaned down to clap a gentle hand on her shoulder, and she nodded in reluctant agreement.

"No games to start with," Chase decided. "Let's get the lay of this place before we put money on the line."

It was the right decision.

Though the casino was mind-blowingly large, the crowd was nowhere near to filling it up. Perhaps it was the time, perhaps it was the day, but it was a light crowd, Chase saw.

Most of them had one thing in common.

They all smelled of desperation.

She'd seen it many a time back home, among her hormone-filled peers. Or when one of them got yearning for something unachievable... which was the same thing in a lot of cases, come to think of it. Chase's ears twitched at the laughter that just wavered near hysterical, and she watched how fingers white-knuckled against green velvet on tables as dice fell. She smelled the sweat as she passed by silent groups fanning cards and trying to keep their faces still.

The ones here now are those that need the money, she thought. *Or something else?* She peered through a gap in the crowd at a break in the wall, a darkened door with a line of nervous-looking men waiting before it, masked and fidgeting. They were older, she thought. The door opened and one came out straightening his clothes. A wash of perfume rolled out behind him, and a throaty female voice bid him well.

"It's not the quartiere carne, but the function is about the same," the Muscle Wizaard said as they passed. "I'd imagine that they cater to more selective tastes."

"What?" Chase asked. "Taste? I don't expect food has much to do with that."

"Ah! No, selective tastes is a polite way of saying that the people through that door do socially unacceptable things for great deals of money. Which is probably why the gentlemen are allowed masks. I'd wager the clothes are loaners too, and there are dressing rooms around here somewhere. They have to take all that stuff off if they want to go back to the regular games."

"Why are they all men?" Chase wondered. "Don't women have special tastes too?"

The Muscle Wizaard coughed. "Well, yes. But... well, it's... I don't know how it works exactly or why, but you only ever see men paying money for things like that." The Muscle Wizaard said. "Mind you, I have had women offer me money for my time before when I was younger, so I know that can happen. I've had more men offer me money for that, though. And I honestly don't know why it's not more equal."

"Weird," Chase said. And it was. Like anyone else her age she'd felt the changes of adulthood, and the hungers of the flesh. But unlike most of her peers she'd realized that her dreams required her to put those aside until she could safely fulfill them.

That said, bedroom shenanigans weren't entirely out of the question, and someday she expected she would investigate them more thoroughly. Starting in the shallow end. With someone that she could trust and was attracted to. Whose time she didn't have to pay for.

Still, her mind wandered, and she angrily tried to get it back on track. *This isn't the time!* So instead of pondering on the fantasies available through that door, she remembered the shock and horror she'd woken to during last night's attempted groping. THAT killed her libido before it got started, and Chase was able to get her mind on business.

She cleared her throat. "So it's a casino and a brothel—"

"And a taverna," Renny whispered, tugging on her hair until she looked over to a corner of the room that had been walled off by wine racks and glass partitions. Good glass, not the bubbly stuff she'd seen in the cheaper areas of town. Men and women sat at tables there, laughing and drinking.

We've reached the end of the room already, she realized as she noticed the corner bar. *It's not quite as big as it seems.*

"This place is an enormous con," Chase realized, as she turned back to the Muscle Wizaard. "It's designed to keep you here, and everything fun here costs money. One way or the other," she said as a richly-dressed man at one of the tables groaned at his dice and slid over a pile of silver.

"But we're not here for money, so we should be safe, right?" Renny whispered.

"To a point. We have to look like we're here for something this place provides, and..." she considered the line of gentlemen and the strong odor of liquor coming from the corner, "...money's probably the safest thing to pretend to be after."

"Well then! Let's see what games they have to offer," The Muscle Wizaard gestured grandly, almost flattening a passing server. "Ah! Sorry!" he said as she ducked him without missing a beat or spilling a drink. "Wow! Such professionalism!"

Chase flushed and grabbed his robes, tugging him as best she could. It was like trying to guide a mountain, but after a moment he got the hint, folded his hands into his wide sleeves, and followed.

We are being watched, she realized as they moved between the tables. The... oh what were they called. The employees who ran the tables? Croppers? Whatever they were, they studied the trio as they passed... or rather they studied the Muscle Wizaard first, and Chase second. None of them took any real notice of the stuffed toy fox head sticking out of her pack.

Best to keep it that way. "Don't say a word, Renny," she told the golem without turning her head, watching a few of the table people's eyes snap to her lips. But hopefully they'd assume the big man behind her was named Renny, if indeed they could lip-read.

As light as the crowd was, as early in the day as it was, most of the attended tables were occupied. Chase passed card games, marking a few she thought she knew. Dice games were a bit trickier, but after watching them a bit most seemed simple enough.

Strangest of all were metal boxes with whirling tumblers rolling around in them, levers sticking out of the sides that people jerked down with satisfying CLUNKS and CLANKS.

"Slot machines," The Muscle Wizaard declared, when she stared at one of them for a minute too long. "Tinker contraptions. All pure luck, really. You drop a coin in, and depending on the symbols that come up, you might get more out."

Judging by the silvers that were disappearing into each machine, and the silvers and coppers that occasionally popped out when tinkly bells rang, might was too strong a word. "It's entirely luck," she realized, turning her head up towards her large companion. "The other games are against people. You can try to trick them—"

"Bluff them," The Muscle Wizaard said gently.

"—right, that's what I said, more or less. You can try to... bluff them, and there's some luck involved, but you're still up against other people. Machines can't be fooled. Not the way they've set them up, anyway. I mean, unless you're an animator or something."

"They're usually built with alarms if anyone tries to force them that way," The Muscle Wizaard said.

She scrutinized him. "You seem to know a lot about these things."

"This isn't my first casino. I've helped work security at them before, during lean times. Even ran my show in a couple. They each have their own style, their own gimmick, but at the end of the day most are the same." He frowned. "Though I've seen slot machines turn up in some truly weird places. Spots where metal is a luxury and nobody knows enough to even come close to unlocking the Tinker job, yet the local gambling hall always has slot machines. It's one of the two big mysteries of these places."

"One of two? What's the other?"

"Come with me. It's easier if you experience it for yourself."

Bemused, Chase followed her titanic friend towards what she realized must be the rough center of the gaming area.

At it stood a raised dais, surrounded by four marble fountains, with the words 'G.O Gamble!' inlaid in gold around it. Tables filled the center, slot machines lined the edges, and the place even smelled better than its surroundings, though she couldn't say how.

And every table, every machine, stood empty.

Chase frowned. This was a nice place, easily the nicest gambling spot in the entire casino. Why was it deserted?

"Go on, head up there," The Muscle Wizaard told her.

But she knew the tone in the back of his voice. Heck, she'd heard it in her own voice, time and again.

PER+1

"You're pranking me, aren't you?"

"Only a little," he confessed. "It won't hurt you or do anything that should set us back. Beyond expose you as a relative newbie, which is all right, I think?"

"It is. I don't mind being underestimated." In fact, it was her preferred method of operation, when she thought about it. She'd only survived the troubles in Bothernot because everyone involved thought they had bigger problems than one small halven.

Trusting in her friend, she tried to climb up the long steps that lined the sides of the dais.

And instantly she was looking back at the gaming hall.

Chase blinked.

She turned around and tried again—

—and again she found herself a few feet away, staring at a nearby table. The man running it shot her a sideways look and moved his jaw, clearly trying not to laugh.

"Ahem," someone cleared her throat, and Chase turned to see a server pointing at a pair of velvet ropes off to the side of the dais.

"Oh, do I go through those to go up there?" she asked, innocently, heading toward the seemingly open and empty queue.

"No. I don't think you can go up there dear," the older woman replied and turned a small sign at the top of one of the poles supporting the ropes.

It read, PLAYERS ONLY.

Chase felt her eyes widen, and she hurried back to The Muscle Wizaard's side.

A chill crawled down her back. This was one of the cracks in the world. This was the work of the demigods, the things that the Camerlengo was trying to keep hidden and away from the rest of the world.

"There's a place like that in every casino I've ever seen," the Muscle Wizaard said, falling in next to her. "I've only ever known a single man who could get inside those places, and he never told me how he did it. Everyone here's a player, right?"

"There's players and there's *players,*" Chase said, still feeling that chill. "But I don't think this will help us talk with the Rossis or find clues to our mutual problem, so I think we can safely ignore it."

"Well of course," The Muscle Wizaard sounded confused. "But you asked, and I thought you'd get a kick out of seeing the oddity. So... we should probably talk. Are you hungry?"

"Ravenous," Chase realized. It had been a long walk to the docks, and she was carrying about an eighth of her own weight in the form of her new armor. Granted, she had good strength now thanks to recent job levels, but she was still a halven. And her stamina was entirely too low. "Let's do elevenses. It's a bit early, but more satisfying than brunch."

"Bars in these places usually have food. And we can talk more freely there, everyone will be more interested in each other," The Muscle Wizaard confirmed.

The taverna in the corner did have food. For certain definitions of 'food,' anyway. For Chase who had been raised on home cooking her whole life, it was a greasy, unappetizing mess. But she ate anyway, wondering at the mismatch. "This food is... not good."

"Well, they don't make much of a profit on it. They also don't want people coming here just to eat, so they have to work to make sure it's nothing that anyone could consider their favorite kind of food." The Muscle Wizaard shrugged, a motion that made his pectorals roll under his robe like calving icebergs. He wasn't eating *his* food, just shoving it around on his plate, so Chase felt a bit annoyed he hadn't told her about this beforehand. But she put it from her mind and focused on business.

"You know casinos. This is good," Chase said, speaking as quickly as she thought, searching for ideas. "We need to learn about the murdered patron. The Rossi patron. But nobody here is talking. They're focusing on the games, or uh, romance." That was a bit too kind a word for it. "The guests are going to be a bust. But the staff might know something about it."

"They won't talk about their employers on the floor," The Muscle Wizaard said. "If this casino is like the ones I've known, they'll have a different floor where the staff does all the work. All sorts of people, doing things from cooking to laundry to moving supplies and money around. They'll talk and gossip, in their own lounges and halls that customers never see."

Chase considered. "Every person I've seen working here has been human."

"They'll have a few other types working behind the scenes, where nobody sees them," The Muscle Wizaard said. "A lot of times humans don't get along with other races. So the casinos play it safe to avoid losing business. It's ridiculous, but it's business to them."

"Still, my odds of sneaking back there are bad. You'd be a better choice to infiltrate... except you're kind of distinctive."

"I thought halvens were good at sneaking?" he frowned.

"The best way to sneak is to look like you should be there in the first place. And no," Chase said, as her mind caught up with her mouth, and she started to decipher the way she'd been watched over the last hour or so. "The more we wandered the hall, the more they looked at me. They think I'm the rich person slumming, and they have you pegged as a bodyguard. Here's what we'll do," she decided. "I'll go out there and start gambling. I'll make a show of giving you my pack, and after a few rounds you'll pull me aside, and whisper in my ear. I'll get angry and send you off, and you'll storm away. Then, you'll try to slip into one of the staff hallways. Renny will help you with illusions if it's tricky."

"Are you sure you'll be okay by yourself?" Renny asked.

"I'll be fine. Once I lose enough money, I'll come back to the bar and nurse some wine for a while, or something. Maybe talk with one of those lonely looking men to see if I can get some useful gossip."

"I've heard worse plans," The Muscle Wizaard said. "It'll be risky, but the worst they'll do is throw me out if they catch me, I think. This doesn't have the feel of some of the nastier places I've had to work."

"If it does get bloody, Renny can help you escape. Either way, if you're not back at the bar in a few hours we can meet at... at the leather shop where I bought my armor. Sound good?"

"It's probably worth the risk." The Muscle Wizaard nodded. "Are you ready to gamble?" The Muscle Wizaard asked.

"Time to lose some money," Chase said, hiding a wince as she got up from the table.

It was a good plan.

It was a solid plan.

And it probably would have worked, except for one thing.

Five minutes later, Chase stood in front of the slot machine she'd chosen to lose a few coins in, eyes getting bigger and bigger as the bells blared and rang, and gold shot like a fountain from its coin dispenser.

LUCK+1

Chase licked her lips, remembering just how *high* her luck was, after sinking so many levels into Oracle and Grifter.

"Er," the Muscle Wizaard said, taking her shoulder again. This time his grip was a bit less gentle, and she turned to see quite a few men in suits around her, looking from her to the pile of gold.

"Uh, hi!" Chase said, beaming. "Beginner's luck, huh? Wow..."

CHAPTER 12: HIGH STAKES GAMBLER

The needle hurt like hell. Chase bit down on the leather of her gag and tried to ignore the pain in her arm.

"There's no smoke," her tormentor declared, and someone else grunted.

Then the blindfold was off her face, and Chase was staring up at a tall, middle-aged human in a white suit. He had a flat-brimmed hat on his head, scars on his right cheek, and blue eyes rendered large and outsized by a rimless set of spectacles.

"Hello?" Chase said. "You know, if this is what I've won I think I would have preferred to lose."

A grunt from off to one side, and Chase turned, angling to see around the humans in the room, until she saw the Muscle Wizaard. He was restrained just as she was, bound to a chair by entirely too many chains, and thrashing about as a man in physician's robes stuck something into his arm.

"No smoke," the physician declared.

Then pieces clicked into place. "That's a silver needle, isn't it?" Chase asked.

A gloved hand caught her face, turned it up to stare into blue eyes behind glass. "Now why would you ask that?"

"Because half this damn city has made me take a silver test whenever I visit their shops," Chase said, staring back, trying not to flinch. But she could feel herself shake. This situation had gone poorly ever since they'd let the casino staff take them back into the secret parts of the casino, to talk with the man in charge. Someone had shouted **"Stunning Blast,"** and it had all gone downhill from there.

At least she thought it had. Her memory got a bit fuzzy after that...

spell? Probably a spell, had gone off in her face.

She turned her head to the side, playing at being afraid to meet the stranger's eyes... though it wasn't play, not really. This was the smallest she'd ever felt since she left Bothernot. The most helpless.

But as she looked around, she noticed something interesting.

Her pack was lying in one corner.

And Renny wasn't poking out of it any longer.

My hidden weapon.

Suddenly her chances of getting out of there were looking a lot better.

"What is the meaning of this?" The Muscle Wizaard barked.

"Calm down, Wizaard," Chase said, turning a much-less-fearful face up to meet her silent captor. "They're afraid, that's all."

The man's eyes narrowed, as she met his stare, unyielding this time.

WILL+1

"You're not wrong," he spoke again, blinking first. "But we're not afraid of *you*. Keep that in mind, young lady." He turned away, whipping his coat back, and striking a match with hands so fast she barely saw them move. Then he was smoking a pipe, his back to her, looking out a long, wide window that angled crookedly.

Chase's vantage point was bad, but she recognized part of a crowd, and the glint of metal machines. *That's the casino hall! We're above it, looking down on it.*

Which was bizarre. She was pretty sure she would have remembered seeing a window of this size from below. But then again, most of this place was based on misdirection, it could easily have been hidden. In any case, it was the least of her worries right now.

"Leave us," the white-suited man said.

"Sir?" One of the black-suited staff replied, looking from the Muscle Wizaard to Chase.

"I can handle them. *If* it comes down to it. It won't, will it?"

"Not if you untie us," Chase told him.

The white suited man waved his pipe in a commanding gesture, and hands freed Chase and The Muscle Wizaard from their chains. Then the servants withdrew, one by one, closing a thick door behind them.

Now that the crowd was gone, the room stood revealed as an opulent office. A heavy mahogany desk filled the space before the window, and golden sculptures and lanterns dressed the walls. The tapestries and paintings in here were a touch more tasteful than the ones on the floor, and a shag carpet deep enough to go up to Chase's ankles coated the floor.

Well, all except the spot where Chase and The Muscle Wizaard had been deposited. That spot had a cheap rug thrown over it, and Chase's blood ran cold for a second. *They did that so they wouldn't stain the good carpet if they had to kill us.*

Then her eyes lit on a small table in the corner. It was draped with gold cloth and held a pair of statuettes holding dice and cards. One was a friendly looking woman, juggling dice, with a set of very thin wires holding them up in the air. The other was a surly looking man slouching at a table, throwing a tiny set of cards down in disgust.

Chase recognized those figures. "That's Rando and RNG, isn't it? That's a shrine to the gods of luck?"

"Yeah," the white-suited man grunted. "Don't touch it, please. They hate that."

"Are you an Oracle, then?"

"Cleric. Which is one of the reasons why you're here right now. They told me you were coming."

"Perhaps you'd better tell us what this is all about," The Muscle Wizaard said. "We certainly weren't cheating, so this treatment is entirely uncalled for!"

The man turned to face them, his scars sliding into shadow as his hat brim blocked the light from the window. "When the next jackpot rings, the hour of your death is here, Enrico Rossi. That's what they told me when I prayed for guidance."

"Enrico..." Chase felt her eyes narrow. "You're supposed to be dead!"

He spread his arms. "They tore me up pretty badly a couple of nights ago. I figured it was best to let them think I didn't survive. I've been hiding out here ever since."

"You faked your death?" The Muscle Wizaard asked. "But why?"

"One last con. For all the good it's doing." he shot a glare toward the shrine. "But if there's one thing I've learned, it's that there's no fate but that I make. I can beat the odds. I was just a piddly archer, back when Dona Tarantino called in her favor and brought me along on a werewolf hunt. This time? They're up against a full-fledged Gambler." He turned toward them, his hand twisting again, and suddenly it was full of shiny-edged playing cards. Shiny *silver-edged* playing cards, Chase realized.

"We're after the werewolves too," Chase said, speaking quickly. "We can help you—"

"Maybe. Either way we'll see. Here's how this is going to go," he said, making the cards vanish as quickly as they'd appeared. "Your winnings are in your pack. I threw in an extra ten percent to pay for your time. You're going to spend an hour with me. At the end of the hour, if nothing happens, then you'll walk out of here with your pack and complimentary buffet tickets. It's all-you-can-eat, you halvens go nuts for that sort of thing."

Chase blinked. She'd never been in a situation where she'd ever had all she could eat. Then she shook her head. "And if the werewolves come?"

The Gambler puffed on his pipe and smiled. "You'll be in the same room as their target. I figure one way or another you'll improve my odds."

"I don't work for free," said the Muscle Wizaard. "And I certainly don't appreciate this sort of treatment."

"Check the pack," Enrico said, pointing with his pipe stem. "And tell me if you don't think that's enough for your time."

The large man did so, and his eyebrows climbed into his hair. Then they narrowed. "Wait. Where's Ren—"

"You drew blood from us without our permission, though," Chase said hastily. "Was that really necessary?"

"Oh yeah. A werewolf with enough cool can ignore the pain of touching silver. But silver that breaks skin? The blood gives it away. Learned that one when we hunted their matriarch, all those years back." Enrico took a seat behind the desk, the leather of his massive chair creaking as he settled in.

But he was sharp, and his eyes lingered on the Muscle Wizaard. "Is something missing from your pack, sir? It's possible it might have fallen out in the scuffle. I can have my people check."

"It's my pack, and I'll see if anything's missing later. Is the gold fair enough, Bastien?"

"It's quite a bit more than I've seen in a long time. Very heavy, I'll have to carry it for a bit, I think."

"Then, since we're here for an hour or so, maybe we could focus on more important matters?" She smiled at the not-so-dead Rossi patron. "We came here looking for clues, ways to investigate that would let us tell our employer where the werewolves might be. Can you help us with that?"

"I wish I could. My family is working like hell to track them down. Me? I'm what they want. I'm hiding, out of touch, minimizing contact with the rest of my family. But if Rando's prophecy is true, then I've been wasting my time." His lips thinned.

I wish I could size him up. But he's used to dealing with Grifters. I'm not practiced enough with silent activations... ah, this is frustrating. I need to get better at this, get better at the subtle skills. She made a mental note to train up once she got out of here. She couldn't risk conversational foresight, not even when his back was turned. He might catch her reflection in the window's glass.

So instead Chase asked, "Is there anything you can tell us? Anything that might help? Maybe something about the night of the attack?"

Enrico shrugged. "They evidently came right over the manor wall. I woke up when my door got broken down. We always sleep with it locked and that saved me. My lover... not so much. Poor Federico never had much luck." His eyes went misty behind his glasses.

Chase sat there in shock for a second. *That's a man's name! Did he just admit to... well, why not? He thinks he's going to die, and who are we to use that to blackmail him? Nobody with any clout, and his family would wreck us. Besides, the man's dead anyway.*

"I'm sorry for your loss," The Muscle Wizaard said.

The fact that he was a lover of men bothered Chase for a few seconds, before she squelched it. *That's a remnant of Bothernot. That's a stupid way of thinking that foolish old halvens want me to think. Why should I let it bother me? I'm on an adventure, we're hunting werewolves, and I just got more gold than I've ever dreamed of having.*

A little more analysis, and her ears twitched as a new thought occurred to her. *He let slip something like this to a pair of strangers. Maybe because we ARE strangers. We're in a weird position. He wants to talk about this, but given the stigma of men loving men, he can't talk about it to anyone that matters. We don't matter, not really. We could be his confessors, in a way.*

That gave her an in.

And... she did feel invested, a bit. He was hurting. She had acted as a confessor, as a safe secret keeper for those who felt as he did, before. This was the right thing to do, regardless of how much information she could milk out of him.

"Please. Tell me about Federico." Chase said, after a bit.

Enrico considered her, puffing on his pipe, letting smoke curl up to the ceiling in patterns to join stains long set into the wood. Just as she thought she'd overplayed her hand, he nodded. "I met him here, actually. Back when we were just a single basement and some plank tables on boards. Back when the family's fortunes were... not so good." He tapped the pipe out into an ashtray. "We'd just lost management of the quartiere carne. We'd settled things with the Tarantino famigilia, but the long fight had exhausted our coffers. Which is why they gave me the go-ahead to set up this place. It actually has a name, you know? Not that most people actually find it out."

Chase itched to ask what the name was, but her instincts told her it was better to let him talk, get it out of his system.

"He was a bookie. Originally we had numbers games, bets, even the occasional river raft races. I had him in my office every other day, arguing about the numbers. He was the only one who ever stood up to me, ever argued with me." Enrico smiled, and pulled his glasses off. "Brave, brave man. Idiot sometimes, no real common sense. Smart as a whip, but dumb. Dumb enough to leap in front of a frenzied wolfman." He closed his eyes. "Idiot."

"Brave," she said. "You meant everything to him."

"A brave idiot, then." Enrico chuckled. "Yeah. Anyone will stick by you when times are good. When times are bad, you find out what your friends are really worth." He stared. "A lot of people separate friends and lovers. They say you can't be both. But to me he was always my best friend. I know a lot of people... hell, I'm related to a lot of people, who decided that their lovers were *lovers*, not friends. And it's caused so much grief, messed up so many marriages. A lot of people live in misery, because they think that's how the gods want it, or because it's good for the soul."

"And how many of those people would stand between their lover and a beast?" Chase asked.

To her surprise, Enrico smiled. "Damn few." He pushed his spectacles up and rubbed his eyes. "You're all right, kid."

"Thank you," Chase said, simply, and though she was bursting with questions, she let the silence work its magic. She let the Gambler piece himself back together.

"Heh. It's funnier because you don't understand," Enrico said, filling his pipe again.

"Then please tell me, so I can laugh at the joke."

"Once we grabbed you, I had you two put through every test you could imagine. We keep a scout on staff. I know every bit of your status screen. Hell, I probably know things about you that *you* don't know. And just by looking at your jobs, you'd be the last person in the world I'd trust with a damn thing."

Chase fought back an angry protest. Her fingers curled around her skirt, at the casual dismissal. Was his mood so fragile that he'd flip-flop so casually?

"Looking at your *jobs* you seem untrustworthy," the Gambler emphasized. "But you haven't fired up a single skill. Haven't tried to get a single edge on me. Jobs are one thing, but they aren't the measure of a person. The status screen shows you some things, but it doesn't tell you what you truly are inside. That's the part that's hidden, that's the part that nobody can see." He smiled. "My screen? It doesn't show that I like men, or women, or anything of that sort. It doesn't matter to these words, these weird things that rule our lives, and dictate how we can excel. It isn't a limitation, or a condition, or anything. It's just how I am. And that's a special kind of thing. And you have so, so many ways to manipulate me, but you haven't reached for a single one of them. That tells me you're all right. And that's why it's funny... because to you it's a casual compliment. Until you know the context."

"Text? I see none here," rumbled the Muscle Wizaard.

Enrico chuckled. "You're all right too, big guy."

"Thank you!"

"So..." the white-suited man said, sitting down and wiping at a speck on his desk, "I like you. And I have nothing to lose by helping you out. I'll help you as much as I can. You wanted clues? I guarantee I don't have all of the picture, but I can maybe do you a landscape or something."

"All right. Let me think," Chase said.

Where to start? Where to even begin?

Well, the basics were a start. "Why are the werewolves hunting you?"

"They're hunting me because two decades ago Dona Tarantino called in a favor with my family. No, I won't go into details on the favor. But I was one of the hunters who teamed up to take down the pair of werewolves that were terrorizing Arretzi." He sighed. "The doge at the time wasn't as competent as the current guy. The underworld had a bigger reach back then. They tapped us and a few other of the noble families, to lend support."

"The Bianchis!" Chase burst out. "Is... did their victim survive too?"

Enrico snorted. "No. Well, I mean I don't know for certain, but she wasn't nearly as clever as me. They're usually more goody-goody. Lotsa Paladins come out of that family. They don't work the angles, like we do."

"And yet they helped out organized crime." the Muscle Wizaard pointed out.

"For a good cause," Enrico puffed on his pipe. "And the famiglias know better than to ask the Bianchis for anything that they'd consider personally dishonorable. It's a self-serving line to walk, but the Bianchis manage. They're doing better now that the doge has been cleaning up the place, anyway."

"So it's revenge?" Chase asked. "That's all?"

"That's all?" Enrico laughed, and cursed gently. "—yeah it's revenge," he finished. "Cities fall, states crumble, because someone got slighted. Revenge is the most primal of all motives, you know. Even I'm not immune to its call..." he said, picking up a small portrait from his desk, and staring at it. His eyes hardened, magnified behind the spectacles, and Chase had a clear view as they turned bleak and cold. "Never underestimate vengeance, kiddo. It can drive a man to points where reason bailed out long ago."

Then he deflated, shrinking back into his chair, his suit wrinkling as he sagged. "Given time to fester, anyway. Me... I'm just hollow. Maybe when I am done mourning. If I live that long. But yeah, it's revenge. We killed the runt's mate. Now the runt's all grown up and hunting us down. And he brought his pack."

"You're sure of that?"

"There's at least three," Enrico said, standing, and moving back to stare out the window. "The survivor, tall and thin and fast. He's the alpha now. A squat one, muscled and beefy, maybe a kid of the old mate. And a small one... a new runt, I'm thinking. We learned that during the attack on our manor. We saw them by firelight, checked their tracks in the blood of our servants and guards."

"A small one. Halven sized?"

Enrico tilted his head, as he turned back to consider her. "Yeah, maybe. The change makes it hard to tell, but the little one could be a halven when he isn't fuzzy. Why do you ask?"

Chase related the story of the leatherworker and the knife. When she was done, she caught his gaze. "Do you know why one of them would kill a leatherworker?"

"No. But it could be that the little one's new, still learning to control himself. Maybe the guy's daughter cut herself or something, and he smelled blood and lost it."

"Maybe," Chase said, remembering the raw stink of the tannery. Would even a werewolf be able to smell blood over that chemical reek? It seemed unlikely. But they were dealing with monsters, when all was said and done. She couldn't say what they couldn't do.

But there's someone here who can help rule out a few things, at least. "You say their blood burns when silver touches it? What other weaknesses do they have?"

"Ah... it's like vampires. There's a few different types so the weaknesses can be different depending on how they ranked up," the Gambler shrugged. "They have to hunt during the full moon. They regenerate like no one's business. Silver that pierces their flesh burns them. Beyond that?" he raised a hand and opened it, palm up. "Dunno."

"They still have bones, right?" The Muscle Wizaard asked. "They're flesh and blood, yes?"

"Yep."

"I can work with that!" The big man slammed a meaty fist into his other palm, and the smack echoed through the office.

"Let's hope so," the Gambler said, pulling out a metal disc and opening it with a snap. "We've got forty-six minutes to see if you need to test that theory."

"Okay. So everyone but the leatherworker that's had a public death has had ties to the hunting party," Chase got herself back on track. "Who's left alive?"

"Me. Don Coltello. Don Sangue. Maddalena Verde." he shrugged. "We all brought some people, some support, but we're the main four left."

"I'll have to ask Cagna about Don Sangue, and whether or not any of Coltello's people have been targeted. They probably have been, since some of the murders have been in the Outskirts."

"Not a bad conclusion," Enrico said. "I think—"

Shouts came from below, muffled by the glass, and the Gambler whirled.

Half the room had gone dark, and as they stared, a howl resounded.

High and keening, it reached out to the back part of Chase's mind, the part that constantly reminded her that she was small, squishy, and tasty, and punched it like a boxer on a speed bag.

Chase gasped.

She hadn't felt such fear since Pandora, since that dark prison, with the Butcher's knife at her throat as he whispered threats.

"So it begins!" Enrico snarled, slapping cards down on his desk, silver edges flaring in the lamplight. "Come on then! Ante up or fold!"

"Chase!" Renny called, and everyone jumped. Enrico turned, eyes whipping around the room, cards in his hands faster than she could follow with her eyes. The Muscle Wizaard was up, hefting his chair in one hand.

"Chase! There's a new scent in the room! There's somebody in the room with us—"

And that was all the warning they had before a cloaked figure lunged out of the shadows and carried Enrico's screaming form through the window.

CHAPTER 13: WHEN YOUR LUCK RUNS OUT

"No!" Chase bolted out of her seat, running around the desk and staring down through the window.

Screaming people fled in all directions, overturning tables and sendings cards scattering like autumn leaves. She watched in horror as one running man tried to go through the player-only area, rebounded so hard that he fell, and was promptly trampled by the people behind him.

And across the hall, the darkness suddenly grew as a chandelier went out.

"Where is he? I can't see him!" The Wizaard boomed behind her.

"Let me look!" Renny hurried forward, and Chase smiled to see him. *He was here all along!* She didn't know how he'd evaded capture, but she didn't need to. The fact that he'd been silent backup made her feel a lot more in control of this chaotic situation.

The feeling lasted until someone started banging on the office door and shouting.

"Oh this is bad," Chase said. "There's no way they won't blame us for this! They'll think we pushed him or whatever!"

"There he is!" Renny pointed, to where Enrico's white-suited form was rising from the ruins of a card table. Miraculously, it had broken his fall almost perfectly.

But then, of course a Gambler would be *lucky*.

No sign of his attacker, though... but across the way another chandelier went dark, and the howl rose once more.

"We need to get down there!" The Muscle Wizaard said and started flexing and intoning his buffs.

"Jump! I've got you!" Renny said.

"Er..." Chase said, looking down at the floor. How high up was it, precisely? It was pretty high.

Then strong arms folded around her as she squeaked.

"Hang on tight!"

She grabbed double fistfuls of beard as the Muscle Wizaard threw himself through the window... taking her with him.

Chase screamed... then stopped, as everything slowed down. *Did I activate Foresight by accident?*

But no. Around her the screams still rose, the Muscle Wizaard's beard still twisted in her hands. They were just falling slower.

Above her, she saw Renny step out of the window onto thin air and hover downward, paws crossed over his chest, borne by air.

I keep forgetting that he's really good at this, Chase thought, and was thankful for it as the world revolved, and the Wizaard flipped himself over landing feetfirst on the ground.

"Excuse me," he said, putting her down, pulling out his hat, then ripping his robes off with a single tug. He stood there in only a loincloth, settling his hat on his head, pounding one fist into an open palm. "It's showtime!"

Enrico's voice rang out across the floor, cutting through the din. **"Cardsharp."**

"What? Ow!" The Muscle Wizaard stumbled backward, as a flash of silver light carved into his side. Blood flew, and a red '128' rose up from his head.

"No! Stop!" Chase yelled. "We're on your side! **Lesser Healing, Lesser Healing!**"

You have healed Muscle Wizaard for 28 points!
Your Lesser Healing skill is now level 31!
You have healed Muscle Wizaard for 29 points!

Enrico hesitated, staring at her...

So she threw one at him for good measure. Going through the glass had to hurt, right? **"Lesser Healing!"**

You have healed Enrico Rossi for 29 points!

He grunted, then looked around. "Who got me? Who pushed me?"

CHA+1

Chase sighed in relief, then lost that relief when Enrico's eyes found Renny's floating form and drew back to throw. "No! The fox is with us! We don't know who pushed you!"

"It doesn't matter who pushed you, little man..."

The guttural voice rumbled from the darkness, and Chase froze. She turned, along with the other three. The bulk of the crowd was gone now, and empty and broken tables stood between them and the darkness. The player's area was still lit somehow, an oasis of marble and gold and fountains, but of the speaker there was no sign.

"It matters that you're down here with *me*. And unlike all those years back, this time I know what I'm doing."

"You got a lot of nerve," Enrico said, drawing himself up. "Attacking me here, in my place of power. Attacking ME! You're in my house, and the house always wins. I know when to **Hold'em.** And when to **Fold'em.**"

The voice laughed. "Of course you do. Let me guess, you also know when to walk away, and when to run?"

"What the caga are you talking about?" Enrico said, drawing back to Chase and the Wizaard.

"Nothing you'd understand. Come on then. Show me what you got, Enrico. Let's see if you can take out an eye *this* time!"

"Quench Light," a different voice growled from deeper in the darkness...

...and the chandelier over the little group went out.

Enrico's voice hissed through the darkness. "Quick! You guys got good fortune?"

"What?" Chase called back.

"Fortune! You got enough of it to take some hits?"

Chase nodded. "Yes!"

"Well, er, not really," The Muscle Wizaard said.

"Sort of, maybe?" Renny spoke.

"Then I'm sorry in advance. **Ante Up!**" the Gambler shouted.

Instantly, a familiar sensation rippled through Chase. It felt like what happened when she overused foresight too much in a short time. It was the feeling of her pool of fortune energy being tapped and drained of a good chunk.

You have taken 50 fortune damage from Enrico's Ante Up!

Calculating winner...

Around her, she saw three white '50's float up from the darkness.... Enrico, the Wizaard, and Renny, she knew.

And to her horror, she saw eight more white 50s float up in a semicircle around them, out in the darkness. "There's eight werewolves!" she called out.

"I know!" Enrico said. "Give me a second, and I'll have enough fortune to take care of— wait, what the hell?"

Congratulations, you are the winner!

Fortune buffed by 600 for one minute!

A surge of raw power burst through Chase, filling her and crackling like raw fire. In an instant she went from feeling scared in the darkness to having the world itself at her fingertips. Crackling with potential, humming with power, she gasped and heard it echo through the hall.

"How did I lose? Agh, fight for your lives! Here they come!" Enrico called out.

"Don't worry," Chase said, feeling things click into focus, knowing just how far, exactly, she could push her luck for the next fifty-five seconds. "I've got this. **Foresight!**"

Seconds stopped and started, stopped and started, as Chase took control of the battle, using her premonition to figure out the best courses of action.

"Renny! Make torches!" she commanded, after seeing how they'd fare in darkness.

"On it!"

Your Foresight skill is now level 23!

"Wizaard, go after that one slinking around behind us!"

"I cast silence! Have a **Chokehold!**"

Your Foresight skill is now level 24!

"Enrico, go all out! **Good Fortune, Good Fortune, Good Fortune!**"

You have healed Enrico Rossi 9 Fortune!

Your Good Fortune skill is now level 2!

You have healed Enrico Rossi 10 Fortune!

Your Good Fortune skill is now level 3!

You have healed Enrico Rossi 11 Fortune!

Your Good Fortune skill is now level 4!

"Thanks! **Cardsharp! Rapid Fire!**"

Your Foresight skill is now level 25!

For a glorious moment, everything was going well.

For a few grand seconds, the surprised werewolves hesitated. Six-to-eight foot tall furry forms wearing torn clothing, now bloodied and beaten back by unexpected resistance, hunched in the cover of the tables and considered the surprisingly competent foe.

But only for a moment.

The shortest among them, a mere six feet tall but so squat and thick with muscle that it looked more like a bear-person than a wolfman, snarled and pointed at Chase. "Geek the mage!"

"What?" another rasped, as Chase whirled to face them.

"Kill her!" the stout werewolf commanded.

"Do it!" another one growled.

"**Bad Fortune!**" Chase yelled, pointing at the one ordering her dead.

Your target resisted your curse!

Uh-oh, she thought, and ran to get behind the Wizaard.

The Wizaard, covered in blood, let the limp werewolf he'd been strangling fall, and turned to face her. "Oooh yeah! Time for my signature move! Are! You! Ready?"

"Do it!" Chase said, diving and sliding between his massive legs, fetching up in a pile of chips behind him.

The big man spread his arms wide and roared in joy! **"Signature Move! YOU SHALL NOT PASS!"**

The entire battle paused.

Everyone looked to him.

Then the werewolves shrugged as one, and surged out from their cover, howling as they came.

Chase just grinned, and whispered **"Lesser Healing,"** a dozen times or so, healing her Wizaard as best she could.

WIS+1

She watched her skill rise and rise, and threw in Foresight between her spells, making sure everyone else was all right as she healed.

Everyone was. Renny was hovering in midair, directing a man-sized column of whirling air against one of the man-wolves, keeping it busy and unable to do much against an elemental.

Enrico Rossi was darting and dodging between tables, flipping over them with a grace that belied his age, throwing silvery cards at the stout werewolf and a tall, thin one. *The former runt,* Chase realized. *Now the packleader.*

One werewolf was unconscious, lying in the remnants of a slot machine, choked out by the Muscle Wizaard.

The remaining three were trying to tag-team the Muscle Wizaard, or get around him to go after Chase, it was hard to tell. They weren't having much luck against his signature move, and the big man was managing to control the battle pretty well... at the cost of blood and skin, whenever one got too near. He'd given up on grappling and was yelling about casting fist... which didn't seem to involve a skill, but just a lot of punching.

Wait, Chase said, realizing that something was missing. *I count seven werewolves. But there were eight people struck by Enrico's ante up! Where's the last one?*

INT+1

She whipped her head around, looking for the last werewolf...

Wait.

Who said it was a werewolf?

"The cloaked man! Do you see him?" She called up to Renny. He had the best vantage point, and wasn't currently threatened, so it seemed safe to interrupt him.

"No!"

She gnawed her lip, looking around. He could be hiding, he could be magically concealed... the lighting was spotty anyway, Renny's torches didn't entirely cover the whole of the darkness. No, her perception wasn't good enough to find the last one.

Her instincts told her this was important. Very, very important.

And as she wracked her brain for a solution, she came up with an answer. "Renny! My pack! I need my pack!"

"On it!" The little fox zipped up, back into the hole in the ceiling. "Oh! Uh, hi there," Renny said, as unknown people shouted.

Oh. Right. Enrico's enforcers. "Your boss needs help!" Chase shouted, "Look at the wolves! Shoot the wolves!"

Renny shouted back. "Yeah they're down there! Excuse me, excuse me. Here, catch!"

Then Chase's pack dropped out of the heavens like a meteor, landing on her and exploding in a shower of gold.

"OW!" she said, tumbling down, feeling pain on her back and knowing something was broken, searching frantically...

...and realizing that she'd be fine, as her fingers touched the stiffened leather of the corset's backing. *Score one for the armor,* she thought, and rose, clutching the pack. She spared the Muscle Wizaard a glance and caught him beating a werewolf with another werewolf... but the third one had taken some nasty slashes out of him, and red numbers were floating up. *He's bleeding. I need to be quick, here.*

Then her fingers caught the edge of a disc of cloth and she shouted in triumph and snapped open Thomasi's hat. "Here we go!" She put it on her head, and cried out, **"Activate Direct Attention to the cloaked skulker!"**

Once more, the battle paused. Once more, everyone snapped their heads around to look at a single point.

A single figure, sitting alone in the player area.

IN the player area.

Oh gods. Another one! Chase's breath hissed from between her teeth as the figure rose, and flipped his cloak over his shoulder, exposing bandoliers full of glass and metal crisscrossing his chest.

"No!" The squat werewolf roared...

...and then he was hurling himself toward the figure.

Left alone, against Enrico, the Alpha glanced between the distant figure and the white-suited Gambler.

"I'd run if I were you. I've got a good hand," the older man said, fanning his cards. "Sweet, **Suit Sorcery!**" The cards burst into flames and crackling lightning.

But Chase couldn't spare it any attention, as she watched the musclebound werewolf charge the cloaked stranger. Watched him stand patiently, knowing as well as she did what would happen when four hundred pounds of charging beastman hit the immovable barrier.

Except...

Except it didn't happen.

Chase gasped as the werewolf passed right through into the player's area... and stopped cold, five feet away from the stranger.

The werewolf could get onto the player dais? That could mean only one thing.

"Run! We need to run!" Chase shouted.

"Okay." The cloaked figure's voice was metallic, scarcely human. Male? Perhaps. Hard to tell. "This is a surprise."

"You know what you have to do if you want my hide!" The werewolf barked, clawing at the air only a few feet in front of him. "Turn your switch on! Let's settle this!"

"So your transformation hides your name and status? Well thass cute," the figure said, drawing out something from his cloak. Something that burst into flame, wicks of it tracing down toward red sticks.

"Oh no, run!" Renny yelled.

Chase was ahead of him, grabbing the Wizaard's loincloth and tugging until he followed. The werewolves on him were distracted, at least, their attention as fixated from the hat as everyone else... everyone save for Chase.

"Options," she heard the cloaked figure say. Then, as the werewolf grabbed him and opened its mouth to bite his head off, he spoke once more. **"Activate Teleport."**

He disappeared.

The bundle of burning sticks fell to the ground.

"NO!" The squat werewolf yelled, hurling itself backward...

The world turned white.

You have been afflicted with blindness!

You have been afflicted with deafness!

Chase screamed or thought she did. She hurt, and she couldn't tell how bad it was.

Groping, searching around, she found a broad chest. Feeling up it, knowing that it had to be the Muscle Wizaard, she was relieved to find that it was still moving. But there was blood, so much blood.

"Silent Activation, Diagnose," she mouthed.

The words appeared, giving her hope, hope that she could still do *something*, even without her sight.

Your Silent Activation skill is now level 10!

Muscle Wizaard (Bastien)
Debuffs: Bleeding, Blindness, Deafness
Conditions: Curse of Obscurity, Curse of Poverty, Unconscious

Curses? What were those doing there? That was unexpected.

"Silent Activation, Lesser Healing," she said, first for the Wizaard, then for herself. And when she checked again, he wasn't bleeding. That was good, because her head was aching, full of static and pain and it was so hard to focus. *My sanity's low. I spent most of that fight healing,* Chase thought and it was like thinking through cotton.

Now what?

Renny and Enrico, she thought. *Did they survive?*

She had to help them. And she thought she maybe had a way to do it. **"Status,"** she whispered, and winced. Twenty-seven sanity left. She could do it, but she'd have barely enough sanity left for a single healing spell.

But then I can't heal Renny anyway. Which means that Enrico's the only one I have to worry about. This is the only way.

"Sorry Wizaard. This is temporary," she told him, even though she couldn't hear herself say it, and she knew he couldn't, either. **"Transfer Condition."**

You are no longer deaf!

Your Transfer Condition skill is now level 5!

"Transfer Condition," she said again, and this time she heard herself say it.

You are no longer blind!

Your Transfer Condition skill is now level 6!

Now blessed with sight once more, she stared around at the room... what was left of it.

There was a massive hole in the ceiling above, and sunlight streamed through down onto the shattered remnants of the hall. Stone and bricks and wood and dust settling in the light. The player's area had been completely obliterated, as had every table within fifty feet of it. The remaining debris had been blown outward, and Chase heard people screaming and groaning in the wreckage...

But her eyes were glued to the white-suited figure of Enrico Rossi.

He was pinned under a massive crossbeam and his white suit was now slowly turning red, as a spreading dark puddle grew under him. The man coughed and coughed again, staring at her with desperate eyes.

"Enrico!" she called out, hurrying towards him, pausing to scoop up Thomasi's hat as she went.

"Kid..." he wheezed. He'd been lucky enough to dodge the deafness, then. Lucky enough to dodge the blindness, too, by the way his eyes followed her as she drew close.

But not lucky enough to dodge the roof. And as Chase knelt beside him, looking wildly for a way to fix this, she knew she couldn't.

"If I heal you, it'll just... the beam will still be crushing... hang on. Renny! Renny!" She stood and yelled. "Help!"

"Kid," Rossi rasped. "Did... good. Thanks."

"It's not over!"

"It's... listen. Gods told me... something else. Said... the Oracle would avenge me..."

"I'm an Oracle," she said, mind stuttering, a step behind. She was low on sanity, and it was hard to think.

"Right. Here." Enrico reached up, and silver-edged cards spilled from his hand. She grabbed them, hissing as the sharp, metal edges cut into her palm. They were metal, thin metal with paint, she saw.

"What? No! What am I supposed to... Renny! Help! Get an elemental over here!"

She heard a muffled response from farther back in the hall, and turned that way-

"*Listen,*" Enrico rasped. "Gambler... is... an Archer and Grifter mix. Experiment. Mix... skills. Unlock it. Kill the... stugats... with my cards. Got it?"

"I don't... no, we can..."

But Enrico Rossi didn't hear her.

He was dead.

The house had lost, in the end. The Gambler hadn't beaten the odds.

"Chase!" Renny yelled again, and she paused, and closed Enrico's eyes. It seemed the thing to do. Then, pushing the cards into her pockets, she hurried over to the fox.

As she did so, rubble shifted, and something... no, several somethings fled further into the darkness. There was a yip, as if a dog had run into something in the dark, and then there was nothing.

Nothing save for a cluster of words scrolling by so quickly that she had to stop, because she could barely see past them.

You are now a level 2 Medium!
CHA+5
LUCK+5

You are now a level 10 Oracle!
CHA+3
LUCK+3

WIS+3
You have learned the Influence Fate skill!
Your Influence Fate skill is now level 1!
You have learned the Short Vision skill!
Your Short Vision skill is now level 1!

You are now a level 11 Oracle!
CHA+3
LUCK+3
WIS+3

"There you are!" Renny said, and she gasped to see him. The stitches on his right side were burst, and stuffing spilled out, white and puffy. One arm was almost off, and he was cradling it, and it hurt to see him like this.

"What?" he asked.

"You're hurt," she whispered.

"Oh. I'll be fine once I get stitched up. Is the Wizaard okay?"

"Yes. He's unconscious, though. And he'll be blind for a while until I can... wait, I can think again!" That was right, the levels had refilled her pools of energy. And with renewed sanity came the knowledge that they were in a bad position. "We... should probably get the heck out of here."

"Alright. Your pack's over there. I'll call up a new elemental to carry the Wizaard. Are we done here?"

Chase looked around at the ruin. At Enrico's corpse.

I only knew him for a little bit, but I liked him. Damn it, he deserved better.

She didn't feel the urge for vengeance, or the drive to punish the werewolves for what they'd done. She didn't hate them or have it in her heart to be driven like they were, or like Enrico had been in the end.

But she rather thought she could find it in herself to honor Enrico's dying wish, if the opportunity arose. And it WOULD arise, she knew that.

The werewolves knew them, now.

There was no doubt in her mind that they'd meet again, and the next confrontation would probably be just as ugly.

CHAPTER 14: SCRYING TIME

Bastien's massive hand clenched hers, and she ground her teeth, ignoring the pain. "I've got you. Hang on just a little while longer," she said, even though she knew he couldn't hear her.

A door slammed open behind her. "I've got them. You're sure about this?" Cagna asked.

"No. But if it fails we'll improvise." Chase stuck out her hand.

Without a further word, Cagna dropped her wriggling, slimy burden in Chase's palm, and the halven closed her fist around a bunch of earthworms.

"Absorb Condition." She said, and the world went dark.

You have been afflicted with Blindness!

"I can see!" she heard The Muscle Wizaard roar.

"Transfer Condition," Chase intoned.

You are no longer afflicted by Blindness!

Your Transfer Condition skill is now level 7!

In her hand, the worms wriggled on, uncaring about the fact that they were now blind.

Another few seconds of work, and they were deaf as well, and then The Muscle Wizaard was hugging her and she couldn't see anything save for massive biceps.

"Easy!" She tapped his side with her free hand. "It worked. Good."

"What happened? What did I miss?" The Muscle Wizaard let her go and looked around the villa's study. Dusty books filled shelves, moth-eaten animal heads lined the walls, and a bear reared in the corner, stuffed and revealing a few wooden ribs where the moths had eaten through to reveal that it was a taxidermied creature.

"Can't say much for the décor," he wrinkled his nose.

Cagna answered. "The Don's fond of trophies. Used to hunt a lot in his youth. And I'll second the big guy's question, what DID he miss? For that matter, what the hell happened?"

"I've got a big question for you first," Chase said, narrowing her eyes as she considered the dog-woman. "Did you know that Enrico Rossi had faked his death, and was hiding in the casino?"

"What? No!" Her ears perked. "Wait. WAS hiding?"

"Dead now. The werewolves came for him. We were there at the time."

"You saw them..."

"Saw them and fought them!" The Muscle Wizaard punched his palm again. "Though it wasn't my finest hour. I fear I was unequal to the task."

"You survived and held off a bunch of them, you did your job just fine," Chase reassured him. Then she shook her head, and glared at Cagna again. "So you didn't know?"

"No! But this explains why Raoul was reluctant to talk about a few things..." Cagna massaged her muzzle. "I'm sorry. I honestly didn't mean to send you into danger. Hell, if I'd known Enrico was alive I could have gone through Dona Tarantina, there used to be some connections there... except no, she died last night. Damn it all, they're killing all the—" she shut up. "Okay, so we need to—"

"They're killing all the old hunting party. Everyone important who took down the werewolves the last time. Enrico told me all about that." Chase held the woman's eyes as Cagna tried to look away. "Is there anything else you're not sharing?"

"No. Nothing related to this, anyway. Can't lie to you, huh?" Cagna considered her.

"Not well. You've got a ton of tells." Chase took a breath. "Okay, we'll have to trust you on this." Wiggling in her hand reminded her that she was holding a bunch of worms. "And can you get me a jar? With dirt and airholes? This earthworm trick was useful so I think I'll keep them around."

"That's gross, but all right."

"They're earthworms. I'm a country mouse, remember? I'm not going to lose it over these friendly little guys."

"Point." Cagna went to the door and spoke with a servant, returning to the table. "Now, please fill me in on everything that happened."

Chase did, holding nothing back.

When she got to the part where the werewolves attacked, Cagna held up a hand. "You heard one of them say 'quench light?' You're sure about that?"

"Yes. It was a growly voice. It had to be one of them."

"That's a Burglar trick. That's a pretty high-level Burglar trick, too. Twentieth level, if I remember correctly."

"Twentieth level? Impossible!" The Muscle Wizaard said. "I'd be a smear on the ground if they were that strong! The ones that I fought weren't anywhere near that effective."

Cagna held up two fingers, putting them down as she made her points. "First off, Burglars don't have any real combat tricks that aren't related to escaping and evading. A twentieth-level Burglar is no match for any kind of decent warrior in a straight fight. Second off, the pack is probably all different levels. We think the pack leader can only recruit when he bites people on a full moon. At least half the ones you faced are probably recent hires, so to speak."

Chase nodded. "I'm willing to bet that the ones the leader sicced on us were the hired help. We were just the obstacle to his goal... which was taking out Enrico. Heck, the Burglar might have been the one you choked out in the beginning of the fight."

"It's possible," The Wizaard admitted. "He did squirm a lot. It was all I could do to keep ahold of him."

"Hey, I have a question," Renny raised a newly-sewn paw. "Does size translate between forms?"

"Excuse me?" Cagna blinked at him.

"If someone's small, do they turn into a small werewolf?"

"Kind of, I think. The basic physical form affects the werewolf form."

"So there's at least one more out there, if the tiny knife is any indicator. We didn't see any halven-sized werewolves in that fight."

"Or gnome-sized," Chase offered, weakly, but that wasn't too likely, to be honest. The gnomes were gone save for a few tiny families, their bloodlines mingled into humans and halvens centuries ago. "Yeah, okay, the leatherworker's killer was probably a halven. Which makes me wonder, why her? She's the one who doesn't fit. If the former runt IS after vengeance, then why is Friatta Castillo dead like the others?"

"They also killed a constable, and I guarantee you he wasn't involved. And some people in the Outskirts," Cagna pointed out. "Some of them worked for Don Coltello, true, but some didn't."

"Still something we're not seeing," Chase paced back and forth in the study, staring at the moth-eaten bear every second turn. "There's something going on here. It's not just vengeance."

"There was also that cloaked guy who pushed Enrico through the window," Renny pointed out.

"Him! How could I forget about him!" Quickly she filled Cagna in on the rest of the fight... leaving out the part about how he'd been sitting in the player-only area.

I can probably trust Cagna when it comes to werewolves. But now that there are players involved, I need to know more about what she's hiding before I say anything about the conspiracy.

For a second she worried that Bastien or Renny would throw in a detail that would force some hasty explanation, but it was a fear that never came to fruition. Cagna's eyes grew wider and wider as Chase described the cloaked figure, and the dog-woman finally gasped, "Poner!"

"Excuse me?"

"That's the legendary murderer, Poner!"

"Owner?"

"No. It's actually spelled P-W-N-E-R. It's foreign. It's pronounced Pone-er. He's... a bad dream. A legend. A hit man that commands ludicrous amounts of gold and never fails. It's rumored that he can't be killed. A friend of mine saw him... or somebody like him, anyway, get filled with arrows. His body disappeared from the morgue a few hours later, leaving only equipment and clothes behind. It was a locked room, with every exit guarded, and the strongest of magical wards, but the body just... it was gone." Cagna had gone pale.

"He was an Alchemist," Renny said. "That was a really big Alchemist's bomb he pulled out at the end, there."

"Pwner's methods and tricks change with every story," Cagna shook her head. "There's a hell of a lot of murders on the books that are attributed to him, but nobody knows for certain."

Cold ran down Chase's spine and collected somewhere around gut level. *He's a player. Of course he can return to life. He's powerful and nigh-immortal, and doesn't care about who he kills to get what he wants.*

And the squat werewolf is a player, too.

An ugly suspicion niggled at the back of Chase's head. The Camerlengo was here in the city too, with two captive players in tow. What were the odds that this was a coincidence? What were the odds that ANY of this was a coincidence?

"The thing I'm having trouble seeing is why he's here," Cagna said. "This doesn't fit Pwner's rumored motives. Someone would have to pay him a wompload of gold to hunt something as mundane as monsters. He's only supposed to take on the really challenging jobs, or the ones that pay ludicrous amounts of coin. Even Don Coltello couldn't afford his price."

"Could a guild afford his price?" Renny asked.

"Of course!" Chase slapped her knee. "Soluzioni Semplici! They're the ones you said were mercenaries, right?"

"They could, I guess..." Cagna puffed her cheeks out, and blew a raspberry. It looked weird as her muzzle rippled. "This is a lot of conjecture. But if he's involved, that's bad news. The man doesn't seem to have any morals when it comes to completing a job. He just focuses on winning, regardless of the collateral damage. This is... we're going to need to bring this up at the council tonight."

"Oh! Right. That." Chase said. "Argh. How much time do we have to prepare?"

"Four hours," Cagna said. "If I were you I'd get some rest—"

A knock at the door, and Giuseppe Coltello stuck his head in. Meeting three sets of unfriendly eyes, he blanched, but walked in anyway. "Here," he said. "You wanted this?" The Don's son pro-offered a glass jar full of dirt to Chase.

"Thanks," she said, and dumped the worms in, wiping her slimy hand on the velvet seat of the chair she sat in. Giuseppe winced at the stain. "Did you want something else?" Chase put a bit of iron in her tone.

"I uh, er, I... well yes, I looked into what you asked me to do. The Rossis are still in mourning, but one of the Bianchi dowagers is attending a Verde masquerade ball tonight."

Verde... Chase knew that name. After a second it came to her. *One of the people Enrico mentioned, one of the hunting party was a Verde. Her name was, let's see...*

"Maddalena!" Chase burst out, and Giuseppe flinched backward. "Maddalena Verde. Will she be there?"

"She's the one throwing the ball!" Giuseppe said, smiling. "It's all very sudden. She announced it two days ago, barely any warning at all. Tabita begged me to go, and we've got our costumes all picked out. It would be no hardship at all to bring some, er, servants." He winked, and his tone turned obsequious. "Though I certainly wouldn't expect you or your honored friends to actually BE our servants, just, er, pretend to be them..."

"When is this ball?" Chase asked.

"Tomorrow night. And rumor has it that the very highest nobles in the city will be in attendance!"

Cagna grunted, and Chase shot her a look. When she turned her face back to Giuseppe, she forced it into a smile. "Thank you. Yes, do take us along. This should pay your debt nicely."

"Ah, good!" He said and coughed.

"I think you can go now, friend," The Muscle Wizaard spoke, and Giuseppe needed no more prompting. He fled, slamming the door behind him.

"I don't know what you did to him, but this is the most useful I've ever seen the guy," Cagna said.

"He climbed into bed with Chase and tried to play with her," Renny said. "But she didn't want to play, and she beat him up."

Cagna shot the halven a horrified look. "Oh gods! That slime! Are you okay?"

"Um... yes. Why wouldn't I be?" Chase blinked. "He didn't get too far, and he stopped once I went for his eyes."

Cagna halted, half-off her chair. "You're fine? Really?" She scrutinized Chase, and her ears lifted in surprise. "You are. That's... not normal."

"What do you mean?"

"Most girls your age would be a wreck. A lot freeze up when someone tries something like that, and... bad things happen. Even when the perverts don't get their way, it's still... most people need days or weeks or even longer to put themselves back together after an assault like that. But you're fine? You're fine, just like that?"

"Oh... I see what's going on." Chase sighed. "Don't take this the wrong way, but you're used to dealing with humans, right?"

"Mostly, yeah. They're pretty much everywhere. Why..." Cagna caught herself. "Are halvens different somehow?"

"So... you're good with jobs. I've gathered that much by being around you and talking with you," Chase said. "I'm betting you're good at thinking about the numbers. And I don't know what beastkin get when they level up, but I'm guessing it includes armor and endurance, yes?"

"Well, yeah. A bit more than humans in some cases."

"Halvens don't get any armor or endurance. At all. All the points that would go to those instead go towards mental fortitude and cool."

Cagna thought about it a bit. Then her eyebrows shot up toward her ears. "Damn. So what you're saying is that you don't let things like that get to you."

"Oh, they get to us. Our willpower is usually low enough that we feel fear, we feel annoyance. But... we get over it. Faster than humans do, usually. We don't really break so much as we bend, and when we bend back we take steps to prevent ourselves from being in such uncomfortable places ever again." *Like locking my door and shoving furniture in front of it every night from now on.* "I guess I could have let it eat at me, but... I've got things to do. And I'm not going to put my life on hold just because one drunk playboy mistook me for his mistress."

"Ah. Is THAT what happened?" Cagna lifted her hand away from her sword. "I guess I can put Giuseppe's gelding off for another day, then."

"It's what he *says* happened," The Muscle Wizaard rumbled. "I will admit to some temptation when it comes to neutering the lad. But a face wouldn't do that, no. If I'd been in heel mode instead, well... you'd have heard his shrieks from the outer walls."

Cagna shared an appreciative grin with the Wizaard. "Starting to like you, meat mountain."

"Right back at you, muttface."

Cagna paused.

"Oh! Er... sorry," The Wizaard said. "Was that bad? I was trying for familiarity..."

"No, it's fine..." she said. "Lachina calls me that. It just made me think of her. And of tonight." Cagna rubbed her muzzle, and sat down. "I'll check in with her tonight, and you'll get to see your flamboyant friend, kiddo."

"Oh! Right!" Chase smiled. Given how hectic the last day had been, she'd almost forgotten about that. Since there hadn't been any news she'd figured Tom was working his magic, so to speak. Hopefully. "So you say we have a few hours to prepare?"

"Yeah." She scrutinized Chase. "I'd recommend fixing the rips in your clothes, making sure your armor's hidden. Aside from that, maybe a nap..."

"Not a chance. I'm still wired from my level-ups," Chase said. "Though I think I'm going to murder some mid-day tea once I'm done here. The walk home was work."

"I'm going to rest. You healed my wounds, but the stamina damage will take a while to heal." The Muscle Wizaard smiled, and then turned solemn. "My usual fighting tactics didn't work so well against the werewolves. I kept them busy, but I couldn't inflict enough damage to put them down. They healed as I watched. I might need some silver knuckles..." he flexed his hands.

"I need some supplies as well," Chase said. "I don't think I'll be resting. I've got some new Oracle tricks, and I've got a Medium skill I haven't been able to try out before now."

"Oh? What changed?" Cagna asked.

Chase upended her pack, and gold coins cascaded out. "We lost a few when Renny threw it down on me—"

"Sorry!"

"—don't worry about it. But now I think I can afford a crystal ball. And combined with a few other things, I think I can maybe get us some information, and also level up Medium before tonight. That'll refill all my pools, and I'll be fresh for the meeting."

Cagna didn't reply. She was busy staring at the gold.

"Believe me, we earned it," Renny said.

The dog-woman got up, shaking her head, and headed out the door.

"Talk to the servants and send them into town with money for whatever you need. Lie low. Trust me on this."

"I will," Chase promised. *On this, if nothing else.*

An hour later, the servants returned from their shopping trip.

Chase hefted a four-inch diameter sphere of crystal with both hands, staring into its depths. It wasn't flawless, not entirely... it had a diffused fog filling the center, that lightened as it approached the edges. "They might have gone a little overboard, here," she said.

"You think? That's a really big chunk of crystal."

"I wasn't sure how much it would cost so I gave them a lot of money. But the stuff left over went to potions, so that's okay." The crystal ball went down to its velvet cushion and he picked up a small red vial and stared at it. Several others like it mingled with different-colored vials nearby, and one by one they went into her pockets. She spread them out... it wouldn't do to have them all end up broken by an unlucky hit, or by landing on them wrong.

"Lucky. You can drink stuff," Renny said, handing her up one last blue potion. "So what is it that your skills do, exactly?"

"Let me double check that. **Status.**"

And one by one, she checked through the skills that seemed useful here.

Influence Fate
Cost: 25 For   **Duration: 1 Turn**
At this level, your foresight extends to the actions of others. You may grant others a brief usage of your own foresight, allowing them to determine the best course of action. This skill is a spell.

Short Vision
Cost: 25 San   **Duration: 01-100 minutes**
The world is full of omens and portents, but sometimes they aren't enough. By taxing your sanity, you can send your mind into a trance, seeking out help from your god. They'll usually oblige by sending you a short vision, related to your question or the situation at hand. It's rarely straightforward, though skilled Oracles can guide the vision, a bit. The harder the question, the greater the wisdom and skill required. The downside of this spell is that it knocks you out for a random amount of time, basically rendering you unconscious and unable to wake up until the vision is over. This skill is a spell.

Crystal Ball

Cost: 50 San   Duration: 1 minute per skill level
Through manipulation of the winds of fate, you can use a crystal ball to scry people, places, or things of interest. Time is mutable in such visions and be forewarned that the winds of fate are fickle and the scenes shown may vary... skill and wisdom are required to reduce interference. This skill is draining and may only be used once per day.

Chase read them out loud to Renny. "Okay. Influence fate might not help all that much. I thought it might, but now that I've read it... no."

"Are there any other useful Medium tricks?"

"At higher levels? Maybe. But not right now, not for this. Good Fortune lets me heal someone's fortune pool. Bad Fortune damages their fortune pool. You've seen what Séance does, and all Stack Deck does is let me choose which card to pull from a deck." She shrugged.

"What if you used those fortuna cards and stacked the deck?"

"Then I'd get a false reading, probably." Chase shrugged. "That book I've got about fortuna readings said that if you cheat it won't work. The author knows her stuff. She doesn't know much about writing or grammar or spelling or... well reality in general, but she knows the cards."

"Okay. So the Crystal Ball sounds like the big winner here. But that one use a day limit is troubling."

"It's powerful. Especially for a skill you get at job level one."

"Job level one in a Tier Two job." Renny pointed out. He put his head to the side and considered, tail lashing. "You should use the vision first."

"First and maybe second and third. It depends on how much time it takes." Chase grimaced. "I'm pretty sure it won't level me in Oracle though, not this close to the last two levels. I'll have to do it first anyway, and use the Crystal Ball afterward... with maybe a few fortune attacks and heals to grind experience, re-level, and refill my pools."

"Sounds like a plan. How can I help?"

Chase looked at the remnants of her meal. Then at the rather expensive-looking clock on the wall. "Guard the door and make sure I'm not interrupted. Please?"

"Okay."

Chase lay back on her bed and got comfy. *Here goes...* **"Short Vision."**

The light in the room shifted.

"Oh, you're awake!" Renny said, as she sat up.

"Nothing happened. How long was that?"

"An hour and a half."

"Oh no..." Chase rubbed her face. She felt off, like she'd woken from a bad sleep. "It should have done something. Let me check it again." Back to the status screen, and she read it over. "Okay... so it looks like I have to ask a question. I guess I've got enough going on that the gods can't just tell what I should be asking about..." She gnawed her lip. "Renny, you're smarter than me. What's a good question to ask here?"

"How about... what will help us find the werewolves?"

Chase thought it over.

"Close. But not quite. What will help us *win* against the werewolves? Yes!"

Before she could lose her nerve, Chase lay down again. **"Short Vision. What will help us win against the werewolves?"**

Chase closed her eyes... and opened them again, to see a cruel, wrinkled face staring down at her. Steel at her throat, and Chase saw more steel glittering in the hands of shadowy figures surrounding her.

But she couldn't look away from that face. She knew it, well.

Camerlengo Zenobia!

"Give me one reason I should let you live," the Camerlengo whispered.

And as though she spoke through water, Chase heard her own voice reply. "I'll give you two reasons."

Then her vision blurred, and Chase's perspective launched through the room, through the lit windows of a city at night, moving so quickly it was like a series of portraits, with a silvery, full moon hanging in the sky like the watchful eye of a god.

And she saw the goblin cave, the dungeon, with furry forms arrayed across the rocks, watching the lights of approaching torches. LOTS of approaching torches.

...Then with a gasp, Chase sat bolt upright. "Oh yeah," she whispered, as soon as she could find her voice. "That did the trick."

Critical Success!

Luck+1

Your Short Vision skill is now level 2!

"You were out for uh... fifty-eight minutes," Renny said, checking the clock. "Not much time left. Do you want to risk another?"

"No." Chase said, checking how the light from the windows had moved across the floor. As a country girl, she was better at gauging that, then trying to read a clock. "But I think it's time to break out the crystal ball."

Two minutes later it was resting on an end table, and Chase was standing on a chair, hands hovering above it. "Now all I have to do is figure out what I want to scry. I'm thinking... I'm thinking the werewolf leader is a good idea. The rest of the pack is going to be with him. What did Enrico call that guy?"

"The werewolf Alpha."

"Okay. **Crystal Ball, show me the werewolf Alpha.**"

She was just guessing at the terminology there, but whatever entity governed the usage of skills seemed to accept it.

Your Crystal Ball skill is now level 2!

Chase felt the familiar strain on her mind as sanity left... she was glad that she'd recovered some from resting, while the short visions were going on. The crystal ball glowed and seemed to fill with clouds. But one by one they thinned, revealing a figure standing in what appeared to be a tailor's shop. He was tall, slim, and dark, with a dashing goatee and piercing green eyes. A pair of servants were fitting him with a crushed black velvet tunic and buckling a rapier at his waist.

"Are you seeing this?" Chase asked Renny...

...and gasped as the man looked up in surprise, eyes narrowing.

Did he hear me?

"Yes," Renny whispered back.

After a few seconds the man shook his head and looked back to the servants. He said something and one of them laughed.

And then the clouds were back, and the crystal ball returned to its previous, un-magical state.

"I don't know who that was," Chase said, "but he was getting fitted for some very fancy clothes. And given that one of the targets on their murder list is throwing a ball tomorrow night, I'm pretty sure I know where he's going to be going, wearing such nice clothes."

"So what now?"

"Nothing, now. I have a lot to think about." The Camerlengo's hate-filled face crossed her mind again, and Chase shuddered. *Will it come to THAT?* "In the meantime, I didn't level. But I've got a few tricks that I can use here, if you're willing to help. Any objection to letting me heal and harm your fortune a few dozen times?"

"None at all!"

And in the time they had left before Cagna knocked on their door, Chase did level Medium and felt just a bit more prepared.

As it turned out, she wasn't prepared at all...

CHAPTER 15: BLOOD AND CANNOLIS

Well, we've got one thing in common, Chase thought, as she looked at the groaning tables full of food. *Both gangsters and halvens love a hearty dinner.*

She really hadn't known what to expect when Cagna led them through the darkening streets. Back alleys or maybe a tavern like the one they'd first come to in the Outskirts, something like that.

What she got was a fortress. A literal fortress! The place was an old stone tower, surrounded by two walls, not even two miles away from the Doge's palace. Sure, it was a little run down, and sure, parts of the wall had lost chunks off the top from sieges long ago, but the place was still not what Chase envisioned when it came to crime lords having clandestine meetings.

While it had looked foreboding and run-down on the outside, the inside was another story. Luxurious furnishings, thick rugs, and roaring fires gave shelter against the late-autumn chill. Works of art stood strategically in empty corners and unused spaces, lined the walls stretching up the spiraling staircases, and sat around the great banquet hall that Cagna had led them to.

Mind you, it took a while to get there. They had been stopped and questioned every step of the way, and her fingers still throbbed where she'd had to prick herself on silver needles. The place was crawling with enforcers, mercenaries, and mages. All sorts of races and professions were represented, patrolling the premises and generally looking badass.

But the strangest thing of all, were the people who obviously *weren't* hard-bitten men and women of action. They wore nice clothes... the men all had suits, the women all had dresses, and they were the sort of people who wouldn't stand out in a crowd.

And though it was risky, Chase started mouthing words as she moved through the crowd. **"Silent Activation, Size Up. Silent Activation, Size Up."**

Four skill levels, sixty moxie and thirty fortune later, she was certain of the commonalities. Most of these ordinary-looking people had charisma and willpower, though only a few could compare to her own charisma. But on the average they were only decent on perception, and wisdom seemed to be lacking in general.

"These are the dons and their people, aren't they?" Chase had asked Cagna on their way up the stairs.

Cagna had confirmed that, then reiterated that she didn't want any questions until they were there...

And *there* had turned out to be the banquet hall, full of food, with guards at every entrance, and long, stained glass windows reflecting the lantern light in bright colors. Above the entire room hung a chandelier that dwarfed those she'd seen in the casino... a massive work of steel and glass with magical orbs playing around it.

Chase would have been a lot more impressed if she, Cagna, Renny, and the Wizaard weren't the only guests in the room at the moment.

"We're here, and it's safe," Cagna said, leaning down a bit to squeeze Chase's shoulder. "You can let the questions fly now."

"I'm not sure we're safe. Or that anywhere's safe right now," Chase said, feeling the truth of the words. "But right now I'm wondering why all the important people are downstairs, and we're up here."

"It's precisely because they're important people that they're downstairs. They're using the time before the meeting to talk business, trade favors, and politick. Us? We've got nothing to offer and little to talk about that involves their business... save for one thing."

"But what about Don Coltello? Won't he want to meet with us before things start?"

Cagna nodded. "He will. I expect him to be along shortly. Really, the only one he did much business with anymore was Dona Tarantino, and well, she's gone. None of the other dons like the old man that much. Which could hurt him in the long run, and us by proxy, if they decide to politic against him."

Damn it, I should be down there, Chase grimaced. She had honed herself for that kind of battlefield, and there was much to gain if she played her cards right.

Instantly her thoughts went to her pockets, and the Gambler's legacy inside them... the cards that were made for throwing, for killing.

Wait a minute...

"They didn't search us for weapons?" Chase asked. "Why?"

But it was the Muscle Wizaard who answered.

"In a place like this, everyone's armed. And given the situation, it would be foolish not to be." He held up his hands, displaying the spiky silver knuckles he'd bought with his share of the jackpot winnings. The letters 'MUSL' and 'WZRD' traced a shiny path over his fingers, and the spikes looked like little conical hats. "I'm going to guess there's a general prohibition against pulling weapons, yes? But nobody cares if you bring them."

"Something like that," Cagna confirmed.

Chase felt Renny shift in her pack, but he kept silent. Probably good, since quite a few of those guards were looking their way. She'd used the time she had left before the meeting devising a series of taps and raps and code words to let Renny know when he could and couldn't do things. *The cards in my pocket are an ace in the hole I suppose, but Renny... Renny's my secret weapon. The werewolves know about him, sure, but the gangsters? Not so much.*

Not that she thought the werewolves would be foolish enough to try anything, not here. She had taken their measure during the casino fight, and they had come up lacking, even with a player involved. If they tried the same thing here they'd inflict damage, sure, but the weight of numbers was against them. Between all the mercenaries and goons who were forewarned and armed with silver, assaulting the famiglias here would be the height of idiocy.

Something flickered in the back of Chase's mind while she considered that.

The fight at the casino *had* been easier than it should have been. Not a cakewalk, not that. And true, Enrico was the one who had been stuck with the most dangerous werewolves, while Chase and Renny and the Wizaard had been hard-put to fend off the lessers.

But still, given their reputation and the care that the familigias were showing here, that fight should have been a lot more difficult.

Had the werewolves been holding back?

If so, then why?

Chase bit at her lip and started to shift her pack to the floor. She needed to check the cards. Not the silver-edged ones, but the fortuna cards. *They've never steered me wrong. One quick reading should help me figure out—*

"Ah, mia piccola nipotina! Welcome!"

Chase pulled her hand back from the pack's lacings and looked up to see a familiar, ugly smile.

"Nonno," Chase said, feeling the wrongness of the word as she smiled back at Don Coltello. "How have you been?"

"Not so great," he confessed, taking a seat at the big table, the only one that wasn't laden with food. Beside him, Lachina stood silent and solemn. The Don took no notice of her as he kept staring at Chase. "Someone I trusted very much has betrayed me. He stole something from my house and vanished."

"That's horrible!" Chase said. "Is there anything I can do to help with that?" She grimaced. "Well, to be honest, the werewolf thing is keeping us busy, so I don't know if I could. But I could try, if you needed..."

About that point she noticed that Cagna had snapped to attention, and the Muscle Wizaard was surreptitiously stepping into position to put himself between Chase and the Don. "Ah... wait, what?"

The tension had crept up on her without noticing. Reviewing the Don's words, now she marked the tone that had been behind them. An expectant, menacing tone...

Chase blinked. She'd been distracted, and now, now this might get ugly.

"Sir?" Cagna asked.

"You really don't know?" Don Coltello asked.

"No sir," Chase said, keeping her reply short, studying him. "Should I know something? Please tell me." *This is frustrating!* Chase thought. *It's just the sort of thing that silent foresight would help me navigate, but he's staring right at me, he'd surely notice...*

The fat man grunted. "Either you're one hell of a liar, or somehow you're being truthful. Cagna?"

"I'm pretty sure that both of those statements are true," said the beastkin. "I'm also pretty sure that she's smart enough not to steal from you and would have the wisdom not to get within arm's length of you if she did. So if you're trying to figure out if she's involved with whatever you're talking about, I'd say she isn't."

"That's very strange," said Don Coltello. "Because that stugat Tom *is*."

Chase's eyes went wide. "Oh gods, what did he *do*?"

That threw him for a loop. The Don's mouth opened and closed, and she saw his eyes narrow as he considered her again. Finally, he grimaced. "Your man came to my home. He sat at my table. He ate my food. He helped me with some minor things, trivial favors, really. And then he stole from me, and fled in the middle of the night. What have I done that he should insult me so? It wasn't anything of real value that he stole! Just that stupid—"

A gong sounded, and the massive doors across the room creaked open.

"We'll talk about it afterwards," the Don said, and the small group turned as pale figures appeared in the darkness beyond. "For the love of gods say nothing more on it until we're done here."

Chase nodded... and then she had no more time for Don Coltello, as the foremost figure approached.

Tall, thin, dressed in black from head to toe, with a sweeping red cape that called to mind shimmering blood, the man glided across the rugs with a fluid grace that wasn't natural, couldn't be natural. His eyes were crimson, his skin pale, and his hair a waterfall of black strands that somehow moved in perfect unison as he turned his head to consider the group before him.

"Massimo..." he whispered, and Chase felt the word push against her ears with unnatural pressure, his dry, deep voice echoing through the room in a way it had no business doing. "I expected you to arrive with the others."

Chase shuddered. Somehow the implied possibility of a rebuke was terrifying beyond words, even if it wasn't directed towards her. But Don Coltello was unruffled. Either the benefits of good willpower or long familiarity, it was hard to say.

"Just some business to take care of beforehand, Prezzo." The Don leaned back in his chair, and Chase jumped a bit as it creaked. "Had to sort some things out with my investigator."

"This is the one, then?" Red, red eyes turned toward Chase.

And she froze.

Every instinct was telling her NOPE.

The back of her mind was reminding her where every exit out of the room was located and busy doing math to figure out how to get her there in the most efficient fashion. This man standing before her... this *thing*, whatever he or it was, this was danger. This was death.

"She is," Don Coltello confirmed, in the silence.

"A strange choice..." the man said, squatting down and somehow making it look graceful, like it was the most natural thing in the world to be crouching, looking her in the eye. "She's paralyzed by fear, just from my presence. So how would she even be effective against those beasts?"

"We, er..." the Muscle Wizaard said, and the hot red eyes left her, just for a second...

But it was all the time Chase needed to recover herself, to bounce back, even just a bit. "We aren't supposed to fight them, just find them!" she said in a rush. "Though, uh..." she quailed again as Prezzo looked back to her.

"Though we already did," The Muscle Wizaard backed her up. "Fight them, I mean. Briefly. They got away."

The pressure that seemed to be pushing against Chase, the raw force of the man's presence, eased up. He smiled then. "Did you? I look forward to hearing all about it. As I'm sure the others will." He offered a hand. "I am Don Sangue. Welcome to my home."

Chase shook it and hid a gasp. His hands were cold as stone.

She wondered if all of him was so. He was easily the palest human she had ever seen... no. No, he wasn't human. She wasn't sure what he was, but it wasn't good and it wasn't human.

But then he was standing and moving toward the head of the table. The other pale figures who had emerged from the doorway joined him, but Don Sangue was the only one who sat down.

"You sit at my left," Don Coltello told Chase. Then he looked to the Wizaard. "You, big guy, you stand behind her, with my bodyguards. See to our needs and keep an eye on stuff. Don't talk unless directly addressed."

"Standard bodyguard rules then," The Wizaard nodded. He was wearing his robes again, newly sewn along the easily-rippable seams.

"Standard rules," The Don confirmed, nodding.

Then the rest of the guests started filtering in from downstairs, and Chase watched them come.

It was a similar setup across the board. One of the ordinary looking people would take a seat, and some of the obviously stronger or more magical people would take up position behind them, or nearby.

As they sat down, Chase's people-watching instincts came to the fore. There was an etiquette to it, she realized. An unspoken dance, as the guests studied each other, and chose their places due to politics or relationships that she couldn't begin to guess at without context.

But as the crowd thinned, and the final people settled around the far edges of the big table, Chase determined two things.

The first thing was that the dance was important, that it was an old custom and respected. Nobody rushed it; nobody showed impatience, or even much emotion at all, really. Keeping your cool was a big part of the game, and that probably affected the seating order too.

The other thing that she noticed was that Don Coltello, by taking his seat before anyone else got here, had disrupted things and pulled attention to himself. And though nobody said anything, the way that the seats around them were the last to be taken spoke volumes. Disapproving, heavy volumes.

PER+1

Chase inhaled and almost coughed as the cool, overly-dry air hit her throat. The fireplaces, though huge and stacked with blazing wood, were far across the hall and the tower was drafty. It had a warm facade, with rugs and well-cushioned chairs, and tapestries and big fires... but it was a facade, really. This place was not built for comfort. *It resembles its owner,* Chase knew and didn't dare lift her eyes toward Don Sangue. *Beautiful on the outside. But death itself, once you can see past the facade.*

But at last everyone was seated, and the dinner began. Don Coltello snapped his fingers and Lachina brought him a plate of goodies. Whole baked pheasants on penne pasta, with a delicious, cheesy sauce over it all, and salads chock full of the finest fall vegetables made up the majority of the Don's selection.

After Chase whispered a few words over her shoulder, the Wizaard returned with a plate heaped full of meat and cheese. A few more whispered words and he brought her bread, and pasta, and a quiet apology. "Sorry. I'm used to sticking to protein."

Chase was worried that he'd broken the 'bodyguards don't talk' rule, but a glance around the table showed nobody had noticed. Quiet conversation rippled and mixed in among the clink of silverware on plates and the subtle slurping of heady wine from tall glasses.

She did note that Don Sangue's own glass remained full of wine as the minutes crawled by. *I suppose he doesn't drink wine,* she thought.

To her horror, the pale don caught her eye and smiled, just briefly. And like a stillness spreading through a rushing brook, one by one the conversations nearest him stopped, and his neighbors looked down at Chase. And then THEIR neighbors looked at Chase. And so on, and so forth, until the entire table had fallen silent.

"Merda," Don Coltello whispered, so faintly she almost missed it.

Chase put her fork down. Doing her best to ignore every other set of eyes, she stared back at Don Sangue. "Signore," she said into the silence. "You serve a wonderful dinner."

"I know. Tell me something I do not know, please." Don Sangue's face was like glass... but at least it lacked the horrible intensity she'd been subjected to at their first conversation.

This is a different sort of Charisma. Far more than mine but focused, and he's got some sort of intimidation effect. He's not using it now... The thought gave her strength.

"I am uncertain what you do and do not know, Don Sangue," she said, and stood up on her chair. "But if you wish, I can **Lecture** everyone here about the results of my investigations into the werewolf problem."

Your Lecture skill is now level 5!
Your Lecture skill is now level 6!
Your Lecture skill is now level 7!
Your Lecture skill is now level 8!
Your Lecture skill is now level 9!

Your Lecture skill is now level 10!

Your Lecture skill is maxed! Level up your Teacher job to increase this skill!

As one, the rest of the table looked to Don Sangue. The red-eyed man smiled back and lifted his wine glass. "Please proceed. And enjoy the experience, I imagine this will net you a few levels once you're done."

A nervous laughter rippled through the room, and Chase swallowed.

She spoke of her trip to visit the leatherworker and how she'd conducted a séance to ask his slain daughter for help. There was muttering and murmuring as she put the knife on the table and grunts of satisfaction.

"Good," Don Coltello grunted. "Now tell them about today."

"I'm just getting to that, Signore..." Chase said. "Okay. Everyone knows the Rossi casino out on the waterfront got blown up, right?"

THAT got a lot of attention on her, very quickly. All save for Don Sangue. She hesitated, watching him speak to one of his pale attendants. The man was dressed in armor, armored like the figures that she had seen coming in through the gates. She watched the Don frown at his minion and nod.

"Ahem," she coughed to buy time. *Should I continue?*

After a bit of reflection, it seemed rude not to. He'd wanted her to speak for the full table, and even if he was in charge at the moment, his attention was his own business. He didn't *have* to listen to Chase.

INT+1

Well, that settles it, Chase thought and started to relate her trip to the casino.

But she'd barely gotten to the point where the cloaked figure had rushed Enrico Rossi, when the doors opened once more, and a contingent of armed guards came in, herding someone between them.

"What the hell?" Don Coltello barked, and around the table the gangsters shot to their feet, as steel sung clear of scabbards, and mages readied to cast spells. "What is this cazza?"

"This is a parley," an unfamiliar voice spoke. "Isn't that right, Don Sangue?"

"You are correct. For now," the Don stood, and gestured. "Get him a seat."

But the gangsters didn't sit down, and Chase was left craning her neck, wiggling around, trying to see through the multitude of people in her way.

Just as she'd given up hope, strong arms wrapped around her, and Chase squeaked as the Muscle Wizaard lifted her...

...and Chase stared.

She might not have known the voice, but she knew that face.

He was wearing different clothes, yes, but that was the face she'd seen in her crystal ball not two hours ago.

"I'm so glad we could meet under more pleasant circumstances," said the werewolf Alpha. "So, could I ask someone to get me a plate? That food smells lovely."

CHAPTER 16: A DUEL OF WORDS

You are now a level 3 Teacher!
INT+1
WILL+1
You are now a level 4 Teacher!
INT+1
WILL+1

The words shocked Chase back into reality, drew her attention off the foolish, audacious werewolf who had come into the den of his enemies. It brought her mind back to the present and reminded her that she wasn't exactly in the safest of positions, either.

However, with all eyes on *him* now, she had a heck of a lot more freedom to act.

I don't know what his game is, but the more I know about him the better.

"Silent Activation, Size Up. Silent Activation, Diagnose." And then, because she didn't know how long eyes would be off her, she decided to throw in a few other buffs. Everything she could think of, really. **"Silent Activation, Silver Tongue. Silent Activation, Quickdraw."**

Your Silent Activation skill is now level 15!

Sizing him up proved helpful.

Werewolf Alpha
Charisma – Moderately worse
Perception – Greatly better

Willpower – Moderately better
Wisdom – Much worse
Influencing conditions: None
Your Size Up skill is now level 4!

Diagnosing him proved less so.

Your Silent Activation skill is now level 16!

Werewolf Alpha
Conditions: Blessing – Agility, Slow Poison
Debuffs: Full Moon Fever

You are now a level 8 Grifter!
CHA+3
DEX+3
LUCK+3

That was a surprise! For a second she was giddy as the energy coursed through her again... and then the joy was replaced with dread.
He's THAT dangerous. Oh gods.
Wait.
Chase's eyes slid to the other insanely dangerous man in the room. She looked upon Don Sangue and found his red eyes fixated on the werewolf.
Do I dare? Well why the heck not! Easy level!
"Silent Activation, Size Up. Silent Activation, Diagnose."
And instantly the Don's eyes flickered to her.
Chase slammed her head away, sweat breaking out on her brow, sweat that turned cold as the words rolled up out of nowhere.

Don Prezzo Sangue
Charisma – Insanely better
Perception – Insanely better
Willpower – Insanely better
Wisdom – About equal
Influencing Conditions: Predator's Gaze

Don Prezzo Sangue
Conditions: Undead, Light Allergies, Predator's Gaze, Wood Allergies
Debuffs: Bloodthirst

Oh gods he IS a monster! And he saw me! Surrounded by a crowd, with his enemy before him, he had the perception to see I was trying something against him!

But after a second she felt the heat of those red, red eyes leave her. He had bigger problems, after all. Though she had no doubt she'd be in trouble, later. If there was a later.

You are now a level 9 Grifter!
CHA+3
DEX+3
LUCK+3

The words confirmed the danger... but then the werewolf was speaking.

Someone had brought him a plate, she saw as the crowd shifted. He wasn't eating any of it, but he did drink the wine. "A subtle hint of wolfsbane. Nice. I wonder how many of your guests will have diarrhea tomorrow."

"A little discomfort is well worth the security," Don Sangue replied. "Please, everyone, be seated. He is a guest at our table. For now."

Chase tapped the Muscle Wizaard's arm and he put her back into her chair before resuming his post. She glanced back to find him looking around the room. Cagna was doing the same thing.

That makes sense. There are enough eyes on the Alpha, and this feels off. He's a distraction? Maybe. There won't be any threat from him, but it's quite likely there will be something from an unexpected angle... if it happens.

"Thank you," the Alpha broke off a small piece of bread, dipped it in salt, and gulped it down. "Your time is valuable. So is mine. I won't waste it."

"Oh, you're welcome to stay as long as you like." Don Sangue smiled, showing sharp, sharp teeth.

What IS he? Chase wondered. Some sort of undead, though it seemed impossible. The undead she'd heard of were rotting or skeletal or ghostly figures, and aside from his coloration, he seemed human. If it weren't for that aura, he could have passed as an exotic living person.

But the Alpha had finished chewing, and she glanced back toward him. "You'd like that, I suppose. You know as well as I do that the moon is calling me. Soon I'll have to hunt and kill. And the higher She rises, the louder the call." He smiled. "And the second I attack anyone in here that'll void my guest right."

"You're not wrong." Don Sangue angled his neck a fraction of an inch. "And you're obviously smart enough to know that I don't have to let you leave. So the longer this goes on, the less likely you are to walk out of here. Not that there was much of a chance of that to begin with. So..." he drummed his pale fingers against his wineglass. "Why then, are you here?"

"To offer peace."

There was a long pause. Then the table erupted in laughter, all the dons howling like the wolves they were fighting.

Even a few of the bodyguards and servants joined in, and Don Sangue himself offered a fang-filled chuckle. Eventually he waved a languid hand, and the table quieted. "If you had come to me with respect, before the Bianchi woman or the Rossi man were killed, I might have considered it. If you had arrived with this invitation before you took Dona Tarantino from us, there might still have been a chance. But now there is blood on your hands, werewolf. And that blood is one of *ours*. And I am hard-pressed to think of a reason why I should entertain this request as anything besides the lunacy it so obviously is."

"There is blood between us. But truly, was she one of you any longer?" The Alpha shifted his gaze around the table. "We found records in Dona Tarantino's house. Records and ledgers and letters. What would you say if I told you she had broken omerta?"

THAT got a response. Rumbling and discussion and whispers throughout the table, and Sangue himself opened his eyes wide, face freezing into a pale, marble-like mask.

Beside her, Chase saw Don Coltello tense up.

And a thread of worry started to grow in the back of her mind as she remembered Cagna had told her that Dona Tarantino was the only one Don Coltello associated with anymore. *This could go to a dangerous place for him... and us, by proxy. I need information.*

Chase leaned over and whispered. "Omerta. What is it?"

The old man shot her a horrified look and shook his head.

"Please! Tell me. I need to know."

CHA+1

The old man again said nothing... but he looked up to Cagna and nodded.

Cagna leaned down and whispered in her ear. "Omerta, among other things, is a vow of silence and loyalty to the famiglias. No police, no talking about business with outsiders, respect for your elders... even when you're trying to kill them. Especially when you're trying to kill them."

"Impossible," Don Sangue said, into the shocked silence, and Chase patted Cagna on the hand in thanks and went back to watching the byplay. "The vow is magically enforced. Her blood would have burned in her veins."

"You didn't think it strange she was bedridden these last few months?" the Alpha replied. "And magic cast by one person can be weakened by another. The Doge had his top wizards and enchanters on the task. I have correspondence and letters between them, that showed she was almost free of the vow. All of these missives I am willing to turn over to you... in exchange for peace and a few concessions."

And now the dons were murmuring, chatting among themselves. Chase saw more than a few lips moving soundlessly... no shortage of Grifters in this crowd, and they were checking things out for themselves, using Size Up and activating who knows what other skills. They could see just as well as she could that his charisma was probably decent but not *great*. Not good enough for him to be able to bluff his way through a lie of this magnitude. Not to Don Sangue.

And one by one, every eye moved to look at the undead thing at the head of the table.

"If what you say is true," Don Sangue replied, "we will need to investigate it. I will acknowledge that the current doge has been troublesome this last decade. If his idealism is leading him to foolishness, we may have to reassess a few matters. In light of this, I think I could perhaps offer a truce. You cease your vendetta, hand over the evidence, and stay with me as a guest for a month. At the end of it, if you speak truly, you will be released. Then, depending on your behavior, we may discuss a longer-term peace."

The Alpha nodded. "That is a generous offer. May I present a counter-offer?"

Chase frowned.

Something was off about the way he'd spoken. He'd spoken just a bit too quickly. His sincerity was a bit lacking, and there was a tension underlying his words. She wasn't the only one who had noticed that, she was sure, as the crowd muttered.

Don Sangue hadn't missed it either. He waved a pale, ringed hand, sneering at the werewolf as he did so.

The Alpha barely seemed to notice. "Our counteroffer is this: we have but one matter of vengeance left to resolve that affects you. Give us Don Coltello, let us take his possessions and estates and servants as our own, let us join you as a new famiglia, and we shall serve you loyally and well in your war against the Doge and his court."

And there it was. Chase's premonition had been right.

They think I'm his servant. So that means...

The entirety of the table turned to stare at Don Coltello, who shot to his feet. "You bastard! You stugat! You ran from me like a coward and I put your woman down, and I can put YOU down just as—"

"Massimo."

Don Sangue spoke quietly, but the word resounded through the room with such clarity that Chase thought he'd shouted for a second.

"You cannot be considering this," Don Coltello said, his face sagging, his corpulent frame sinking back into his chair, as if the world was pulling him down.

"If he has proof that Dona Tarantino betrayed us, we must investigate this. All of this. Including anyone she has had business dealings with." Don Sangue's red eyes bored into Don Coltello.

Chase licked her lips... *Don Sangue is trying to regain control of the situation. He's not as in charge here as he's pretending to be. He needs these people, even if he is a... whatever he is. This is politics.*

She looked back to the Alpha. His face was still, and he barely moved, but Chase looked over his posture, looked for the tells...

And found what she needed.

PER+1

"You're desperate!"

And only when every eye at the table turned to her, did Chase realize that she'd spoken out loud.

The Alpha sneered at her. "You're one of Don Coltello's servants, aren't you? I expect you're feeling pretty desperate yourself, right now." He took a drink of wine.

Chase inhaled, and she knew that if she stopped, if she gave in to her nerves, then it was all over. This was the best and only chance to derail the way this conversation was going. If she didn't, then there were far, far too many consequence, both for her and her friends.

"No, *you're* desperate. That's the only reason you're here. Up until now you were winning."

Muttering around the table, some irritated tones, and Chase spoke more forcefully. "You were *winning*. We—" Her tongue caught on the word. She wasn't truly one of this council. But it made sense, now that she thought of it. 'We' was appropriate here. *The more I establish myself as a part of the dons and their circle, the more they'll listen to me, here. Solidarity, and maybe they'll hesitate to throw me to the wolves. Literally.* She gathered her breath and spoke again. "We couldn't find you. You were striking out of the night, holding the city hostage, taking everyone you aimed at. You would have won eventually, if you kept on this path. So why change? Everything was going your way. Why put your head into the noose? No, you are desperate, signore, and I think I know why."

She didn't, not really. But it would buy her time to think. An accusation of the sort she had posed required a serious rebuttal, and it would take the werewolf some time to put up his counter argument. But it didn't matter what he said, because she wasn't going to listen to him anyway. Chase was going to be doing something else. She just... had... to wait...

There!

The werewolf spoke again, and all eyes turned to him. But Chase wasn't listening. Chase was mouthing words. **"Silent Activation, Foresight."**

It took three tries before she got the vision she wanted. Three tries, three frantic attempts while the pain grew in her chest, but finally, finally she had the words that got the reaction she wanted.

She came back to herself, hearing the tail end of the werewolf's speech. "—ultimately, we know this bloodshed serves no purpose. Arretzi is a profitable and convenient city, and together we can—"

"You're here because Pwner is after you!" Chase blurted out.

Your Foresight skill is now level 28!

The werewolf's head snapped back as if he'd been punched.

The chamber erupted into noise as roared as the dons started shouting. A few rose and headed for the exits, and for a second Chase was tempted to join them—

—And then a cold, unyielding hand clamped down on her shoulder with strength that rivaled the Muscle Wizaard's.

"I will have *order*." Don Sangue snarled, and she almost hurt her head as she whipped it up to stare at him. Somehow he'd gotten around the table, around all of the table in a heartbeat.

"Hey, back off—" the Muscle Wizaard said, but Chase shouted.

"It's all right! Yes sir!" Chase forced herself to pat Don Sangue's hand. "I can explain."

The Alpha said nothing, staring at her as the table slowly fell silent, and everyone took their seat again. His eyes were hard, but compared to Sangue's dead gaze, his ire was something Chase could meet without flinching. "I never got to tell the rest of the story, of what happened in the casino. A cloaked figure threw Enrico out of his office onto the casino floor when the werewolves showed up. They fought, but I noticed the figure off to one side. In the Player's area."

The Alpha blinked, and Chase saw a bead of sweat start up by his perfectly-groomed hairline.

Don Sangue's hand tightened for a second. Then it was gone from her shoulder, and his voice was friendly, almost conversational. "And then what happened?"

"One of the werewolves went to confront him. He pulled out a... my friend called it a bomb. Then he used magic to get away but left the bomb there. Then the casino blew up. I have no idea how many werewolves made it out of there. Later on, when I told Cagna about it, she identified the figure as Pwner."

The Alpha blinked. "Wait. Cagna?"

"Is this true, Cagna?" Don Coltello spoke up for the first time.

"It is," the dog-woman replied. "I didn't see him personally, but his appearance and methods match the description. If it isn't him, it's someone pretending to be him and doing a damn good job of it, which is just as bad."

"You're Cagna?" The Alpha rose from his seat. But he halted as Don Sangue raised a hand in dismissal, then pointed to Chase.

"You are certain, that he was sitting in the *player's area* of the casino?"

And now Chase saw something in the very, very back of Don Sangue's crimson eyes.

Fear.

Only a bit, but it was there.

He knows, she realized. And oh, the next thing she was going to say was going to change everything here.

But she had set this arrow in motion, launched it as if she'd shot it from a bow, and she had to follow its path regardless of where it landed. "I am sure of that. I saw it myself. Just as I saw one of the werewolves go in after—"

"Cagna is one of the names in the ledgers! It's the name of one of the Doge's infiltrators!" The Alpha blurted, and every eye turned to him.

No! Chase thought. She tried to salvage the situation, stave off what was to come. "I saw one of the werewolves go in after Pwn—"

"Cagna and Lachina are the two secret police assigned to infiltrate and bring you down!" the werewolf roared. And Chase's small voice and halven-sized lungs were no match for a loud, loud werewolf.

And then it sunk in, what he was saying, and Chase whipped around to stare at Cagna...

Cagna, who had gone back to back with Lachina, as the rest of the table glared at them and weapons began to sing free of sheaths.

The werewolf stood and stalked around the side of the table, and nobody stopped him. Even Don Sangue was silent.

He's collecting his thoughts, Chase realized. *He's got massive charisma, but his personality is such that he's not very adaptable. When he's not in control of the discussion, he goes on the defensive. This is the wrong way to handle this guy. The wrong way to defend against such outrageous lies...*

And then she glanced back to Cagna, and several pieces fell into place.

They aren't lies. They aren't lies at all.

Cagna, who had never killed anyone in Chase's sight, even when she'd been ambushed. Cagna who had disapproved of the Don's business but was working for him anyway. Cagna, who had shown nothing but ease walking through a guard station and known the signals for various things such as dignitaries arriving. Cagna whose jobs would definitely NOT support the level of perception she had.

It made sense.

Well, Chase thought as the werewolf stalked around the table and angry confused gangsters rose and followed him, *when have I ever let the truth of something slow me down?*

"You liar!" She jumped up onto the table, gaining what height she could and narrowly missing putting her foot into her soup. "You're desperate! Pwner is after you and you want to sacrifice us to slow him down! You want to kill two birds with one stone!"

The Alpha said nothing. He was sweating now, advancing on her...

...and then with an abrupt motion he twisted aside and moved toward the wall. He stopped there, and the crowd murmured, confused.

"You don't even deny it?" Chase asked...

...but he seemed to ignore her, turning and smiling. "It doesn't matter now. I did my job."

"What? What have you done?" Don Sangue said, stepping forward. "Besides bring chaos to my house?"

"Oh, we've brought more than that. Let's just say Pwner inspired us. **Wallwalker.**"

Then he whirled and threw himself back.

Back through the nearest stained glass window.

There was a pause for a long second.

"What is that fool doing?" Don Sangue asked, almost rhetorically. "He can't escape me, not here! **Wallwalker!**" And then, with a snap of his blood-red cape, he was through and after the werewolf.

But Chase didn't hear him. Chase's eyes were going wide.

Pwner had inspired him.

"We need to leave right now!" Chase shouted, hopping down and grabbing the Muscle Wizaard's hand. "Cagna, Wizaard, let's go!" She tried to drag them toward the window.

"What? Why?"

"Hold on!" said Don Coltello. "Cagna, was what he said true—"

"No time!" Chase yelled.

There was only one way that Pwner could have inspired the werewolves to deal with a high tower full of their enemies.

And then it was too late, as the first explosion went off far below, and the tower shook...

...and fell.

CHAPTER 17: THE TOWER

There was no time to think things through. There was no time to plan, no time to hesitate, no time to panic.

There was only the collapsing tower, and the mob of panicking... well...mobsters, between her and the only way out.

"Foresight!" Chase screamed and saw what she needed to do. "Bastien, run out the window! Make a path! We're playing this like the casino! Renny, get ready to fly us all! Cagna, pick me up and hang on!"

Your Foresight skill is now level 29!

The Muscle Wizaard lowered his head and charged forward, shouting **"Reckless Charge,"** as he went.

Chase's world blurred, as Cagna's arm whipped down and snatched her up. **"Always in Uniform,"** Cagna literally barked.

The halven girl clung tight, seeing Lachina hot on their heels, the two women leaping and bounding over trampled gangsters and past shocked bodyguards, seeing the first cracks appear in the walls, seeing the bricks starting to fall from the roof above...

...and then there was an upward surge, and for a second Chase was looking down on the shocked crowd...

...as the screaming cut out, and she saw the edges of the window appear and tilt, saw the walls around it...

Cagna jumped out the window. We're falling, she realized as her perspective tilted, and the starry sky appeared overhead, the moon just on the horizon.

"Renny!" Chase screamed.

"I'm trying! Stop squirm... ah!" The fox shouted in her ear. "There!"

Everything slowed.

Chase felt her hair snap downwards, felt a jerk that ripped through her entire body. Cagna grunted, and Lachina swore.

"Got you!" Renny cheered. "Uh oh. Um..."

Chase squirmed, looked around, and saw why he was panicking.

The tower wasn't coming straight down. The tower was tilting their way. Bricks showering from its exterior, metal reinforcing struts starting to rip free, mortar flying in a cloud of dust against the moon... and the darkness of the old stone, crunching directly toward the small crew of slowly falling friends.

"Oh my gods," Lachina croaked.

The tower shuddered. Then it stopped. Bricks cascaded down, and for a second Chase thought they were safe.

CREAKKKKKK....

It was a groan of old wood, stressed far beyond its tolerances.

Chase's eyes snapped to the holes in the bricks, seeing the exposed wooden ribs they were passing, the guttering flames of fallen lanterns catching old tapestries and illuminating the hole in the tower's side. She saw crossbeams popping out and crunching, giving way bit by bit.

PING! Something whipped past her, tugging at her hair, and Cagna grunted in pain. Hot liquid spattered onto Chase's neck.

A nail or something, Chase thought, and said **"Lesser Healing,"** without looking back.

You have healed Cagna for 30 points!
Your Lesser Healing skill is now level 37!

Then they were past the open wound in the tower.

"We need to fall faster!" Chase yelled. "Or get around the tower!" Her voice was lost in the wind, but Renny managed to hear her just fine.

"This is really, really hard! Hang on! **Summon Minor Elemental!"**

A tornado with eyes whirled into view a dozen meters away—

—then they were past it, falling fast, the tower whizzing by...

...another jerk, and Chase was snapped around, her teeth clacking shut, her spine screaming in agony. That *had* to have done damage, but no time to think about it. She was now facing downwards. Cagna must have lost her grip then caught her again by the waist, and that was okay.

Because now she could see the Muscle Wizaard, falling just below them, fifty feet down or so.

And beyond him, two figures running down the tower. *Running* down it as if it were a flat field, and they were having a casual footrace. Except the one in the lead was fuzzy, huge, and running on all fours, and the one behind him had a red cape snapping straight up like a falling flag. She watched breathless as below them a support gave way, and wood and stone showered out of a broken wall. The werewolf Alpha swerved and the undead followed him, and then they were around the curve of the tower and out of sight.

Then something massive rushed past Chase, so quickly that the air screamed and the little crew bobbled, and started to follow it down.

"Oh heck no!" Renny yelled, and they stabilized...

...but Chase gasped, as bodies followed it down, screaming. Bodies in suits and dresses and sparkling jewelry, flashing in the mad moonlight. And then a table fell past, the same table she'd been seated at not long ago.

"It's coming down from above! Renny, get us around the tower!"

"I'm! Trying!" The little fox shrilled at full volume.

I'm not helping, Chase realized. She watched the air elemental dart down and scoop up the Muscle Wizaard, whirling him around and around as it pulled him back to the group. Then there were a few bumps, and for a second she thought they'd been hit...

"Got us!" Renny shouted. "Oh boy. Uh... look out above!"

Chase twisted, tugging at Cagna's arm.

"Mother of Nurph!" Cagna howled, as she glanced up... and Chase caught what she was staring at.

A mass, a black mass of the tower was coming down on them. She saw stars through the holes in it, holes that were growing as the floors and walls and ceilings broke apart mid-fall, but with a sudden clarity Chase knew that it wouldn't spread out fast enough. They would be crushed.

Unless...

This. This is something I can help with.

"Foresight!" Chase shouted.

The falling mass paused, and she watched them all die. **"Foresight!"** she screamed again as soon as time resumed.

This time the outcome was different. "Take us left NOW!" Chase yelled.

They bobbed, air whipping at her, the city lights coming into view as she whirled right, and then they were gone as a chunk of brickwork screamed past.

Your Foresight skill is now level 30!

But there was no time to rest, because more debris was coming, and Chase screamed **"Foresight!"** again and again. She burned her fortune freely, spent it like water in a bath. And six skill levels later, they were around on the other side of the tower, and she blinked to see the werewolf and undead now racing the other way, hopping over windows... and straight into a huge cloud that was rising to meet them.

Dust, she realized. *Dust from the initial explosion. From the tower collapsing at the base.*

"Hold your breath!" she called and then grimaced. *I can't tell Renny which way to go if I'm holding my breath.*

But wait, I've got a skill for that, don't I? I don't have to be the one telling him to do things, if he can see it for himself...

Then she couldn't see a thing; they were in the dust, and the smell of charred chemicals filled her nose. **"Silent Activation, Influence Fate: Renny,"** Chase muttered.

Your Influence Fate skill is now level 2!

"What the heck?" she heard Renny say, then she heard a groaning and a massive SNAP.

The wooden supports, the big ones, had finally given out.

"Are you doing this?"

Chase reached over her shoulder and squeezed his nose.

"Oh, okay then! Give me another!"

Your Influence Fate skill is now level 3!

Your Influence Fate skill is now level 4!

Seconds passed by, blind seconds, with massive bits of rubble and other things falling from above. Enormous chunks falling around them, whipping the dust and smoke up, and Chase couldn't see a thing.

"Again!" Renny called.

"Silent Activation, Influence Fate: Renny," Chase mouthed.

But this time, the words that appeared made her heart sink.

Insufficient Fortune to cast that spell!

"I'm out!" Chase called then put her face into the furry crook of Cagna's elbow, scrunching her eyes shut and coughing from even the brief inhalation of fumes.

There was nothing to do but wait. Wait and hope.

A second passed. Three. Five, as they whooshed down through the cloud.

For a moment, Chase dared to hope that they'd escape. For a second, it looked like they might.

Then, everything tilted, and Chase felt Cagna's grip leave her. "No!" The dog-woman barked, and Chase was spinning, falling out of control...

"Ha! I've got us!" Renny called out.

Then it was back to the slow fall. Alone this time, holding her skirt down, Chase drifted down with Renny in her pack. She fell to her knees and put her hands on the ground the second they touched down, shaking, feeling sick to her stomach. No clue where the others were; no idea where *they* were for that matter.

She just knew that she wasn't safe, that this was the very *opposite* of safe.

The dust was thinning, she noted absent-mindedly. *I can almost see....*

KRAK!

Then a chunk of wall was right in front of her, and Chase yelped as fragments screamed and ripped past her, cutting her clothes and skin in equal measure.

Time to go!

She didn't know where. She didn't have time to examine her skills, or figure out a good strategy, or do anything beyond run and hope for the best. No time to do anything but flee and trust to her luck.

Which, fortunately, was her best attribute.

Shrieks and screams from above intermixed with crunches and cracks as stone and wood and bodies met ground in a roaring cacophony that sounded like a groaning giant, a bass moan that went on, and on, and on.

The dust thinned ahead of her and she turned toward it, turned toward what seemed like a light, hoping against hope that it was the way out, that it would lead to safety.

No place in this city is safe, the thought stuck in her head and wouldn't leave.

Then she was out. Out, and coughing, and the noise behind her was finally coming to a stop, the giant's groan dying with its occupants. More pattering, a few more creaks, and the occasional, forlorn crunch... but Chase didn't care about that. Chase sat on the ground and laughed or sobbed, she couldn't tell, and her vision filled with words, words, words.

You are now a level 10 Halven!
AGL+4
CHA+4
CON+2
DEX+4
INT+2
LUCK+4
PER+2
STR+2
WILL+2
WIS+4
COOL +5
MENTAL FORTITUDE+5

You are now a level 10 Grifter!
CHA+3
DEX+3
LUCK+3
You have learned the Feign Death skill!

Your Feign Death skill is now level 1!
You have learned the Old Buddy skill!
Your Old Buddy skill is now level 1!

You are now a level 11 Grifter!
CHA+3
DEX+3
LUCK+3

You are now a level 12 Oracle!
CHA+3
LUCK+3
WIS+3

You are now a level 13 Oracle!
CHA+3
LUCK+3
WIS+3

No, Chase realized as she squatted on all fours on the ground; no, she was laughing after all. Laughing as the energy rushed through her once more, giving that oh-so-tantalizing buzz.

"I wanted ADVENTURE!" she shouted and climbed to her feet, thankful for her shoes for the first time. The ground was littered with rubble and sharp bits and maybe some people; she didn't want to look too closely at those lumps which bled darkly in the moonlight. "And I got a halven level because I just spent the worst minute of my life regretting that CHOICE!"

Honestly that might not have been why, but Chase didn't have much time to reflect on it. Her newly-increased mental fortitude reasserted itself, and the orders of business became clear to her.

"We need to find the others. Got anything that'll help with that?"

"I'm alive..." Renny whispered.

"Yeah. We need to check on the others. Got anything to help, there?"

"Yes! Yes I do. And now that we're not falling, manipulating this air should be easier... oh, and let's have a **Phantasm**, because it's kinda dark out."

The dust peeled back, as Renny hopped up out of the pack and onto her shoulder, waving his paws. Lanterns with wings appeared all around them, pushing back the darkness.

The still lumps on the ground *were* bodies, and Chase stared at them, acknowledging them and not feeling a thing. She remembered once how the sight of dead people made her vomit. Now? Now after all that had occurred, it didn't faze her. Now she searched them, and the only emotion in her heart was concern... concern that the people she'd cared about in that tower had made it out okay.

As it turned out, she had to settle for two out of three.

The Muscle Wizaard found them, dust caking his beard, robe torn and tattered as he staggered out of the darkness. Metal gleamed on his silver knuckles as he shook his head. "I hope that's you! My spectacles are quite gone and my eyes aren't what they used to be."

"It is. Have you seen Cagna and Lachina?"

"Oh. Yes. Yes I have." His tone told her all she needed to know.

Something had gone wrong.

They found Cagna by a large chunk of bricks, holding Lachina's arm. Just her arm. That was all that was sticking out of the masonry.

The dog-woman wasn't crying. She wasn't making any noise at all. She just sat there, occupying space, and holding Lachina's hand.

Chase's nose twitched. She stared up at the gutted shell of the tower, and the bits still falling off it, now and then. They were not out of danger, by no means were they out of danger. But...

No.

Cagna needed this.

So Chase moved up next to the woman, reached up to her shoulder, and rested her small hand on the dog-woman's sleeve. Then she quietly got to work healing her friends, until they were full up again.

It was hard to say how long the moment lasted. She was distantly aware of yelling from the city, alarm bells ringing, as Arretzi woke to its danger. The tower was far enough back from the rest of the district that it would take some time for anyone to reach them, but Chase had no doubt they'd have visitors in due time.

"What the Alpha said was true, wasn't it?" Chase asked. She hated to do it, hated to break the silence, to pressure the mourning figure next to her. She hated to do it... but she had to. Time waited for neither, halven nor beastkin alike. Only the gods were above it all, and even then only to a point.

"Yes," Cagna said. "We were working a long-term operation. Just bad luck that the werewolf stuff came up when it did. Just her bad luck. Again." Cagna's muzzle lowered. "Orcs never have luck that isn't bad luck."

"You come to my table," a cold voice spoke from the darkness, and Cagna bolted upright, throwing Chase's hand off as she twisted.

"You damned bloodsucker," Cagna snarled.

"You come to my table..." Don Sangue said, striding out of the shadows, his cape gone, his fine clothes torn by debris, and covered in gray dust. "You come to my table under false pretenses, and you plot against me. These are not the actions of a guest."

Old Chase would have quailed in fear.

New Chase had just survived falling down his godsdamned tower and knew that hesitation would get her friend killed.

"Don Sangue!" she said, stepping between Cagna and the undead. "It is a moot point, now. You have no more table. And we are not the ones who took it from you."

The man paused, and Chase marveled at how... untouched he looked. His skin was unmarred; his hair was still an oily black. And his red, red eyes bored into her.

The pressure was still there; the fear still gripped her heart... but Chase found it easier to speak, easier to push it aside, for now. "Regardless of what she's done, it's really a moot point, isn't it? If you lived, then your enemy lived. Your TRUE enemy. And MINE as well."

"Ours," Cagna rasped. "The Doge wants the werewolves put down. That is more important to him than my department's own goals."

Chase risked a glance. The dog-woman's ears were back, her fur was in hackles, and her hand was on her sword...

...but her eyes were human. And they were weary. Weary and sad.

She'll fight if she has to, but she realizes that it wouldn't help matters. She sees it as I do, Chase mused.

When she looked back, Sangue was there, towering over her, inches away. The Muscle Wizaard cried out in shock.

"I could kill all three of you without much effort at all," Don Sangue said. "What do I care that your enemies are mine? What help do you think I need here?"

Chase swallowed. "And yet you worked with people a whole lot less competent than us, to try and stop the werewolves. If you COULD do it alone, you wouldn't have bothered with the famiglias."

"You think yourself more competent than they were?" The undead raised a thin eyebrow.

Chase looked back at the tower and swept an arm around, gesturing at the field of bodies. "We're alive. They aren't."

"That is easily fixed," A voice growled from the darkness.

"Uh-oh," Renny whispered in her ear, as Chase stared at the hulking, furry shapes moving out of the shadows.

The Alpha stepped forward, clothes in tatters, holding the rapier that Chase had seen so long ago. The squat werewolf was next to him, cracking his knuckles... and glaring at Sangue with green glowing eyes.

"You!" Sangue hissed.

"Me." The Alpha growled. "Take the beastkin alive. Kill Sangue, and the rest of them."

"Not a chance!" The Muscle Wizaard roared. **"Flex! Strong Pose! Signature Move, You Shall Not Pass!"**

But the Alpha shook his head. "You've pulled that one on us before, big man. Did you think we were *fools?"* He snarled the last word and flourished his rapier. "We're already behind you!"

Chase whirled, as forms bolted from the darkness...

...and then Cagna's arm was around her again, hurling her in between the dog-woman and the Wrestler, tossing the halven like a sack of potatoes. Chase watched, dazed, as Cagna pulled something from under her cloak...

BLAM!

Some contraption of wood and metal exploded in her hand with a flash and a puff of smoke, and one of the werewolves fell. **"Stand Down!"** Cagna yelled, and another hesitated... but then three more were rushing in, and Cagna swore and drew her blade. **"Always in Uniform!"**

"Time to **Let My Muscles Do The Talking!"** The Muscle Wizaard roared, and Chase shot her head around in time to see a charging werewolf meet a silver-knuckled fist. He flew backward with a yelp, leaving a trail of smoke and an odor of burnt fur behind him. "Aw yeah! Whatcha gonna do, furballs? Whatcha gonna DO!"

They're doing it again, Chase realized. *Sending the extras, sending the lower-trained ones in to keep us busy while the Alpha and the short one kill Sangue.*

Do they have a chance?

She stood up and turned, but time was at a premium, and she didn't have—

No.

No, wait. I have ALL the time I want. In ten-second chunks, anyway. **"Foresight,"** Chase said, and instead of examining a course of action, she used the still time to take stock of the battlefield.

There's probably a Tier Two job in this somehow, she said, finally realizing some of the more martial applications. *Combine it with a fighting type job, and it's something like Time Warrior, or Chrono General, or something of the sort.*

But that was a musing for another time.

With a few seconds left on the spell's duration, she saw Don Sangue. He and the Alpha were caught mid-stride and mid-strike, far from their starting position. They were both fast, and both looked like they knew what they were doing, so that left...

She found the squat werewolf just as the Foresight's grace period expired.

Fortunately, it was easy to synch up with her vision, this time. She turned, hearing Renny mutter words behind her, hearing the air elemental come down and smash into the ones trying to take down Cagna. But she didn't spare that much attention.

She was too busy watching the squat werewolf pull out a big pack and start tossing down flowerpots.

It was a surreal moment. The blurred figures of the Don and the Alpha were silhouetted against the moon, fighting along a fallen support beam of the tower, while the Muscle Wizaard's grunts blended into the snarls and growls of his opponents, and Cagna's blade whistled behind Chase and left yelps and sizzling noises in its wake. And here the player, the most dangerous werewolf on the field, was throwing what had to be flowerpots around. Yes, those were flowerpots, complete with random flowers poking out of them.

Then, the werewolf spoke and Chase understood why. **"Call Vines. Call Thorns."**

A mass of twisting, writhing vegetation burst up, thorns lengthening in the flickering illusory torchlight. Lengthening into stakes.

Wood allergies, Chase remembered absently, as the mass obscured the place where the Don and the Alpha fought. *Don Sangue is vulnerable to wood. Does this count?*

The Don screamed.

Well, that answers that, Chase thought. She licked her lips.

"Chase! They need healing!"

Renny's cry interrupted her, and she gasped.

There were a LOT more werewolves this time around.

And unlike the fight in the casino, they weren't holding back.

There was no time to watch the most powerful creatures on the battlefield duke it out. There was only time to keep her friends alive...

And it was damned hard.

"There's too many!" Renny said, as his elemental shrieked and died. He threw blasts of wind at werewolves, knocking them around, and caught a moment to say, **"Minor Elemental!"** A new whirlwind roared to life... and got tag-teamed by two werewolves. "They heal as fast as I hurt them!"

"Keep! Them! Busy!" Cagna snarled back, blade flashing, cloak over one arm as a makeshift shield. But blood ran down her legs, dripping around her boots, blood from where claws had caught her, time and again. The Alpha had wanted her alive, but the moon was full, and the beasts were out to play...

And the Muscle Wizaard...

Oh, Bastien, poor Bastien, Chase's breath caught in her throat. Where Cagna was dripping blood, the Muscle Wizaard was a river. She watched as a werewolf lunged in and clamped jaws on his side. The Muscle Wizaard bellowed, dropped to one knee, clenched his hands together, and slammed the werewolf's neck into his knee with a brutal double-punch. But the werewolf's jaws still tore a hunk of meat from him, and Chase frantically threw Lesser Healings at him, trying to keep him alive. Then a few Foresights, to shout directions... but the more she used it, the more she realized it was like trying to plug up a failing dam with her bare hands.

We're losing, she realized. *And this time I don't have the fortune from Enrico's Ante Up trick. There's just too many, and they heal too fast. We don't have enough silver weaponry...*

Or do we?

Chase's hands crept downward, and found the cool, thin cards tucked into her pocket, and pulled out Enrico's last hand. Silver gleamed in the torchlight, and she took a breath. "I have another job! And plenty of stamina for *all* of you!" she shouted, and to her surprise, the ones nearest her paused. Then they jumped back, as she shouted, **"Rapid Fire! Razor Card!"**

Silver cards flew and danced, and werewolves staggered back as she unleashed a one-woman barrage. Each card split into two as it sang through the air, and those that hit sliced through fur with hideous sharpness.

Your Razor Arrow skill is now level 2!

For a second, she thought that they could win this. For a second, Chase dared to hope. The lights in the distance were coming closer, the city taking notice of the ruckus or coming to investigate the fallen tower, she couldn't say. But whistles were sounding, and the constables would be here, before long. All they had to do was hold out. And though Chase was burning through her stamina, it was working... she wasn't killing them, but she was driving them back, and it was working...

...and then Don Sangue shrieked.

Everyone paused and looked up to the mass of thorns and vines.

The Don writhed there, hanging from hundreds of thorns, blood dripping down from him like the world's most macabre lawn sprinkler. He twitched, one last time, and was still.

And then the Alpha turned to *her*. "What is it you say, dear?"

"Geek the mage!" Roared the squat werewolf.

"Bastien!" Cagna shouted. "Plan Gimli!"

"What?" Chase asked, confused.

"Do it!" Renny hopped out of her pack. "We'll be fine, we've got this!" he reassured Chase.

"I don't understand," Chase said, pausing in mid-throw...

...and then the Muscle Wizaard scooped her up one-handed and threw her.

Sailing out beyond the torches, sailing into the black, Chase gulped and dropped her cards and tucked herself into a ball. She heard the Wizaard yell one last time, voice fading behind her...

"I hate to do this! But you asked for it! **Rage!** RAAAAAGGGGHHHH!"

"Phantasm!" Renny shouted, and the torches disappeared, replaced by a cloud of evil-looking green smoke. She heard a whole lot of werewolves yell... and then the sounds of the furry mob vomiting filled the night air, even drowning out the shouts and alarms and whistles approaching from the rest of the city.

Then she struck the ground, and everything went black... for a second. Maybe? It was hard to tell.

CON+1

Everything spun, and she got to her feet and used a bit of what sanity she had left to heal herself. "Score another point for the armor," she muttered, brushing herself off. Bruised, yeah. Broken, no." Then she narrowed her eyes and stared at the cloud. "Those jerks! They planned this!" Chase took off running, heading back to the fight, halven instincts momentarily deserting her...

...up until the point that a figure stepped out of the shadows of the rubble.

A fuzzy figure.

The smallest werewolf she'd seen yet, barely twice her height. Chase's mind flashed back to the halven-sized knife, and she gasped.

...and somehow that sound drew his attention, as red eyes turned her way.

Chase turned to run, but it was on her in seconds, grabbing her shoulder and spinning her around. Its breath was hot and foul on her face, and Chase had nothing, had spent her energy in the fight; he had her dead to rights...

"Berrymore?"

It took her a second to realize that the creature's growl was a word. She squeaked.

"Chase Berrymore?" it asked again and released her.

"What?" She said. "Yes, I'm... who are... wait, hold on, how do you know me?"

The werewolf just stared at her, then it looked back at the city, and the roiling cloud. "No time. Where is the skin?"

"What?"

"Where is it? The skin! She needs the skin!"

"I don't... I don't know what skin you're talking about," Chase said. "Please, just tell me, who are you?"

But then he was gone, loping off into the darkness, and his final words rang back to her. "Leave the city! Don't come back!"

Chase slumped to her knees, exhausted...

...at least until the words roused her once more, driving past exhaustion, revitalizing her weary muscles and tattered mind.

You are now a level 6 Archer!
DEX+3
PER+3
STR+3

You are now a level 7 Archer!
DEX+3
PER+3
STR+3

With entirely too many questions and dread in her heart, Chase headed back into the darkness to save her friends.

CHAPTER 18: CSI ARRETZI

"You think this'll work?" Cagna rasped.

"Only one way to find out." Chase said, reaching into her dress and pulling out the miraculously-intact jar of earthworms. A second later she had one hand plunged down into the slimy wrigglers and the other clutching tight in Cagna's gloved grip. **"Absorb Condition."**

You have been afflicted with Curse of Lycanthropy! (5:36)
"Transfer Condition."
You are no longer afflicted with Curse of Lycanthropy! (5:36)
Your Transfer Condition skill is now level 9!

One of the earthworms twisted frantically under her hand, as Cagna breathed a sigh of relief.

"Did it work?" Bastien asked, from his corner.

"Yes," Chase said, giving Cagna's hand one last squeeze before heading over to him. "The worms sure don't like it, though."

"I'd recommend killing them before the moon rises tonight, just in case," Cagna said. "I don't know what lycanthropy does to earthworms and I don't want to know."

"It's probably time for a fresh batch," Chase agreed, taking Bastien's massive hand and working her magic. **"Absorb Condition. Transfer Condition."**

You have been afflicted with Curse of Lycanthropy! (5:33)
You are no longer afflicted with Curse of Lycanthropy! (5:33)

"Thank you," The Muscle Wizaard said, giving her a hug. "Coming so close on the heels of my rage, it was... harsh. I've spent a long time learning to master my anger. This was stress I didn't need."

"So. Berserker, then?" Cagna asked.

"I had a misspent youth. But it was one pillar of my true vocation.

Combined with the Model job, it led to Wrestler, and that changed my life!"

"Wait," Cagna asked, surprised humor just underneath her words. "Model?"

While the others discussed the ins and outs of proper self-care and muscle maintenance, Chase studied Cagna's safehouse.

It wasn't much.

It had taken them about ten minutes to reach it from the slums, after mutually agreeing that heading back to the villa would be unwise. And now that her cover was blown, Cagna had offered up this place as a probably-safe compromise.

The crumbling tenement hadn't looked like much from the outside, but once inside...

...well, it still hadn't looked like much. Shouts and thumps echoed through the building on their way up through the cramped halls and past the slumped forms of vagrants and drunkards. But the apartment had a thick door with many locks; the windows had bars, and the walls were lined with cork that muffled the sounds from outside. "It also keeps us from being overheard by the neighbors," Cagna explained, sweeping a mess of papers and dirty clothes from a table with casual disregard for cleanliness that made Chase wince.

Chase picked up a box full of circular pastries that looked to be days old, hesitated, then took one and munched as she tried to ignore the smell of smokeweed and the flaking plaster that occasionally fell from the ceiling. *At least there aren't any bugs,* she told herself.

And the pastry *was* kind of good, if a bit sugary and stale.

Ten minutes later, after everyone was un-lycanthroped, Chase sat in a circle with the others. Renny had just finished clean-and-pressing every bit of furniture in the cramped apartment, so it was probably as safe as it could get. "Well," the halven broke the silence, taking off her headscarf and flexing her ears. "That could have gone better."

Cagna just looked away.

"I'm sorry for your loss," Chase said. "If you want to sleep on it, take a rest before we talk this over, that's okay. We can do that."

"No," Cagna said. "No, I won't get any sleep tonight. There's no sense in trying. We should move on and deal with the mission. That's what she would want me to do."

But her voice was raw, hiding pain. Chase knew that pushing ran the risk of breaking her. So she ignored the immediate, more serious topics, and moved on to something that might ease her friend a bit. "All right. So... Plan Gimli? Seriously?"

Cagna and Bastien laughed simultaneously, Renny joining in a second later. The little fox spoke up."We talked about tactics earlier. You're the squishiest of us all. But tough enough to survive being thrown, and lucky enough you probably wouldn't land anywhere bad. And you've got that hat that can make people ignore you, so you'd be safe once you were out of their direct attention."

"Ah. Right. The hat." Chase coughed. She had totally forgotten about that, earlier.

Fortunately, Renny didn't notice her embarrassment as he continued on. "I can make illusionary barf-clouds, but they're hard on anyone who doesn't have much constitution. It might have knocked you out."

"True..." Chase admitted, wincing. Her constitution *was* a problem.

"We decided to combine our strengths!" Bastien said. "And werewolves have sensitive noses, so..."

"Like me and Renny, they can turn that off, sort of," Cagna said. "But they weren't expecting it, so it bought us time to get out of there, and with their noses turned off their chances of tracking us were bad. Renny's illusions did the rest."

"Not that they had much time to chase us, since the guards were almost there." Bastien shrugged. "I am sorry for throwing you without warning, but they wanted you dead, and I wasn't sure if we could stop them."

"I guess it makes sense. I'd like to be invited to the next tactics talk though," Chase said. "I'm okay with being handled like that if I expect it."

"Fair enough," Cagna shrugged. "So. The famiglias are effectively dead. Don Sangue, the old terror of the underworld, is finally gone. We failed, and now they'll have a clear shot at the last of their targets. We *failed*."

"Not completely," Bastien pointed out. "They wanted to take you alive, for gods know why. They didn't get that, at least."

"That's an oddity," Chase mused. "I... I'm starting to think that they're not after vengeance after all. Or maybe they are, but it's secondary to what they're really after. I got a clue, but..." she sighed. "But it just raised more questions."

Cagna considered her. "Everything's a jumble? You've got facts and clues and no way to put them together?"

"Pretty much. Or I'll have a way, but maybe not in time, or..." Chase shook her head. "It's difficult to explain."

"No. It's a mystery. And you're in luck. See, I'm not actually a Highwayman. That was just my Undercover identity."

"Your what now?"

"I'm a Detective. We get skills related to policing and solving mysteries." Cagna went to what Chase had taken to be a screen and twisted it, revolving a central square on wooden supports.

It was a corkboard, and Cagna rummaged around in a nearby cupboard and pulled out a set of metal pins, small pieces of parchment, and bits of yarn. **"Tackboard,"** she said.

Nothing seemed to happen. Bastien, Renny, and Chase shared a look between them.

"It's more subtle than that," Cagna said. "Basically you talk about clues, and the board helps connect them, put them into context. It's annoyingly vague at times, and if you're completely off base it'll try to connect the wrong things, but it's good for sifting through and separating assumptions from facts."

"Like a fortuna reading!" Chase said, eyes wide.

"Bah, it's much better than that mystical crap."

"That mystical crap got me through some pretty bad things, in the past," Chase pointed out. "And it saved me from a shallow grave when Don Coltello wanted me dead for passing Fool's Gold."

"What?" The Muscle Wizaard stared at her.

"I was framed. Long story. Gah, Tom, you idiot..." Chase rubbed her face. "I'll worry about that later. Okay, so how does it work?"

"Well, this case is about werewolves. So let's start at the beginning." Cagna held up a piece of parchment. "The werewolf murders fifteen years ago."

The parchment disappeared from her hand, and popped onto the board, up top with a soft "whump." Now it showed a pair of cartoon werewolves killing stick figures.

"Ha! Neat trick!" Bastien said.

But Renny was studying the figures.

"There's two werewolves. Was that all there were?"

"All we ever found," Cagna said. "The Alpha and her mate."

She held up pieces of paper as she spoke, and they flickered to the board, showing a werewolf stick figure with exaggerated hips and round circles for breasts, and a charcoal sketch of the Alpha's face, looking sinister. Tacks and yarn appeared at the board, connecting between the three pictures, forming a small triangle.

Then a red X, almost bloody, slashed itself over the female werewolf's note.

"That's... an odd difference," Chase said looking from the crude art of the stick figure to the well-done drawing of the current Alpha.

"I've personally seen the male. I never saw the female. Nobody ever figured out what she looked like when she wasn't a werewolf." Cagna shrugged. "The tackboard pulls from the collected experiences of everyone in the room while we talk this over. It's not a god's eye view or anything."

"I can maybe help with that later," Chase said. "You bring the logical; I'll bring the mystical. But let's keep going this is working out."

"All right. So the next part is the group that went out and hunted the werewolves. A mix of the city's elite and its best killers in the underworld." One by one, the parchment flickered, and one by one, charcoal portraits appeared on the board, with names in neat letters under their faces. Sonora Bianchi. Don Coltello. Enrico Rossi. Don Sangue. Dona Tarantino. Maddalena Verde.

"That's one short of a full party," Renny noted. "Are you sure there's not one more hunter who never got named?"

"Positive," Cagna said. "We investigated this angle. Sonora was a paladin, and she insisted her horse be in the party to benefit from the buffs. And no, before you ask, the horse died a few years back so he's safe from potential furry vengeance. In fact, there's only one target left." Red X's scrawled themselves over every one of the hunters, save for the stern-looking woman that was Maddalena Verde.

"Wait." Chase said, squinting at the tackboard. "We need a new note. Call it... the new werewolf murders."

"All right." Cagna complied, and the new note whumped onto the board and started connecting itself to the hunting party.

"I see where you're going with this," Cagna said, after studying it a second. "These are vengeance kills, and then you've got the bystander kills." New notes appeared. One showed Friatta Castillo, the leatherworker's daughter.

There were other faces there, but Chase ignored them and stretched up to tap the board under Friatta. "This one. The small werewolf killed Friatta."

"Small werewolf?"

"Enrico Rossi said that three of them attacked his compound. The over-muscled one, the Alpha, and a tiny werewolf."

"Oh, right, the thing with the knife. You're sure that's a valid clue?"

"It is," Chase said, as the paper disappeared and reappeared on the board, putting the squat werewolf and the tiny one next to the Alpha. They got lines to Enrico, and the tiny one got his own yarn strand all the way over to the leatherworker. "In fact, I ran into him, after you threw me."

"What?" Cagna stared at Chase, and Bastien and Renny whipped around to face her so quickly she thought they'd given themselves whiplash for a second.

Chase described the meeting, and at the end of her story, there were two new posts on the board. One smiling portrait of herself, and a post that read simply 'Skin?'

"That." Chase said, tapping it. "That's a really strong suggestion that this isn't about vengeance at all. This is something else entirely."

"I'm more interested in knowing how the little werewolf recognized you. He might have heard your first name, if he's spying on Don Coltello. But Berrymore is your last name, yeah?" she frowned. "He might be a Scout. Could have read it off your status screen."

"No." Chase said, although something about Cagna's statement sparked in the back of her mind and she wasn't sure why. "He was going to bite my face off. Then he recognized me and stopped. That's the only reason I'm alive right now. I'm sure of it! And he told me to leave afterward... he cared. For some reason he cared."

"Halven solidarity, maybe?" Cagna asked.

Chase snorted. "When we're done, remind me to tell you about Jooger Hunnybudger and how he killed off the honey business in Bothernot forever. Trust me, halvens can be just as nasty to each other as humans. No, he *knew* me. I'll sleep on it. It'll come to me later, I'm sure. I don't know THAT many halvens, really. Process of elimination will sort it out."

"The skin..." The Muscle Wizaard said, tapping his chin. They looked at him, and saw his eyes widen. "I just got an intelligence boost! One step closer to true wizardry, oooh yeah!"

"What did you think of?" Chase asked. "That means it's probably important. Share, please!"

"There's a legend where I grew up, about Loup Garous. They're like werewolves... okay, they're pretty much werewolves. Only instead of turning into one after being bitten, they skin a wolf. Then they skin themselves. Then they put the wolfskin off, and boom! You've got a loup garou."

Another whump, and a note entitled 'loup garou myth?' tacked itself above 'Skin?'

Chase took a breath and frowned at the two of them... and then her eyes went wide. "Don Coltello had the old alpha skinned. And he put her skin on his wall. He bragged about this when I first met him." *I still have the female's skin on the wall!* The old man's voice resounded, in the chambers of her mind.

Instantly a line of yarn snapped between 'Skin?' and Don Coltello. And the question mark vanished with a popping sound, she was pleased to notice.

And another thing occurred to her. "She *needs* the skin," Chase said. "That's what the halven werewolf said to me. She. SHE needs the skin."

The yarn snapped to the deceased Alpha werewolf... and the red X undid itself.

Of course it did, Chase nodded.

"What the hell?" Cagna barked. "She's dead!"

"No. No, she's not. She's like Pwner." Chase said, as the cloaked assassin's picture snapped onto the board, and yarn connected them. "She's a *player.* And only one other werewolf has been confirmed as a player, so far...."

The squat werewolf disappeared from the board and took the place of the old werewolf alpha. The yarn reconnected itself along new lines accordingly.

"What?" Cagna stared at her, uncomprehending.

"This is going to take some time. Do you have anything to drink?"

Cagna retrieved some sort of bitter stuff that was like tea only nastier, but did the job of keeping Chase awake as she talked and related the story of Bothernot, the secret prison, and the immortal demigods who walked among the unknowing mortals of the world.

That necessitated explaining the Camerlengo's role in things and how Chase was... technically probably a fugitive from whatever conspiracy the baroness was involved in.

One by one the players she'd met snapped onto the tackboard below the Camerlengo...

...and at the last one, the Muscle Wizaard gave a bellow and shot to his feet. "Thomasi? You know Thomasi?"

"Yes!" Chase jumped up, surprised beyond reason. "Wait, you know him too?" She slapped her forehead. "Your wagon is the same color and make as his! He made that wagon for you, didn't he?"

"Yes! So long ago... Back when I was in his circus, with everyone else. He was the only one I knew who could go into player's areas in the casinos. Not that he did that all that often, just when he wanted to get people's attention."

"How was he, overall?" Chase asked. "Was he a good man?"

"The best! He looked after us, cared for us, made sure we had nothing but good opportunities and the best venues." Bastien sighed. "After he disappeared it all turned to merde. It was like everybody had forgotten our name, and people started charging us more for supplies and taxes, for no real reason."

His curses are obscurity and poverty, Chase remembered. She would *really* have to sort this out with him at the earliest opportunity. When they weren't on the run and fighting werewolves. "Wait. He disappeared?"

"Just up and gone, one night." The Muscle Wizaard shrugged. "Along with most of the wagons and horses and all. For a while we thought he had betrayed us... He had this trick where he could miniaturize the wagons, you see. But now... now I don't think he did. I think he got taken. We were on the border of Ferrari at the time. I think your Camerlengo or her people came and grabbed him."

"This is above my paygrade," Cagna shook her head. "And now the Camerlengo's here... and Coltello had Thomasi."

"Until he didn't. Thomasi stole something from him and ran. Thomasi stole something that Don Coltello thought was worthless." Chase said...

...and a line of yarn ran between Thomasi and the skin.

"That's an assumption," Cagna said.

"How can we confirm it?" Chase asked.

"Well, we could go to the Don's house, but we risk running into werewolves." Cagna rubbed her muzzle. "If I'd only had time to talk to Lachina. Gods, she could have..." Cagna cleared her throat, as her voice wobbled.

Chase took a breath. "We can. If you're up for it."

"What? How... ah. Oh. That."

"That," Chase said. "Got any candles? And you don't have to do this, if you don't want to."

The dog-woman was quiet for a long moment. "No. Let's do this. At the very least I can properly say goodbye."

It took a few minutes to hunt down candles in the clutter.

It took another few minutes to call up Lachina.

Your Séance skill is now level 3!

At Cagna's request they went into the cramped bedroom of the apartment, giving her privacy. Only when she knocked on the door, did they come back in.

"It was the skin," Cagna said, sagging in her chair, staring at the floor.

"So. All this..." Chase said, thinking. "This isn't about vengeance. Or vengeance is secondary. And Tom figured that out, somehow. Tom grabbed the skin, but why? To try and protect the Don?"

"More likely to protect YOU," Cagna said, and yarn snapped into place between Chase and Thomasi. "Pretty sure if he was as good a man as Bastien says, he wouldn't give a toss about the Don."

"He was... is," Bastien confirmed. "He had no love for the wicked. I'm fairly sure he cheated many of them, as we traveled."

"Except... both of them are players," Chase pointed out, and lines snapped over to the old alpha and Pwner. "He's helped players before, even evil ones. He could be trying to give her the skin, for... for whatever player reasons he has."

A line stretched from all three of the players on the board and snapped into a large note that just said "?"

"Ouch. That's a bad one, I've seen it before. It means that anything we figure out along these lines is going to be conjecture."

Chase rubbed her eyes. It felt like they'd been at it for hours. "This eats sanity, doesn't it?"

"Yep. Hence why we're drinking coffee. That restores it."

"Oh, I hadn't even noticed." Chase glanced at her cup with new respect. "Still tastes like a butt."

"How do you know what a butt tastes like?" Renny asked.

"Anyway!" Chase said, shaking her head. "New line of thought. There's one survivor from the original hunting party."

"But vengeance isn't necessarily the goal," Bastien said.

"Right. It's the skin. Or the skin's a bigger goal, anyway," Chase realized. "They didn't just want Don Coltello, they wanted his estates and people. They wanted to check for the skin without anyone knowing they were doing that... and that would explain why they were holding back at Enrico's place and why the little one wasn't there! He's stealthy! Odds are he was casing the casino, and looking for it while the others dealt with the Gambler."

"That's a hell of an assumption," Cagna said. "Actually a bunch of assumptions."

The yarn crawled across the board, and the 'Skin' note shifted into a central position. "Yes, but..." Chase said, and grinned as a line stretched up to Friatta Costello. "It explains the leatherworker's daughter. He did exotic, even magical stuff for shady clients. What do you want to bet he's the one who skinned the werewolf for the Don fifteen years ago?"

"I could check that," Cagna said. "Wouldn't be hard to run down in the morning."

"If that's the case..." Renny said and floated up in midair to poke one plush paw at Maddalena Verde. "If that's the case, then they will want to check through her stuff."

"And she's throwing a party tomorrow night," Chase said. She grinned, in that wide, wide way that was disconcerting to humans. "The werewolves won't miss this opportunity to look for the skin, even if it's an obvious trap for them. Fortunately we're invited, thanks to Giuseppe and his...dwarven... mistress..." Chase's voice slowed as pieces snapped into place, mind blazing with fire, as she saw the full scope of it.

"Tollen Wheadle. The halven werewolf is Tollen Wheadle! And that means I just figured out a very important thing," Chase whispered.

Portraits whumped into view on the tackboard, and everyone gasped, as they stared at it.

"No way," Cagna whispered. "Clever, clever girl."

CHAPTER 19: PARTY PLANNER

The carriage rattled through the cold streets, past the mobs gathered in the deepening twilight. Past broken glass windows, past charred buildings, past the guard patrols that watched every intersection.

Arretzi was at its breaking point. It had gone over last night but recovered... another one like that and it might be lost forever. Desperate and under siege, the mood was... murdery, Chase thought. It had had *enough* of werewolves.

She couldn't blame them. She was hitting her breaking point there, too.

Tonight, she told herself. *Tonight this will all be over. One way or another.*

The carriage slowed, and Bastien tensed. Renny squirmed around her neck, where he was playing the part of a fox-fur stole, thanks to some creative sewing and a minor illusion. Chase's hand slid down to the silvered cards in her pocket... the few remaining now, after the showdown last night.

Then three knocks resounded on the door, followed by two quick taps. They relaxed, as Cagna opened the carriage door and took a seat. She wore a loose robe that covered her from head to foot and wrappings over her muzzle.

It was dangerous to look canine tonight.

"Good news and bad," Cagna said.

"Good news first," Chase said. The mood of the city had infected her, and this could be the medicine she needed to find her heart again.

"The guard knows where the explosives came from and has figured out how they got into the tower. An alchemist's guild laboratory was robbed after the casino blew up, and they think just about everything the werewolves took went into the old tower's detonation." She pulled her muzzle free of the bandages. "Along with some stuff that wasn't explosives at all. Apparently they just piled everything they got up in there and set it on fire."

"How did they get past the guards?" Bastien asked. "That was good security, last night."

"See, the old tower used to have tunnels that connected to the other fortifications that were around it. Those fortifications are gone, but there were some tunnels still intact, evidently. And since we know that the Alpha... the male Alpha... is a top-tier Burglar, that's something he could have found and gotten into. Walked them right back to the tower." She snorted. "It wouldn't surprise me if Sangue had left a few of them open as escape routes. Sealed his own fate with his paranoia."

"Fate's more flexible than people think," Chase said, checking over her props and tools. "The visions showed me that."

She'd spent the day binging visions and trying the cards, but nothing had been certain. The critical success of her initial Short Vision hadn't been repeated. She'd gain some skill levels out of it, but the future was still troubled. "There are just too many ways that things could fall out, here." Chase said, into the silence of the carriage. "I've got two, maybe three linchpins identified. Three things I really need to try at this party. Beyond that, we'll see how everyone else reacts and adapt on the fly." Chase nodded, more to herself than anyone else. "Okay. You had bad news as well?"

"The guard can't give us any backing," Cagna said. "The second I brought up players, the chief shut me down and told me to stop talking about that."

"I was afraid of that," Chase said. "It *is* a conspiracy."

"Yeah. He said that it's being worked at higher levels and if I got involved it would end my career, or worse. He also told me that it's taking everything they have to hold the city together. And that's *with* the Doge's personal guard and household backing them up."

"This is a chance to end the problem at the source, and he can't help?" Chase asked. She'd expected something like this, but it had cost nothing to ask, and there had been the possibility that they might get support.

"Well... that's the third problem." Cagna sighed. "They have no jurisdiction on the Verde estate. It's city law that the nobles take care of their own law enforcement. They can't go breaking the law, but the polizia aren't welcome without express permission. And since Maddalena's obviously rigging this trap with her own forces, I don't think we'd get it." Cagna's nose wrinkled. "Honestly, if I weren't going there on my own business, rather than guard business, I'd be breaking my code of chivalry. And now is a *bad* time to be without defenses. Fortunately I found a loophole. I'm off duty right now. Chief approved my leave slip."

"I'm going to pretend to know what that means, but honestly I'm just glad you're with us." Chase reached across the carriage and patted Cagna's hand. For the first time since she'd met the dog-woman, her hand was bare and gloveless. It was covered with short, dark-brown fur that made it seem bigger than the flesh beneath.

Cagna caught Chase's hand and gave it a squeeze. "This is my chance to get Lachina some payback. She'd want it this way."

"All right. Just... remember the plan. Such that it is," Chase said, squeezing Cagna's hand back. "We don't want a fight here. This is not the best place to bring things to a head, not with one side trying to spring a trap, and the other side expecting a trap. The honest truth of it is..." Chase bit her lip. "The honest truth of it is that there are players on the field. The ones I dealt with had ludicrous amounts of power and weren't afraid to use it. Even Thomasi... especially Thomasi, now that I think of it, all of them are dangerous in ways that we can't match. And they have our number, now. They know a lot of our tricks and limitations. If it comes to a straight-up fight again, we'll lose."

"So we have to make it not a fight. Not a physical fight anyway," Renny said, keeping his voice low so he didn't shout in her ear.

"Right. And the best way to do that is with misdirection." She looked over at the Muscle Wizaard, and the duffel bag he held on his lap. "You've got the most important part of this plan, really. If you've got any questions, now's the time."

He shook his head, the new spectacles on his nose flashing in the light of the setting sun. "I just hope it's worth the money we spent on these. The enchantments sure weren't cheap! Even minor magic is expensive magic."

Chase shrugged. "Now that I know casinos exist all over, gold isn't a big deal. I can get more of it." It was a shock to admit that, but it was true. "Or I can get it some other way. Heck, one of my jobs is kind of geared toward..." she glanced over at Cagna, and caught herself. "...my job is geared toward getting us through tonight. So let's get this straight, you're actually a Scout?" she asked Cagna.

"Yep. Not a bandit. Scout, Knight, and Detective are all the jobs I've got." The dog-woman confirmed. "My task is to cover the Muscle Wizaard, and relay any interesting things we find with my Wind's Whisper skill."

That particular Scout trick let her send silent messages to any target she chose, within range. It was how Cagna had reported back to her handler without breaking cover. Now it would help Chase coordinate the little group.

"And you're going to come back to where we are every half hour or more, so I can do the same! Sort of," Renny said. "I mean I'll have to see you, so I can make phantasmal sounds at you. Remember that, okay?"

"We will," Cagna promised. Then she sighed. "I'm going to have to get changed, aren't I."

"I'm afraid so," Chase said. "I hope you don't mind."

"You," Cagna said, shooting the Muscle Wizaard a glare, "look away."

"I'd rather not; you're quite lovely," he smiled. "But if it makes you comfortable, of course I will! We are partners in a performance. You have nothing to fear! I've often changed in tight quarters as the show's requirements demanded."

Cagna just stared, mouth hanging open slightly.

"What?" Bastien asked, confused.

"Lovely? You think so?"

"Well, yes."

She snapped her mouth shut. "Just turn away."

Chase hid a smile. *Well, well, well!* Her antenna had been well-trained and calibrated for this sort of thing. She was certain the dog-woman was blushing under her fur.

But the Detective hid it well, trading out her robes for a ruffled red dress and orange corset arrangement, long gloves, and a thoroughly ridiculous feathered hat and a bird-like mask that covered her muzzle entirely. "This is a lot of trouble to go through for a few minutes of deception," Cagna said when she was done. Then she pointed her beak at Bastien. "Hey! Shouldn't *you* be changing, too?"

"Of course! **Call Outfit!**"

Cagna jumped in surprise, and she wasn't the only one as Chase scooted back. Out of nowhere, a bundle of orange and yellow covered the Muscle Wizaard, resolving into a huge tunic and pantaloon set that made his legs look like drumsticks. He had a beaked mask as well, and a cape that stretched up to attach to his wrists, that suggested wings. The effect was a bit more ridiculous, but somehow he made it work. Where Cagna's outfit looked elegant, his was entirely gaudy.

"You can DO that?" Cagna asked.

"Yes! It's an easy model trick. Costs a bit of Moxie, but with something this complex it's easier than trying to get it on without damaging it."

"Good, good," Chase said. "This'll save us some money when we return it, as well. Say, can you do that for other people?"

"Sadly, no. Just me. But what about your own costume?" Bastien asked.

"I'm not certain I can get what I need, here. It's worth a shot, but I need to get confirmation before I change. And remember, we want her to be focused on YOUR costumes. Which reminds me, you have the perfume?"

"Cologne, in my case. And yes, I do. Should I apply it now?"

"In this enclosed carriage? No. We all want to smell different. And you'll want to make sure to get it on your costume, not your skin, remember?"

"I do. Gods, am I glad you're a Tailor, too," Cagna nodded toward Bastien. "Make sure to save some sanity for a Clean and Press."

"We're here," Renny said, as the carriage rattled to a stop.

"Cagna?" Chase asked.

"Let me check." She opened the roof hatch of the carriage and peered out. "Nope. They're not here yet."

"Could it be possible that they arrived early?" Bastien asked, testing the range of mobility on his feathered arms.

"Not a chance," Cagna said. "When I went by to scope out the villa, the servants hadn't gotten the carriage out of storage. It takes a while to set up, then they'll have to prepare the horses, then there's the trip over... no. Besides, he never arrives early anywhere. He thinks it makes him seem less desperate."

"He could have rented a carriage for this one," Chase pointed out.

"Unlikely. The old man keeps... well, *kept* him on a tight budget. And he doesn't know his father's dead yet."

"You're certain of that?" Bastien asked. "He might skip this party, if you're wrong."

"The cards say he's ignorant," Chase nodded. "But it doesn't matter. Even if he'd be tempted to give it a miss, *she* won't let him. They'll be here. It's just a matter of time."

While they waited, Chase moved to the front of the carriage and slid open the window, peering past the hired driver to stare at the estate beyond.

She'd thought Don Coltello's villa was magnificent.

As it turned out, that was more of a reflection on her own inexperience than it was an accurate assessment. Whereas the entirety of Bothernot could have lived in Don Coltello's villa with room left over, the manor before her could house the entirety of Bothernot, with buildings and livestock included. The grounds around it could get a significant amount of the gardens and fields, too. And the stone outbuildings that surrounded the main manor house were all taller and much-better crafted than any her old village could boast about.

But something niggled at her mind, and the more she stared, the more it bothered her. Finally, she realized what it was. "This is near the heart of the city, but there are no walls. The neighboring houses have walls, yes, but not this place. Not here. Why is that?"

"Because the Verde family doesn't need them. Security is not a problem... in most circumstances," Cagna said.

"Is their magic *that* effective?" Chase frowned. "It seems like a bad idea to put all your eggs in one basket. I know you said they were really good mages, but this is just tempting fate."

"Okay. Maybe I undersold them," Cagna said, watching each carriage as it rolled past, heading to the coachhouse at the outskirts of the estate. "The three major noble houses of Arretzi each brought something to the table, back when the troubles happened, and Arretzi won its independence from the remnants of old Toothany. Without going into history TOO much, they each had their specialties. For the Bianchis, it's war and direct combat. Their estates look like fortified keeps."

"They're the ones who make a lot of paladins," Chase said.

"Yep. They got a dose of religion along the way. Nurph and Ritaxis, mainly. The Rossis, on the other hand, are masters of intrigue and... shady business." Cagna grimaced. "But they're good at keeping it quiet, so we can't do much."

"If they're so good at it, then how come the famigilias got so big?" Renny asked. "From what we saw, they were running a lot of the shady business."

"Some of them had or have Rossi backing. Others, well... they DID get too big. The Rossis take risks, and they don't always pan out."

"They're big on gambling," Chase said, feeling the silver cards in her pocket one more time. "Kind of ironic, the way it worked out."

"I suppose so. The Verdes... they don't HAVE mages. They ARE mages. Everyone in that family gets some sort of arcane training. You don't become a Verde adult without being an Elementalist, Enchanter, Wizard, or something like that. Rumor has it that a few of them even have Necromancer levels, but that's something you definitely don't want to bring up. Not here, probably not anywhere in this city or near it. So no. There are no walls here. There are probably bound guardians and invisible sentries watching us right now, looking for the first sign of hostility."

Chase gnawed her lip. "Renny? Do you have anything we can use to check that?"

"No, not really. Elementalist magic isn't big on subtle things, or detecting other magical stuff. That's more like what Wizards and Enchanters do."

"Then there's no telling what we might activate. We'll just have to be careful and play it by ear. Like the rest of this."

Then a sudden motion caught her attention. She turned and almost caught Cagna's tail in her mouth as it wagged, beating Chase in the face repeatedly. "Gah! Hey, what the heck?"

"Sorry," Cagna said, and her tail stilled. "Here they come."

"That's our cue!" Chase knocked on the slab separating the passenger part of the carriage and the driver's seat. "If you please, sir!"

The driver grunted and pulled forward. He'd been paid triple his standard rates to ignore and forget their conversation, and Chase and her friends had taken care to avoid discussing the plan in the carriage, so she didn't think there would be trouble from that end. His job was over once he dropped them off anyway.

Finally the carriage stopped, and the motley crew spilled out. They were ignored by the bystanders, as people with far more influence, expensive outfits, and personal retinues disembarked their own carriages and were met by the Verde servants.

Safely protected by relative obscurity, Cagna and Muscle Wizaard adjusted their own costumes, and Chase turned her attention to her own outfit.

No cleavage panels here. Just a good, simple dress... or it had been, before someone had sewn a few thousand sequins on it. A 'fox stole' hung around her neck, bangles lined her arms, and her shoes had a curve at the tips, culminating in points that suggested an exotic foreign look.

Then she scowled at the piece de resistance... a turban, fully big again as her head, with a gaudy gem in the center of it and a feather that would add a full six inches to her height. "This is the part I'm least certain about."

"Don't forget the earrings!" The Muscle Wizaard boomed, helpfully.

"Oh. Right. Them." Chase dug into her purse and pulled out the two orbs. As big and shiny as halven Yuletide-ornaments, they snapped onto her lobes with tiny clamps, and dragged her ears downward. It wasn't painful, but it was definitely uncomfy.

Then, with a sigh, she tucked her hair up and planted the turban on her head.

"Cloak too!" Renny insisted.

"Right, right, right..." Chase dug in the purse, pulling out a square of fabric that unfolded into a half-cloak. Emblazoned across the back of it in sequins were the words 'Madame Mysteria!!!'

"You put three exclamation points on here? Really?" She glared at the

Muscle Wizaard.

"It suits the overall role you're trying to play!" Bastien said. "They'll eat it up, trust me!"

Chase took a long breath and let it out. *I should have checked all of the costume parts before we got here,* she thought to herself. *Oh well. This is the least of my worries, at this point.*

"They're almost here," Cagna said, nodding at an approaching carriage... a bit bare and plain, compared to the others in the queue already. "We should perfume up."

"Technically it's cologne in my case," Bastien said.

"Is there a difference?" Chase asked.

"Yes," Bastien said.

"No," Cagna spoke, at almost the same time.

The two of them shot each other a glare, and Chase bit back laughter. Cagna was definitely blushing under her fur.

"Get it over with," Cagna said, raising her gloves. "Then I'll do you. I, I mean, apply the cologne to you."

"Of course!" Bastien said, holding his hand out to Chase. "If you please?"

A few squirts from small bottles later, sharp scents filled the air, and a passing valet paused to glare at the little group. The glare turned to puzzlement, as his eyes fell upon Chase. After a glance around to make sure all the more important people were being attended to, he hurried over, zeroing in on Bastien.

"Your invitation, sir?"

"Oh, we're with HIM!" Bastien said, pointing just as the awaited carriage's door opened and a figure stepped out.

Giuseppe Coltello froze, gaping in shock at the trio waiting for him. "What... do I know... wait, *you!*"

"Me!" Chase bubbled merrily and bounced over to him. "Here to serve you, milord! And your lovely lady!"

Giuseppe blanched. "Oh. Right. Yes, I did say..."

"They're with you, milord?" the valet asked. "Who are you again?" He pulled out a notepad, and started flipping through it.

"Ah, well, haha, I'm actually... here, it's easier if I explain who gave me their invitations..." Giuseppe gave Chase a quick nod, handed her his cane, and hurried over to the valet, gesturing with gloved hands as he explained the circumstances that allowed him to be here.

But Chase didn't move, peering into the shadows within the carriage. Keeping her face a friendly mask, and smiling widely, she tried to ignore the tension she felt from the figure still lurking within. Despite the danger that screamed its way through the back of her mind.

"Hi!" she chirped. "You must be Tabita!"

A pair of hands emerged from the darkness, took hold of either side of the carriage, and the occupant emerged into the lantern light.

She was a dwarven woman, wearing white furs and strings of emerald 'vines' over her coat that straggled up to disappear into her ample cleavage. She was pale skinned, far paler than Chase's own tawny skin tones, with red hair that definitely wasn't from around these parts.

Tabita was broad. Thick as a barrel, for all her four feet of height, with none of it fat and that was the first confirmation. The mask of her smile radiated warmth but her eyes were hot and hateful, and that was the second confirmation.

The halven knew that death stood before her. And the only thing keeping Chase alive at this very moment was that the predator didn't know Chase had her number.

"And you would be Chase," Tabita said, looking her up and down. "Giuseppe's told me a lot about you. Though I wasn't expecting you to be quite so... colorful."

Chase weighed her options and decided to play the 'humble country girl out of her element' card. "Ha, well..." Chase spread her arms. "I'm not normally gussied up like this, but this is a fancy occasion, and I do hope I won't clash too badly."

"Oh, I wouldn't worry about it," said the werewolf, as she turned and started toward the rest of the group."I have a suspicion that you have great taste."

CHAPTER 20: A STUDY IN VERDE

It was just like the storybooks Chase had read, so long ago. Just like the ones that had showed her that there was more to life than her little boring village.

A stately manor that sprawled over space that would normally be filled by city blocks. A long, glowstone-lit promenade at the entrance, with a spotless green carpet stretching back to the entrance, and an arched stone ceiling above to prevent the weather from ruining the occasion. Light spilled out of windows that gleamed like emeralds set against black velvet, and the servants were liveried to complement the scheme and grandeur of the ball. A long line of carriages rattled up and were met, one by one, with the servants disembarking to the side just as Chase and her friends had.

At any other time, Chase would have stopped and stared, enjoying the spectacle... and engaging in her favorite hobby: people watching.

She'd been worried that she'd be the most gaudily-dressed person here. She needn't have bothered. There were women walking around dressed in ropes of gems, with gossamer filling in the gaps in between. There was a woman with a hairdo so large that it had supporting buttresses and a small birdcage on top... complete with a very annoyed-looking parakeet in residence. There was a man whose beard was fire... not ON fire, it WAS fire.

At first she mistook them for performers, but no, judging by the way the crowd moved around them and entourages of servants followed behind, these had to be guests.

Fortunately, Chase had an outlet for her wonder. She walked next to her 'new best friend' and let her mouth go without engaging her brain.

It was part of the plan. And kind of fun, to tell the truth.

"Oh! Look at that one! How do you think she gets out of that corset?"

Bemused, the dwarf glanced over then snorted. Her eyes lost a bit of their heat, as she glanced back to Chase. "I'm betting smithing tools are involved. Maybe some light surgery."

Chase laughed, not having to fake humor, then wound down, as she saw a set of furry outfits ahead. "Oh. Now that's just in bad taste."

"What..." Tabita had been staring at Chase when she thought the halven wasn't looking, licking her lips. She hastily shut her mouth and wiped away a string of drool, gazing in the way the halven was looking. Immediately the dwarf stopped, and her smile disappeared. "Oh no. Oh HELL no."

Someone either very brave or very foolish had decided to poke fun at the city's current werewolf problem. A gaggle of nobles wore crude furs, with exaggerated muzzles and lolling cloth tongues over their faces. A few of them were stumbling around on all fours, making a show of sniffing each other's tails and chasing servants as a nervous crowd tittered laughter at their antics.

Chase and Tabita watched in silence for a moment, and the rage roiling off the dwarf was almost palpable to the halven's social senses.

She wasn't the only one who was exhibiting anger at the display, though Chase imagined it was for different reasons...

...and this gave her an *in*.

"I'll tell you a secret. I've faced them. Twice." Chase gestured with one hand. "Giuseppe didn't tell you, but he didn't know. This was on his father's business, not his."

"Ah, right. Giuseppe didn't mention that. Twice, you say?"

There was that faint tonal shift that Chase had been watching for. Now she knew what Tabita sounded like when she was being deceptive. Forcing herself not to smile, Chase glanced away and moved her face to convey the notion that she was remembering something horrible. "They're nothing like that. They're terrifying and... oddly beautiful, in a way. I don't know how to describe it..."

"Like any predator acting out nature's will," Tabita supplied. "The cycle of life, nature red in tooth and claw but with its own grace."

"Yes!" Chase shot her a carefully-measured 'spontaneous' smile. "Still terrifying but with a grace that THOSE morons could never appreciate. It's a shame that we had to go up against them. But... thankfully, that's over now."

"I'm not sure what you mean," Tabita said. "They're still hunting in this city."

"Oh. Yes. But..." Chase bit her lip. "Without going into too much detail, my obligation to Giuseppe's father is done. He'd threatened us into service. Now we're free, and we'll be leaving soon. I won't have to face them a third time, and that's all right too."

"What? Just like that?" Tabita's face shifted, as Chase started walking again, and the dwarf hurried to keep up. "It's not personal for you?"

"They haven't killed anyone I care about," Chase shrugged... a small lie, here. She didn't think Friatta Costello had deserved death. The leatherworker's daughter had been innocent of all but doing a good job.

But the lie slid past without trouble. Tabita might have been many things and charismatically presentable enough to be the social point woman in the werewolf's scheme, but she was up against *Chase*.

And Chase Berrymore had been practicing her whole life for an operation like this one.

"No, not personal at all." Chase shook her head. "So I'm going to take one last opportunity here to get some coin for the road and put this city behind us."

"It's not personal for your beastkin friend, either?" Tabita asked, as they came up behind the rest of their crew, who were flanking Giuseppe and engaging him in conversation every time the mobster's son tried to shoot Tabita a needy look.

"Cagna? Ah..." Chase sighed. "She's more of an associate. And now that certain facts have come to light, her... work has to reassign her elsewhere. She might travel with us to her next duty assignment; it's hard to tell. Or we might help her with some business in a different city." Chase pulled in. "Don't tell her I said this, but she's kind of a mess. For her it IS personal, but she's barely holding it together. Which is why we brought her here. No werewolf would be foolish enough to start anything HERE, not tonight."

"It does seem pretty unlikely. Who would expect that?" Tabita shrugged, bare shoulders rolling with muscle.

"I know, right? Well, anyway, thank you for letting us come along on this. If you need anything, just call. I've got one or two things to tend to, but after that I am your humble servant, tonight." Chase put on a wide, smarmy smile. "Got to keep up appearances, after all."

"Oh, I can sympathize," Tabita said, studying her with hungry eyes... but there was no trace of the malice that Chase had seen, beforehand. "In fact, if you're looking to leave the city, I have some friends I can introduce you to."

"I'd like that! I'm sure we can find a private room to discuss matters in at some point. This mansion looks like it was built for that sort of thing."

And then Giuseppe was hurrying back to take his lady-love's arm, and only Chase's finely-tuned eyes caught how she tensed, ever so slightly, as he touched her.

He probably thinks she's being demure.

Leaving those two to their own charades, Chase hurried to catch up with Bastien and Cagna. They were waiting by one of the many sets of double-doors leading into the foyer, and once Chase had joined them, the three entered into the Verde mansion.

Five stories high, stood the entry hall. A wide, double staircase rose at the back, branching out into sweeping balconies at the third and fifth stories. A stained glass skylight shown complimentary reds and oranges and purples down onto the forest green carpe. Geometric patterns that shifted and danced as the glowstone lights shifted, seeming to drift in idle, glowing courses above the high glass. To one side of the stairs, a band played a courtly waltz. Up among the balconies, scandalously-dressed performers were assembling a trapeze and tightrope rig. And on the right-hand side of the cathedral-like room, tables lay heaped with food and drink.

It was a bit inferior to the spread in Don Sangue's court, Chase noted with a quick glance. Nonetheless, she gravitated that way.

Free food *was* free food, after all. And she was beginning to like these not-having-to-pay-to-eat opportunities that hobnobbing with powerful people provided her.

"Those are the Acrocats!" The Muscle Wizard muttered, staring up at the balconies. Chase caught a slight hint of envy in his tone. "To land such a prestigious performance venue... ah, there was a time when I'd be right up there with them, diving off the top rope. Oh, what an elbow drop I could do from that top balcony!"

"You may get the opportunity yet," Chase said. "And what it took them probably days to line up? I'm about to score in ten minutes, if I play my cards right, so don't feel too bad."

"You're really going ahead with the show?" Cagna asked.

"I have to pull attention off you somehow. And besides, Renny would be disappointed if I didn't try."

"It's just my dream and all. No pressure," the fox stole around her neck whispered.

"Now that I've taken the measure of this crowd, I'm pretty sure you don't have to whisper," Chase told the little golem. "Birdcage wig lady raised the bar. I'm pretty sure a talking stole is pedestrian after that."

"It looks like we've got some time," The Muscle Wizaard said. "Now what?"

"Go with the standard delaying plan. Make a show of being around if Giuseppe and Tabita need anything, then blend in as best you can. If I get the okay, then you'll know it, and that's your opportunity."

"Good luck," Cagna said.

"You know... I don't think I have any other sort," Chase said, tempting fate and knowing it.

After a quick stop at the food, Chase had two rolls in her pocket and one in her belly. Next it was the simplest thing in the world to march right up to the most well-dressed servant, put on her most unhappy face, and say, "Who's in charge of tonight's entertainment?"

"That would be the major domo," said the nonplussed waiter, staring down at the scowling halven.

"Well I haven't received a schedule, and I don't know WHEN I'm due to perform tonight!"

"Er..." the waiter stared.

"What? You think I'm wearing this costume for my health, here? I have a job to do, and Madame Mysteria is NOT to be kept waiting!" She leaned in. "Between you and me I saw your mistake coming. It was in the cards."

"My mistake?" The waiter looked around, nervously. A few other servants were finding their way over, looking to back up their obviously-troubled friend.

"Look, I know it's above your pay-grade. Just tell me who's running the entertainment and I'll go take the issue up with him."

And in roughly ten minutes she was talking with the major domo, a harried-looking elderly woman who kept getting interrupted by servants running up to check with her on the thousand-and-one little details needed when you're running a grand masquerade ball and given roughly three days' notice beforehand.

Chase was kind Chase was polite, and the woman's moxie was already down quite a bit thanks to the myriad troubles and problems that she'd had to solve tonight. It didn't take much more beyond a minor exertion of charisma and a quick demonstration of her talents to get what she wanted.

She returned to the foyer smiling, even though she had to navigate a full crowd to get to where she needed to be. The band was playing louder now, and a few couples were waltzing around the floor. Chase noted with amusement that Cagna and Bastien were doing a few turns, and she smiled to see that the beastkin was leading. They looked happy.

Above, the Acrocats had finished their preparations and were limbering up, the first few out on the trapezes, swinging in brief, gentle arcs. Every time they completed a set, some of the supporting crew would work the pulleys above them, and the trapezes would slide lower.

But Chase had no time for that. She had her window of opportunity, and the more she waited, the more likely it was that the major domo would come to her senses.

Chase found the stage she had been told to go to, one that had missed her attention during her initial assessment of the room. A small dais, about big enough for a harp or some other large instrument and a single player. It added three feet to her height, and for the first time she was grateful for her ridiculous turban, and its big, floppy feather.

The stage is set, Chase thought to herself, as she looked around. The growing crowd was gathering into cliques and pools, some dancing and others noshing on the food. It was much more relaxed than the gangster meeting had been, and why wouldn't it be? These were nobles and social climbers, and didn't have the werewolf threat to unify them. That was for the little people to worry about, and nothing to concern themselves with.

"It'll be their problem if the city riots and their villas burn," Chase muttered. There were some definite similarities between these people and the stuck-in-the-mud ignorant farmers of Bothernot, though both would be offended at the comparison.

But she didn't see who she was looking for.

"Are we ready?" Renny asked.

"Not yet. Where's Tabita?"

"Um..." The fox stole twisted as Renny raised himself up and looked around, and she got a mixture of admiring and confused glances from the nearest passerby. "I don't see her."

There was Giuseppe, against the wall and desperately trying to talk up a bored-looking noblewoman. But no dwarf. At least not one with red hair. Had she switched costumes?

Then Cagna's voice whispered in her ear. "Tabita left with the fake werewolves. I think she was pretending to seduce them."

Chase's eyes went wide. She stood on her tiptoes until she found Cagna, caught her eyes, then gave her a nod back to show the message had been received. *Thank goodness for good perception. Now why would Tabita have dragged the fake werewolves off to a private place?*

The obvious answer seemed to involve a lot of blood and pain and screaming, but... no. No, it was too early in the party. They weren't the werewolf's real target anyway, just a means to an end. There was more here.

"We need Tabita here before we can start," Chase said. "Be ready. I'll give the signal the second I see her. She *has* to come back here."

But did she? Did she really? The werewolves obviously had a plan. They'd had a plan the last two times, and it had been pretty effective. They weren't stupid, and there was a chance that their plan involved ditching the party and getting in and out as quickly as possible.

So Chase waited, watched, and hoped. It was a matter of luck now.

Mostly luck. Since Tabita was out of the room that meant she could kick Phase Two into motion early. Chase whispered to Renny, who sent Cagna the message. And after a moment, she saw her two bird-costumed friends head out of the hall down a side corridor.

Then she waited.

Chase made a show of fiddling with her purse, and the bag of props that she'd brought along. Minutes crawled by, and after a time Chase looked up to find the major domo looking her way, talking to several servants. After a brief conversation two of them started to head over, and Chase's heart sunk. The clearest vision she'd had earlier today had involved a performance. If she didn't do that, then things got hazier. A *lot* hazier.

But fortunately it was a moot point. A few seconds before the servants reached her, Chase caught a flash of red hair over white fur. She saw Tabita walking back in with the dopey werewolf costumed crowd, and breathed a sigh of relief.

"Excuse me, Miss?" the lead servant said. "If you're not going to—"

With the best imperial glower Chase silenced him with a look. A flourish, one finger upraised, and she whispered "Now, Renny."

"LADIES AND GENTLEMEN!" Renny's amplified voice boomed out, as the oncoming servants found themselves at the front of a suddenly-interested throng of nobles. "PREPARE TO BE DAZZLED BY THE DIVINE INSIGHT OF MADAME MYSTERRRRRRRIIIIIIIAAAAAAAAAA!"

Chase had to admit that drawing out and yelling the last word worked a lot better than she thought it would. That part had been Bastien's suggestion, and she was glad she'd trusted his expertise.

But she could only appreciate that for a second. Time mattered, now... time and audacity. **"Silver Tongue, Lecture,"** she muttered, as the last echoes of her stage name faded.

And then, as planned, Renny shifted his talents to amplifying her voice.

"I command fate!" Chase declared, throwing modesty to the wind.

"I see the future!" Chase stated, entirely truthful.

"I am the harbinger of messages from BEYOND..." Though Chase knew she wouldn't be using *that* trick here. Given the anti-necromancy laws she didn't want to get arrested.

"Nobles and goodfolk of Arretzi? I am your Medium!" She said and hopped into the air.

Out of nowhere a chair materialized and caught Chase as she rose above the crowd. They gasped, and then applause rained from around the room.

Then the chair settled down to about human head height and was joined by a whirling round table. It slowed, and as it did, Chase pulled a purple, starry-patterned tablecloth from her props bag and threw it over the illusion that concealed a mass of air beneath. Unlike the chair, other people would be interacting with the table, so a little reinforcement couldn't go wrong.

"Now..." Chase said, pulling out the cards and shuffling them, as Renny made illusionary cards the size of wagons appear and float above. "Who dares to see what fate has in store for them tonight?"

CHA+1

The crowd ate it up... and in short order, a line formed. And Chase told fortune after fortune, keeping it brief. Above her Renny showed the cards in all their glory, animating them to oohs and ahs of the crowd, and personalizing them to whichever partygoer was present.

And more importantly, drawing attention from Chase.

"Silent Activation, Stack Deck," she'd mouth whenever a bad card came up, or the Fortuna wanted to be more brutally honest than she was comfy with. The fortunes were generally good, and those that were questionable could be spun or slightly tweaked to ensure that nobody walked away insulted.

And as she worked, she snuck glances at Tabita... Tabita, who watched with wide eyes.

Come on, take the bait.

But the dwarven woman never budged, and Chase started to despair. Her vision had shown her reading the werewolf's fortune. It had been very clear about that. Had the vision been incorrect? It was possible. There were many futures, and fate was not set in stone.

Just as Chase was certain she'd have to pack it in, a furry shape lumbered out of the crowd to the laughter and jeers of the crowd. It raised two oversized paws and did a fake dance as it waltzed forward...

...and Chase recognized the black clothes showing under the fur suit. She'd seen those clothes before, in her very first vision.

This is the werewolf Alpha! The new one, the Burglar.

She smiled at him, marking his wary eyes showing from behind his ridiculous mask. "Ah... I see we have a beast among us!" Chase's voice boomed out.

"Rawr!" he replied, but his eyes narrowed.

"Well then, good sir! Would you know your own fate... or that of the werewolves, that trouble our fair city?"

The laughter and shouts from the crowd paused.

"The wolves!" Someone chanted from the back, and Chase was sure it was Tabita's voice. The halven girl grinned wide as the crowd took up the chant and knew her vision hadn't been wasted after all.

A fortune by proxy is still a fortune, Chase said. "Then we shall do something new, here!" Chase said and held out the deck. "Shuffle them, sir! Shuffle them, and think hard upon the werewolves that dare terrorize Arretzi!"

Interested murmurs, and the crowd pressed forward.

The Alpha nodded and shuffled, amazingly dexterous despite his large fuzzy gloves. Up close and watching, Chase could see that they didn't fit very well at all. In fact, his entire costume was a bit loose and baggy...

No. No, he definitely hadn't started the night in this costume. And as he shuffled she found the other fake werewolves in the crowd and marked how they were moving differently from the comical antics they'd exhibited earlier.

She swapped out the fake werewolves for real ones. Clever.

"Here you go then," The fake-real Alpha growled, handing the cards back.

Chase gave him a wide grin and started stacking the deck.

"The first card represents *you...* Or rather, the werewolves." She flipped up the Party, the card that showed four successful adventurers dividing up spoils. It animated, and the crowd oohed and ahh'd as the mage cast spells to identify various bits of treasure, and the rogue quietly pocketed coins when the fighter and the cleric weren't looking. "Unified as a pack, unified in purpose and enjoying their victories. But are they right to do so? The next card shall say, for it represents the dilemma at hand..."

She flipped over the Treasure Chest, reversed this time. A massive box appeared in midair, bulging with gold and gems and scepters and wands... and then it upended, spilling the treasure onto the laughing crowd. "They are seeking something valuable! They're not after simple murder; there's more at stake here. Something... physical."

"Really?" The Alpha said, slipping up and using his real voice. He cleared his throat. "What could that be?" He asked, in a much growlier voice.

"Ah, perhaps the cards shall say... first, let the cards reveal their ally, the traitor to the city itself!"

Boos from the crowd, and another card spun into existence above Chase as she drew it. The Healer: a woman in white robes with a staff, laying hands on an ungrateful looking knight. It animated, and the woman healed the knight, only to have him go charging off to stand in a bonfire for no reason, then run back alternately yelling abuse and whining, still on fire. The Healer rolled her eyes and got back to work, endlessly patient. "Your... the werewolves' best ally for this task is a healer of sorts..." Chase let her voice show tones of surprise. "Someone who's wise and good at keeping her friends alive. I'm getting a hint of other abilities too... Strange." She let the silence linger for a bit too long. Then she shrugged, as the crowd muttered.

"Well, let us see what their key choice is. This is the crux of the matter, the decision that the werewolves can make that will gain them their goal or lose it..."

And Chase pulled out Death.

The room gasped as the bony skeleton rose up on high, red eyes glowing, scythe sweeping to the ongoing celebration of the party. But it paused, as Chase revealed the card was reversed.

Instantly the skeleton twisted, eyeing the Healer instead. It raised its weapon, and hesitated. "They stand poised to kill their best ally!" Chase gasped. "Their own bestial nature will undo them! This is truly good news for Arretzi!"

Cheers from around the room, and the Alpha leaned back, arms folded.

"But the fortune is not yet done!" Chase declared, voice booming around the hall. "For their worst enemy awaits declaration. Let us see what noble scion can stand against these horrible creatures!"

And with a flourish, Chase pulled the Griefer. The Noob's hapless figure faded into existence, scratching his head with his wooden sword, mismatched armor clanking as he walked through a dark wood. Then a murderous figure, wearing glowing armor and wielding a sword twice his height faded out of invisibility and killed the Noob, laughing all the while.

"The Griefer..." Chase hissed. "A powerful and bored man, who kills for joy. A cruel man but one who is on the side of the angels, for he shall vanquish the beasts that trouble our city!"

"Oh my gods," the Alpha whispered.

"Yes... the choice is clear! The werewolves are certain to fall now. They will kill the woman who is their own best chance at finding the treasure..." Death's scythe fell and the Healer died. "...and the Griefer shall gank them all." The Griefer, wiping his sword free of the Noob's blood turned and chucked a bomb over his shoulder, blowing the Party to smithereens. "Their treasure shall be lost forever." The empty box cracked and fell apart, crumbling into nothing. Death saluted the Griefer, and the two walked off hand in hand, almost skipping away.

Chase smiled as the Alpha nodded. "Thank you," he whispered and made a show of pulling out a money pouch, opening it, and pouring silver onto her table.

"You're welcome!" she said, but she was looking past him. Across the hall, Tabita was talking furiously with the other fake/not-fake werewolves, gesturing and pointing at various parts of the manor. Chase watched as costumed furry figures ran in various directions.

"I fear that is all," Chase declared, as she stood. Her chair disappeared and she drifted to the ground. The Alpha nodded and slipped back into the crowd, and Chase retrieved both cards and tablecloth with a flourish, before tucking them away. "But cross my palm with silver, and I may perhaps find it within me to perform again!"

The coins rained down then, and Chase snapped her fingers at the nearest servants, gesturing at the rapidly-disappearing floor. They got to work gathering, which was good because the levels were rolling in now, and Chase was too busy reading the words and enjoying the rush of energy.

You are now a level 12 Grifter!
CHA+3
DEX+3
LUCK+3
You are now a level 4 Medium!
CHA+5
LUCK+5
You are now a level 5 Medium!
CHA+5
LUCK+5
You have learned the Focus Vision Skill!
Your Focus Vision skill is now level 1!
You have learned the Fortuna skill!
You have learned the Palmistry Skill!

You are now a level 5 Teacher!
INT+1
WILL+1
You have learned the Red Ink skill!

Chase blinked, not sure she'd read one of those correctly. The Fortuna skill? She was already doing quite a lot with the cards; she wasn't sure what else she could do with them.

Maybe this would open more options!

"Milady," a voice whispered in her ear.

A very, very familiar voice.

Chase turned, keeping her face under control as she smiled up at a green-liveried servant, a dapper man with a sharp face, angular cheekbones, and a black goatee.

He hadn't even changed his hairstyle. But if he hadn't spoken, she wouldn't have seen the truth of him. "Can I help you?" she said, feigning ignorance.

He smiled, ruefully. "The mistress of the house summons you. Will you come?"

"I shall." Chase said and followed him through the crowd. Many of the partygoers bent to congratulate her, or try to grab her for a talk, but she used quiet apologies and nimble dodges to get out of the way and leave them behind.

And in a matter of minutes she found herself in a deserted hallway in the upper stories. The carpet was a different shade of green, but the walls were dark wood, rich imported stuff that seemed to reinforce the notions of serious business and subtle power.

"You're in danger," the 'servant' spoke.

"I know. I was wondering when you'd turn up again," Chase said.

Thomasi Jacobi Venturi sighed and ran a hand through his hair. "You don't understand. She's here. Zenobia. She's waiting for you at the end of this walk. I can get you out of here, but you have to leave *now*."

Chase winced. "The timing is about what I expected. But it's okay. She'll listen to me."

"What are you... No, you don't understand what you're doing!" Thomasi whispered. "You're playing with fire!"

"And you're keeping secrets. Tell me about the skin and do it quickly."

Thomasi ground his teeth. "Tell me your game first! What do you think you're *doing?*"

"I'm stopping the werewolves. They're killing people."

"So am I! Once they get the skin, they'll leave!"

"Tell me why! Why is it so gods-damned important!" Her voice was rising, and she reigned it in. Too much risk of other ears around. They were being watched; she was certain of it.

Tom's face was a study in irritation. Finally he sighed. "I promise I'll tell you all about it later. It's very, very complicated. But you have to come with me, now. If Zenobia gets you, you're dead. Maybe not immediately, but she won't leave such a loose end to trouble her again."

"Give me the short version," Chase said. "Or no deal."

"Fine! Fine..." Thomasi shook his head. "The skin is an artifact from before we got stuck. Tabita made it before everything went to hell. It's also tied to her, intimately. She thinks she can use it to get home. I'm not certain she's wrong, and if there's even a chance, she deserves to give it a try."

"Okay," Chase said, considering the matter. "So you are going to give it to her here?"

"No! There are too many wards, and the skin is magical. I've stashed it, and I was going to tell her where, but then you started your show. What is your *game?*"

"Tell me one more thing."

"Damn it—" Thomasi choked off his own words as his voice rose. "I've taught you too well," he whispered. "Now you're trying to get levels from *me.*"

"I'm honestly not, but your priorities are lousy," Chase said, glaring back up at him. "This skin might let Tabita go home or whatever. But will she take the rest of the werewolves with her?"

Thomasi hesitated, and in that hesitation Chase had all the answer she needed.

"Then I'm going to go talk to the Camerlengo," Chase said. "Because of Friatta Costello, and Signore Costello."

"Who?"

"An innocent daughter who didn't deserve to die when a werewolf murdered her," Chase whispered, holding his gaze with all the willpower she could bring to bear. "And a father who showed me his heart when he wept for her."

Thomasi looked away.

They walked in silence, down the long, long hall. It was far too deserted, even with the servants tending to the party. No, there were watchers: there were guards.

"You must think me a monster," he finally said. "For helping her, despite what she has done."

"No," Chase said. "I don't understand you yet. Or her, or any of this. Not truly. But I want to. I want you to tell it to me, so I can understand. Our destinies are intertwined now, so if you keep doing things like this, I WILL think you a monster. And I will work to stop you, eventually. Or more things like this will keep happening, where we end up at cross purposes."

Thomasi tightened his lips. "What would you have me do?"

"Seek out the Muscle Wizaard and Cagna. Make contact quietly, and they'll fill you in on the plan. Do NOT make contact with Tabita. Do NOT tell her where you stashed the skin."

"Muscle Wiz... he's here?" Thomasi's eyes rose, and she saw the first honest smile she'd had from him tonight.

"He is, and he missed you greatly. You probably don't want to reveal yourself to him in a public place and be ready to get a few ribs broken. He's a hugger."

"Ha! I remember him well! No worries, I'll take care." Then his grin faded. "You're sure this is how you want to do this? She's not to be trifled with. She's an Inquisitor. They are built to counter Grifters like us."

"I'm sure," Chase said. "Because I won't tell her a single lie. Now go. Get to the others and get out of here. Do NOT tell me where."

"All right. The room you really shouldn't go into is six doors down, to the right, with a pair of lanterns above it. Good luck."

Chase nodded, and walked halfway to the door. Then she paused and looked down to Renny.

"Problems?" The fox whispered.

"Complications. Tom..." Chase ran a hand through her hair. "I don't know."

"You don't trust him?"

"I trust him to be Tom. Beyond that..." she let the words vanish in the silence of the hall.

"Do you want me to..."

"Yes, please."

Chase walked the rest of the way alone.

The door was ajar, and a woman's voice called "Enter," when Chase raised her hand to knock.

She walked into the room, a dimly-lit study with an overstuffed armchair silhouetted against a roaring fire.

Then came a whisper of steel, and the shadows resolved themselves into guards with swords, a ring of them, closing in blade-first. There were more people behind them, but Chase ignored them for now, turning before the blades got too close, searching the faces for the one she was expecting.

And she found it. A stern face, pinched and lined with worry and cruelty, glaring down at her with loathing. Zenobia the Camerlengo. Zenobia, who had tried to drown Chase like a housewife would wash away vermin. Zenobia, who Chase had left facing one of her worst enemies... and oh yeah, then the halven had dumped a mountain's worth of water on HER.

"Give me one good reason that I should let you live," Zenobia choked out, and Chase couldn't remember if those had been the exact words of the vision, but the rest of the scene matched up so the Oracle surrendered to her fate.

"I'll give you two," Chase said, ignoring the blades inches from her neck. "And their names are Tabita and Pwner."

INT+1

CHAPTER 21: BAD LADY, GOOD DOGE

If looks could have killed, then Chase would have been dead many times over.

Come to think of it, Chase thought giddily, *there probably is a job out there that lets you kill with a look. Fortunately she doesn't have it, since I'm still alive.*

The Camerlengo's eyes hadn't left her, but the older woman's jaw was working up and down like she wanted to take a bite out of the halven in front of her. Finally, it shut with an audible snap of teeth coming together, and Zenobia made a sharp, slashing gesture with one gloved hand.

"No, I don't think so," a gentle voice said from the back of the room. "Come join us at the fire and tell me about those two names you just dropped."

Zenobia flushed red, and her eyes flickered away from Chase. She shifted slightly so that her spectacles were mirroring the fire.

The blaze held less heat than the Camerlengo's gaze, and Chase let her shoulders sag in relief. "Thank you," she said, but nobody spoke. The blades between her and the armchair did withdraw though, so she followed the path left open to her.

For the first time since she had come to Arretzi, she was taking the path of least resistance. It was somewhat a relief, actually. The main part of her plan was done.

To her surprise, the figure sitting in the armchair was *not* Maddalena Verde. It was another dog beastkin, this one a corgi-headed man wearing blue and green velvet. He was fat, and furry, and his tongue hung just a bit out of his mouth as the warm fire crackled away just five feet from his layers of robes. He held up a hand festooned with jeweled rings, and

Chase took it, bowing. "I'm sorry," she said. "I don't think I know who you are."

"You're in the presence of Doge Fedelta himself, girl," the Camerlengo's voice snapped the silence like a whip meeting flesh.

"It's all right." The beastkin waved a hand idly. "You are a visitor to my city after all, Chase Berrymore. How do you find it so far?"

"Well, up until yesterday I would have said that it was full of criminals, hounded by rampaging monsters, and on the edge of chaos."

"And now?"

"Now most of the criminals are dead, the monsters are smarter and less chaotic than they appear, and the edge of chaos is back above it as it merrily falls toward the gods only know what."

The doge slurped his tongue into his mouth. "A bit harsh. But not entirely untrue. Still, Arretzi has faced worse crises."

"Yes." The Camerlengo spoke again. "And it has done so under management that is no longer here to cause such crises again."

"If the Baroness disapproves of the way I do things, she can come down and tell me so to my muzzle," the Doge flipped his ears dismissively. "My priority is the city. My own career is less important and should she wish to replace me and find the support among the noble houses to do so, then I will gladly retire to my estate and tend my garden for my last few decades. I'll rather enjoy it! It'll be easier than keeping everyone happy, that's for sure. Or safe, for that matter." The Doge heaved a sigh. "Speaking of that... those two names you mentioned, Miss Berrymore, are definitely not safe names to drop."

"I wouldn't if I didn't have to. But they illustrate the seriousness of the matter." Chase looked to the Camerlengo, caught those burning eyes again. "May I speak to him about players?"

The woman paused. For a second she considered the question, shifting her glasses out of the firelight. "To a point," she finally stated. "Doge, may I ask you to share what you know about them?"

"I can..." the Doge opened his mouth, only to be interrupted as the Camerlengo kept talking.

"Child, if you have additional information about their nature beyond what he has told you, you will keep it to yourself or you shall suffer for that. Do you understand? This secret was not meant to be yours. You are in enough trouble already, and the damage you would do by indiscriminately sharing everything would take lifetimes to undo."

Chase flushed. "I understand that! I may not have the full picture, but I'm not an idiot. That's why I asked your permission in the first place—" Chase shut up midsentence. The Camerlengo had been baiting her; she was sure of it. *I really, really need to work on my willpower,* she thought.

"Enough. Camerlengo Zenobia has told me quite a bit about you tonight, Miss Berrymore. But she was unaware that my agents had assembled a file on you before you showed up on our doorstep... so to speak."

Chase listened to both what he said and what he didn't say. After a second, she thought she got the message. The Camerlengo had given a biased account, obviously, or one that was tailored to her own agenda. The Doge had watched Chase's actions in Arretzi, though, and had noticed discrepancies. That was probably the reason he'd called off the guards... Chase spared a quick look behind her and found the shadows empty once more. Had they been illusions? Hard to say. She thought not, though, invisible bodyguards were a far more likely possibility.

The Doge continued. "But let me acquiesce to Zenobia's request and inform you of players. They are monsters akin to demons or old ones. Things from outside this world that wear bodies of flesh. But unlike such 'dark' creatures, the players are chaotic, disorganized, and lack a universal goal beyond the pursuit of their own individual pleasures. They have a method of rebuilding their bodies after death, although it is limited or painful in some fashion. And it is the agreement of every ruler in Arretzi that they are to be turned over to the Inquisition when they are found."

"The Inquisition?" Chase blinked. She had no idea what that was.

"That is none of your affair," The Camerlengo snapped. "Now, tell me everything you know about Pwner."

Chase hesitated and looked to the Doge. He was her only hope of salvation here. She wasn't naive enough to consider him an ally, but he was certainly better disposed toward her than the Camerlengo.

But he gave her an encouraging nod, and Chase resisted the urge to hug him. He was just so *adorable*.

Then the Camerlengo's words sunk in. "You don't want to know about Tabita?"

"After tonight she will not be a cause for concern."

"You really should ask me about her. You're mistaken about her goals, here."

"Pwner first."

"Well, their fates are intertwined anyway." Chase shrugged, sitting next to the hearth. "Our best conjecture is that Soluzioni Semplici hired him to avenge their fallen guildmate."

The Doge groaned. "Oh Vincente... I told you not to go off half-cocked."

"You knew about this?" The Camerlengo shot him a surprised glare.

"I knew he'd do SOMETHING. Not THIS."

Chase blinked. *They believed me, just like that?*

Then she chastised herself. They knew she'd be here. And they'd planned to interrogate her to some degree, obviously. Of *course* they'd set up magic and buffs and other things to catch any lies she might tell. "He's the one that blew up the Rossi casino. Tabita challenged him when she caught sight of him sitting in the player area down there. He accepted her challenge, dropped a bomb, and teleported out. So I really hope Maddalena Verde has some anti-bomb magic going here, otherwise it could get messy. If it gets to that point."

The Doge and the Camerlengo shared an inscrutable look. "Hmmm... is there anything else?" The Doge asked, turning back to Chase.

"Not as much as I'd like. He was clearly hunting the werewolves and sacrificed Enrico Rossi to do so. And the casino. But he wasn't at the tower when the werewolves took down Don Sangue. Which means that he doesn't have a reliable way of finding them. And that's a problem."

"You want Pwner to kill Tabita?" The Camerlengo sneered. "Foolish."

"I said nothing of the sort. But it's a problem because anyone who knows Maddalena Verde was involved in the last werewolf hunt will recognize this party for the obvious trap it is. And I'm willing to believe that Pwner's smart and tenacious enough to figure that out and come here to hunt his quarry. Am I wrong about that?"

"You're not wrong," The Doge said, staring morosely into the fire. "This changes the plan."

"We can still go through with it," Zenobia considered him. "If you have the strength."

"This isn't a matter of my strength. It's a matter of risk to my people! Arretzi has already bled enough from this matter!"

They argued, and Chase took the opportunity to look around the study. It was tastefully decorated, windowless but the air seemed fresh despite the roaring fire. Magic, perhaps.

The room was missing something. Chase narrowed her eyes and pursued that feeling in the back of her skull until she figured out what it was. And when the argument ceased, and uncomfortable silence reigned, she dared to speak up. "Is the lady of the house here? Maddalena Verde? What does she think about all this?"

The Camerlengo and the Doge shared another look. The Doge shrugged. "I see no harm in it. Do you?"

"At this juncture, no." Zenobia considered Chase. "She'll be under my governance from this point out, so you may as well tell her."

Oh, that boded. But Chase pushed the trickle of fear away for now. "Tell me what?"

"Fifteen years is a long time, and Maddalena Verde wasn't exactly a young person when she helped hunt down the werewolves. She died of her age a few days ago. Her heart, my own Inventor confirmed it." The Doge looked down, ears drooping. "The family was about to send out death notices when Sonora Bianchi died. After we confirmed that the werewolves were wreaking vengeance, we had a talk with the family. They agreed that Maddalena would have wanted to play one last trick on the beasts, and we hatched this scheme."

"The beasts will find no target for their vengeance until we want them to do so." The Camerlengo smiled and held up a green mask. "At the appointed time I shall disguise myself as Maddalena and greet the party. And once Tabita is within my blade's reach, we shall act!"

"And so will Pwner. But there's a problem with that plan," Chase said. "They're not really after vengeance."

The fire snapped and crackled.

"Explain yourself. Quickly," Zenobia spoke.

"They might *want* vengeance, but it's a secondary goal. When Tabita died the first time, Don Coltello had her skinned. She wants her skin back. She thinks it's the key to returning to her own world."

"What...." The Camerlengo breathed the word, dragging it out. "Inconceivable!" Then her hand came up, and she rubbed her chin. "Then again, that was before... dear gods. Agnes scourge me, she might be on to something there!" For the first time, Chase saw fear on the woman's face. "Can she do this?" Zenobia asked, plainly.

"I have no idea. She thinks it's possible." Chase shrugged.

"And she's also smart enough to recognize that this is a trap. And if vengeance isn't her goal, then she won't try for you when you're out there in disguise." The Doge pinched the upper part of his muzzle with two fingers, massaging it.

"She absolutely must not be allowed to do this," The Camerlengo said. "Ah, it makes sense now! She wasn't just killing the members of the hunting party, that was the cover. She was sending her people in looking for it. She didn't know who *had* the blasted thing!"

Chase remembered how the werewolf Alpha had sat there, looking over the room during his confrontation with Don Sangue. *Yup. That's why he came in and risked a face to face. They didn't want to blow up the tower if the skin was still in there.*

The Camerlengo continued. "Where is this skin now? It must be destroyed."

"I don't know where the skin is," Chase shrugged. "But they think it could be here. Which is why I've set my plan in motion."

The Camerlengo closed her eyes. "I'm going to hate this."

"What is your plan?" The Doge asked, gently.

"This is a big grown up party," Chase said. "I know how those go at home. There's strong drink and dancing and music, and people sneak off into the shadows and come back all sweaty. It's what happens, and you have to turn a blind eye. Is that how this goes here?"

"You're not too far off," The Doge smiled.

"Right now my allies are pretending to do that, but what they're actually doing is looking for good places to stash the fake skins that I bought before I came here. All we need is for the werewolves to find one, just one, and that's when THIS will come into play." Chase rummaged in her pockets and pulled out a compass. The needle quivered, throwing reflections against its glass case in the firelight, as it danced and swept around, over and over again.

"Simple magic," the Camerlengo said, squinting at it. "A tracking enchantment... ah, you've tied it to the false skins."

"Are you sure that will convince her?" The Doge asked. "How do you even know what her skin would look like?"

"I've seen her as a werewolf. It's not perfect, but it's been fifteen years, and none of the skins are intact. Hopefully it works." Chase sighed. "Honestly that's the weakest part of the plan. She might recognize whichever skin she gets as a fake. But my divinations all seem to confirm that this plan has the best possibility of success."

Well, it has *a* possibility of success, she thought to herself. Chase remembered the multiple visions that showed the outcome of her other ideas. Most of those ended up with her being ripped to shreds by werewolves, in gory detail.

"So they take a skin and return to whatever lair they're using. Then you would use the compass to track them there." The Camerlengo plucked it from her fingers, and Chase didn't fight the grab. "And then what, girl?"

"Then I was either going to find Pwner, point him at them or find someone else who could handle things. After contacting the guard so they could clean up whoever was left over in their weakened state."

"You're fond of that maneuver," Zenobia glared at her.

"It worked." Chase shrugged. "My friends and family got out alive, and you sorted out your differences. Win-win, as far as I'm concerned."

She never saw the blow that exploded on her chin and sent her sprawling. She only saw stars, and the red '53' rising upward. And the pain in her tongue, where her teeth had gouged out flesh.

"Your crime shall not be forgotten," Zenobia hissed. "Remember your guilt and know that you shall pay for it. Repentance is good for the soul, and I shall show you Agnes' Mercy until you walk the righteous path once more!"

"Zenobia!" The Doge stood. "That was uncalled for! Alfonse, would you?"

"**Greater Healing,**" one of the shadowy figures spoke, and instantly the pain left Chase. She stood, tasting blood in her mouth, feeling her cut tongue knit together.

"I did not come here lightly, priestess," Chase said, staring at Zenobia. "I foresaw this. Hoon granted me this sight. He is willing to overlook our differences to accomplish our mutual goals. Is Agnes so petty she cannot do the same?"

"The grace of the master is unmarred by the flaws of the servant;" the Camerlengo's eyes were slits behind her spectacles. "There is no gain without sacrifice, and there is no sacrifice without pain. But your own methods, as distasteful as they are, seem acceptable in this matter. Tell me more of your plan."

"You're the first of three parties I needed to contact tonight." 'Needed' was a strong word, but the visions and cards seemed to agree that the more factions she got to, the better the odds were. "That performance in the atrium? That was to give Tabita the notion that I was a rogue third party and could be dealt with in a friendly fashion... or at the very least, bargained with. That and a few other things should let me talk to them without getting murdered horribly. I will be able to convince them that the fake skin has been cursed, and they'll need to go to a place of my choosing to undo the curse."

"And the third party?" The Doge asked.

"Pwner. I need to give him the compass."

The Camerlengo considered, then shook her head. "No."

"I have no other way to guarantee that he'll get to them!" Chase protested. "And we'll need a player's power to counter another player."

"We will not. You have *me*." The Camerlengo smiled. "And I am not alone."

"It's better this way, I think," the Doge nodded. "Let Zenobia keep the compass; you have no way to get it back from her, anyway. In return, we'll hold off on *our* plans. You can try to make contact with the werewolves and sell them on your con game. Leave Pwner out of this entirely. By all accounts, dealing with him is like playing with fire. Nobody gets out of that unburned."

"And one more thing," Zenobia sneered. Chase barely had time to twitch, before the woman's gloved hands whipped out and pulled the fox stole smoothly from her neck. "I'll be keeping your little friend as collateral."

"No!" Chase shouted. "You leave Renny be!" She lunged for the

Camerlengo, but the taller woman easily held her back, laughing.

The halven girl raged, letting the sorrow and stress and frustration of the last few days out, ranting and raving her hate at Zenobia. Eventually the older woman's face settled into a mask of boredom, and she slid out a knife, holding it to the stuffed throat of the stole. "You now have incentive to see your plan through. I suggest that you get to it, child."

Chase stepped back, sagging, letting tears run from her eyes. She'd jabbed them with her own fingers during the fight to get real tears, and oh, did they ache. But she focused through the blur at the Doge. "You can't let her do this!"

He looked down. "I'm sorry. You have both been reported as criminals by a trusted agent of the Baroness. I cannot legally help you with this." Then he looked up. "I can, however, insist that both you and your friend be treated with all respect prisoners are due under the law, while you are in our care."

"Technically he's in Inquisition jurisdiction," the Camerlengo said, holding up the fox stole.

Then her eyes narrowed.

"Wait...."

Chase grinned through her tears.

CHA+1

"**Scouter,**" the Camerlengo declared, then her eyes narrowed. "This isn't the golem!"

"No. No, he's off on other business," Chase smiled through her tears. **"Lesser Healing,"** she said, and her eyes stopped aching as the words told her she'd healed herself four points. "But now I know what kind of people you are, and what's awaiting me if I work with you, so why the hell should I do anything to help you?"

"Insolent little chit!" The Camerlengo turned...

...but the Doge caught her hand, rising from his chair to do so. "Enough. Chase Berrymore, you and all your associates are under arrest."

"Oh, gee, guess you better bring in the Jailers," Chase said, snorting. "Better make it seven, I might resist."

"No, you don't get it," the Doge said. "You are under ARREST. That means you are now in the custody of MY guard."

"What? Hold on! You can't do this!" Zenobia declared, dropping the stole and turning purple.

Chase got it a beat later. "So you're responsible for what happens to me... to us?"

"While you're in Arretzi or the environs thereof," the Doge shrugged. "But I seem to have forgotten to bring handcuffs, and all my guards are busy, so please be patient and wait for a duly appointed agent to take you to a cell. In the meantime, do as you will, so long as you don't harm my city."

"She was mine! You agreed to Inquisition custody for this little hooligan!"

"You said she was your problem and I said you could handle her. But clearly, she's now both our problems, so I'm handling her first, since you're incapable of putting aside your vendetta!" the Doge barked.

The Camerlengo's face was plum purple. "No! She's mine! Per the agreement, I demand to take custody of this prisoner!"

"Then you can submit a written request that will be tended to by the arresting official at the earliest convenient opportunity!" the Doge snarled back. "Which isn't now, so SIT DOWN."

A long, tense moment passed. Zenobia removed her spectacles, holding them with shaking hands. "Hoonites," she whispered. "Hoonites are chaos. Letting them run free, giving them agency, it leads to *more* chaos. You can't fight evil with chaos. It breeds more evil."

"Well, our plan is in ruins anyway. We've got nothing, Zenobia. This is our best chance to salvage it with minimal bloodshed. I... look. I respect your religion, and your zeal, but this is the most pragmatic course for my city."

Chase fought to keep her face neutral, as Zenobia looked her over. The Inquisitor looked tired, just so tired. Then the look was gone, replaced by steel and stern wrath. "After this matter is done, know that I am your enemy, girl. I will hunt you. I will find you. And I will reform you away from the god whom you foolishly chose to trust with your fate."

"You're welcome to try," Chase whispered back. "And I'll be ready for you."

There wasn't much left to discuss, she felt, and the guards didn't stop her, as she opened the door and found her way out of the dark study.

Nobody stopped her as she walked through the wide hall, feeling the cool air on her neck for the first time that evening. The stole was gone and thank goodness for it. Renny had followed Thomasi, and if he hadn't then he'd be a hostage. *Lucky, lucky little golem.*

Chase was just glad that she'd brought an identical stole along in her props bag. It had gotten the Doge on her side... well, as much as he could be, anyway. In this matter. The man clearly cared about his own people first, and she was just a visitor here. That was fair.

I wonder how Cagna is going to take the fact that I've been arrested, she thought with a totally-not-hysterical giggle.

Her humor ended when Cagna's voice whispered in her ear. "Get to the main hall, right now! We've got trouble!"

CHAPTER 22: GREEN AND WHITE AND RED ALL OVER

At first glance, the main hall didn't look any different. The dancers were dancing, the musicians had switched to a faster-paced tune, and the Acrocats were flipping and diving with grace between the balconies.

Then Chase stopped and gazed down from the stairs and really *looked* at what was happening down there.

The servants were the first clue. There was a tension there, a concealed panic, a hidden urgency to the way they moved. And once she found that out, it was simple to watch them for a minute and track where they were putting their attention. She watched as heads turned, quick little glances, but every time they happened the servant in question seemed to grow more worried.

She followed their line of sight... and found herself looking at the front doors of the manor.

They were shut now, and Chase frowned to see it. She wasn't an expert at matters of high society, but she knew that you always left the doors open in an autumn party. That part of protocol her mother had drummed into her at an early age. Unless the weather was absolutely hideous, the doors were to stand open so that the guests felt invited and didn't feel pressured to stay while they were there.

But no, the front doors were shut, and a pair of servants stood in front of them. Just behind them, a man wearing a conical hat and a set of green robes peered over the sealed portal, poking at it with growing urgency.

And a few of the guests were starting to notice, Chase realized as she drew her gaze back to the crowd. The more inebriated and the less perceptive were gathering and looking around with eagerness, expecting an announcement or some surprise, or another spontaneous performance or spectacle.

The warier guests had gathered their servants to them and were slowly pulling in their friends and allies, ready for trouble.

Just like Cagna called ME here, Chase thought with a chuckle.

A chuckle that faded, as face after face lifted and turned to her.

Chase blinked, as the entirety of the crowd fell silent.

And in the silence, came a tap from behind her. A footfall of hard leather on stone.

Another tap. Another echoing footfall.

Coming from behind her, and she dare not turn. Whatever was happening, this was the culmination, and her weirdling luck had put her on the stairs with whoever... whatever... was here.

But halvens are resilient, and Chase had an audience now. And so she followed her instincts and half-turned and curtseyed, putting her head down and her eyes to the ground. Her turban, loosened by Zenobia's slap or just by the wear and tear of casual movement, slipped and fell to the ground.

Someone above her chuckled, but it was muffled and quiet and went unnoticed as the next footfall echoed.

A boot came into her view. Leather, reinforced, and black as pitch. Golden buckles in the shape of skulls held the straps in place. Chase flicked her eyes up, tracing up the hose-clad leg until it vanished into a mass of green rags and black leather patches, a crazy quilt of fabric and hide. A massive green cloak billowed out behind it, and atop the costume sat a beaked leather mask with glass goggles, topped by a flat, round-brimmed hat.

In one hand a bronze winged scepter glittered.

In the other, a set of scales swayed and wobbled.

And before it, Chase knelt, keeping her curtsey, ignoring the turban that slowly rolled down the stairs as if the garment itself wanted to flee the scene.

The figure considered her for a second, and the rod swept down, tapping her lightly on one shoulder and then the next, and she rose, smiling, reaching up to take the figure's elbow. It was the most natural thing in the world to descend together, and the relieved laughter of the crowd below erupted and filled the atrium.

Surely this tension was nothing, the laughter seemed to say. Surely, this was just some guest or host making a noteworthy entrance, the laughter reassured the crowd.

But the servants were still on edge, and the door remained shut, no matter what the mage did to it.

"I saw that taro shazz you did earlier," the beaked figure said, and Chase nodded. Even though she had no idea what taro or shazz might be. "That was wickin' cool."

"Thanks," she said. "Your entrance was pretty, uh, wicky too."

"Duelist's got skills to pay the bills, yo," the figure said, as they reached the bottom and swept into the crowd. "Keep your head down shorty. Don't panic, okay? Everything's sang."

"Would you like your own fortune told?" Chase burst out. She was pretty sure who this was, but this was definitely not the place to meet him. Not with so many people around, not with... whatever he was doing.

"Naw. I'm working now. And the flashy shazz with the cards and stuff ain't exactly conducive to tonight's bidness."

The two walked. The figure brushed aside the first wave of social engagement, ignoring or staring at anyone who tried to stop him. Chase hurried along in his wake, her hand jostled from his elbow by the pressure of the crowd.

Then she stopped.

Is by his side the best place to be?

No. And Cagna's looking for me. But before I go...

"Size Up. Diagnose." Chase said, staring at his back in the split-second before costumed figures closed in around him.

Green Masque
Charisma – Moderately Worse
Perception – Greatly Better
Willpower – Much Better
Wisdom – Moderately Worse
Influencing Conditions:

Green Masque
Conditions: Poison Immunity, Disease Immunity, Elemental Immunity - Fire
Debuffs: None

Weird, Chase thought. She was expecting a different spread. *Maybe I'm wrong here,* she thought as she moved through the crowd.

"Ah, there you are!" Bastien's voice boomed, and the Muscle Wizaard beamed down at her. His feathery clothing was rumpled, and under his bird mask, his face gleamed with sweat.

"Had a good time, then?" Chase smiled.

"The best! Everything worked as you said it would," he fell in next to her, and they wandered toward the edge of the hall.

Cagna was waiting by a nearly-empty canapes table there, her own dress mussed. No sweat for her, not with her fur. "We got things done," the dog-woman said as soon as Chase got within earshot. "No problems, and no one bothered us."

"It was fun!" Bastien said, grinning and patting the hollow spot in his costume. Now empty, it had once held three enchanted wolf skins.

It had been a fairly simple plan, really. At the first opportunity, once eyes were off them, Cagna and the Muscle Wizaard would slip away like a pair of lovers seeking privacy. There they'd change out of their perfumed costumes and use the Muscle Wizaard's clean and press skill to alter their scents. Then it would be easy to don new, differently-scented servant's clothing that Chase had purchased earlier today. They'd move from room to room as Chase dragged out her fortuna performance and find good places to put the skins.

Then it was back to their costumes, a little artistically applied salt-water to mimic sweat, and back to the ballroom. Just another tryst among dozens that would happen that night.

At least, that was how things would go normally, Chase expected.

"Pwner's here," she said, once she was next to Cagna. "He's the one I walked into the hall."

The dog-woman sucked in her breath. "**Scouter,**" Cagna said, studying him. "Sorry. You're wrong. According to my skill, he's some guy named Bruce Wayne."

"That's an odd name," Bastien tugged on his beard.

"Scouter. What does the skill do, exactly?" Chase asked.

"It lets me see his status screen. Parts of it, anyway. He must have some pretty good willpower." Cagna frowned. "I've got his name and attributes, and one of his jobs is Playboy, but that's all I can see. Wow, that's some good charisma."

"Yeah," Chase nodded. "My Size Up confirmed that he's only moderately worse than me there."

"What?" Cagna shot her an irritated glance. "No, that's not right. You're somewhere around one-hundred and sixty, right? That's what you had last time I scouted you."

"You scouted me?" Chase frowned. "And I'm up to one-eighty-four, thank you very much."

"He's got a charisma of two-hundred, according to my skill." Cagna's eyes narrowed in her mask's eyeholes. "And you say you register him as moderately worse?"

"Yes..." Chase said. "How hard is it to fool the Scouter skill?"

"It's... not impossible. My own Undercover Identity can do it. Or..." Her eyes widened. "Cazza. Fanculo cazza!"

Chase gasped at the vulgarity, but Cagna grabbed her elbow and the

Muscle Wizaard's and pulled them even further to the sides, away from the crowd. "Cultists," the dog-woman said as they got clear of the crowd. "Cultists have a skill that lets them fool the Scouter."

Oh, oh that was bad. Chase's breath caught in her throat. Everything she knew about Cultists was bad, bad news. "Does Pwner... is he a Cultist?"

"He's been seen in the company of djinn before. And some djinn can Teleport, too, now that I think of it. Gods, I should have remembered that." Cagna's tail drooped, where it stuck out of her dress.

"Wait. Djinn, as in genie?" Bastien asked, frowning. "What do they have to do with Cultists?"

"There are three types of Cultists," Cagna said. "Daemonic, old ones worshippers, and djinn sealers. All of them let things from outside this world access and change Generica." Cagna was watching 'Bruce Wayne' like a hawk, now. "Gods, if he's a Cultist he'll have a nasty bag of tricks to apply here."

"He mentioned he was a Duelist, too," Chase gnawed her lip. "I think he was bragging. I..." she thought it over. "I don't think he knows we're on opposite sides, here. This is my opportunity to talk with him! But I can't do it here, and it needs to be private. How? How can I get him alone?"

"Leave that to me," a nearby servant said.

"Tom!" Chase jumped and stared up at him. It really wasn't much of a disguise. She wasn't sure how she'd missed him... but then, that was one of his tricks, wasn't it? She could do it too, just not as well.

"I'll handle him," Thomasi said, glaring at the masked figure. "You deal with the werewolves. There's one heading your way now, and I expect they want to talk."

"Wait! Bastien, Cagna, did you fill him in on the plan?"

"We did, but—"

"It's a good plan," the Ringmaster interrupted, "but I'm adding a bit to it. Be ready to improvise."

"Improvise how?" Chase asked, but Thomasi hefted his serving tray, handed her a wine glass, and swept off into the crowd.

Then Cagna tapped her on the shoulder, and Chase turned.

It was a small werewolf, a tiny man in a furry suit far too big for him. It had obviously been adjusted and hacked up, much to the amusement of passer-by who made little barking sounds at him. "The Lady Tabita wants you," he said, ignoring the dog-calls.

Chase grinned. "Tollen Wheadle! It's good to see you again. By all means, lead on!"

He had been the key to the whole puzzle.

Tollen Wheadle, who she had last seen guarding a dwarven woman. A woman who she found out later was a *player*.

Then when she'd gotten back from the prison to Bothernot, there had been signs of violence, and both of them were missing. Obviously, the dwarf had turned Tollen into a werewolf and escaped with him, gone off to find her old mate and reclaim her skin.

Sheer luck that they'd come this way? Or had Thomasi *known* they would come this way? Many questions, and no chances to question the manipulative Ringmaster.

But once she'd realized who the small werewolf could be... *had* to be, really, she had realized that Tabita, the dwarven woman, was the player werewolf.

As she greeted him, Tollen flinched. "Hey there, Berrymore."

Chase smiled and flapped a hand in a 'lead on' kind of wave.

"Right, right." Tollen turned. Charisma had always been his weak point. *Gods, this ballroom must be hell for him. And they're laughing at him! They think he's a joke!*

Indeed, he seemed to walk easier once they were out of the main room. And as they passed doors ajar to darkened rooms filled with quiet conversation and quieter moans, he was walking with confidence again.

"Millie's doing all right," Chase broke the silence. "The last time I saw her, I mean. She survived the zombies."

"What are you talking about?" Tollen shot her a look from under his wolf mask.

He was shaking, she saw. The eyes of his mask didn't quite line up with his own, and every time he twitched, it broke his gaze. She couldn't get a good read on his eyes... but she didn't need it, really. His body language was telling her he was holding back something. Holding back anger? No, that wasn't quite it.

"The zombies. One of the prison escapees raised a lot of zombies and tried to wipe Bothernot off the map. He tried to kill everyone, Tollen."

Tollen made a sound deep in his throat. It didn't sound like anything a halven should make. Chase took a step back—

—and he followed.

And it was about that point that Chase realized she was alone in the hallway with a monster.

How long has the full moon been up? How long has he been a werewolf? Not that long. He doesn't have practice controlling it... I'm in danger, she realized.

"Did she send you to kill me, Tollen Wheadle? Were those her orders?"

"Not... her command." Tollen shook his head, sweat running down into the jaws of the wolf mask, and dripping like drool. "Bring you..." he said, voice rumbling. "But... I'm hungry... so hungry..."

"And what would Gam Wheadle say if she saw you like this, Tollen?"
CHA+1

Chase's voice cracked like a whip, and the Scout rocked backward as if he'd been struck. Gam Wheadle had been a terror, as halven matriarchs go, and the memory seemed to shock him out of whatever raw urges his new state seemed to be troubling him with.

"Follow me!" he gasped out and ran down the hall, almost loping as he went.

Chase pursued him, mind working furiously. There were four competing plans in motion here, tonight. The Doge and the Camerlengo were one, and she'd defused *that*: the information she'd given them had rendered it useless. There was Pwner's plan, whatever it was, and she had to leave it to Thomasi. Chase didn't really have a choice there, so she had to hope that he could pull out a win. There was her plan, and it had mostly gone off... but it was the werewolf plan that she had to deal with now.

I have to get them to dance to my tune, or this is all for naught, Chase knew. *I have to get them to where they need to be. To a place where they think they hold all the cards.*

"Here," Tollen snarled, pounding a door with force belying his halven frame. "Go... in."

Chase looked at him, and his eyes flashed yellow. He was still now, not trembling anymore. And the sense of danger from him rose like a stench, filled the corridor, told her it was far, far too late to run.

Without taking her eyes from his she moved up to the door, turned to the side, and opened it. Then with a smooth, unhurried motion she backed through the door and shut it behind her.

"Hello, Chase," Tabita said from behind her.

"Hi!" Chase forced her face into a smile, before she turned around. "How can I serve you, Miss... Tabita..."

Blood spattered the study.

Blood coated the books lining the shelves.

Blood dripped from the desk, where Giuseppe Coltello's head sat, a horrified expression frozen forever on his dead face.

And blood stained the mouth of the dwarven woman who sat naked in the chair behind the desk, casually taking bites out of a human heart. Completely at ease, ivory skin flawless under the slick red juices that coated it, hair primly back in a braided ponytail, kept out of the mess by design beforehand.

"Oh," Chase said, realizing just how much she'd dove in, gone in over her head, overinflated her chances of victory here. She'd screwed up, she'd screwed up bad, and here there were monsters.

"Oh," the werewolf Alpha growled in agreement, and she turned to the side to see him in full furry form... tall, thin, black, and wearing only a sword belt with a rapier. "Little girl, you have one chance to get out of this room alive. Will you help us?"

Chase took a breath, gagged on the smell of blood and offal. To the side she saw a pair of pointy shoes poking out from under a screen, and blood slowly spreading in a widening puddle. Giuseppe was dead, the Coltello line gone for good.

"I'll help you," Chase said, and when she jerked her attention back to the Alpha he was in front of her, her head right at the level of... Oh. Oh, he definitely should have worn pants. But she was far too scared to blush, and she forced her gaze higher still, staring up at the monster's muzzle.

"Good," Tabita said, finishing her meal with a snap of flawless teeth. "Mercutio, take her. We can discuss matters on the road."

"Wait, hold on!" Chase squeaked. She wasn't done *here!* There was too much to do *here,* and the plan required getting back to her allies, and...

...and then the bag went over her head, as her plan fell to pieces.

CHAPTER 23: NO PLAN SURVIVES FUR'S CONTACT

Well, at least they haven't killed me yet, Chase thought to herself as the sack shuddered and bounced. They were moving her again. They had been at this a while, a long while, and she had the bruises to prove that they'd been none too gentle about it.

If it had been a cage or a box she would have tried to escape. You knew where you stood with one of those. Something solid like that was an admission that they weren't watching you all the time, that your captors expected shenanigans, and wanted to slow you down because those shenanigans might work.

But a sack was a different sort of statement. A sack offered the prisoner no real barrier... and no real protection.

And when the world outside of the sack was guaranteed to be filled full of angry werewolves, well...

Chase didn't need Foresight to see how an escape attempt would go.

One last bout of self-pity rocked her, and she cried a bit as she jounced and bounced in the sack, keeping her sobs muffled. Chase knew she had fallen prey to hubris. She'd gone in expecting the wards and magical guardians of the Verde mansion to prevent bloodshed and at least slow down the werewolves, but clearly the wards hadn't presented any real obstacle. She had managed to derail what she thought was the Verde trap, but the Verde trap had been entirely different than she expected, and at best the final outcome had been a draw.

But the worst crime, the worst crime of all was that she had thought that she could handle the werewolves with nothing but words and chutzpah. And if they had been people, then she might have had a chance.

They weren't. They were only people half the time. The other half of the time they were monsters, and when you were up against monsters words didn't cut it.

The second worst crime was that she had gone in there with a plan and expected it to work even though everyone else involved had their own plan going.

Why?

Why should she be special? Why should her plan get some sort of carte blanche to succeed even though it was one among the many? Sure, she was lucky, but that was only one attribute out of ten. And at no time had she ever been fully in control of all the variables or been able to influence everyone she needed to influence to make sure things fell out her way.

This wasn't Bothernot, where she could clearly figure out the impact to everyone her machinations and gossip would impact. This wasn't her home town... which she saw now, was easy compared to dealing with a city full of factions and monsters and nobles. No wonder most halvens shunned adventure and things like this! You went in with your best toe forward, and then you ended up in a werewolf sack! Nobody should have to end up in a werewolf sack. That sort of thing didn't happen to reasonable halvens.

The thought made her giggle, and she tried not to. The stuffy air was making her loopy.

Would they mind if she poked a hole in the sack? She shrugged, slid out a playing card, and whispered, **"Foresight."**

She couldn't see too well, but she saw a shadowy hole appear and let in a bit of light. Nothing happened for the other eight seconds, so Chase let her ghost self fade away and followed through with the slice.

Your Foresight skill is now level 39!

Instantly, cool air rushed into the sack. Chase pushed her nose against the hole and breathed deep...

...and she could smell none of the odors of the city around her.

This was the scent of the field, of fall leaves and dead grass. It was cold, and it contrasted with the warmth of whoever's back the sack was currently slung over. It also put paid to her budding headache, and let her think a bit more clearly.

Halven temperament asserted itself once that last obstacle was gone. Self-pity did no good to help the situation, so now what was she going to do about it?

Fighting was right out. Without allies, the best she could do was throw a couple of silver cards and then die. Even with her Oracle tricks, they'd only delay the inevitable.

Sneaking away? That had more merit. But there were problems with that notion. The first being that Chase couldn't see in the dark, and her captors probably wouldn't be so hindered. She put her eye to the hole, and peered out for a long moment... nope, dark as heck. Occasionally she got a flash of moonlight from above as the sack jounced up on her bearer's shoulder, but most of the time it was hidden by tree branches that closed down like the claws of great black birds seizing their prey.

Also even though she wasn't a slouch at sneaking, she had no real way to hide her scent and she'd be up against creatures that were built for hunting down fleeing prey. No, this would be giving them an advantage, and right now she couldn't afford to do that.

Talking. It would have to be talking, and fortunately she was very good at it. But would they listen? That was the problem.

Then again...

They thought they'd won, hadn't they? Maybe? If they had found one of the skins, then they would think they'd done what they set out to do. They had to have found a skin... she couldn't imagine a reason they would have left the party otherwise.

And there, in the darkness of the sack, her captor's back hot against her own through the layer of canvas and being carried off to gods knew where, Chase took stock of her advantages and prepared for a battle of words. Because if words failed her, she was pretty much screwed.

When the long run finally stopped, when the night air was still again, save for panting and the occasional muttered growl, they finally dumped her out of the sack.

She wasn't sure what they were expecting.

What they *got* was a small figure, picking herself up off the ground and dusting herself off, completely ignoring the ring of dark shapes around her. With a final sigh, she pulled out a headscarf and snapped it open, causing the ring to draw tighter, and a few growls of warning to echo forth. But she ignored that too and calmly fastened the scarf over her black locks, tying it under her chin.

Finally one of the werewolves coughed, and cleared his throat.

She looked up at him, squinting in the moonlight. "Yes?"

"I rather expected you to be sobbing, at this point," said the Alpha.

"Oh, I did all that in the bag." She turned around, taking in the scene. The familiar shapes of the carved logs, the dark mouth of the cave, the faint smell of rot... all those things told her they had returned to the dungeon that she had found three short days ago. *Back where it all started, even if I didn't know it had begun at that point.*

And oh, didn't that raise questions? Thomasi, surely, had known

Tabita was a werewolf. How else would he have recognized the skin? Why else had he taken it? Was it truly coincidence that they had both come this way? Chase thought not. *He's been playing his own game. And... I don't think I should mention him to Tabita and her pack. That's a card I can play later, if I have to.*

"Well, if you're not going to sob and wail that's a relief, I suppose." The Alpha loped over to her and squatted down on his haunches. His breath smelled of blood and dog, as he brought his face to hers, long muzzle nearly touching her chest. She flinched back, despite herself, and he seemed satisfied by that. "Though I wonder how much of this is an act, and how much is true bravery."

"Most of it's logic," Chase said, not daring to look away. "If you wanted me dead, I'd be dead. So you want me for something. And after that fortuna reading, I have some vague idea why... but not any specifics. Maybe you can tell me what you want from me? I'd love to do it for you then go away, far far away from here. Alive and intact. Maybe with my pockets full of gold?"

She wasn't sure which werewolf started laughing first, but it caught on fast, and soon everyone but the Alpha was literally howling.

As the sound echoed from the hills, he stood up and gave a shake, twitching and shuddering and shrinking...

...until the lean, black-haired man she'd seen at Don Sangue's final feast was standing in the monster's place. He was clothed, thankfully and took a second to adjust his sword belt.

"Did you have that on you when you were... fuzzier?" Chase asked, confused.

"It's complicated. Basically it's still there, but it looks like it isn't. One of the perks of my condition."

Condition? Chase filed that away for later usage. But the Alpha was continuing. "Anyway... my name is Mercutio. If it's gold you want we can do that. That's meaningless to us, for the most part."

The ring of werewolves around them shuffled, and a few of them muttered. He shot a glare back over his shoulder. "For the most part!" he reiterated. "You can always get more gold."

"But you can't always get home," Tabita's voice rang over the clearing, and Chase turned to see the squat werewolf sitting on a ledge up above the dungeon, peering out at the forest beyond. "I want to go home, girl. And I think maybe you can help me with that."

"I... you're her, aren't you? Tabita?"

Chase knew very well who she was, but she put uncertainty in her voice anyway. She worked better when people underestimated her.

"I am. You're a clever one, but really you're coming in late in this

sordid little play. Used as a pawn by those who care nothing for you."
Tabita hopped off the ledge, landed with a meaty THUD and a casual
ease that displayed a strength that made Chase shudder. Even the Muscle
Wizaard would be hard-pressed to match that sort of brute strength, she
thought.

"Don Coltello basically threatened me with the choice of death or
helping him." Chase shrugged. "Now he's gone."

"And yet you told Don Sangue we were enemies." The Alpha paced,
circling her. She turned as best she could, without putting her back to
Tabita.

"An angry undead whatever-he-was right in front of me, about to
maul us? Yeah you better believe I told him that!" Chase laughed. "I
would have told him the moon was made out of cheese if it got us out of
there alive!"

"Enough. She'll help us or she'll die. Since she was so good at
opposing us when Coltello threatened her, I figure we can do the same."
Tabita stalked closer. "You're a healer. Are you good with magic that
isn't healing?"

"Divination," Chase said, caught with both werewolves flanking her.
"I'm both an Oracle and a Medium. That's what we do is figure things
out by asking the gods and the cosmos in general."

"Mmm. That last part, I can usually do," Tabita growled. "I'm a
Shaman. But it will take me time, probably the rest of the night to
perform a dream quest. If your work is faster, then perhaps we can figure
something out."

"Mostly. I have one skill that can knock me out for an hour and a half
or so," Chase said, still equidistant between the player and the Alpha.
"But the more I know, the more reliable my work is. I don't have to
spend time separating my assumptions from the reality, if that makes
sense. Can I ask you a few questions before I start firing up my magic?"

To Chase's relief, the Alpha hesitated, then walked around to join
Tabita. The ring of werewolves spread out and slipped into the trees
ringing the hillside or headed down slope. She'd passed a test of some
sort. Now all she had to do was stall... stall and maybe figure out a few
things that Thomasi couldn't or wouldn't tell her.

"I think that's fair," Tabita said. "But we can't waste too much time.
This needs to be done while the moon is full, and I don't want to wait
another month if we take too long tonight."

"I'll try not to waste time with the stupid stuff, then," Chase took a
breath. "What do you need help with?"

Tabita gave herself a shake... and then she was standing there in her
dwarven form. Wearing clothes this time, thankfully. She opened an

overlarge purse that Chase vaguely recalled seeing at one point and hauled out a rolled up piece of fur. She shook it out in the moonlight, and Chase's breath hissed from between her teeth as a small pair of chains on one side of it jingled.

She'd gotten one of the skins Chase had planted, and that meant that there was some hope of salvaging things.

"What is that?" Chase asked.

"My skin. My old skin." Tabita sighed. "Do you know how I got this skin? Do you know how I got my Job?"

"No."

"Shaman and Berserker didn't cut it. Shaman and Scout didn't work out. No matter what I did, or how many people I hunted down and ate, it just didn't unlock."

Chase's eyes went wide, but after a brief struggle, she kept the emotion off her face.

"Shaman and Tamer... that one worked. It got me to Lycanthrope, but the downsides outweighed the upsides. Then at level ten I got rank up options, but none fit... Until I got a lead off Readit."

"Off what?"

"A secret repository of lore. Some of it's lies, but occasionally it worked out. And this lead told about the legend of the loup-garou... as the devs saw it, anyway."

"The loup-garou... you skinned yourself?" Chase burst out, horrified.

"I did." Tabita smiled. Then the smile faded. "This was before I felt pain." Now she was frowning. "Now it's going to be a different story."

"Before you felt pain? You didn't used to? Is..." Chase swallowed and threw a silent Foresight out there. She didn't see herself get gutted for asking, so she chanced it. "Is this a player thing?"

"You know about that?" Tabita considered her warily.

"Very little," Chase confessed. "Cagna told me about Pwner, but I don't think she had the full picture, either. You don't die, or you come back, and you're from another world?"

"A dull world, a dreary world." Tabita said, her voice rising bit by bit. "A world full of sheep who don't know they're being sheared, a world where the powerful and greedy won years ago, and turned everyone else into slaves, and everyone is okay with it!" Now she was stalking around the clearing, fuming, but her anger wasn't directed at Chase and that was a good thing. "A world where the rich buy up the wilds and fence them off and rape the land, ruining it forever! A world where you're not free to be what you want to be. Where you have to work jobs frantically, if you want to even survive. A world without magic, where dreams die and nobody cares because that's just how it is." She spat.

The Alpha sat a warning hand on Chase's shoulder, leaning down a bit to do so. Chase nodded to him. She was smart enough not to interrupt, but it was good he cared. It made her chances of survival that much easier.

"You don't know how lucky you have it here," Tabita said, finally. "How good it is here. And how little I really want to go back. But I have to."

"Why?" Chase asked. And this was really what nagged at her. Thomasi had hinted at things, danced around them, and she needed the answer, if fate or whatever else out there was going to keep throwing her up against players. "Why do you have to go back?"

Silence for a bit longer. And for a minute, she thought Tabita wouldn't answer. But eventually the dwarf chuckled. "What does it matter? You'll deal with it or you won't. This world? This world isn't truly real. It's a game we created. Nothing but a game."

"What, like Chess or Seven-card Spatzle?" Chase shook her head. "That's not making much sense."

"No. Think of it like a dream, brought to life with magic. People from my world created this one. It's a Hyper-Reality... no. How can I explain this?" Tabita rubbed her eyes. "We have machines in our heads, in my world. In the real world. They give us access to made-up dreams. Shared dreams. This is one of them."

"Wait. Everything's a dream?" Chase blinked and followed that to its logical conclusion. "I'm a dream?"

And the pieces of the puzzle slid together.

It explained so MUCH of the players' behavior.

They acted as they wanted they did what they pleased, because to them it was nothing more than a dream. Just something to pass the time between wakefulness and slumber, with no real meaning or consequences, no matter what you did.

"And there's the existential dread," Tabita sighed. "Try to get over it quickly. We still need you to do things."

"If it's a dream..." Chase said, knowing that she probably wouldn't sleep again for a few nights with all of the questions now chewing at her. "If it's a dream, then why can't you wake up?"

"That. That right there is the ten million dollar question," Tabita said, sitting down on a log and kicking a goblin skull down the slope. "This isn't the first game of its sort. It's a cheap darknet feelie, an uncensored gray area sort of game, but even the cashgrab devs who made it weren't dumb enough to turn off the safety protocols. You can't! They're literally wired into our heads!" She raised her hands and slapped them down on her meaty thighs. "The worst that could happen is that you'd get adware piped onto your retinal HUDs until you got a malware scrub! Hell, I'd just purchased advanced antiviral for that I expected that. But... well, it's more than that.

"Things are more real now. Like ludicrously more real. Pain, I feel pain now. All the pain. Before it was muted feedback. Just annoyance, letting you know your character was in trouble. Now... it hurts. And I don't know why." Tabita's voice dropped to a whisper, as she spoke the last words. "Nobody could code that. There are no receptors rigged up to even DO that sort of thing. And it's more than that, there are details, insane details..." She reached down and scooped up something in the darkness. "This twig. Before when I picked up a stick, it would have the same basic shape. It would do that because the developers were lazy. But now each twig is different. Each twig is individual. Who would DO that? Who would waste the computing power to..." she shook her head. "It's crazy. And I wonder if I'm the crazy one, maybe? I wonder if this is somehow another world, and not a dream, despite everything." She turned to look at Chase, and her eyes were wide and wild in the moonlight. "And I need to go back, need to go back and see. I need to make sure that this is the dream, and the other world is the reality, because if I'm wrong or confused somehow then I've done some really, really horrible stuff and I don't know how the hell I can live with myself."

"It's not you," Mercutio said. "It's the beast."

"The beast that I wanted to be!" Tabita stood and glared at him until he lowered his eyes. "The beast that I made of myself," Tabita finished, softly.

Chase swallowed. "How will the skin help you do that?" she asked.

"It might not. But it's the best chance I have," Tabita held up the fur. "I was killed and skinned in Arretzi just before the... whatever-the-hell-it-was happened. Call it the crash."

"Okay... still not seeing how it will help you."

"So you see the words, right? I'd be surprised if you didn't, everyone can now."

"THE words? Yes." Chase frowned. "What do they have to do with this?"

"I'm getting to that!" Tabita snarled. "Players like me, we can see additional words. Including the patches. No, shut up, don't ask. All you need to know is that the patches tell us when they affect our jobs. And the Loup-Garou job requirement got waived. Now you don't need your skinsuit to change. Skinsuits are not supposed to be IN the game. But here it is..." she shook it. "And it still has magic within it! Just as I'd suspected!"

"Ah," Chase said. It had magic within it because she'd had it enchanted.

"It's a glitch," Tabita continued, ignoring Chase's response. "And if I do the right ritual and put it on, I just might glitch out of the game!" She stood, and her shoulders sagged, dragging the skin on the ground. "Might. Might is the keyword, here. It's a long shot. I won't lie."

She looked up then, and her eyes were yellow and practically glowing in the moonlight. "That's where you come in, Oracle. You divine me up a future where that happens and tell me how to get there. And Mercutio will make you the richest halven in this little fake Italy."

"All right," Chase said, holding out her hand for the skin. "Let me see what I can do."

And she did. She pulled out her cards and did several readings; she studied Tabita's palms; she lit candles and studied the patterns left in the smoke. And after Tabita and Mercutio started getting restless, she lay down for a Short Vision.

But what she saw made no sense at all.

A dark room, with green pillars, and numbers and pillars flickering by overhead. Werewolves in those green pillars, and Tabita in the center of it all, cutting, cutting, cutting at her skin. Chase looked away as the blood flowed, and her gaze went on endlessly, staring into a dark void.

It was a place not meant for sanity. It was a place that couldn't be, and she didn't know what it meant, and then the vision started to fade...

...No! She thought. And then she remembered she had a skill for this now.

"Focus Vision," she thought, and her view snapped back to the room.

Then it pulled back, showing a cave lit by guttering fires, a throne room strung with thatch and bones and dead goblins all about. And a green light shone behind the throne; a doorway closing on the void, a hole in the world sealing... just as Mercutio went charging through it, leaving the goblin massacre behind and hurtling into the darkness.

That's the room that Renny told me about! Chase thought. The core chamber.

Your Focus Vision skill is now level 2!
Your Short Vision skill is now level 9!

With a gasp, Chase sat up.

The moon was a lot higher in the sky than she remembered, and then two shapes blocked it, a squat silhouette and a tall, lanky one.

"Well?" Tabita asked.

"I know where you have to go to do the ritual," Chase said. "The dungeon. The dungeon is the key. Well, any one would work, probably, but this one's right here, and time is short."

You are now a level 6 Medium!
CHA+5
LUCK+5

"What does the dungeon have to do with anything?" Tabita frowned.

But Mercutio's eyes grew wide, white in the moonlight. "I've heard something about dungeons. That each one has a vault that's between worlds..."

"That sure matches what I saw," Chase said and explained her vision in detail.

"That's it, that's got to be it!" Tabita said. "It's probably supposed to be a dev-only room, but... well, something's wrong. So it'll be a glitch on a glitch! That's my best shot at getting home!"

"Well, it is what it is," Chase shrugged.

"Did you see Mercutio there?" Tabita asked. "How MANY werewolves in pillars?"

"About six, and no, I didn't see Mercutio there," Chase admitted.

"All right. Then that settles it. Stay here." Tabita pulled Mercutio to the side and spoke with him. He didn't like what she had to say, and they argued for a time, breaking into low, guttural growls at one point. But finally he raised his head and howled, a long, high call that made Chase shudder to hear it.

The call was answered, from all around the forest. And inside of ten minutes, the pack had assembled again. After a brief bit, Tabita chose six of the pack, formed a party, and marched into the cave without a backward glance.

Chase read the anger and humiliation in Mercutio's stance and said nothing.

But he must have read something in her body language, because he marched over and unceremoniously picked her up.

"Wait, what? Hey! Hold on!"

"If she succeeds, you go free and I'll make you rich. If she fails or dies, you'll die," Mercutio said, his earlier civility gone. "Until then, you wait with us. And just so you don't get any ideas...

Chase cried out as he pulled her silvered cards from her pocket, handling them deftly with gloved fingers. "I'll be keeping these," Mercutio finished.

"I wasn't going to use them anyway!" she shouted. "I'm not insane! You'd pulverize me!"

"Keep remembering that, and you might just live through this after all." Mercutio said. Then he turned, as something small pelted up the hill, something that crashed its way through the underbrush. "What? Tollen?"

"Torches! It's an army!" Tollen Wheadle rumbled, still half-beast. "Coming from the road!"

And Chase exhaled with relief, staring out into the darkness and seeing faint pinpricks or light. The compass had done its job. The tracking spell led her 'allies' straight to the werewolves.

Her relief died in her throat as Mercutio whirled at the sound... and though her charisma let her quickly rearrange her features, his perception was just too good. His eyes narrowed. "You. You did this."

"How could I do this?" Chase protested, backing up. "I've been with you the whole time!"

"Yes. Yes you have..." he growled. "We've covered our tracks every time; we've made sure to turn the farmers whose lands we crossed, and we've avoided light and other things that would draw attention. The only difference is that *you're* here."

"Hey! Hold on!" Chase held up her hands. Her back hit the side of the cliff, and Mercutio stalked closer. "I'm trying to help you! I want gold and to get out of here. Do you honestly think that those people won't murder me horribly as well? Silver arrows through the heart will kill me just as bad as they will you!"

He scrutinized her for a moment. "There's a simple way to test this. Tollen, go take her out into the woods, down by the creek bend. If the hunters turn toward you, then kill her and return. If it stays after us, bring her along and hit them from the rear."

Chase folded her arms. "This is a waste of time, but okay."

"Girl, do you really think I need your agreement to do this? Do you think I care?" A hint of the beast crept into Mercutio's voice, and she didn't have to fake the fear that must have shown on her face.

"Come on then," Tollen said, grabbing her shoulders and pulling her back so hard that she stumbled. "Let's go!"

Chase weighed her options, glanced a final time at the Alpha's face, and decided to let her fellow halven pull her away from the obviously angry and possibly-still-going-to-eat-her werewolf.

You are now a level 11 Halven!
AGL+4
CHA+4
CON+2
DEX+4
INT+2
LUCK+4
PER+2
STR+2
WILL+2

WIS+4
COOL +5
MENTAL FORTITUDE+5

Then it was down the hillside, through the trees, and Chase's recently-improved agility let her move without stumbling *too* much as Tollen practically dragged her along. She knew better to complain, or look back, or do anything to make Mercutio change his mind. He could and would gut her right there and then, if he knew what she'd done.

And he'd almost guessed it, she thought, feeling sweat gather at the edges of her headscarf. *With only the barest suspicion, he figured out that there was some sort of tracking effect in play. He just thought it was me and not the skin.*

"You're afraid," Tollen whispered, as the silence of the dark forest was broken by distant gurgling. Water ahead, the creek most likely. "You're afraid and I can smell it. Don't be." Tollen said. "I won't kill you."

"You won't have to," Chase said, putting confidence in her voice. "I'm not the one who drew them here."

"Then why are you afraid?"

"Because I'm alone in the woods with a werewolf. And because you almost killed me earlier tonight, Tollen Wheadle, and I'm not sure why." She stared at him, unable to see very much of him beyond a shadowed shape, in the darkness of the woods.

"That were... that were the beast," Tollen said, his voice rising a bit. "It needed to feed. Needed to hunt. I took care of that after they took you. You got nothing to fear from me, Berrymore."

"You killed someone," Chase said and the words hung in the air as the water ran merrily, dark and hidden.

"They deserved it," he said, but she caught the hint of uncertainty in his voice.

"Did you deserve it, when Tabita attacked you? When she burst out of the summerhouse at nightfall and tore into you?"

A hiss of indrawn breath. "How did you... no, it doesn't matter. I'm stronger now. Better. Don't have to hide in the woods to get away from stupid people who talk too much and won't let me be. I can hide in plain sight, and ain't none the wiser."

"So long as you kill a few every month, that makes it all right?" Chase knew she was pushing her luck here, but this was Tollen Wheadle. She knew enough of his buttons and triggers to avoid them. And this was a vital chance to learn things that the other werewolves wouldn't tell her. "Never mind that," she said, as he growled. "What I can't figure out is how you did it in the mansion. Or how Tabita killed Giuseppe, for that matter. There were supposed to be magical wards and guardians and things like that! Everyone told me about how magical the Verde family was, but that manor did NOT live up to its reputation."

"Oh. That." Tollen seemed to relax a bit, judging by how his shadow shifted. "It is pretty secure... but the Thieves' Guild here cracked it decades ago. Mercutio paid them a wompload of gold for the pass phrases. After that, so long as we didn't target any family, or go to the secure vaults there weren't nothing the guardians could do and the watchers looked the other way."

"She was never after Maddalena Verde." Chase closed her eyes.

"Would have taken her if she could have. But the old biddy was supposed to be a Conjuror. Bad odds on a good night. And that weren't a good night."

"No." Chase picked her way towards the water sound, stopped as she came to a break in the trees. Moonlight glimmered on the water.

Tollen moved up behind her and put a hand on her shoulder. She flinched.

"Been thinking about it," Tollen said.

"About what?"

"You and me."

A trickle of unease crept down her spine, and she stepped back from him. "I don't think we should have this conversation."

"That's the thing," he said, stepping closer. "I think we should. I can't look at you, I can't smell you; I can't hear you without thinking of meat, Chase Berrymore. Even with the kill I had, even with the beast sated... I want you. I want to sink my teeth into your throat and chew."

It wasn't what he was saying.

It was the fact that he was saying it matter-of-factly, that he was saying it like the most natural thing in the world, that filled her with dread.

Chase started to run through her methods of stopping him from tearing her throat out, and came up short. There... weren't many. And he was a Scout, with high, high perception. She mouthed, **"Silent Activation, Foresight,"** and let her ghost self try to deflect the conversation. She watched as he ignored her and his ghostly form stepped closer.

"Silent Activation, Foresight," she muttered again and tried to bluster. It worked no better. And the pain in her chest rose, as paradox threatened.

But the third try, that was the charm.

"Is that what you told Friatta Costello?" Chase asked, standing her ground. "Is that what you did to her?"

Tollen flinched backward. She saw him slink back into the shadows, away from the open patch where the moonlight shone over the brook. "I didn't mean to do that. That were a mistake."

"Then why did you kill her?"

"They sent me! They sent me to find out who had ordered the skin! But she didn't know." He sighed. "I went in, pretended to be a customer looking for a new sheath. Tried to chat her up. Sending ME to chat someone up. Don't know why they expected it to go well."

Privately, Chase agreed. The loner Scout was one of the least charismatic people she'd known back in Bothernot. "And what happened, exactly?" Chase asked. She kept her voice gentle and neutral. No hint of judgment.

"She didn't know. It was her mother did the work, back then. But her mother was dead. It was just her and her father, and she was lonely. And then she..." Tollen's voice hitched in his throat. "She said she was lonely. That her father was dead drunk. Wouldn't hear nothing. And she leaned into me, and her throat was right THERE."

"Ah." Chase said.

"It was indecent! Didn't even know if I was married or not!" Tollen snarled. "She weren't no good woman. Just a loose city trollop!"

"And now she's dead," Chase said.

"Which brings us back to you and me," Tollen said and moved back into the light.

Damn him. Damn his single track mind... Chase took a deep breath. "There isn't a you and a me."

"No. But there could be." Tollen considered her. "One bite and some time is all it takes. Not even a full night."

"Did Mercutio tell you to offer me this?" Chase said. "Because I don't want it. I have trouble keeping well-fed anyway, I don't want to have to go running all over the woods on top of that."

"No. But I know how he thinks. We ain't letting you go. You know too much. You're with the pack now." Tollen stepped closer. "I'll have to smell you every day. Every night. And Berrymore? You smell delicious."

"Thanks," she said, taking another step. Her foot splashed in the water, and she was thankful for her shoes for once.

Then... then she had an idea. Not a great one, but it was worth a shot. She squirmed her foot, tore it loose from her shoe, and stepped deeper into the creek. Mud and rock under her foot, and she felt around with her toes as Tollen advanced on her.

"Two ways this ends," he said, his voice dipping lower, heading toward the beast but not quite there. "I'll kill you. Or... you join us."

"Mercutio said he'd let me go," she protested.

"Mercutio might. We won't. Your scent is on my mind. In my head. And the others, the others you beat up... it's there, too. We all want you, Berrymore. We all want to feed." That last word rattled into a growl.

"And what would Gammer Wheadle say about this?" Chase asked. Nothing... nothing... there! She stopped moving, her foot on a rock that was just the right size.

"Gammer Wheadle ain't here!" Tollen said, stepping all the way into the moonlight. The leer on his face was horrific to see.

"Oh. Well, in that case..." Chase bent into the stream, swept up the rock, and yelled, **"Rapid Fire!"**

Tollen barely had time to blink before three rocks slammed into his face, with audible crunches. He fell backward, crying out, and Chase backed up further into the stream, squirming out of her last shoe as she shouted over and over again, **"Bad Fortune! Bad Fortune! Bad Fortune!"**

You have inflicted 47 points of fortune damage on Tollen Wheadle.

Your Bad Fortune skill is now level 7!

Tollen Wheadle resists your Bad Fortune curse!

You have inflicted 48 points of fortune damage on Tollen Wheadle.

Your Bad Fortune skill is now level 8!

By the time Tollen was on his feet again, Chase was across the stream and down about a hundred points of her own fortune, from casting the spell as quickly as she could. But it paid off, in the end.

Your Bad Fortune is ineffective: Target has no fortune.

"Berrymore!" Tollen shouted and grew, grew a full foot and a half as he expanded and his skin swapped out for fur. "You're MINE."

"That's no way to talk to a lady!" a cheerful voice called from above. "I cast fist from **Off the Top Rope!**"

And Chase laughed, laughed in hysterical relief, laughed as a massive form plunged from the trees, elbow first. Laughed as Tollen Wheedle disappeared under the mountain of flesh that was the Muscle Wizaard. She laughed until she cried, then sat on the ground and shook while Renny and Cagna rushed over and folded her into their embrace. She even ignored the words that rolled by.

You are now a level 7 Medium!

CHA+5

LUCK+5

All told it only took about a minute and a half to get over it. Her cool was far too high to let it get to her for too long, and she had stuff to do. Finally she patted the dog-woman's arm and stood.

"Ahem," another familiar voice cleared its throat, and Chase looked up into the moonlight.

"Thomasi," she said. "I was wondering what was keeping you."

"I had to make sure his attention was properly directed elsewhere."

"I helped! I masked Bastien's scent!" Renny piped up.

"And Cagna's the reason we were able to pick up your trail in the first place," Thomasi continued. "So it was a team effort. Sorry for the delay though, we had to stop by our old campsite up the ridge a ways. I had to retrieve the skin."

"We have a lot to talk about," Chase said, not taking her eyes off the man. "But there's no time. Tabita's in the cave. Now is our chance to take down Mercutio and the rest of the werewolves. All we have to do is hold them until the Doge and the Camerlengo arrive, then get away in the chaos."

"No good, I'm afraid." Thomasi shook his head. "We passed by above and upwind of them while we were looking for you and caught some of the conversation. Mercutio's gone into the dungeon to warn Tabita."

"What? No, he can't... he can." Chase realized. Like a fool, she'd told them that any dungeon would work for their purposes. They could escape and try the ritual in a month, at a new dungeon.

"Yes. It's over. I'm going to leave them the skin as a peace offering and a note asking them to leave the country," Thomasi said. "It's probably the best outcome that we can get out of this."

Chase turned around and thought. And after a moment, the answer rose up... along with anger. "No. Not good enough."

"Don't fight me on this. If she has a chance to get home— "

"Not good enough!" Chase shouted, and stomped up to him, glaring up at his wide, wide eyes. "We're not dreams! This isn't a game! You don't get to murder us or turn packs of us into monsters and get away unscathed!" Still keeping her eyes on him, she knelt and started picking up stones from the creek, finding the ones just the right shape and size for throwing. "This ends here and now, and they go down. And I'll do it with or without you, do you understand me, you... you... player?"

"Oh cheese us," he muttered. "She told you." He seemed to shrink... then rallied. "Look. It's a moot point. They'll withdraw into the dungeon and wait us out. Wait the army out, for that matter. It's full of goblins to eat, probably has water to drink as well, and they're off in their own private instances. There's no way to get them out."

"Actually, there is." Renny spoke up. "Do you remember what I said about sealing dungeons?"

CHAPTER 24: CONFESSIONS OF A RINGMASTER

The rock whistled through the air, forming a perfect arc just above Renny's head, and smacked into the stomach of the twisted little black-and-green man who was charging him. The breath left the goblin with a whoosh of air, and he crumpled to the ground, sliding across the floor. Renny stepped to the side and let him go by.

The fourth goblin screeched and threw his spear at Chase...

"Whip It!" Thomasi said, and with a snap of his Ringmaster's whip the spear went clattering off a wall and into the gorge below, vanishing into darkness.

Then the Muscle Wizaard was on the fourth goblin, and that was pretty much that. Chase turned away as the little creature squeaked and stared at the bodies on the floor.

"You do this sort of thing for *fun*?" Chase muttered, sparing Thomasi a glare.

He had the good grace to look abashed. "Some do. I never got the taste. It's mostly those for who are obsessed with getting powerful magic items and fighting challenging monsters."

Chase just looked at the bodies and the black blood spreading beneath them. One of the goblins had a little bracelet. Just some little thing with charms on it.

"They eat babies," Cagna said. "Don't mourn them."

"So does Tabita, I'm pretty sure. Or she's done things about as bad." Chase turned her back on Thomasi and pointed at the low entrance to the next cave. "But here we are, on our way to help her."

The Ringmaster sighed. "She gets to leave. You get her out of your world. It's a win-win situation."

"And if it doesn't work, what then?" Chase scowled, falling into line behind Cagna. "Will you help us fight her? Will you help us capture her?"

Silence, just for a heartbeat. Two heartbeats. "Yes," Tom said.

He sounded sincere.

It meant nothing.

"I wish I could believe you," she whispered.

"If it comes down to it, you'll see the proof. Let's hope it doesn't come down to it. You don't know what I've given up for you."

"What?" Chase looked back for the first time...

...just as Bastien yelled a warning. "Six of them! Archers too! Let's get ready to rummmmblllllle!"

"Down!" Cagna barked. Then her pistol fired, a bark completely unlike her own. "Renny, take the left!"

"I'm on it!"

This was the fifth room in the goblins' dungeon that they'd come to, and by now they had things down to a rhythm. Bastien went in first, took any hits that were necessary and drew attention to himself, while moving up to administer beatdowns. Cagna focused on taking out any magical attackers or ranged shooters, then charged in to guard the Wizaards's flanks with her shortsword. Renny had Manipulate Air going and an elemental he directed to scatter any organized resistance, and keep lone goblins busy until Bastien or Cagna could get to them. Thomasi used a bullwhip with consummate grace, guarding their flanks and watching for ambushes. Chase healed, and threw rocks.

Cagna had set up this order, and it was working well.

To be honest, Chase had expected... something more, really. The goblins weren't a match for them. If she'd been alone she would have been in danger, but if she'd been alone she wouldn't be here in the first place. With everybody in the party combined, the little twisted creatures really hadn't had a chance.

It wasn't adventure. It was pretty much slow slaughter, with the occasional attempt to murder them right back.

Chase sighed, and then followed Cagna into the room. She and Renny didn't have to duck to clear the low doorway, at least.

The upside was that it was over quickly.

The downside was that it wasn't very challenging, so they must have been getting fairly low experience. Chase hadn't leveled once, and her throwing skill had only gone up once, for all her rock hurling ways.

The fight was over quickly, the barricade the goblins had set up kicked apart by Bastien's big boots, and Cagna did a quick search of the area. She came up with a small wooden box.

"Yay, more treasure!" Renny clapped his paws together.

"Great," Chase said. "Maybe it's another couple of copper pieces and a half-chewed bone. Totally worth it."

"Oh for the love of the Nurph," Cagna growled. "Can you *not?*"

"What?" Chase blinked. "Can I not what?"

The dog-woman stared at her. "We're in a dungeon. We're in a dangerous spot, and if you don't get your head in the game, you're going to get someone killed! I know you. You're better than... this. What the hell is your problem?"

A meaty hand patted her shoulder. "I've got this. Give us a few minutes," Bastien said.

"What are you talking about?" Chase glared. "This isn't my doing, I'm trying to... hey!" She protested as Bastien walked past her, swept her up with one arm, and carried her over to the corner of the low cave.

"So," he said, sitting between her and the rest of the group. "Let's talk about this."

"There's nothing to talk about," Chase said. "We need to get there fast, seal the dungeon, and get out before the werewolves realize what's happening."

"And give Tabita the skin before we seal it," Bastien said, adjusting his spectacles.

Chase felt her lips twist. "Yes, that too."

Thomasi had insisted on that part.

The Muscle Wizaard's eyes were magnified. The glass made them seem bigger, and the kindness in them made her look away.

"It's easy to forget that you're still so young," he said, barely a murmur. Behind him, she could hear the clink of coins as they sorted through the treasure, and Renny and Thomasi tried to figure out what this or that item might be.

"Well... yes. Not too young. I'll be sixteen next October." Chase frowned. "So what?"

"You've gained so many levels for one so young. So much experience! And it was in a really short time. And I'm betting most of those jobs boosted your charisma, am I right?"

"Oh yeah...." she said, trying to mimic his voice.

He laughed. "See! From anyone else I might think they were mocking me. From you, it's cute. Look... have you ever really thought about what high charisma *means?*"

"Aside from making me better at talking with people? Not really. It only helps me when talking matters. It doesn't help me with... this. Whatever this is." Chase waved a hand at the slaughter dungeon.

Bastien nodded. "High charisma means that people pay more attention to you. Even when you're not trying to get them to. And they feel more empathy towards you. Which means that when *you're* in a bad mood..." he let his words trail off.

Chase was bright enough to see where it was going. "Everyone else feels bad."

"Yeah. And we can't ignore it, because gosh darn it, we like you! You're the heart of this group! You pulled it together; you've healed our wounds; you help keep us alive... you're the reason we're here, Chase." Bastien removed his spectacles and rubbed them on a handkerchief. His eyes were a little misty. "My life was going nowhere. Now I have friends again, one old and three new. I can maybe even be a proper wizard someday!"

"You already are." she put her hands on his shoulders. "And don't let anyone tell you otherwise! Muscle magic beats book magic any day!"

He laughed. "Hey, I'm giving the pep talk here!" But he was beaming now, the shadow of sadness gone from his eyes. "So... tell me what's eating you, and maybe you'll feel better. And then we can get back to it, get our heads in the game. Dungeons eat people who don't get their heads screwed on properly."

Chase shook her head. "You really think this place is dangerous? It's more pathetic, really."

"See, you haven't been listening to Renny. This one's easy so far because we're higher level than it. But they get deadlier the further you go. Cagna knows it. I know it. Thomasi sure as heck knows it. Nothing is safe; nothing is certain."

She closed her eyes. "That's how they thought in Bothernot. That's what my mother would say. I couldn't stand that place..."

Just for a second, a wave of homesickness washed over her. Nostalgia and a longing for a place where the biggest decision of the day was whether or not to skip second breakfast for more reading time.

Chase shoved it down. She'd wanted this, wanted adventure and risk and excitement, and here it was...

...and she found her eyes wandering to Thomasi. He was standing alone now, watching down one of the corridors. His face was half in shadow, but the part she could see looked saddened.

As well he should be, Chase felt a worm of anger gnawing in her breast, and realization came to her. "I trusted him. And he's... he doesn't think I'm real. He doesn't think any of us matter. We're not real to him," Chase whispered.

"What?" Bastien turned. "Thomasi? Man, he was happy to see me when he came to us at the Masquerade! He was so sorry he'd been taken away from us. He asked me about the others, but..." Bastien's brow furrowed. "It's funny, I can't remember them so well. We all went our separate ways. For some reason... ah, it doesn't matter. Look, Thomasi's good. He cares."

"How can he?" Chase burst out, a little louder than she intended. "It's a game! It's all a game to him. Not even a real dream."

Cagna shot her a glare. But Thomasi flinched and turned away. She felt an odd sense of triumph at that, mixed with shame. This was the sort of thing her mother would do, that she'd seen other Bothernot matrons do. Get ahold of something and never let it go, inflame guilt to get the others to fall into line. They didn't see a thing wrong with it. After all, their own relatives had done the same to them, over and over...

"It's not just him you're mad at, is it?" Bastien's hands enveloped her shoulders, then pulled her into a hug. She buried her face in his beard and tried not to cry.

"No," she whispered. "I'm mad at me for acting this way but I can't STOP." Her voice twisted as she spoke, pain and sorrow blending together. "I can't stop and I don't want to be this way."

"There was a time I didn't want to be the way I was either," Bastien said, hugging her more tightly. "So I decided to be a wizard. And I never looked back. I'm not there yet, but I'm the best one I can be, and I'm better for it. Because the more I was a Wizard, the less I was the old me. And eventually I could look back and take the best parts of old me without bringing the bad stuff along. And that's magic, kind of. I'm rambling, I'm sorry."

"No, no, it's okay," Chase said, letting him go. "I'm an Oracle. I'm a Medium. I'm a Grifter and an Archer, and I'm not done yet. I can't forget where I came from, but I don't have to let it rule me. And that's what it was doing. Old me was sitting in the back of my head, trying to scramble for control." She spoke the words, feeling the truth of them as she went. Some part of her had been trying to hold herself back, through all of this... but there was no going back. From the second she'd met her god in that rustic tavern, it had all been downhill from...

No.

No, it wasn't downhill. Her life had gotten better. She was alive because of it. Everything from there had been rising up, facing insane odds and beating them. Rising above them.

For a second she remembered Enrico Rossi, that tired, beaten man who had gone down fighting in a blaze of glory because he couldn't do anything else, knew the odds were against him and played the game anyway. Her hand felt for his cards... then she remembered that the Alpha had taken them.

I'll have to even that score. For Enrico, she thought.

Her eyes found Thomasi again. He had helped her, in his own way. He was about as reliable as a barn made of paper... but he cared. He did, even if he was really, really bad about keeping secrets when he shouldn't.

Maybe... maybe she could kill two birds with one stone here?

Halven mental fortitude did its job then, and she gave Bastien a final squeeze and pulled free of him.

He let her go. "Better?"

"Better. Thank you." Chase mopped her eyes, and headed over to Thomasi. "Hey. You."

"Hey you," he said back, looking down at her with wariness.

"I haven't forgiven you yet. But I'll make you a deal. I'll forgive you, if you tell me... no, you tell us everything else. Everything you're hiding that I need to know. No shenanigans! Do you accept this deal?"

His face twitched. "Yes. But I'm not sure we have time. There's a lot I haven't told you."

"Then you can tell us the less-important parts later. The existential crisis stuff can wait."

"All right." He rubbed his eyes. "May I have my hat back, by the way?"

"Oh. Right." She rummaged in her pack. "I keep forgetting to use the thing anyway."

"Thank you. It completes a set bonus when I've got it on." He tried to put it on, scowled as the low ceiling got in the way. "Well, that's irritating."

She laughed. She couldn't help it. Part of it was his high charisma, she knew, but part of it was that she genuinely liked Tom. He was fun. Also he was a part of her new life, and she owed him for his part in her escape from Bothernot.

Putting that aside, she brought her mind back to the task at hand. Like the Muscle Wizaard had said, you had to keep your head together while you were in a dungeon. "So. Tabita. Tell us about her."

"We were imprisoned together. Like most of the others she'd more than earned her place in the prison."

"Most? No offense, but everyone except maybe for you seemed pretty horrible."

"Compared to you and the villagers, yes. Zenobia... well, let's just say her tortures made us all look like saints." Thomasi looked away for a second, then shrugged. "Dijornos and Speranza were probably the least worst. Dijornos was brutal and loved violence, but he was in a line of work where that was not unknown, and he could channel his aggression to constructive ends. So long as he wasn't bored he was pretty decent. Speranza could enslave people's minds, but she usually held off on that unless the need was dire. She was big into lore and story, learning people's backgrounds and working her own adventures into that."

"And Vaffanculo?" Her lips curled as she remembered the Necromancer. "Please don't tell me about his good qualities."

"He was in this for the stress relief, I think. Honestly a pretty horrible guy all around. Self-centered and shallow." Thomasi shrugged. "I still didn't want him dead."

"What *does* death mean to you, exactly?" Cagna asked. "We might have to kill Tabita here. I'm not looking forward to her coming back a decade later for vengeance."

"It's..." Thomasi rubbed his chin. "Okay. Without going into too many details, we used to be able to revive from death after a few hours of time. Also, we had things called tokens that could bypass even that waiting period and let us respawn at a time and place of our choosing... well, from any waystone we'd touched, anyway."

"I thought those things were just for teleporting?" Renny asked.

"For you, they are. For us they have a few more uses," Thomasi shrugged. "Anyway, not all of us bought tokens when we had the chance, and it's pretty easy to blow through the meager amount you start with. Which is a problem, because there's not many ways to get more of them now. You can't just go out and buy them anymore."

"What about reviving regularly?" Cagna asked. "If it only takes a few hours, that's still a problem."

"You don't have to worry about that," Thomasi said. "I do. You see, it doesn't... it doesn't work anymore." He sat on the ground, hugging his knees to his chest.

"Something stuck in my mind," Chase said, moving up to him. "Back in the village. You didn't want to kill Vaffanculo because it would send him to a fate worse than death."

"Yes," Thomasi said. "If you choose revival, you get dropped into a gray place. You can talk with everyone else who's waiting for revival. Or you can pay tokens to revive early. Those are the only things you can do, the only options you can see. And Chase..." he looked at her, and his face was filled with dread. "Some of the people in there have been waiting for revival for a very, very long time."

"Oh no," Renny said, putting his paws on Thomasi's arm. "It's like soulstone madness!"

"That's hell," Thomasi said. "Plain and simple. Dijornos told me about it... he died a year after the revival stopped working and was there briefly. They've gone mad in there. It's screaming, and babbling, and threats, and thousands of voices talking all at once, and you can't shut them off. If you weren't mad before, that place will do it. I don't want to send Tabita there. Even after what she's done."

"She made herself a monster," Chase said. "But... what you described? Nobody deserves that. Not even a monster." Chase let out her breath in a sigh. The others echoed their agreement.

And as they did, Thomasi relaxed. He chewed his lip for a moment, eyeing Chase, then seemed to come to a decision. "The good news is that it won't kill her permanently here, no matter what we do. She has at least enough tokens for one more revival. Which also means that she won't waste time or effort on vengeance." He nodded to Cagna. "If the rest of the pack dies here, she'll cut her losses and revive, probably on another continent. She was one of the few of us who traveled a lot before she got incarcerated. So if we have to... yes, you can kill her. I won't stop you, and I'll help as best I can. Although... it probably won't come to that."

"No?" Chase asked.

"I'm taking a leaf from how you handled Pandora." Thomasi smiled. "All we have to do is pop this dungeon, then leave her for the Camerlengo and Pwner to sort out."

"Pwner?" Chase frowned. "He's got no way to find her."

The others shared a look. "We forgot to tell her," Bastien said.

"To be fair, we were busy and she was sulking," Cagna offered.

Chase frowned, but it was true.

"Pwner's waiting outside," Thomasi said. "I cut a deal with him back at the Ball. Remember when I asked you to leave him to me?"

"Oh!" Chase blinked. He had, hadn't he? That seemed like almost an eternity ago. Then she shot Thomasi a glare. "Hold up. What kind of deal did you get from him?"

"A temporary truce, and he used his magic to get us here before the army. In return, he gets to take a whack at Tabita without interference from us."

"Sounds fair. I'm fine with that, actually." Chase nodded. "And he's here, so that'll fulfill my bargain with Zenobia and the Doge."

"Wait, the Doge is involved?" Cagna looked up.

"Yes. Also I'm technically under arrest."

"Oh don't tell me that. Wait, I'm off duty. Okay, you can tell me that, don't tell me that tomorrow."

"What? Never mind," Chase frowned. "Hold on. Only a temporary truce?"

"Yes. Once Tabita's off the field, it's open season. He'll probably go after me." Thomasi looked her in the eyes. "And this is the important part. If he does, you must *not* interfere."

"What? No, hold on—"

"You must *not.*" Thomasi thundered. She took a few steps back, surprised. He lowered his voice. "Do not. He's lethal. He's designed for assassination, and I'm not just talking about the job. He'll kill you. And unlike me, you don't have any way of reviving."

"Actually..." Renny said, then shut his muzzle.

"You don't. Not here at any rate, which is the same thing," Tom shot the little fox an apologetic look and ruffled his head.

"You have a way of reviving? You have tokens?" Chase asked. Then she frowned. "You can't lose them, can you?"

"They're only physical when I trade them. Big old golden coins, and so valuable..." he looked wistful for a second. "No, I can't lose them. Not unless I give them to someone else. Which I won't," Thomasi shook his head, and held up two fingers. "By my calculations I've got two fast revives left. If Pwner kills me, so be it. You know where to go, and I'll meet up with you later." He shot Chase a look.

She nodded. "I don't like it. But if we have to... I still don't like the idea of you just letting him kill you."

"Now who said anything about that?" Thomasi smiled. "I'll fight back or try to escape. But... frankly, this is what he does. I'm outmatched."

"You're sure you can't talk your way out of it? Use some Grifter tricks?" Chase frowned at him. "I've sized him up. His willpower isn't good..."

Thomasi hesitated... then shook his head. "There's something you don't know. It's complicated."

"Then enlighten me!" Chase threw up her hands in frustration. "That's the deal! You come clean, and we can do this! This isn't the time to keep secrets!"

The Ringmaster frowned in irritation. "I'm not! I'm just trying to work out how to say this... okay. I think I have a way to put it. Bear with me. Simply put... our physical attributes limit and affect us, to a degree. But our mental ones don't, not as much anyway."

"What?" Cagna furled her lips back from her muzzle. "Why wouldn't they?"

"Because our brains aren't really here! And that's the complicated part and don't ask me about it. Things like perception, that's partially tied to our brains, so the best this world can do is sharpen our senses, but it's still on our brains back at home to tie things together. Intelligence? Wisdom? Sure, they affect what our skills do, but they are at best an influence rather than a limitation."

"So what you're telling me," said Chase, eyes going wide, "is that even though Pwner's willpower comes up as relatively low, he's free to ignore my charisma, and he's not as likely to be fooled if I lie to him."

"Yes," Thomasi said. "That's why I couldn't work a better deal. Without the system influencing how charisma interacts with willpower, it's his brain against mine, so to speak."

The ramifications were horrific.

"No wonder the Camerlengo fears you," she said, slowly. "You're unpredictable. You're chaos."

"Even the better among us cannot be controlled, not truly." Thomasi nodded. "Some spells can force us not to do things, but those are only temporary. Nothing can truly make us do things that we don't want to."

Chase nodded. Then she offered him a smile and a pat on the knee. "It's all right. I didn't do what my folks wanted me to do either. That's their problem, not ours. They can just deal."

Thomasi stared at her for a moment, then laughed. "Birds of a feather! Equals, then! I'm good with it." He stuck out a gloved hand, and she shook... and then the others gathered around, and they spent a second shaking hands and laughing, tension released in hysteria. "Well." Thomasi said. "We shall not be hanged for nothing. All right. Any more questions?"

"Just a few," Chase said, sparing the goblin bodies a glance as they dissolved. From what Renny had said, they'd be respawning soon, so time was even shorter now. "Since I know now that I can't depend on charisma alone, I need to know everything you can tell me that might give me an edge over Tabita..."

CHAPTER 25: MY NAME IS ERROR

The rest of the dungeon went quickly. Chase felt mollified by Thomasi's openness, enough so that her mood didn't affect the others anymore.

There was still much to discuss, but if she died here she'd at least die knowing some of the secrets she hadn't known before.

Wow. Morbid, Chase thought to herself, as the notion occurred to her. Then again, it was hard to escape.

The goblins in here didn't act like regular people should. Or even like monsters should. They charged when the odds were impossible; they never ran even when they were losing, and they went to their deaths without a second thought. It was creepy, really. Like they were goblin-shaped puppets, acting out a play.

That made it a little more tolerable. The death and blood still irked her and seeing her friends killing their way through bothered her more, but if she could pretend the goblins weren't real, then it wasn't so bad.

That's what they think of us, though, Chase's eyes lingered on Thomasi.

But that way lay dark moods and pursuing that wagon train of thought down its particular path would only lead to the others noticing and suffering again.

Finally, after the eighth cavern, they emerged into a big room. Hewn from rock, it was covered in stolen tapestries, strewn with thatch and bone, wickerwork supporting skulls in a sort of awning leading up to a throne that had once been an outhouse. Someone had knocked three of the walls off, leaving one bloated goblin sitting there, wearing a crude crown of wood and metal scraps.

"Hoomans!" he yelled, and the warriors kneeling before him turned, glaring. "You have invaded my cave! Storied cave of Gnawtoe tribe! Once you is hear our rich and colorful history, you will be honored to fall before us! It all started when—"

BLAM!

The king's head jerked back, black blood painted the back wall of the 'throne', and Cagna lowered her smoking gun. "Pass," the Detective said.

Thomasi wasn't much help during the short but brutal fight that ensued. He was too busy leaning on the wall and laughing.

Chase wasn't laughing. She was too busy healing, because the goblins were literally coming out of the walls. Cagna and Renny's elemental both took flanks, while she pressed her back to a solid patch of cave next to Thomasi and Renny and focused on keeping everyone alive.

"Signature Move: You Shall Not Pass!" Bastien roared, and suddenly it got a lot easier. Instead of having to split her attention between healing Cagna and the elemental, she could focus on the Muscle Wizaard alone... which was good, because he was taking the brunt of pretty much all the goblins' ire.

This was the only fight they'd run into that truly worried her... and it *did* make Chase glad for her talk with Bastien earlier. Complacency might have made her lax, and it would have been his life on the line.

But she was not complacent. She dumped most of her sanity into healing, while the others got to the business of killing, and by the end of it she was down pretty far.

Doesn't matter, Chase knew. *In a second here...*

She waited. Nothing happened. Her friends looked around then relaxed, tending to their injuries and checking over their weapons in their usual post-battle rituals.

"Um," Chase broke the silence. "Shouldn't we have gotten a level from that?"

"No," Thomasi said, shooting her a look. "Why?"

"We... just survived a dangerous situation?"

"Not really," Bastien said. "I've had worse. Only had to use one or two skills. And you had my back."

"This is a low-level dungeon," Thomasi said. "You can see the party screen, right? You can see my levels?"

"I can," she said, eyeing the list.

Thomasi Jacobi Venturi
Human 17   **HP 227**
Duelist 11   **SAN 175**
Grifter 18   **STA 320**

Model 12	**MOX 536**
Ringmaster 28	**FOR 268**
Tailor 12	

"Well, those goblins we've been killing have been between levels five and seven," Thomasi said. "I've been deliberately holding back to see if you'd get more experience that way, but no dice, it seems. And since I was ready to step in if things got tough, the system knows that and refuses to give you the experience that you'd get otherwise."

"Wait..." Chase said, frowning. "When we were talking with Don Coltello, and it looked like he might murder me, I got levels for talking my way out of that. Are you saying you WOULDN'T step in if he'd decided to do that?"

Thomasi shot her a hurt look. "Of course I would have stepped in! But we weren't in a party then, so the system didn't count it."

"That makes no sense," Chase furrowed her brow... then she shook her head. "We're getting distracted. And I'm low on sanity, so that's probably why."

"Guys!" Renny said, from next to the throne. "I found it!"

Chase closed her eyes. *I'm too low on sanity for this. But... I prepared for this, didn't I?*

A quick rummage brought out her blue potions, and she drank two of them, let them settle.

Mana Potion recovers your Sanity and your Moxie by 50!
Mana Potion recovers your Sanity by 50 and your Moxie by 13!

And as sanity returned, so did clarity. She checked her status screen soberly... still down a few sanity points, but not enough to be worth another potion.

Then Chase looked over to where Bastien and Cagna were drinking their own potions, and she dug out her second-to-last mana potion and drank it anyway.

Their lives were on the line. They were depending on her to be their healer. She would not let them down. Not over a five-gold potion.

Moving around the throne, she stared at the hole in the world.

Black-edged, hard to see until you were up on it, an eerie green light flickered and played out into the small space behind the throne.

"Is there something there?" Thomasi asked. Chase started in surprise, glanced up to find him squatting behind her, peering over her shoulder.

"It's right there," Renny said, putting a paw into the hole...

...and he was gone.

"No!" Chase said. "Crud! Go, go, everyone go!" And then she took her own advice and jumped in after her friend.

This was *not* the plan... but few of her plans had ever gone without hitches, now had they? No time to think about it, the only thing she could do was improvise. Trusting her instincts, trusting her visions, trusting that Hoon wouldn't have empowered her so if he were going to throw her life away here... trusting the world and her place in it, Chase jumped in and hoped the others wouldn't hesitate.

It wasn't like she thought it would be.

One second she was in the goblin throne room. The next she was nowhere. Blackness darker than night, darker than a moonless overcast sky, crushing and absolute filled the world, was the world... yet somehow she could see.

And from off to one side was flickering green light, eerie and inconstant, dancing and foreboding.

Chase turned...

...and then something crashed into her, and she went tumbling. Above her, Cagna swore.

"We're blocking the entrance," Chase said, rubbing her head as she stood and half-ran forward. "Let's..."

She came to a halt, as she saw what lay ahead.

Green pillars, standing on black nothingness, and stretching up to a... sky? Green numbers and letters flashed and flickered in patterns that her mind couldn't quite catch. It reminded her of when Hoon had shown her the world— the true world, shorn of mortal perceptions.

But that wasn't the worrisome part.

Shapes were moving through the pillars, great hulking shapes that she knew too well by now. The werewolves that Tabita had brought in with her moved among the pillars, reaching into them and pulling out screaming goblins. Blood followed, and Chase froze in horror. Somehow, though she couldn't say how, she knew that these weren't like the goblins in the dungeon. They LOOKED like them, but they screamed; they wept; they begged for mercy... and mercy was not given.

Then one of the werewolves looked her way, and she scrambled, reaching for a rock...

...only to stop as a plush paw whacked her on the knee with strength unbecoming to a toy fox.

"Ow!" She choked off her yell.

The werewolf looking her way shook his head, then turned back to the goblin he was eating.

"We're behind an illusion," Renny whispered. "Sight and sound. It's not perfect and they have really sharp senses so try not to move or be loud."

"Renny, did I tell you I'm really glad you're smart?" Chase whispered. "Because I'm really glad you're smart. Really, really glad about that," she said, trying to peer through the grove of pillars.

"No but thank you." The little golem stood a bit taller.

Behind her, the Muscle Wizaard grunted as he came in, and Chase turned in time to see Thomasi following. She whipped a finger to her lips and shushed them, as Renny bounced over and explained the situation.

Chase left him to do that and kept peering into the darkness.

And after a moment, she found what she was looking for.

PER+1

It was comforting to see the words, as her eyes sharpened. Comforting to know that even in this weirdling space, the rules that she'd lived with all her life still applied.

But that comfort was secondary. She'd found Tabita. And just like in her vision, the werewolf was sitting in the central part of things. She had the false skin in one hand and a knife in the other.

With a shudder, she became a dwarf again and started undressing.

She looked like she was going to throw up, and for a second, for just a second, Chase had sympathy for her. Chase knew what Tabita was going to do, and it was a nightmare.

Then another goblin screamed and died, and Chase lost that sympathy.

"She made her choice long ago," Chase whispered.

"Yes." Thomasi said, squatting next to her. "And there's the new Alpha."

"Mercutio," Chase said, staring at the black-furred werewolf. He was talking with a few of the others, gesturing toward the pillars and back to the entrance. "I'd hoped we would beat him here. This is going to make things tougher."

"My Scouter skill says he's a top-notch Burglar and a middling Duelist," Cagna said. "That rapier's going to be a problem."

Chase rubbed her chin. "Thomasi, can you help? You're a Duelist too."

"No."

The answer derailed her train of thought. Chase stared up at him, and he was staring at Tabita, his face stern and sad and angry all at the same time.

"Why?" she whispered.

"You need to distract them. Renny, help me get over there without her noticing. Can you do that?"

"Yes, but... why?"

"I'm going to swap out the skins."

"She's holding it!"

And just as Chase said that, Tabita put the skin down, put both hands on the knife, and started *cutting.*

"Oh gods," Chase whispered, and looked away. "Fine. Do it. Just... this is your shot. If you fail..."

"I won't. Not this time. Not again," Thomasi whispered, and then he was moving.

"I'll have to drop the screen, Chase!" Renny whispered.

"We're ready," Cagna said, moving up to her left. Bastien gently pushed Chase behind him.

"Are you?" he rumbled.

And just as he did so, Mercutio looked up, eyes narrowing as he stared at the screen. He waved the werewolves along with him, and they dropped their goblins, moving toward the hidden group.

"**Silver Tongue.** Do it," Chase patted Renny, then pushed on Bastien until he let her pass.

The four friends stepped out and the werewolves stopped. Growling rose from the first couple.

"Tollen tried to bite me," Chase called out. "Just like you knew he would."

Mercutio was silent for a bit, and Chase used the time to Diagnose him. Something he'd said earlier had caught her attention, something about conditions...

...but no. He had no conditions. No debuffs. He'd either been misrepresenting his powers or confused about the terminology.

"I'm sorry about that," Mercutio said. "But that doesn't matter now. You need to turn around and walk out of here."

"No." Chase said. "We have questions, and we need answers." She couldn't see Thomasi anymore and supposed that was a good thing.

"Questions." Mercutio rumbled. "If that's all you want, is to talk then come out from behind the old man there."

"I have a name," Bastien rumbled.

"Your name is meat..." one of the other werewolves growled.

"Shut it, Giacomo," Mercutio cuffed him. But he kept his eyes on Chase. "Come closer, Medium."

It was a trick.

It was obviously a trap.

There was no way it wasn't...

Beyond him, Tabita paused in her gruesome work and looked up, staring around wildly. For a second Chase's heartbeat raced...

...then the woman shuddered, throwing drops of blood everywhere. Again she looked down, and again she raised the knife.

I have to give him his chance, Chase knew.

For Thomasi, for her friend, she shoved aside caution and stepped forward. "My hands are empty," she called. "You know I'm no match for you. I am no threat and mean you no harm. Can you say the same?"

"Spoken like a true Grifter," Mercutio rumbled.

But he stepped forward. His rapier stayed belted around his waist. Step by step they walked toward each other, heading for the halfway point behind the groups.

"Silent Activation, Foresight," she mouthed.

Your Silent Activation skill is now level 30!

Chase watched her shadowy self walk forward and stop before Mercutio. He didn't kill her, so that was good. But she knew that ten seconds was a short time, painfully short.

Letting fate work, she finished the movement, feeling the tension in her chest ease as Mercutio did the same.

The werewolf spoke first.

"What I'm trying to figure out, what's got me puzzled and confused is why you're here. Why the HELL are you here, girl? What do you hope to achieve?"

"She's a player, and she's going to where players go. I want to see how this works."

Your Silver Tongue skill is now level 19!

"It's not a place we can follow." Mercutio closed his eyes, but not before Chase caught a glimpse of emotion in them. Sorrow? That was the most likely candidate. That would make the next bit tricky... there were a couple approaches here, and they all had seemed risky.

"Silent Activation, Foresight," she mouthed, barely moving her lips. She watched herself speak, watched the werewolf snatch her up and roar in her face. Okay, nope, not that way. **"Silent Activation, Foresight,"** she spoke again while Mercutio's eyes were still closed.

There. THAT one went better. The pain in her chest turned to an ache, but she rode it out until she could speak. "What if we could?"

Your Silent Activation Skill is now level 31!

Your Foresight Skill is now level 40!

"Don't be ridiculous. We're her dreams. She's the sleeper here. She gets to go back, and we don't."

"Really? Are you sure about that? Is she sure about that?" Chase spared her a glance then looked away. It was hard to tell how much of the player's grisly work was done; the blood was everywhere. "She said that she doesn't know how this works, pretty much admitted this was a long shot. What if the magic she works, the... glitch? What if the glitch can pull *other* people through as well?"

She looked back to find Mercutio leaning closer. "You have my full attention," he said, clearly pondering the matter. "Go on."

Well that's good, but not good enough, Chase said, rubbing her chin... *where am I going with this? I need to see how he reacts.* She muttered **"Silent Activation, Foresight,"** as she took her hand from her face, and his eyes followed her fingers for a second. Fortunately the answer she chose seemed to work.

Your Foresight skill is now level 41!

"Basically I'm seeing a chance for ALL the gold. Not just a one-time payoff." Chase spread her hands. "A new world? One without magic? What's to stop us from going in there and taking what we want? What's to stop us from using our magic to be kings or queens or whatever?" She smiled.

Your Silver Tongue skill is now level 20!

Tap.

Tap.

Tap.

Chase's eyes flicked over to the werewolf's clawed hand, where it tapped against the hilt of the rapier.

"I admit that's tempting," Mercutio said.

This is a new tell, Chase thought. *Why is he...*

Then it occurred to her.

He was marking the seconds.

He's marking out the seconds from when I used Foresight!

INT+1

Panic then, and as his finger tapped the hilt for the tenth time she tried to run, found herself frozen, frozen for just a bit too long...

...as he lashed out and the world blurred. She squeaked and found herself pushed up against a furry chest, with one of his arms holding her snugly in place.

Chase heard the whining of steel on leather as the rapier slid free and a coolness on her throat as he twisted it to her neck.

"Chase!" Renny yelled and raised his paws.

"Drop her!" Cagna snarled, pulling out her pistol and aiming above Chase... until Mercutio shifted her, and she was looking down the barrel of the gun.

"You're making a mistake BIG TIME, buddy!" The Muscle Wizaard boomed.

"Ten seconds. Ten seconds, that's your trick, isn't it?" Mercutio growled. "Ten seconds into the future."

"How did you know?" Chase didn't have to fake the quaver in her voice.

"You think you're the only Oracle out there? That first time we met, you were shouting Foresight like a lunatic! We went and found an Oracle and asked him what the hell you were doing. And I know you can silently activate things, so it was just a matter of counting time from when I saw your lips move."

She closed her eyes. It was irritating, finding out that she'd underestimated somebody. Chase knew full well the value of your enemy underestimating you and finding it turned around here was galling, to say the least. "Well played," she murmured.

"Thanks. You lot, relax, you'll get her back." Mercutio raised his voice. "Put down your weapons, and we wait. As soon as Tabita's back home, we're leaving this place."

"Okay! Okay, that's fine. You can put me down, I wasn't planning on trying anything anyway!" Chase said, flailing her feet a bit for dramatic effect.

"Nope. Stop kicking or my hand might slip. I don't trust you one bit."

Chase stopped flailing. Her feet had told her what she needed to know, anyway. Her head was resting on Mercutio's lower chest, which meant her hand was... yes, there was the leather of his belt.

She had the glimmerings of a plan, but it was a desperation move. "This is pointless. The army is coming for you. And if Tabita succeeds you'll have to face them alone! If she fails, then..."

Chase thought about using foresight, discarded the idea. Mercutio was holding her close, he'd likely feel or detect her talking, hell at this distance he could probably smell her breath when she opened her mouth.

So she decided to risk it. "If she fails, then the Inquisition will get her. They're sending someone along with the army. Some evil witch named Camerlengo Zenobia."

"H'aht?" Tabita shrieked.

"What? Who? What are you talking about?" Mercutio twitched, and for a horrible second Chase felt cold pain on her throat...

...but then it was gone, and the blade was off her neck. "Sorry, sorry!" Mercutio said. "She's alive! Seriously, drop your weapons! I was surprised, that's all!"

"Zeno'ia..." Tabita roared, and her voice was filled with such distortion and rage that Chase almost shook to hear it. "Here? Noh? I'll ... no. No, I hah to go. I hah to..."

"Grace."

Thomasi's voice rung through the room. And though it wasn't loud, it cut through the noise, stopped the rising tension cold, and drew all eyes to him... even Chase, though she had to turn, and she felt the blood ooze from her neck as she beheld the Ringmaster emerging from between the pillars.

"Grace," he repeated, staring at Tabita. "I've got her taken care of. Let it go."

"Hoh..." the skinless thing that had been Tabita said, and Chase felt her gorge rise, forced herself to shut her eyes as it spoke without lips.

Off to the side Cagna vomited, and that didn't help one bit.

"Oh Grace... what you've done to yourself," Thomasi said, stepping forward.

"Tay ack! Tay ack you gihter!" Tabita screeched.

"As you wish. But look... look at this. You have to go through with it. You have to try. You really think you'll get up the nerve to do this TWICE?"

Dead silence, as green letters flickered between worlds.

"No," Tabita gasped. "No."

"Then do it. And if the gods are grateful, then maybe you'll pull me along with you."

Silence again, broken only by the Loup Garou's gasping. "Noh I see. Noh I see your lan. How nuch of dis? How nuch uss you acting eehind de scenes?"

And Chase wondered the same thing. Had he intended this all along?

But it didn't matter. He was her friend. If he wanted to go home, then he could try it here.

"Otay. Otay. Hine. No ricks."

"No tricks. Do it before you lose your nerve! Do it, Grace!" Thomasi shouted.

"Hnnnn.... **Ritual Skin!**"

The world stopped.

Everything slowed down.

Not in the same way as her foresight. There were no ghosts here. There was just a sense that everything was stuttering; everything was caught between the seconds, that the world itself had come up against a great invisible wall and was beating itself senseless and shaking everything and everyone in it to bits. She turned her head and for a second, she saw the world as she'd seen it with Hoon, and everyone was numbers and letters, coiled together so tightly that they were garbled and incomprehensible... but they weren't, because somewhere something was reading them.

Then the screaming started, and stopped again, and started again as the world did its thing, breaking like an arrhythmic heart, gasping along and shuddering, and she realized that everyone in the core chamber was screaming, and she was screaming, too.

But none of them screamed louder than Tabita.

Another jerk and the numbers were invisible again, save for those flowing overhead. Another skip, and the world stopped stuttering, as everyone turned to stare at Tabita...

...or rather, the garbled mess where Tabita had been.

No longer skinless but not whole, a bloody hand poked out above her, fading in from blurry air. One of its fingers was replaced by an eye, which blinked. Her head was half bisected by a patch of the fur, that drifted down impossibly long and stretched, disappearing into the blackness that served for a floor, here.

Those were the most recognizable parts of the woman. Everything in between was blurred and glowing but in weird patterns, square like blocks, flesh and fur colored blocks that melded into each other. The overall effect was like colored crystals of salt or something similar, all jumbled together in a standing heap.

"Mother of gods," one of the werewolves whimpered.

And then it *moved*.

It thrashed and swirled, and the blocks moved around within it, and to her horror, Chase realized that the blocks were *spreading*. Like one of those crystal growing kits that her parents let her buy from Mimby Doonel sometimes, only sped up a thousandfold.

Chase knew, just knew that touching whatever that was would be death. It would be worse than death.

Which is why she screamed herself, when Mercutio moved toward it. "You! You're an Oracle! Fix her! Fix this!"

"I can't!" Chase wailed and knew it was true. Knew that even trying to diagnose this would invite doom.

Then his blade was back at her throat. "Fix it or die!"

"All right! I'll do it! Put me down!"

Your Silver Tongue skill is now <ERROR>

Oh, oh that was bad: even the words that governed the world feared this thing!

But it didn't matter. It didn't matter, because Mercutio had believed her.

And as the rapier slid away from her throat and he lowered her to the ground, she waited until her hands were passing his belt and mouthed, **"Silent Activation, Pickpocket."**

Your Pickpocket skill <ERROR ABORT RETRY FAIL!>

She had no time to read the words, because her hands were full of silver, now. Silvered cards, stolen back from Mercutio. And with a scream she shouted, **"Rapid Fire, Razor Card!"** as she threw them all into Mercutio's face at point blank range.

He screamed, dropped his rapier and staggered back...

...and then Bastien was there, diving into a tackle and grabbing the werewolf Alpha's heels. He shouted "I cast magic missile! **Throw!**"

Mercutio flipped head over heels—

—and sailed right into whatever the hell Tabita had become. With a cry his body crystallized too, fragmenting apart and spreading.

Then words filled the sky;

ERROR! NO MASTER DETECTED. DUNGEON SEALING IN 30.

"I've got the core! We need to go!" Renny shouted.

The werewolves howled in rage, and Cagna's pistol blew a big hole in one of them. That made them pause. By then Chase was already running. Then big arms came down and Bastien was running with her on his shoulders.

"Run to *where?*" Chase screamed.

"I don't know!" Renny yelled back. "I didn't take the advanced class!"

The world flickered, moving from creepy green and black darkness to regular dark darkness... then it flickered back.

Behind them, the remaining werewolves bayed and gave pursuit. Or maybe they were trying to get away from the spreading mass that had been their leaders, it was hard to say.

From her position on Bastien's shoulders, Chase watched the world break and crystallize. Now Tabita filled up a field's worth, and most of it was mouth judging by the screaming that seemed to grow, seemed to rebound through the void, screaming that was joined by Mercutio's voice as the two werewolves howled their last...

...*maybe,* Chase realized, with a sick horror. *This might not kill them and that's worse,* she thought and gasped as one of the werewolves was too slow and fell, screeching, his legs converted to the mass that now spread faster.

"Ten seconds!" Renny shouted, and Chase pondered Foresight, then decided against it.

If this was going to catch them, she didn't want to spend the last ten seconds before eternal torment knowing she was doomed.

So Chase closed her eyes and buried her face in Bastien's beard and waited.

"Whoa, stop!" Cagna yelled, and for a second Chase was confused because stopping was literally worse than death...

...and then she realized that the screaming was gone.

"Whoops!" Bastien said, and then they were bouncing off a wall and hitting the ground and rolling, and it hurt but she was laughing and they were all gasping and some of them were laughing because they were alive. Alive and not... not *whatever* that had been.

And only after Chase had settled down, did she realize that she had new words hovering right in front of her face.

You are now a level 14 Oracle!
CHA+3
LUCK+3
WIS+3

You are now a level 15 Oracle!
CHA+3
LUCK+3
WIS+3
You have learned the Grant Vision skill!
Your Grant Vision skill is now level 1!
You have learned the Random Buff skill!
Your Random Buff skill is now level 1!

Congratulations! By combining deception with gambling-implement based murder, you have unlocked the Gambler job!
Would you like to become a Gambler at this time? Y/N?

Chase flopped her head back on the stone floor of the grungy cave and studied the ceiling. It had goblin pictograms carved into it. The ones she was looking at showed a little guy bringing down a wolf with a good spear toss, and she giggled a bit at the appropriateness of it. "This has to be an omen," she murmured, still punch drunk. "Sure, let's do it. Yes!"

You are now a level 1 Gambler!
LUCK+5
PER+5
You have learned the Ace in the Hole skill!
Your Ace in the Hole skill is now level 1!
You have learned the Assess Challenge skill!
You have learned the Cardsharp skill!
Your Cardsharp Skill is level 1!
You have learned the Gambler's Fortune skill!
You have learned the Hold'em skill!

"Know when to **Hold'em**," she whispered, remembering Enrico's words.

And she jumped in surprise, as silver cards appeared in her hands. Blood-stained silver cards that now glowed with runes. Runes that faded back into nothing as the blood dripped off them and away. "Of course they were magical. Gods knew he could afford it," Chase whispered. Her new skill had called the cards back from wherever she'd thrown them.

"Everyone okay?" Thomasi said, striking a match.

"I'm good," Cagna confirmed, pulling out a rod and starting to reload her still-smoking pistol.

"Never... oof... never better!" Bastien boomed, taking stock of his bruises.

"I'm great!" Renny called out, studying a glowing crystal that he held cupped in his paws.

"I'm jus' fine, thanks for asking," said Pwner as he drew a pair of bombs.

CHAPTER 26: PWNED

They looked at Pwner.

Pwner looked back. He was still wearing his birdlike mask, but he'd swapped out the rest of his masquerade garb for the gear she'd seen in the casino. The glass vials on his chest gleamed evilly in the light of Thomasi's guttering match.

"Gods *damn* it!" Chase burst out. "We won! We just won! This isn't... this isn't fair."

"Did we win?" Cagna asked. "Still not sure what happened back in there."

"Nothing good," Thomasi said. "Don't talk about it in front of him."

"Now that's rude."

"I'm going to insist that you let us pass," Bastien said, standing.

"You wanna go?" Pwner thrust a bomb at him.

"No!" Thomasi shouted. "No. I want to bargain."

"We already bargained. You told me to go to a different place, so you already tried to cheat me once, old man. Fortunately for me I had a backup plan." He nodded at Chase.

"Wait. What?" Chase looked back. "I'm not your backup plan!"

"You weren't. But the Bounty Hunter mark I put on you *was*."

...and Chase remembered how he'd tapped her on the shoulders with that scepter back at the party. "Oh. Oh no..."

Thomasi bowed his head.

"I'm sorry. I'm so sorry," she told him, feeling miserable.

They'd *won*.

And now, this.

"It's not your fault. We're no match for him," said Thomasi.

"S'all good, my man. Just give me Tabita and we're square. Even give you that head start, though you cheated me."

Thomasi sighed. "We don't have her. She's gone. Gone in a weird way. I'll tell you about it if you let my friends go."

"Don't think we got time for that. Got the Inquisition out there, old man. They'll be here before long. But you're surprising me. Wanna do the hero thing? Trade their lives for yours?" He surveyed the little group.

"Thomasi..." Renny said. "We can do this. We can fight him."

"No!" barked Thomasi.

"Naw," said Pwner, contemptuously. "No you can't. This bomb? Poison. This other bomb? Plague. Even if you had a shard of a shot, even if I didn't have thirty levels on you in my main, even if you're hot shazz like that, e'ery one except you is gonna die, little golem. You I'll just take and disenchant for parts later."

Renny stepped back. "You can't do that... can he do that? He can't do that, right?"

"He can. And yes," Thomasi said, stepping forward. "I'll trade my life for theirs."

"Not good enough," Pwner said, stepping back. "And keep your distance. No trying to pickpocket my bombs outta my hands."

"Then what's good enough? You don't want information on Tabita's fate. What do you want?" Thomasi asked.

"I don't know. But make it good. And you got like three minutes, or it's all moot."

Chase licked her lips.

Thomasi stared at him, uncomprehending. "I'll... let me think... gold?"

Pwner called him a vulgar name and laughed, the beak shaking. "My guild gives me all the gold I need! Try again, fool!"

"I can help," Chase spoke up, and they turned to her.

"What? You? How?" Pwner looked her over. "You done enough for me, shawty. Done helped enough."

"I can check the cards. See what would work, here."

"We don't have time for a full-on reading," Thomasi warned.

"It won't be one!" Chase burst out. "I have a skill. I'll use it, if it's all right."

"No tricks. One use. If I think you're fooling, e'ery one dies. Got it?"

"Got it," Chase said and reached into her pack. **"Fortuna,"** she said and drew a single card.

She stared at the card revealed. At four rogues around a table, each clutching a strongbox to themselves, eyeing the others. Coins were visible within.

She'd been hoping for a major arcana, for something earth-shattering, but she didn't get it. "I don't understand," she whispered.

"What does this card mean?" Thomasi asked, and it was only from her long experience that she could tell he was choking back emotion.

"It means wealth saved or hoarded. Scarcity and control of money. But he doesn't want money..."

"Oh gods." Thomasi covered his face. "I know your price."

"Thass a neat trick, 'cause I sure don't," Pwner said, folding his arms. "Surprise me."

And then Chase knew. Knew just what she was asking of Thomasi.

"Tokens!" She burst out. "You want those tokens that give you extra lives!"

"No!" Cagna shouted.

"Hold on there!" Bastien said, raising his hands.

"No, don't do it!" Renny said. "You'll go to the screaming place!"

Pwner looked to her... and that was what she wanted. That was what Chase was hoping, because she had an idea and one shot at this. "Don't do it!" Chase said. "It'll be like working for Coltello all over again!"

And she fought to keep the relief off her face, as words appeared at the edge of her sight.

Your Silver Tongue skill is now level 32!

Chase didn't look at Thomasi, not directly. She kept her eyes on Pwner, locking her gaze on his. But in her peripheral vision, she saw Thomasi mutter something into his palm.

"Oh gods." Thomasi whispered. "This is... not a light thing you ask of me."

"That would 'bout do it, though," Pwner said, tilting his mask. "Ain't none of us are crazy enough to turn down that kind of deal."

"How do I know you'll keep it?" Thomasi asked. "How do I know you're not going to renege the second you have my tokens?"

"You don't. But I got no reason to. I'll let 'em go and get my pay from you after that."

"That's... uncommonly generous." Thomasi narrowed his eyes.

Chase saw it before he did. "I'm still marked," she said. "If you renege he'll just come after us and kill us."

"She's right," Pwner said, flipping a bomb up in the air. Everyone flinched back but he caught it, with dexterity that made Chase flush with envy. "So. Ten tokens sounds fair."

"That will clean me out," Thomasi said. "Five."

"Inquisition's gonna be too close to escape in like three minutes. "Nine tokens."

"If they get me, you get *nothing*. Good day sir! But seriously, six."

"Hahaha! You even look like shazzin' Will Wonka. Yeah, okay, tell you what. Eight. Final offer. I'll even move my mark off shawty, here."

"You'd do that anyway if I remember how bounty hunters work, but... fine. Just fine. And kill me quickly. No torture. Eight."

Thomasi took his hat off and reached into it, pulling out fat gold disks, oversized and elaborate.

"What the heck?" Cagna asked, staring at them. "Gold coins aren't supposed to look like that. All coins are supposed to look the same."

"Don't waste time," Thomasi's voice was strained. "Go. Now!"

"I don't want to lose you a second time, boss!" Bastien protested.

"Go!" Thomasi turned to him. "Fly, you fools!"

They ran. Out of the cave, up the hill, and into the night. Away from the torches and the sound of shouting.

And behind them, Chase heard Pwner laughing. Not in a mean way, but an honest laugh, and that was somehow worse. "You know they ain't gonna get the irony of you telling a wizard that, right? Ain't none of them seen that movie!"

"Just get it over wi—"

Then Tom was silent, and Chase closed her eyes.

Her luck carried her through the darkness until she could bear to open them again, and when she couldn't run any farther Bastien scooped her up without asking.

"Now what?" Chase asked, as they broke into a familiar clearing. "I don't see where we can go from—" She blinked, as a shape resolved itself under the moonlight. "The wagon? You brought your wagon?"

"No, it's Thomasi's."

"Oh, it's Dobbin!" Chase said, moving up to pet the old horse. He blinked at her, then briefly searched her head for edible treats. She giggled as his tongue tickled her scalp. Somewhere along the way she'd lost her headscarf, but that was all right.

"How can you laugh!" Renny burst out.

"What?" she turned to him.

"Thomasi's dead! Maybe forever! That guy took a lot of tokens, and he didn't have that many to begin with, right?"

Chase smiled, as she started loading up the wagon. "He took zero tokens from Thomasi."

The clearing went silent.

"We saw him hand them over," Cagna said. Then she scrutinized Renny. "Wait. Did you use an illusion to fool him?"

"No!"

"You're close though," Chase said, with her too-wide grin. "Remember when Thomasi was first describing those tokens to us? Big gold coins, he called them? Well, there's a Grifter ability called Fool's

Gold."

"What? You... how?"

"He spent a good amount of time paying his debt to Don Coltello by making Fool's Gold for him. That was why I brought up Coltello's name. Thomasi caught it and ran with it." Chase smiled, as she climbed into the driver's seat of the wagon. She hadn't personally done this, but Thomasi had done it many a time, and how hard could it be?

She'd just have to improvise.

It had worked out okay so far, right?

"That glorious man!" Bastien laughed, hopping into the wagon as it started to roll off. "That's the Ringmaster I remember!"

"Yep. Which is why we're going to meet back up with him as soon as possible," she said as the others climbed aboard. "Except maybe..." she looked up at Cagna.

Cagna looked down. "Oh, I'm in. You know how many crimes Pwner has committed in Florian, and the other city-states?"

"Yes, but we're not going after..." Chase's voice faded away.

"You might not. But after he figures out those tokens are fool's gold, I think I know who just made his list."

Chase stared into the darkness.

Then she shrugged. "He can get in line. Let's go! Gnome awaits!"

Her enemies were growing daily; she was wanted in at least one city-state, and chaotic entities from beyond time and space were hunting her, but for the first time Chase found she didn't care.

She'd wanted adventure, after all.

And fate had given it to her!

EPILOGUE

Once upon a time, a halven girl had to hunt werewolves. She made new friends, got in trouble, and had to get out of town in a hurry. For the second time in a row, actually.

She also found out a great secret... one that her enemies would and could kill to preserve.

But first they would have to catch her.

So when the morning came and she decided to figure out her next move, she said **"Status,"** and this is what she saw.

Name: Chase Berrymore
Age: 15 Years
Jobs:
Halven level 11, Cook level 4, Archer level 7, Gambler Level 1, Grifter level 12, Medium level 7, Oracle level 15, Painter level 2, Teacher level 5

Attributes		Pools	Defenses
Strength: 65	Constitution: 38	Hit Points: 103	Armor: 10
Intelligence: 67	Wisdom: 117	Sanity: 184	Mental Fortitude: 55
Dexterity: 128	Agility: 66	Stamina: 194	Endurance: 0
Charisma: 205	Willpower: 54	Moxie: 259	Cool: 65
Perception: 85	Luck: 213	Fortune: 298	Fate: 43

Generic Skills
Archery – Level 1
Brawling – Level 8
Climb – Level 15
Dagger – Level 2
Dodge – Level 12
Fishing – Level 14

Ride – Level 10
Stealth – Level 14
Swim – Level 7
Throwing – Level 28

Halven Skills
Fate's Friend – Level N/A
Small in a Good Way – Level N/A

Cook Skills
Cooking - Level 15
Freshen - Level 10

Archer Skills
Aim – Level 6
Demoralizing Shot – Level 1
Far Shot – Level 1
Missile Mastery – Level N/A
Quickdraw – Level N/A
Rapid Fire – Level N/A
Razor Arrow – Level 6
Ricochet Shot – Level 10

Gambler Skills
Ace in the Hole – Level 1
Assess Challenge – Level N/A
Cardsharp – Level 1
Gambler's Fortune – Level N/A
Hold'em – Level N/A

Grifter Skills
Feign Death – Level 1
Fools Gold – Level 1
Forgery – Level 1
Master of Disguise – Level 3
Old Buddy – Level 1
Pickpocket – Level 12
Silent Activation – Level 30
Silver Tongue – Level 32
Size Up – Level 4
Unflappable – Level N/A

Medium Skills
Bad Fortune – Level 13
Crystal Ball – Level 2
Focus Vision – Level 1

Fortuna – Level N/A
Good Fortune – Level 8
Palmistry – Level N/A
Séance – Level N/A
Stack Deck – Level N/A

Oracle Skills
Absorb Condition – Level N/A
Afflict Self – Level 1
Diagnose – Level N/A
Divine Pawn – Level N/A
Foresight – Level 41
Grant Vision Level 1
Influence Fate – Level 4
Lesser Healing – Level 44
Omens and Portents – Level N/A
Random Buff – Level 1
Short Vision – Level 8
Transfer Condition – Level 9

Painter Skills
Fast Dry – Level N/A
Painting – Level 5

Teacher Skills
Lecture – Level 20
Red Ink – Level 1
Smarty Pants – Level N/A

Unlocked Jobs
Farmer, Herbalist

Gear
Light Leather Armor – level 5
Enrico's Last Hand

APPENDIX I: CHASE'S JOBS AND SKILLS

HALVEN
Smaller even than dwarves but nowhere near as sturdy, halvens normally hate excitement and love regular meals. As such, normally only the weirdos among them go adventuring.

Level 1 Skills
Fate's Friend
Cost: N/A   Duration: Passive Constant
You gain a bonus to your fate equal to your halven job level.

Small in a Good Way
Cost: N/A   Duration: Passive Constant
Sure, you're small, but you know how to use that! Whenever your size would be an advantage for the situation you're in, you gain a bonus equal to your halven level. This doesn't apply to combat situations unless you're fighting in very small tunnels, or the foes are all the size of giants, or some other similar factor applies.

CRAFTING JOBS

COOK
Cooks specialize in treating and preparing food for consumption.

Level 1 Skills

Cooking

Cost: Cooking Ingredients   Duration: Permanent

The Cook spends thirty seconds and a variable amount of ingredients and either attempts to craft a known recipe or discover a new recipe. This skill is influenced by wisdom.

Freshen

Cost: 10 For   Duration: Instant

This small charm has a chance of removing any rot and reversing any decay or spoilage on a particular ingredient or foodstuff. Luck weighs heavily in the success of this spell, as does the amount of time the food has been spoiled. Beyond a year, sorry, there's no salvaging the foodstuff.

TEACHER

Teachers pass on valuable knowledge and skills to their students.

Level 1 Skills

Lecture

Cost: 10 Mox   Duration: 10 minutes per Teacher level

When used before starting a lecture or otherwise passing along information, this skill increases the chance that your audience will remember your lesson accurately. This is dependent on both their intelligence and your skill level.

Smarty Pants

Cost: N/A   Duration: Passive Constant

Teachers are good at recalling information, no matter how strange! Your smarty pants skill increases the odds that you'll remember trivia and other useful facts. It scales by your Teacher level.

Level 5 Skills

Red Ink

Cost: 10 San   Duration: 1 use

This skill instantly marks a single held manuscript, underlining errors and flaws. It is not perfect, and uses the Teacher's intelligence and the rating of the skill to determine how many errors are caught. It can also be used to detect forgeries in written media.

ADVENTURING JOBS

ARCHER

Archers are experts with ranged weaponry, focused on fighting at a distance. They earn experience from shooting foes or otherwise engaging in missile combat, and by making trick shots at crucial moments.

Level 1 Skills

Aim
Cost: 10 For   Duration: 1 Turn
The Archer takes careful aim and adds their aim skill rating to the next shot they take. This is an increase, not a buff. Note that the shot must be taken within the next turn, so the maximum amount of times the archer can effectively use it is twice before they have to shoot.

Missile Mastery
Cost: N/A   Duration: Passive Constant
The Archer's obsession with ranged weaponry makes them an excellent shot, even with weapons that they haven't practiced to the same level. When attacking with ranged weapons, they may substitute half of their highest ranged weapon skill, instead of the skill they would normally use. The experience for this attack goes off the skill that missile mastery replaces, instead of the one actually used. This makes it an excellent way to train up sub-par skills. The affected skill groups are archery, throwing, guns, and siege engines. This skill has no levels.

Quickdraw
Cost: 5 Sta   Duration: 1 minute
The Archer uses supreme skill and reflexes to draw a weapon at the speed of thought. For the next minute after using this skill, the archer may draw any weapon or item on their person at incredible speed. This skill has no levels.

Rapid Fire
Cost: 10 Sta   Duration: Instant
The Archer may take two shots in the next ranged attack, instead of one. All costs must be paid as per normal. This attack can only be used once per turn. This skill has no levels.

Ricochet Shot
Cost: 5 For   Duration: 1 attack

The Archer can bounce a shot off a hard surface to strike a target behind cover, or around a corner, or otherwise not easily targeted. Activating this skill reduces the penalties required to make the shot.

Level 5 Skills

Demoralizing Shot
Cost: 10 Sta   Duration: 1 attack
The Archer fires a warning shot, designed to break the target's will, rather than cause physical damage. This skill has no levels.

Far Shot
Cost: 15 Sta   Duration: 1 Attack
The Archer strains his muscles to throw or shoot an attack as far as possible. Activating this skill reduces the penalties required to make the shot.

Razor Arrow
Cost: 10 For   Duration: 1 Attack
The Archer fires a supernaturally-sharp shot that bores through the target's armor. Activating this skill lets the attack ignore a portion of the target's armor.

GAMBLER
Gamblers use their skills to beat the odds, both at gambling and at killing things at a distance via gambling-themed weaponry. Some of their more powerful skills have an element of random chance... good thing they've got the luck to back it up!

Level 1 Skills

Ace in the Hole
Cost: 10 For   Duration: 10 seconds per Gambler level
Produces either a playing card or a razor-edged throwing card. The card can have any appearance the Gambler wants, so long as it is clearly a playing card of a reasonable size. The damage of the card is modified by the Gambler's Ace in the Hole skill.

Assess Challenge
Cost: 5 San   Duration: Instant
Use this spell right before you or an ally attempt an action, and you

will know the odds of success. This skill doesn't work for sinister long-term plans or anything beyond actions that take longer than a minute to resolve. This skill has no levels. This skill is a spell.

Cardsharp
Cost: 5 For   Duration: Instant
Increases the odds of scoring a critical hit with your next gambling-implement-based attack.

Gambler's Fortune
Cost: N/A   Duration: Passive Constant
You gain a bonus to your fate equal to your Gambler level.

Hold'em
Cost: 10 For   Duration: Instant
Instantly recalls all gambling-based weaponry that you've thrown back to your person. You can choose to exclude specific items when activating this skill. This skill has no levels. This skill is a spell.

GRIFTER

Grifters are conmen (and women) who specialize in tricking and fooling their targets. They gain experience from lying and bluffing; the bigger the stakes the better.

Level 1 Skills

Fools Gold
Cost: 10 For   Duration: 10 minutes/Skill level
The Grifter always seems to have some fake coins on hand! This spell creates one gold coin per Grifter level. However, the gold is only temporary, and it soon dissipates. This does not tend to engender feelings of goodwill in those so fooled. The gold coins register as magical to various detection spells. This skill is a spell.

Master of Disguise
Cost: 10 Mox   Duration: 10 minutes/Skill level
The Grifter puts on a masterful disguise! The difficulty of seeing through it is modified by the Grifter's charisma and skill level. The difficulty may be negatively modified if the disguise is extraordinarily different from the Grifter's regular appearance... such as a raccant disguising themselves as a giant, or a human attempting to costume

themselves as a dragon. This skill can mimic faction inclusion.

Silent Activation
Cost: 10 Mox   Duration: 1 Skill activation
Grifters are the masters of subtlety! As such they can silently activate any skill they have, by taking an action and spending ten moxie before activating the skill in question. They still have to move their lips, though... Anyone looking at the Grifter's face has a chance to spot this lip movement, influenced by the Grifter's charisma and their silent activation skill.

Silver Tongue
Cost: 10 Mox   Duration: 10 minutes/Skill level
The Grifter buffs their charisma by an amount equal to their skill level... but this bonus only applies to lies.

Size Up
Cost: 5 For   Duration: 1 Turn
With a good hard look, the Grifter sizes up their target. If the Grifter succeeds, they learn the target's charisma, perception, willpower, wisdom, and any detection or observation skills that might interfere with the Grifter's lies or deceptions.

Level 5 Skills

Forgery
Cost: 10 For   Duration: Permanent
With some carefully-aged parchment and a few pen strokes, a Grifter can quickly craft a suitable license, authorization, or document that appears to be the real deal! Anyone scrutinizing the document may detect that it is indeed false. Fair warning: appraise and other item-reading skills will see right through this deception.

Pickpocket
Cost: 10 Sta   Duration: 1 Attempt
What's mine is mine. What's yours is negotiable. The Grifter gains a buff to his dexterity rolls... but only for the purpose of performing sleight-of-hand or pickpocketing a target. This is usually paired with silent activation, as it otherwise attracts undue attention.

Unflappable
Cost: N/A   Duration: Passive Constant

When you trick people for a living, you become fairly resistant to things like shame and guilt. You gain a bonus to your cool equal to your Grifter level. This skill has no levels.

Level 10 Skills

Feign Death
Cost: 20 Mox   Duration: 5 minutes/Grifter level
Sometimes death IS the best option. Though a rather permanent one, mind you. This gives you the best of both worlds! While this skill is active, you appear to be dead. Anyone failing to pierce your bluff, which is modified by your charisma and skill level, is convinced that you are dead. Needless to say, while this skill is active, you cannot move or speak or do anything to draw attention to yourself or the skill abruptly ceases.

Old Buddy
Cost: 25 Mox   Duration: 1 minute/Grifter level
With the appropriate act and attitude, you can fool anyone into recognizing you! Even if they've never met you before in their life. If you succeed, then they believe that you're an old friend, even if they can't place you exactly, or remember when they met you. This confusion renders them moderately friendly in most non-combat situations. It isn't much use in combat, or other tense situations. When the skill expires, they'll realize that they never met you before in their life, and react accordingly.

MEDIUM
Mediums take prophecy and visions a bit farther, interpreting them for clients and allies. They specialize in divination and getting the most useful advantages out of fate... even if they're not above skewing the interpretation a bit here and there to accomplish their own goals.

Level 1 Skills

Bad Fortune
Cost: 10 For   Duration: 1 Action
Curses the target, inflicting damage upon their fortune. This skill is a spell.

Crystal Ball

Cost: 50 San   Duration: 1 minute per skill level

Through manipulation of the winds of fate, you can use a crystal ball to scry people, places, or things of interest. Time is mutable in such visions and be forewarned that the winds of fate are fickle and the scenes shown may vary... skill and wisdom are required to reduce interference. This skill is draining and may only be used once per day.

Good Fortune
Cost: 10 For   Duration: 1 Action

Soothes a target's fate, healing fortune damage. This skill is a spell.

Seance
Cost: 25 For   Duration: ???

Allows the Medium to perform a short ritual, involving darkness, candles, and a loved one or relation to the deceased. It calls up a spirit-like memory of the deceased, which is not undead and cannot be manipulated by necromancy. The deceased sticks around for a short time influenced by the Medium's charisma and the strength of the bond to the loved one or relation, and may or may not be helpful as they see fit. Also, the longer the subject has been dead, the shorter the séance will last. This skill is a spell.

Stack Deck
Cost: 5 Mox   Duration: Instant

Allows the Medium to pull any card they choose from a deck of cards. This skill has no levels.

Level 5 Skills

Focus Vision
Cost: 20 For   Duration: Instant

Activate this skill during any sort of vision to grant clarity to a specific area, or uncover a new wrinkle on the fate being shown. This skill is a spell.

Fortuna
Cost: 10 For   Duration: 1 Action

Pull a card from any fortuna deck. The card will act as a minor omen, shedding some enlightenment on the situation at hand or question asked. Of course, it's up to you to interpret it. This skill has no levels.

Palmistry

Cost: 10 For   Duration: 1 Reading

By inspecting a creature's hand, you gain a limited portent related to a random facet of their life or fate. This skill has no levels.

ORACLE

Chosen by a god or affected by proximity to a divine influence, Oracles serve to embody the concepts and will of their patron. They can heal, remove and transfer conditions, and eventually overcome time itself with foresight and wisdom. Oracles gain experience by predicting the future and aiding those around them to cope with twists of fate.

Level 1 Skills

Absorb Condition
Cost: 10 For   Duration: 1 Action

This skill transfers a condition or debuff from a target that you're physically touching to yourself. Note that it doesn't restore drained pools, so if a target's dying, and you take the condition, then the target will instantly start dying again because their hit points are still zero. This skill has no levels. Regardless of the debuff or condition absorbed, the Oracle shakes it off after a day's worth of time if it isn't cured before then. This skill is a spell.

Diagnose
Cost: 5 San   Duration: 1 Action

This skill reveals all debuffs and conditions on a target. It never fails and has no levels. This skill is a spell.

Divine Pawn
Cost: N/A   Duration: Passive Constant

Congratulations! The gods have selected you to be one of their agents on Generica. Good luck with that. You gain a bonus to your fate equal to your Oracle level. This skill has no levels.

Foresight
Cost: 10 For   Duration: 1 Turn

Time is malleable to gods. They'll share a little bit of that with you, spinning out predictions of the next few seconds. You get a glimpse of the near future, and the results of an action you choose at the time of using foresight. Bear in mind that failing to follow through with an action similar to that chosen has a risk of backfiring, as the feedback and dissonance from the false visions throws off your precognition for the rest of the day. The higher your skill, the less the chance of dissonance.

Lesser Healing
Cost: 5 San   Duration: 1 Action
Instantly heals a living target within a hundred feet of the Oracle, restoring a small amount of HP, influenced by the level of this skill. This is light-based healing, and when used upon an undead or negative-natured target, it inflicts damage instead of healing. This damage bypasses all defenses, and automatically hits. This skill is a spell.

Level 5 Skills

Afflict Self
Cost: 5 For   Duration: 10 seconds per skill level
Afflicts you with a random minor condition. The condition fades when it is cured, or when the afflict self duration expires, whichever comes first. This skill is a spell.

Omens and Portents
Cost: N/A   Duration: Passive Constant
The gods send you signs, sometimes subtle, sometimes blatant. Your dreams are occasionally filled with visions, or sometimes sticks will fall in mystical patterns around you. But it's up to you to decipher them! This skill has no levels.

Transfer Condition
Cost: 10 San   Duration: 1 Turn
This skill lets you put a condition or debuff that's affecting you on another target. After casting this spell, you have a short amount of time to touch them, boosted by your transfer condition skill. If you succeed, then they gain a condition or debuff of your choice from those currently afflicting you. Note that the duration of the condition or debuff is unchanged. This skill is a spell.

Level 10 Skills

Influence Fate
Cost: 25 For   Duration: 1 Turn
At this level, your foresight extends to the actions of others. You may grant others a brief usage of your own foresight, allowing them to determine the best course of action. This skill is a spell.

Short Vision

Cost: 25 San   Duration: 01-100 minutes

The world is full of omens and portents, but sometimes they aren't enough. By taxing your sanity, you can send your mind into a trance, seeking out help from your god. They'll usually oblige by sending you a short vision, related to your question or the situation at hand. It's rarely straightforward, though skilled Oracles can guide the vision, a bit. The harder the question, the greater the wisdom and skill required. The downside of this spell is that it knocks you out for a random amount of time, basically rendering you unconscious and unable to wake up until the vision is over. This skill is a spell.

Level 10 Skills

Grant Vision

Cost: 30 For   Duration: 0-100 minutes

This skill lets you grant a willing participant a prophetic dream. You must touch them in order to use this skill.

Random Buff

Cost: 30 San   Duration: 10 seconds per skill level

Grants you or one target a minor but useful random buff.

Level 15 Skills

NOTE: General skills are self-explanatory, and do not have activation costs or require explanation.

Made in the USA
Columbia, SC
24 November 2023

26982376R00178